GLORY DAYS IN THE REARVIEW

A STORY OF LOVE, REDEMPTION, AND HOPE

A NOVEL BY

MARK NEPPER

LITTLE CREEK PRESS
MINERAL POINT, WISCONSIN

Little Creek Press
5341 Sunny Ridge Road
Mineral Point, WI 53565

ORDERING INFORMATION
Quantity sales. Special discounts are available on quantity purchases by corporations, associations, and others. For details, contact info@littlecreekpress.com

Orders by US trade bookstores and wholesalers.
Please contact Little Creek Press or Ingram for details.

Printed in the United States of America

Cataloging-in-Publication Data
Names: Mark Nepper, author
Title: Glory Days in the Rearview
Description: Mineral Point, WI Little Creek Press, 2024
Identifiers: LCCN: 2024918415 | ISBN: 978-1-955656-80-1
Classification: Fiction / General
Fiction / Family Life / General
Fiction / Family Life / Marriage and Divorce

Book design by Little Creek Press

For Dad and Mom

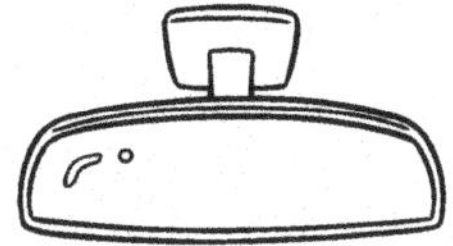

CHAPTER 1

The futility of this conversation with a client literally and symbolically represented the folly of what my life had become.

I really wanted to tell him rather forcefully to just shut the fuck up. Of course, I can't speak like that to a client. No good would come from that. But, oh, how I wanted to scream at him.

I wanted all of the discordant noise from my job, from my life, to just disappear.

As my frustration grew, I sensed this would not end well. Proper phone etiquette dictated that I avoid telling him what I really wanted to say. I tried to listen to the drivel oozing out of the client's mouth, hoping I could make some sense of it. I shook my head frantically. Maybe that would shake everything back into sensible order. It didn't.

Sometimes you have a bad day. Sometimes you have a bad week or month. Sometimes it seems so much longer.

Sometimes it seems that everything just sucks.

Times like these, most times, actually, I hated my job, and a lot of other things if you want to know the truth.

I hated working in a cubicle farm. I hated making nice with clients because mostly I hated my clients. I hated my boss. I hated how I had to play nice because I needed the paycheck. All of this hatred intensified because I knew I should look for another job, maybe one that would actually bring me some satisfaction and pay commensurate with my talents, which far exceeded the mind-numbing work I was currently doing. That would mean, however, that I saw the possibility of a better life for myself. In high school, I was voted most likely to have a great life. Seriously, it says that in my yearbook. What I had become would surprise most of my classmates—and immensely please the others. I hated how unsatisfactory and disappointing my life had become. I hated how I could only view myself as a failure. Mostly, I hated my life and what I had become—a walking, talking cliché.

As the conversation continued, I pulled the phone handset away from my face and stared at it in disbelief. Fixating on the phone provided no clarity. I still could hear the nonsense my client was spewing.

"No, sir. I'm not being disrespectful to your demands. I'm just not clear how I can make this work the way you want to," I said, working hard to maintain a polite demeanor. If only I could let him know what an absolute moron he was. I kept looking at the clock, willing it to just skip ahead to quitting time. The moron on the phone was making it particularly difficult to avoid making disparaging comments at his expense. After listening to him rant for a full minute, in which he shouted an impressive string of profanities while I held the phone a good foot from my head, it still felt like as if I were standing in front of him, the spittle hitting my face would feel like driving sleet. I finally interrupted him.

"Sir, I will look into your suggestions and get back to you. Thank you for calling, and have a nice day," *and fuck off while you're at it*, I thought, gently cradling the phone. If I didn't force myself to be gentle, I would have smashed the handset down with such force I would have shattered the plastic piece of shit all over my desk. The boss wouldn't appreciate me breaking a third phone this month. I took a few deep breaths to fight off the anxiety that rose in my throat like bile. I tried to center myself in calmness, quickly searching out the four waterfall photos I had hung on the back wall of my cubicle. Sometimes it worked. I could stare at the photos and find myself transported. The water would rush with the pull of gravity, creating a long, silky stream of milky white water, plunging into the pool below. The sound would fill my head, and I would feel the spray wash over my face. A smile always blossomed at the memory.

I was just about lost in the memory when I felt a presence looming over me. I looked up and saw my boss. "I just got off the phone with Steve Duggan from Digital Design," Jennifer said.

"Really? He and I just had quite a chat," I said, hoping to go on the offensive.

"He wasn't happy," Jennifer said. I was about to protest, but she cut me off. "It behooves us in this business to remember the customer is always right. We provide a service to the customers. You're part of that service. Our goal is to ensure that our clients can effectively use our computer software, and if they can't, then we have to help them. We most certainly don't say to them, 'Fuck off' at the end of the phone conversation."

"What?" I said, and then I thought, *Shit. Did I say that out loud?*

"And yes, you did say that out loud," Jennifer said. "Steve found it offensive enough that he called to report what you said."

Tattle is more like it, I thought. But I made sure that the thought did not escape my mouth.

"We don't treat our customers like this," Jennifer said.

I found my unease growing. I subtly glanced at the clock on my computer screen. One hour and fourteen minutes left until the end of the day. Could she continue this tirade that long? Something told me she could.

"So, Robb, here's what you're going to do. You are going to call Mr. Duggan back and make a contrite and heartfelt apology. Then you are going to reassure him that you will make sure we meet all of his demands. You will also give him a 10 percent discount for this service. Go ahead. Make the call," Jennifer said, folding her arms across her chest.

"You're going to stand here and watch me make the call?" I asked, incredulous.

"Yes, I am."

"Jesus Christ, Jennifer. It was an honest mistake. Haven't you ever wanted to tell a client to fuck off and done so under your breath?"

"Actually, Robb, I haven't because, as I said earlier, the customer is always right."

Yeah, right, you tight ass, I thought, again worrying about saying the words out loud.

Then Jennifer reached for the phone on my desk and handed it to me. "Make the call."

"This is just a little humiliating," I said.

"Then maybe next time, you won't be tempted to make such crass statements to our clients. Make the call."

I did as she ordered and then fumed when she walked away from my cube. I took the koosh ball that Trev and I played catch with over our half walls and threw it as hard as I could against the actual wall. It left a dent in the thin layer of plaster. I picked it up and went into the windup to vent more anger when Trev said, "Hey, man, don't ruin our koosh. We need that for catch."

"Here, catch," I said. I threw it as hard as I could, bouncing it off the ceiling into the corner of his cube. Silence hung in the air, and I found myself breathing hard. Then I heard Trev's disembodied voice again.

"That sucks, what she did to you." Of course, Trev heard every word, the risk of working in a cube farm, where no real privacy existed, just the illusion of it. I heard one side of every word of every one of Trev's conversations with clients, just as he did with me. And when a person showed up at one of our cubes, we shared that, too. Even though I worked in close proximity to Trev and called him a friend, the relationship always seemed surreal. We chatted often throughout the day but only laid eyes on each other during the start and end of the day and when we rushed out for lunch. Occasionally we would stand up and poke our heads above the wall to look at each other, like groundhogs taking a peek. We never ate at our desks or in the plastic cafeteria for employees. Even though we had to rush, we both needed to get off campus for lunch just to connect with other people in the world, even if they were beating a path from their own cubicles, too.

"Yeah," I said, and that was about all I could manage. I slumped into my ergonomic chair, holding my head in my hands. I looked at the clock. 3:50. Only another hour and ten minutes. I could make it through another shitty day if I just hung on, right?

Trev seemed to be reading my thoughts. "We're almost done for the day. Beers after to celebrate the end of the week."

"Yeah, sure, beers after work." I leaned back in my chair. Beers after work. Another weekend. We had been locked in this same routine for years now. Once we hit the bars, we would bitch about work, and lately, we bitched most about Jennifer, who seemed to thrive in the cube environment, where contact with other human beings mostly occurred through email and the occasional conversation. God, how I hated the impersonal nature of work in the cubicles. I hated waiting for the sacred five o'clock *ding*, which signaled we could all leave work, but only if we had finished all of our work for the precious clients.

On Fridays, especially, most people made their last phone calls around four thirty to ensure they would be free to leave at the *ding*, which, though muted, still felt like a school bell setting us free for the weekend. Once the ding pinged, people would dash for the exits. Participating in yet another Friday afternoon controlled rush for the exits disgusted me. I grabbed a piece of paper from the printer, scribbled a note, folded it into a paper airplane, and sailed it into Trev's cube.

Still on the phone, he stood up with the note unfolded and a quizzical look on his face. By this time, I had thrown into my briefcase a legal pad, the latest copy of *Sports Illustrated*, and the plastic container that carried the pistachio nuts I would nibble on in the late morning. The briefcase established the illusion that I did important work. I was just grabbing my coat off the hook on the wall separating me from Trev when my paper airplane returned to my cubicle like a delayed reaction boomerang.

I reread the note and nodded at him. He held up his hands with a quizzical look on his face. So I mouthed what I wrote: "Fuck it! I'm leaving early. Join me now or later if you want. But right now, I'm gone." I turned and walked out, giving him a wave without turning to face him. I made it to the elevators without seeing anybody else. You really never saw anyone else except at the beginning and end of the day and at lunch.

When I hit the street, I took a deep breath. It smelled like freedom. On my way, I pulled out my cell and gave Cameron a call.

"Friday afternoon, Cam. Wanna join me for a couple of tall cool ones?"

"Love to, Robbie, but Stac and I are leading a seminar at the Ramada this weekend in Janesville."

I laughed. "Ah, another one of your seminars. Cam, you live a life that most people would be jealous of. How many people wouldn't love to be married to a stunningly beautiful woman with whom you operate a sex therapy business where, at your seminars, you get in front of people and talk about every iteration of sex possible in the name of improving relationships?"

"Every teenage boy's dream job, right? Hey, we've all got to make a living. And I've got two kids to put through college," Cam said, and from the tinge in his voice, I knew he found the irony succulent. As the guy who couldn't buy a date in high school, who called the live sex chat lines where they would hang up on him, as the guy tabbed in the yearbook as least likely to ever get laid, no one could have predicted he would become a guru of sex, the creator of self-help sex books, self-help sex videos, and self-help sex therapy weekends like the one he and his wife were about to lead. But that was our Cameron. They didn't actually have sex in a conference room at the Ramada. But they sure talked about it. I went once and blushed for the entire three hours of the session and another three hours afterward.

"How 'bout a beer Sunday night? Green Mill, nine o'clock. The usual," Cam said. After agreeing to continue a ritual we had practiced for the past fourteen years, Cam gave his signature parting. "Goodbye and good sex," but with me, this rejoinder always contained a healthy guffaw, as if I was the only one who could really appreciate the joke. Truthfully, I probably was. And believe me, I did appreciate it. Talking with Cameron always lifted my spirits.

I got in the car and drove to Pedro's, where we always went on Fridays.

The margaritas were big and cheap. They also had a nice selection of microbrews. On Fridays, they put out a table of appetizers. Normally I ordered a beer, but this time I ordered a goldfish bowl-sized margarita. Given the end to my day, I guessed I'd order another two or three before I decided to make my way home. Sitting there, sipping my drink, I watched *SportsCenter* on ESPN, which is a pointless endeavor. After all, how can you hear the talking heads when they have shut off the sound and the heads make no noise? If a tree falls in the forest, what would the sports commentators have to say about it for the next eight hours? Thank God for closed captioning. The trailer matched what the talking heads said, which allowed me to gather insights on which football teams would likely draft whom in the next day's draft.

While I sipped my margarita and honed up on the draft, a woman came in and plopped down on the barstool next to me. "Give me a Dewar's, double, neat," the woman said when the bartender approached.

She looked at me. "That sounds like a serious drink," I said, wryly. "You must mean business."

"I do. I'm trying to forget what a bitch my boss is," she said.

"I hear you on that one," I said. The bartender brought her drink. She raised her glass and looked at me. "Here's to bitchy bosses." We bumped glasses and took the obligatory sip. I remembered the rule from college: whenever someone proposes a toast, you must drink, out of politeness, out of obligation, out of thirst. Sometimes you drink just because you can.

"So what made today so bad?" I asked. If she wanted to tell me about her day, I might find a kindred spirit who would listen to me spout about Jennifer.

"Some days, I think my boss is incompetent, and I'm the one who has to put out all of the fires and keep saving my boss's ass."

"Line of work?"

"Advertising. Today the issues were a printer's strike in Chicago, probable missed deadlines, lost revenue," she said, taking another sip of her scotch.

"So how did you save your boss's ass?"

"I located another printer, who would do the work as a rush job, with the verbal understanding that we would shift our business over to him. So, tell me about your day."

"Just another routine day at the office, dealing with customers who don't know what they want but then blame me when I can't deliver, and a boss who would kiss the harvest moon of any client who bent over in front of her."

The woman laughed. "And let me guess. You're not one to ever kiss the client's ass?"

"Only once in a blue moon." We both laughed and bumped glasses again.

Her attention drifted to the television. "So, do you think the Pack will draft a quarterback to replace the irreplaceable Rodgers?"

"They better get another body in with some ability to serve as the superstar's backup because I'm not so sure the guy they have is the guy. As a diehard Packers fan who remembers decades of losing, I've gotten kind of used to this winning stuff. So they better find a replacement before Rodgers loses the golden touch. Seems like his prime is fast fading. Are you a fan?"

"Hard not to be in this state."

A little more idle chatter passed between us about the Packers.

"So tell me about this boss of yours," I said.

"A real bitch. Let me tell you," she said. "But let's talk about something else besides work. I'm Alex."

"Robb."

"So, Robb, are you married?"

"Divorced. Two kids. We sort of share custody, but the kids are in high school and have started to protest the residences that shift each week, so we're trying now to just move them once a month. It doesn't work either, but at least the kids get more of a routine. How about you? Married?"

"Divorced. God, when I think about it, isn't everyone?" Alex said.

I watched her. I could tell she was trying to think of couples who hadn't gone through at least one divorce.

"Think of anybody?" I asked.

She laughed. "Two couples. One seems like the real deal. The other couple should probably be divorced, but they're hanging on for the kids."

We had tried, we really did. Amy and I met in high school, and we seemed like we would have the juice to keep a marriage strong and vital. But the juice glass went dry. My fault, maybe. No, definitely my fault. And suddenly Jimmy Buffett's "Margaritaville" flashed through my music memory. When Amy grew tired of being the only one really committed to making the marriage work, she begged me to try. When my efforts fell short, she begged me to go to counseling.

I thought marriage would come easy for me, just like everything else had. I was the student who attended a lackluster high school and never had to work to get the A's, but when I went to college, I couldn't handle the academic rigor. I made it—barely. But that meant that I had fewer options in the job market after college. So I took shitty job after shitty job until I ended up in my current situation. The shitty job started affecting my life. Pretty soon everything was shitty. I stayed in the shitty job because it was easier than leaving. Amy finally made the call, ending our shitty marriage.

I thought Amy would always love me like she did when we were in high school. But then marriage got tough, and I did what those struggling college students do: I got really stinking drunk and dropped out. Getting stinking drunk regularly when you're unhappy with the marriage is never a good idea. It led to things, more indiscretions, which Amy discovered indirectly. So when Amy proclaimed her absolute dissatisfaction with the marriage, I finally decided to try. But I didn't really know anymore how to work to make a relationship work. When I gave up on counseling after three sessions, she begged me for a divorce.

But at least the divorce proceeded amicably. No *Wedding Crashers* divorce mediation scenes.

"We talked about staying together for the kids," I said, munching on a giant pretzel the bartender had just placed in front of us. "In the end, Amy and I decided we deserved a chance at happiness, and maybe we could find it with someone else." I grabbed another chunk from the pretzels. Alex's hand grazed mine as she reached for her own pretzel chunk simultaneously.

Actually, Amy decided she wanted to be happy. I would have been perfectly willing to go along indefinitely in a meaningless marriage because the thought of being suddenly alone terrified me. I hadn't been alone since the summer between my junior and senior years of high school when Amy and I started dating. We kindled the relationship after getting to know each other in our summer marching band. I lapped up another gulp of my margarita, getting a tongue full of salt. "At any rate, I think we, I, have totally screwed up my kids."

"Don't be so hard on yourself," Alex said. "That's what parents are for. It took me years to get past my brutal childhood."

"What made your childhood so bad?" I wasn't sure I felt comfortable with this conversation. I usually prefer generally meaningless chatter, especially when I have just signaled the bartender for my third margarita fishbowl. Take me back to the lengthy conversation about the Packers, and I would have been perfectly content. The direction of this conversation made my stomach roil. If we continued at this level of honesty, I would probably bare my soul to Alex. I just didn't do that kind of thing. Not anymore.

"They treated me like a neighbor's pet—happy when they saw me but felt no real obligation to spend time with me."

I just nodded my head. I had friends in high school who suffered because of the same kind of absentee parents. Even though Amy and I divorced four years ago, I never abandoned my kids. Somehow, out of a sense of obligation or true desire, I remained as much a part of their lives as if I were living under the same roof.

"So, they ignored you," a statement of fact, not a question.

Alex nodded and sipped her drink again, which now seemed perilously close to being gone. If I wanted this conversation to continue, I would have to buy her another drink, and she was drinking Dewar's, top of the top shelf scotch.

"They left me home with a nanny every day while they made their fortunes. In high school, I was driving a BMW. I would rather have had supper with them every night."

"You know, Alex, you were right before. We do. As parents, we do terrible things to our children. How did you escape the children issue?"

"My ex and I were both so focused on career advancement that we just took children off the table. And then it became obvious we should take marriage off the table, especially when I found him and a coworker having sex on, well, on the dining room table."

"I bet you got rid of that table, too," I said.

"Bet your ass I did. Burned it." We both laughed. "There's irony here, though, Robb. I wasn't really that broken up about the marriage ending. Anger just seemed to fit the moment. You know, it's like when you dated someone in high school, and they broke up with you. Really sad for about two days and then pissed off for two more days, and then you looked for someone else."

"I never had that experience in high school. I dated a few girls and ended up marrying the last one. But I wasn't even really that pissed off when she divorced me. Just sad. On the other hand, she was really pissed at me." Amy wore a scowl for the year leading up to the divorce and for quite a while after that. At least she wore that scowl when she was around me. I think she was so angry because I was the love of her life. She used to tell her friends, "I'm going to marry Robb Cesario." She made that statement prophetic. I had totally let her down. She ended up married to the guy who peaked in high school and never figured out how to live as someone less than the "it" guy.

Alex caught the bartender's eye and ordered herself another scotch. The bartender had just delivered my margarita. "I'll get his, too. Robb, the next round is on you."

I nodded. I already planned on getting three or four of these bad boys. If she was going to make the gesture, it would be fine with me if she paid for a round or two. Although I didn't learn much in college, I did learn a very important rule, one I still followed: never turn down a free drink or a free meal.

The bartender delivered the scotch. Alex paid. I raised my glass in a silent toast of gratitude. He also brought over a basket of tortilla chips and a bowl of salsa. More snacks. The pretzel had disappeared. Yet another in a long line of fine dining experiences for me. Alex reached in first. Then I took a turn.

"So, tell me more about this boss of yours," I said, trying to maneuver the conversation back to a safer topic. "Did you end up bailing her out today?"

"Yes, as usual," Alex said and laughed.

Something about her laugh made me feel a little suspicious. The cadence of her laugh and then the roll of her eyes seemed playfully deceptive. It dawned on me to ask another question.

"Just which advertising firm do you work for?"

"Shenk and Company," Alex said.

"And what position do you hold there?"

"Ah, I think you've got me," and she started to laugh. "I'm president and CEO."

I joined her in the laughter. We took a sip of our drinks. "I don't think I've ever heard a boss talk in such pejorative terms about themself. It's actually refreshing."

"Robb, I was being totally serious. I really screwed things up today, and I was trying to blame everybody else until I took responsibility for the dump truck of shit I dropped into my office. So when I finally regained control of myself, I apologized and then cleaned up the mess."

"Admirable and honorable. I'm impressed. You have restored my belief that bosses can actually be good people. I would love to work for a boss like you. It would be refreshing."

The conversation with Alex stretched long into the evening. I lost count of the number of margaritas I had. Fortunately, Alex offered to share a cab with me on the ride home. We ended up sharing a bed, too.

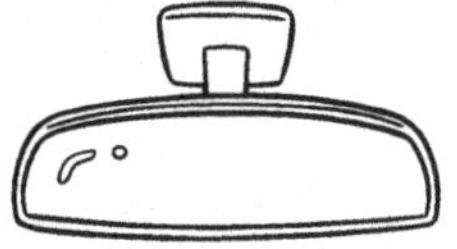

CHAPTER 2

I'm forty-four years old, and my life didn't turn out how I expected it would.

Hell, nobody who knew me then would believe the train wreck of my life. If my high school classmates could see me now, they wouldn't know what to think. That's why I do all I can to avoid them. I'm sure many of them achieved great success in their lives. I was supposed to have that, too. My classmates didn't vote me most likely to succeed. Why waste the time and effort? To them, the success of my life was a foregone conclusion.

I dated and then later married Amy, the prettiest and coolest girl in school. Not just my opinion, but I was biased. We had it all. Then I lost Amy. I spend a lot of my time thinking about her. When I think about Amy, I can't help but look back on our senior year, a magical and wonderful time when everything in the world looked new and sparkled like diamonds in the morning sunlight, when everything was not only possible but likely, when we knew we would live lives they could immortalize in poetry and movies, when we felt as if we were the next generation of Camelot.

If you know your mythology or your musicals, you know how that story turned out.

Sadly.

Some of those people who have carved out a nice or even a great life for themselves might feel a bit of smug satisfaction if they could see me now. They might nod sagely and conclude that nobody can live their whole life on the upswing. No one can expect only good things and then wait for them to happen, knowing the wait would never be too long.

That was exactly how I lived my life, though. I waltzed through high school. Senior year was a continuous display of joyful success, moments of happiness on repeat. Life was easy.

I knew my life would continue along that same easy path, no boulders or detours on the journey through life. The road ahead always appeared freshly paved, with minimal traffic and no posted speed limits to force slowdowns—just a steady, wonderful cruise through life.

Some would actually like to know I had failed because, let's face it, in high school that didn't seem possible. Looking back, I know I didn't look down on others. In fact, I liked my classmates. Don't take this as bragging, but I genuinely liked my classmates, and they liked me. We talked, laughed, shared stories, did crazy stupid things together, the kinds of things you can get away with as a kid, where adults might shake their heads sternly, turn away, and then laugh at the sheer audacity or stupidity of it.

Most of it was harmless and innocent. Like the infamous M&M suck contests. Every lunch hour in the commons, when we were seniors, crowds gathered around the center table. Someone would set out two long lines of M&M's straight down the center of the table. Two people would step up, put their arms behind their backs, and the contest began. The idea was to see how many M&M's you could suck into your mouth in one Hooverific motion. People cheered. Administrators laughed at the spectacle. Someone actually sucked a record twenty-seven M&M's into his mouth. The M&M suck became so popular that the cover of our yearbook shows a long line of M&M's snaking around a shadow of the school and our mascot. Innocent stuff. Every spring our jazz music program put on a variety show. The show featured the jazz band throughout the performance. It also featured other acts, singers, dancers, boys and girls kicklines, and emcees who told slightly risqué jokes that alluded to the sexual antics of high school students. Innocent stuff.

—x—x—x—

When I woke Saturday morning after drinking the previous night with Alex, I felt a body pressed against mine. I realized I hadn't spent an innocent night alone. This definitely was not high school. It took me a moment to remember that I had come home with Alex, and we engaged in the kind of frantic, fumbling sex that drunk people stumble into, thinking that meaningful companionship will result. And it all seems so right when you start exchanging those sloppy, sexy, drunken kisses. But then in the morning, when you wake up, your first thought usually runs along the lines of, *Oh, shit*. Awkwardness follows. Since my divorce, I have experienced this enough to know how it would go.

I lay quietly for a few minutes, steeling myself for the rest of the morning because this thing could stretch into a prolonged continuation over bagels and coffee at the nearest Panera. As I lay there, I thought about the conversation with Alex. It developed a natural rhythm that sometimes occurs when you first meet someone. Their choice of words, the level of their honesty, and the stories they tell grab your attention. It seems as if you might have fallen into a situation that could lead to a meaningful friendship. Sometimes that actually does happen. With me, more often, though, it seems conversation at the next meeting starts and stops like Beltline traffic at rush hour. The original fascination and rhythm disappear, especially if the next encounter occurs across pillows the next morning.

Alex had obviously experienced these situations before. She woke up a few minutes after I did.

"Morning," she mumbled. We chatted for a few minutes while she woke up. Then she gave me a soft kiss, slipped out of bed, and began dressing. "Thanks for last night. It was special." Then she kissed me again and quietly left with a little wave as she crossed the bedroom threshold and, a moment later, softly closed the apartment door.

Recreational sex does have its benefits, I thought as I pulled myself out of bed. My ruminations before Alex awoke and left got me thinking about that bagel and coffee at Panera. After I showered and dressed, I grabbed my cell, left the apartment, hopped on my bike, and made the five-minute ride to Panera on University Avenue. I settled into a chair in their outdoor café—why spend time inside when spring mornings can be so glorious? I wanted to read the paper and ease into the day. I had made it into the sports section when my cell rang. Dad, checking in as usual on Saturdays. I checked my watch—10:45 a.m. I smiled. Long ago, after aborted conversations when he and Mom would call me freshman year in the dorms at 7:30 Saturday morning and expect meaningful conversation, he learned to call later in the morning.

"Hi, Dad," I said, but before I could say anything else, he interrupted. "Robb," his voice choked. "We're on our way to the hospital. They're taking her to University Hospital."

"Taking who? Dad, what's wrong?" I felt like a boa constrictor had just wrapped itself around my neck.

Though he wasn't talking, I could hear small sobs. "Your mother. Robb, she had a heart attack. I gave her CPR until the paramedics arrived. Call your sister and let her know, and then come to the hospital. Oh, God. Oh my God."

"Dad, I'll be there. Just hang on. Everything will be okay." As those words hung in the air, I wondered why people made such pronouncements.

The thought quickly disappeared. I ran from Panera, leaving my waste on the table. Someone else could do the cleanup. I hopped on my bike and peddled like Lance Armstrong through the Pyrenees, except I wasn't on performance-enhancing drugs. With the panic and adrenaline, I didn't need them. My speed carried more significance than a possible yellow jersey. When I got home, I made a quick call to my sister, shared the news, and then told her I would call later with an update, and she could start making travel arrangements. When I found my dad at University Hospital twenty minutes later, he fell into my arms. It felt like I was holding a heavy, lumpy sack of potatoes with no possible way to support itself. It felt like dead weight.

"How's Mom?" I asked.

"They're still working on her, stabilizing her. God." He exhaled deeply and started to cry. I continued to hold him. Time passed slowly, like it always does in a hospital waiting room. Dad took my hand and held it. "I hope she doesn't die in there, that way. She would want to die with us around her, holding her hand," Dad said.

"Dad, let's not jump to conclusions. The doctors here are good, the best in the state. They're going to do all they can for her. Let's wait for the doctors to give us an update before we jump to any conclusions." I said all the things people say in those situations. I didn't know that you were supposed to say these things. They just spewed from my mouth.

"Did you call Shelly? She needs to be here."

"I did. She was shocked and scared, just like us. She was going to catch the first plane, but who knows what kind of jumps she will have to make from Atlanta. She had no way to predict when she would get here. I told her I would give her an update, and then she could make her plans."

"They talked last night," Dad said. "They had one of their usual little fights."

"I've never understood that," I said and shook my head. Shell had always been a wonderful little sister, but when she discovered that our parents weren't perfect, she lit after them like they were the worst child abusers in the world. She found fault with almost everything Mom did and said. But Mom never showed anger other than in the moment. She always forgave Shelly. I asked her once how she could forgive when her youngest child called her Satan's wife, which logically made Dad Satan. Shelly, though, often said she really didn't have problems with Dad. Mom replied with a smile that you could only describe as beatific.

"She's just angry right now, Robb. And when she's angry, she doesn't filter. But she doesn't mean it. Not really. The truth is Shelly loves me every bit as much as I love her."

At that stage, I had learned an important skill, and it seemed appropriate at the time. I rolled my eyes and walked out.

Dad continued. "Ever since Shelly hit puberty, it's like she started to hate your mother and never really quite got past it. It's been one long fight. The truth is that I get angrier with Shelly than your mother ever does."

"Shelly never told me why she always got so angry with Mom, but it seems like there must have been something that set her off."

"It's rarely one thing. You know this from being married. It's usually an accumulation of a lot of little things."

The truth of that statement stunned me. In my marriage, the little things started to occur as frequently as the warnings about climate change. But just like the rest of the world, we didn't heed the warnings. Eventually the little things became big and then bigger and then insurmountable.

"When did you get so smart, Dad?" He smiled and squeezed my hand tighter. We sat quietly as doctors and nurses scurried past the waiting room or stood outside and engaged in what amounted to office chatter.

An hour later, I stood. "Where you headed?" Dad asked.

"I'm going to get us some coffee, and I need to call the kids and let them know."

"Let Amy know, too. She and your mother were always close."

They were. Amy filled the void of loving daughter and dearest friend that Shelly could never quite manage. The bond Mom and Amy had became even stronger when Shelly moved away after college and then took a job as far away from home as possible. They talked about everything. Amy told Mom we were getting divorced before she even told me. In the years since the divorce, Amy kept in touch with Mom, calling her several times a week. Amy wanted to maintain the friendship, and she also wanted my mother to remain close with her grandchildren. I asked Amy once if the level of friendship felt awkward. "No," she said. "I love your mom."

Everywhere I went in the hospital, I saw signs forbidding the use of cell phones. I went outside and stood about fifteen feet downwind from the smokers, solitary travelers with angry scowls.

When I called home, or, my former home and still the home of my children, Amy answered. I knew she would. Jessie was at dance class. Every Saturday from nine to three she danced. And TJ would still be in bed. Also, predictable.

"Hi, Amy. It's Robb."

"I thought I recognized that voice. So how is the father of my children?" She seemed to be in the mood for light banter. She obviously couldn't read the concern in my voice from the brief salutation.

"Amy, I've got some bad news. I need to tell you ..." I faltered. I had never had to deliver this kind of news before, and I wasn't sure what to do, how to say it. Do you just blurt it out? Do you lead up to it? Do you hem and haw and hope they pick up the gist? "I wanted to let you and the kids know that—"

"Robb, something's obviously wrong. Just tell me," she said. Her voice had dropped soft and low, full of concern. She settled the issue. She always seemed to know just what to do, what to say. The revelation surprised me. I had forgotten about that quality of hers.

"Ames." Without thinking, I called her by the nickname I gave her before I kissed her for the first time. "Mom has had a heart attack. She's at University Hospital. The doctors are working on her now."

"Oh my God, Robb. Oh, no. Are you okay?"

"I'm a little numb. Dad and I have been sitting in the waiting room for the past hour, holding hands, talking, and crying. I'm scared. I know that."

"How's Bob? Did he find her?"

"Yeah. He gave her CPR until the paramedics arrived. He's really scared. I think he's contemplating the possibility of her dying. They've been together for fifty-two years. I don't think he would know how to go on without Mom."

"Don't get ahead of yourself. She's at the best hospital around. Wait until you get some information before you start going down that road. That's something I learned with my mom. Wait for the information. Then you can deal with the reality."

"Okay. You're right. Anyway, I wanted to let you know what's going on. Maybe you could tell the kids and then bring them down at some point. I'd tell them myself, but I'm stuck here at the hospital, and I'd rather they not hear news like this over the phone."

"Of course. I'll tell TJ, and we'll go get Jessie. We'll be there this afternoon."

"Thanks, Ames." I paused. I wanted her to keep talking. Her voice had already comforted me. I wanted that to continue. It also seemed like I needed to tell her more, but no words came.

"Okay, Robb. We'll see you soon." Then she hung up.

I bought some coffee from the cafeteria. It appeared Dad hadn't moved since I left. Leaving the waiting room would mean that he could miss news about Mom. He took the coffee I offered him and just held it. About an hour later, he set the plastic cup down. It was still full.

Amy brought the kids. We all hugged. It reminded me of the group hugs Amy and I used to make a part of our family ritual. Each family seems to develop their own rituals. As a kid, Mom and Dad insisted we have supper together every night. We also did things like picking strawberries and corn together, cutting down the family Christmas tree, shoveling the driveway and sidewalks, and doing yard work together.

Amy and I developed similar rituals, but the family meal became more and more difficult as the kids' lives became busier. We held onto the group hug for a long time. We would form a small circle and drape our arms around each other. I smiled at the memory. We started doing it when the kids were wee little ones, and we had a simple rule. Anybody could call for a group hug, and we all had to join. In our family, you could never take a pass on a group hug. As the marriage deteriorated, though, so too did the frequency of the group hugs until they disappeared like the bees.

After staying for about an hour with some stiff attempts at conversation with Dad and me, they left.

At three o'clock, I went downstairs and rejoined the smokers. I wanted to call Shelly and leave her a message with another condition update on Mom. Her flight to Chicago would land in an hour. Then she would get to Madison by six that evening. I promised to pick her up at the airport, which I did.

Shelly scurried out of the security area and ran to me. She hugged me as if she were drowning, and I had just swum up to save her. Tears slid down her face, which she buried in my shoulder.

"Am I too late?" she asked.

"No, Shell. Mom's resting now in the CCU. Let's get your bag and get to the hospital. She's been asking about you. She will definitely want to see you." The ride from the airport to the hospital took twenty minutes. Shelly looked out the window the entire time. When we drove up East Gorham toward the capitol and State Street, she perked up, smiling at some of the landmarks, like Tenney Park, which in the winter had a beautiful ice-skating rink on the frozen pond. We used to skate there as kids. Mom used to say it looked like a Currier and Ives woodcut that became the basis of a series of popular Christmas cards in the early twentieth century.

Then we passed James Madison Park, where she spent much of high school getting high with her friends, and State Street, where she logged many, many hours during college waiting to get into the hottest bars and clubs. Brief smiles played on her lips as she remembered. I knew what memories she was reliving. I had done most of the same things, except the getting high adventures. We often compared notes.

"Happy memories?" I asked.

"Some."

The rest of the ride passed in silence.

After a long hug with Dad, Shelly and I walked into Mom's room. She lay awake, entangled in tubes. Monitors tracking her vitals beeped and whooshed. Her skin had turned sallow, and she seemed to have aged fifteen years since I left to get Shelly. But she was awake and lucid. She looked like a different person than the vibrant, alive Mom I had always known.

People say you never get over seeing your parents like that for the first time in the hospital. Now I knew what they meant. When Mom saw Shelly, her eyes sparkled. She held out her hand, stretching the IV tube taped into her forehand. "There's my girl. Come and give me a hug."

Shelly shuffled over to Mom's bed and leaned toward her, unsure what to do because of all the contraptions affixed to Mom. Finally, she rested her cheek against Mom's. They held the hug for a long time. Shelly brushed away a tear and sniffled. Mom rubbed her back.

"Oh, Mom, I was so scared. I didn't know if you'd be.... I didn't know how you would be when I got here."

"I'm still here, baby. You made it, and I'll tell you I feel a lot better right now than I did this morning. The sumo wrestler sitting on my chest seemed to have found another place to rest. So I don't think I'll be going anywhere yet."

"What happened? I mean, I guess I know that. You had a heart attack. But have you been experiencing any symptoms?"

"Shelly and Robb, you might as well hear this, too. I've been a bad girl, and now I'm paying for it."

"What do you mean, Mom?" I interjected. I moved to the side of the bed opposite Shelly and took her hand. When Mom patted the edge of the bed, Shelly sat, perched like a bird on a wire.

"At my last physical I struggled with the stress test. The doctor said I had some blockage and would need to take care of it. He put me on statins and beta blockers and was talking about inserting a stent. I never told your father and, against doctor's orders, kept putting off doing anything."

"Mom, why would you do that?" Shelly seemed exasperated, and I could hear the edge in her voice. I gave her a stern look, which she ignored. The last thing Mom needed right now was more judgment from Shelly.

"A couple of reasons. First of all, I was afraid. You know, you hear something like that, and the natural reaction is to say to yourself, 'But I feel fine.' Or, in my case, the thought of surgery scared me. A lot. Heart surgery, probably a bypass, unless they could use a stent to open the arteries, is a big deal. I was surprised the doctor didn't call an ambulance for me at that moment and have me taken to the ER. When he gave me a choice, I just never actually decided. It turns out it wasn't something I should have put off. So I guess it was a big deal."

"Mom, it is a big deal," I said, offering her a smile. "But a lot of people have heart surgery nowadays and get through it just fine and come roaring back into life."

"I know, honey. What you've just told me makes perfect sense. But I'm afraid I didn't think very rationally about this. The other thing was I convinced myself that I couldn't go through something like that with your father being sick. His diabetes is getting worse."

"Worse? How?" This news surprised me. Dad hadn't mentioned anything like this to me. In fact, throughout the entire day in the waiting room, he never talked about himself or any health issues. As I thought about this, I nodded my head. Neither of my parents put themselves first in the marriage. Their first concern was always the other person. Mom shared that he was having more difficulty walking because neuropathy had started. His legs had weakened. He was having some vision issues. He had lost some weight—typical symptoms.

"Okay," I said. "I understand." And I did, too. I wasn't just trying to make her feel better. Shelly didn't say anything. She continued to hold Mom's hand.

"So what happened today?" Shelly asked. "How did you know you were having a heart attack?"

"I had pain in my upper back before I went to bed last night. I woke up this morning and vomited. The chest pain immediately followed. I finally told your dad I thought I was having a heart attack. Then I passed out. He was calling 911 and had them on the line. I guess they told him how to do CPR. I woke up here."

"So what happens next?" Shelly asked.

"They're going to keep me here a couple of days, get me stabilized, then they are going to perform a double bypass surgery, keep me locked up here for another week, and then I will go home."

"So, the surgery is definite?" I asked.

"It is."

Shelly's shoulders shook, and tears cascaded down her face. "Come here, baby," Mom said, and she pulled Shelly to her. "It's okay, honey. I'm going to be okay."

I rubbed Shelly's back. Mom must have thought I needed a hug, too, because she pulled me into a little group hug on her hospital bed.

—x—x—x—

Before Mom went into surgery, she spent time alone with each of us, including Amy and our kids. Shelly went in crying and, an hour later, came out smiling and crying, so at least something changed for her. I went in smiling and came out crying.

The four of us, including Amy, who took time off from work for Mom's surgery, clustered in the surgery unit waiting room. People from other families slept, which I didn't get. Mom's surgery kept my fingers drumming a staccato beat. One eye twitched with the regularity of a turning fan. Every two minutes I looked at the clock or down at my watch. Every hour I made a trip to the bathroom, where I sat behind a locked stall door and cried. I even tried to pray, but it had been so long since I'd gone to church that I couldn't remember any of the standard prayers. I kept saying over and over again, "Please, God. Please, God. Please make this surgery go well." There was no way I could have slept.

Five hours after we left her, the doctor found us in the waiting room. "Everything went well. She did great. I completed bypass surgery on two arteries. I'm optimistic about the prognosis."

The four of us collapsed into a spontaneous group hug. Then we asked the doctor some questions. "She'll have to make some lifestyle changes. A different diet. We recommend the Mediterranean diet. Exercise. She'll go through physical therapy. She'll be on a daily dose of medications for the rest of her life. But everything looks good."

—x—x—x—

After Mom got out of recovery, we went into her room briefly. I thought she looked bad after the heart attack, but I wasn't prepared for what I saw post-surgery. This was a high-speed crash on the interstate. When she saw us, she tried to open her eyes but couldn't. She tried to reach out her hand but couldn't. She tried to smile but couldn't. Shelly and I gave her a soft hug. We pulled up a chair for Dad, who sat beside her for the rest of the day. He wasn't going anywhere. At some point, Shelly and I left and went for a walk through the university playing fields that abutted the hospital. We talked little, just slowly walked, essentially alone with our own darkest of thoughts. We both admitted we were wondering what our family would become if Mom died.

Eventually, Mom came out of the anesthetic haze, but she could hardly talk because of trauma from the intubation tube. Conversation flowed like hardening lava. Shelly and I left. Dad stayed, sleeping on a cot the hospital staff had pulled into the room. We grabbed some dinner, a couple of good greasy burgers at the Village Bar, an old traditional night out in our family. Then we headed over to Mom and Dad's house. It seemed appropriate to stay there during this family crisis. Shelly slept in her old room. I slept in mine. We often joked about making our rooms into shrines when we left, draping a velvet rope across the door. Our parents had essentially met our wishes. My room remained unchanged from when I moved out for college.

Packers, Badgers, and Trojans pennants hung on the walls. My old stereo filled a bookshelf in the corner of the room. My computer, which Mom and Dad passed down to me when they replaced the family computer, still filled up most of the desk in front of the window. I also tacked album covers to the walls, including several Bruce Springsteen covers. At the end of my senior year, Amy put together a collage of photos to commemorate our year together. I sat down at the desk and stared blankly at the photos. At that moment in my life, high school seemed like a phantom memory.

When I found Shelly in the family room, I handed her a beer. She read the label. "Warped Speed Scotch Ale. Any good?"

"Yeah, it's actually very good. Better than the Leinenkugel's crap we drank in high school."

"Hey, don't knock Leinie's," Shelly said. "I was weaned on that stuff. So were you. In fact, I lost my virginity because of it. I'm guessing the same is true for you, too. "

"Yeah, but you know I don't think I could even drink it anymore. I decided a long time ago that if I were going to drink beer, I would drink beer that tasted good. I pay homage to the gods every day for bringing us microbreweries." I was rambling, just talking nonsense to keep from pouring over Mom's condition again. I needed a break from it. Shelly apparently did, too.

"How old were you when you had your first beer with friends?"

After pondering for a moment, the answer came quickly. "The end of junior year, I mean the absolute last day. For lunch a couple of guys went to Bo's house. We raided his old man's beer fridge. Over a couple cans of Old

Style, we planned our summer workout schedule. You know, to get ready for our senior football season."

"Oh, nice irony. You know I was probably having my first beer with friends at exactly the same time that year, the last day of ninth grade," Shelly paused and took a sip of her beer for emphasis. "I think I spent most of the next four years in some altered state, but rarely was I ever in a state of bliss. And most of my fights with Mom, in one way or another, resulted from my fondness for substance abuse. Man, did I drink a lot of this shit, and I smoked a helluva lot of weed."

"That was a long time ago, Shell. You don't party like that anymore. At some point you need to forgive yourself for that."

"Someday, maybe. But I feel so guilty because fighting became the natural way for Mom and me to interact. It's almost like I felt her love the most when we fought. The worse the fight, the more I felt her love. Subconsciously, I picked the fights just so I could feel that love. You know the weird thing, Robb? Mom knew it. A couple of years ago, after I figured that out with the help of a therapist, I talked with Mom about it. She smiled and said, 'I was beginning to wonder if you would ever draw that completely apt conclusion.' And then she smiled at me again and said, 'Any time you feel the need to fight, just call me.'" Shelly lapsed into silence. The more I learned about Mom in the past few days, the more amazed I became.

Shelly and I talked long into the night. Then we returned to the hospital as soon as visiting hours began the next morning.

When we arrived, we found Dad pacing the hallway outside the CCU. He saw us, and he just stopped. His shoulders sagged. He ran a hand through his hair, which, from the tousled look, he had apparently been doing frequently.

"Dad? Dad, what's wrong," I asked.

"During the night your mother took a turn for the worse." He started to waver on his legs. Shelly and I rushed to him, wrapping his arms around our shoulders. We led him to a nearby chair. Dad stared at the ground. Shelly rubbed his shoulders in soft, sweeping motions as if she were gathering shards of glass into a pile. I kneeled in front of Dad.

I didn't want to hear bad news. The Rolling Stones said it best. "You can't always get what you want." If you're a pessimist, you end the lyrics there.

"During the night, your mother became feverish. She's developed some sort of infection." He paused and took a deep breath. Saying that much seemed to have exhausted him.

"But they're treating her, right? They're giving her antibiotics or flushing out the surgical wound?" Shelly asked.

"I guess."

"What did the doctor say? Did he offer a prognosis?" I asked.

"Yeah. The next twenty-four hours will be critical."

I stood and walked toward the window at the end of the hallway. Looking out, you could see the university campus, the tall buildings, the historical sites, the new technological monoliths the university built to remain on the cutting edge, but which required demolishing its history, Lake Mendota, and the final curve of the capitol dome. I looked but saw none of this. All I could see was the image I held from the day before of my mother lying in her hospital bed, looking like no one I ever knew. Now she would appear even more foreign.

Dad had reported that the next twenty-four hours would be important. The body can heal itself in amazing ways, especially if the mind joins in the fight. I found some hope in that. The variable, though, would be Mom's physical strength. After a heart attack and then a double bypass, would her body and mind be strong enough for one more major fight? Throughout her life, Mom had demonstrated her strength. You don't live to be seventy years old without showing strength. But Mom had faced some major tests in her life.

When people ask me about my family, I tell them I'm the oldest of two. Not exactly an accurate appraisal, but easier. I was the middle child, but my oldest brother died when I was two, and he was four. My grandparents had come to visit. They parked across the street from our house. Stevie grew so excited at seeing Papa and Nana that he slipped from Mom's arms and ran across the street toward them. The driver said he never saw Stevie, who darted between two parked cars. Mom, six months pregnant with Shelly, watched in horror, as did Papa and Nana. Somehow Mom got through those horrible days and the burial of that small casket. Mom found a therapist, who she saw daily until Shelly arrived, and then twice a week for the next five years.

"That woman saved not just my life, but Shelly's life, too," Mom said of Helen, who became a close family friend. Helen helped Mom grieve but also made her continuously work on finding joy in life. She also helped Mom get through a naturally overprotective state of mind. This traumatic period in Mom's life only became clear to me years later when Amy and I were expecting our first child, and Mom told us to love and cherish our children every day without fail, to always appreciate the special gift of family, of children, of love. And then she told us, in detail, about how often she almost gave up in those first two or three years. "Sad things happen in life," she said, "but that doesn't mean you have to live a sad life."

After a corporate merger, Mom lost her job as a mid-level manager, but she took her marketing skills and became a major success as a realtor. "If you can sell one thing, you can always sell another thing," Mom said. She entered the real estate market at the start of the big boom. She listed homes for a few clients who drastically overpriced their homes, strictly against Mom's advice. But she worked hard, of course, and then the first home ended up creating a bidding war between three potential buyers. She ended up selling the home for $5,000 more than its listed price, a significant amount at that time. Through the years, many of her colleagues thanked her, crediting her with single-handedly changing the pricing structure in the city.

My divorce from Amy hurt Mom. She looked at Amy as another daughter. She made us talk with Helen, but I had pushed Amy too far. During those days, Mom rarely smiled. She lost weight. She started chewing her fingernails, something I had never seen her do. "I'm worried about you, Robb. I'm worried about Amy. I'm worried about my grandchildren. A family is the most precious thing we have in life. And the end of your marriage makes me so sad. I'm having trouble dealing with it," she said when I asked her what was wrong. She pleaded with me to continue with counseling on my own, even after the divorce. I did—for three months. It didn't take.

Mom sat with her sister, her best friend, as she breathed her last breaths, succumbing finally to a battle with breast cancer she fought for more than three years. In the final four months, Mom brought a home-cooked meal for her sister and husband almost every day. It seemed that when Mom wasn't showing homes, she worked over the stove, cooking three or four meals at once and storing them in labeled and numbered plastic containers for easy matches when she collected the plasticware for refilling. I complimented Mom once on this heartfelt effort. "She'd do it for me," she replied simply. "This is what people do." *I guess I just haven't run into a lot of people like that lately,* I thought then.

Oh, yes, she had shown strength.

But did she have enough left now?

We gathered around her bed the next day as she labored to breathe. Strained efforts came out as gurgles. We sat with her for hours, holding her hand, touching her arm, hugging her. That entire time I gently touched her,

her arm, her leg, her hand, without break, afraid that a loss of her touch would be a loss of everything. She looked at each of us as if to remind us to heed the message she had given us the night before in separate, labored conversations. Then the look softened, and I don't think I will ever again see a look so full of pure love. It said more than any words could ever convey.

"So tired," she whispered as she closed her eyes.

"Don't go, Mama. Don't go," Shelly pleaded.

Mom's face contorted in a grimace. She took another deep breath and then another many seconds later.

"Rest now with God, Grace. We love you," Dad said in a hushed tone as tears slid down his face.

Mom took one more breath and then settled into the bed. Peace relaxed her face.

After the initial tears, I slipped out of the hospital, mumbling an excuse that I had to call Amy and the kids. I sat in my car and sobbed.

A half hour later, the sobs that wracked my body subsided, and I made that painful, sad call to Amy. I took a deep breath and simply said, "Mom died a little bit ago." Then I shared some of the details of her final moments.

"I'm so, so very sorry for you. For your family. For our family. We lost such a bright light today." She started to cry. I resumed crying. We cried together but separately. I felt more alone than I have ever felt. Who knows how much time passed, but we finally muttered our goodbyes. Then I returned to the hospital's cardiac floor. My body moved, but it felt as if I were walking through Jell-O, and the exertion left me numb. Dad and Shelly stood outside Mom's room.

"We thought you might want a little more time with your mother," Dad said simply.

I walked up to him and held him. He cried in my arms for several minutes. He touched my cheek with his fingertips. Then he kissed my forehead. I touched his cheek in return and walked into Mom's room. Dad had opened the shades. I knew it was Dad, honoring Mom's love of the light and shadows the sun cast throughout the house. During daylight hours, no shades ever remained closed at our house. She found the rectangular patterns of light the sun cast through the windows as beautiful as a stained glass window in a cathedral. I sat in the chair beside Mom's bed.

She looked peaceful, truly peaceful, so beautiful. But her skin had already started to lose its vibrancy, graying even more. I wanted to remember her as she was alive and vibrant, not like this, and not by some ridiculous attempt by the mortician to breathe life into her. I reached out and held her hand. It already felt cold. I stared at her for a long time. Sitting there beside her, thinking about what it would mean now that she was gone, the tears flowed again.

I wondered what traditions, like the Thanksgiving feast, tree-trimming party, Christmas dinner, and birthday celebrations, would continue and which would fade away. I wondered who I would now turn to for the sage advice I craved and the tough love I sometimes needed. I wondered who would encourage me to pick up the pieces and fix the mess I'd made of my life. I wondered how I could ever survive knowing I could never talk to her again. I wondered how my father would handle the emptiness and silences of the house. And I wondered how deep into darkness this sadness would plunge me, how long it would last. The despair at that moment almost overwhelmed me. The wracking sobs began again.

Shelly and Dad honored my time alone with Mom. When my painful breathing eased, I looked at her with some clarity. In my mind, I heard her say what she always said at the end of phone conversations and when I left her presence: "I love you."

I always responded with the same standard reply, "I love you, too."

She would then respond, "Good, good!"

Before I left the room, I took one last look.

"I love you, too," I said from the door.

I swear I heard, "Good, good." I let the door close softly behind me.

—x—x—x—

We finally left the hospital and headed back to the house. While I spent my final minutes with Mom, Dad had called the funeral home. When they retired, they decided to make some of their funeral arrangements. "Just planning ahead," Mom said when she told me.

"Mom, I don't want to think about you dying," I said.

She took a pragmatic approach to life and death. "We all die, hon. And it will be hard for you and Shelly when we die. You will face immeasurable sadness. You will find yourself desolate with sadness, but you also will find strength you never knew you possessed. You will get through it, and your life will go on, probably better than before. You just have to be patient with yourself." That conversation came back to me after Dad told me he had asked the funeral home to pick up the body. She had ceased being Mom and now had become the body. I mused about how quickly life changes. It's like flipping a light switch, going from light to dark—in an instant.

Shortly after we got to the house, Amy arrived with the kids. We did a group hug. Jessie couldn't stop crying, and she needed to hold Amy's or my hand constantly. TJ didn't cry. After the family hug, he slipped away, and I later found him in the family room staring mindlessly at the television, unaware he was watching a show about beautiful brides. When I slipped into the kitchen to bring some beverages out, Amy found me. She slipped into my arms and held me tight. Neither of us said anything for minutes. We just held on. She touched my cheek, stared into my eyes, and whispered, "I'm so sorry."

The next day, Shelly, Dad, and I went to pick out a casket and flowers. The funeral director led us into a showroom and pointed. "These represent the caskets we offer. You'll see the prices, which include the cement vault. Please take your time and let me know what you decide." He stepped out. The showroom featured twenty-five caskets in the tightly packed space. Like cars on a car lot, they were lined up in rows. Most had half the lid up so potential buyers could look under the hood.

"How in the hell do you do this?" I said, looking bewildered at Dad. "It's too much like picking out a Ford." He just shrugged. We made one quick circuit of the room and picked a lavender metal casket with a cream, satin interior. It was a lot like covering your eyes and pointing.

Before we left, the funeral director asked us to bring clothing we would like Mom to be buried in, along with any special effects. "If you would like to bring photos or any memorabilia for display at the visitation, you can bring that when you bring the clothing. Some people create photo boards or video memorials. Sometimes people like to display memorabilia that highlight important moments of their loved one's life. Even though Grace died on Friday, we were scheduled to hold the visitation and funeral on Wednesday to allow time for relatives and friends to get here." His delivery of information seemed as impersonal as it would have been if he had been explaining to prospective buyers about the special accessories in their new car they thought they might buy.

With that daunting task completed, we drove to the florist and spent an hour looking through floral display books. As Dad talked to the florist, I turned to Shelly. "We should probably buy an arrangement from the kids and grandkids." Then we picked one out for $150. The casket and funeral expenses would top $10,000. The funeral luncheon we ordered at Luigi's for the family and guests would be another $2,500.

I marveled at the amount of money it takes to die.

When we finally got back to Dad's, friends and family started to show up. The doorbell rang. I jumped up to answer it. "Hi, I'm Sandra Weiss, and your mother helped me buy my home. I'm so sorry for your loss. It is our loss, too. I thought your family might appreciate a nice meal. I brought a hot dish, salad, and dessert." It sounded like she had prepared a speech. "Your mother was such a wonderful person. When we moved into our new home that day, she came by in the middle of the afternoon. She brought us our first meal. She prepared a casserole, baked a loaf of bread and an apple pie. 'This meal will be the first step in turning this house into a home,' she said. It was such a beautiful thing," Sandra paused and brushed a tear away. "She was such a good person, a beautiful person. Again, I'm so sorry for you and your family." She patted my forearm and turned and left.

That moment happened again and again. People actually did bring food and drink to the bereaved. That surprised me. I just thought of the well-wishers who were full of kindness and compassion as a Hollywood myth. I didn't know if I would ever feel like eating again, but seeing the counter covered with casseroles, bread, and desserts, I found myself thinking kindly of good people who would take the time to help others in need. As I became so jaded after the divorce, I stopped believing in the goodness of people. Even in death, Mom, as always, helped me see that goodness.

—x—x—x—

"You gave a wonderful eulogy for your mother. So beautifully written. I've known your mother my whole life, but you made me remember how full of love she was. She was lucky to have you."

"I was lucky to have her, Aunt Susan. Thank you for the kind words." I didn't reveal to Aunt Susan or anyone else the anguish that went into writing that eulogy. Amy would have understood, though. It became apparent she went through the same thing.

On Sunday morning after Mom died, I left Dad and Shelly, who sat quietly in the living room, Shelly wrapped in Dad's arms. I grabbed my laptop and shuffled four blocks to a local coffee shop. After buying a chai latte, I pulled out my computer and checked my email. I smiled at the condolences friends had offered me, responding to a general email I had sent out to inform people of Mom's death. Many "friends" offered similar condolences on Facebook. I had made a heartfelt post on my own page and also added a note to Mom's timeline.

I spent an hour writing emails and notes on Facebook to show my gratitude for people's kindness. I mused for several minutes about how people try to show compassion but also create distance with personal/

impersonal comments. Many people expressed "sorrow for my loss" with "hugs" or "prayers" but said nothing personal or meaningful. And some people absentmindedly clicked the "like" button on my post about my mom dying. What did they like about that? I scratched my head, sipped my chai, and pondered how social media creates the illusion of closeness but often just creates distance. After another half hour of these rabbit hole meanderings, I browsed a few more websites and realized I was delaying. I took a deep breath and started to write.

How do you write something that becomes both a tribute and a summary of someone's life? How do you also help friends and family remember those special qualities? And how do you convey your own deep love and sadness? Having never done so before, I wrestled with writing a eulogy for someone so important in my life, for someone I so loved. I tried to write down some memories, just to get going.

Instead, I ended up writing a poem:

She is Gone

The May flowers blooming rampage paused
The birds halted singing in mid-song
The stars blinked
And the sun covered its eyes
Behind a passing cloud.

And for all of us
The spinning earth faltered
As we stood beside her
Hopeful for more time
But knowing the end had come.

Now we live on memories
Already made, already lived
No new ones to come
Her voice now silent
Like an early January morning.

She will impart no more wisdom
We must make do
With what she labored to teach us
Recalling her sayings and philosophies
Always hoping to make her proud.

She gave us life

She dedicated a lifetime to us
In our youth she set us free
To live our lives as best we could
Now she has done so again.

We invite the mourners to come
And sing their sadness and memories
It will be a sad tune they sing
But still full of echoing chords and beautiful melodies
The notes written on tear-stained sepia pages.

She is gone, we keep saying
And wondering how such a thing
Could have happened so soon
But when we leave from here to go out there
We will carry her with us out into the world.

Then, without really planning to, I wrote a paragraph about my wedding reception:

> Everyone wore smiles along with their fancy clothes. Unlike many people who bemoan all of the mishaps of their wedding day, we experienced no problems, and it might just have been because Amy and I didn't care if anything went wrong. We just felt so happy about the life we had just formally started together, and we were taken up by the bigness of this idea, so nothing could intrude on that happiness. I think all the guests felt that, too. All night long, everybody seemed to smile, especially Mom and Dad, who stood arm in arm as they wished us well at the end of the night. Mom hugged Amy and then me, and she whispered in my ear: "Be happy. Your love is one for the ages."

As I wrote about my wedding and thought about Mom, I found myself sobbing uncontrollably, looking out the window but seeing nothing. Other patrons looked away, uncomfortable with the awkwardness of sitting near someone in so much pain. They sipped their expensive drinks and scrolled down their phones, leaving me in my solitary grief, trying not to show their curiosity about how anyone could be so sad on such a fine Sunday May morning.

After Mom's funeral, conversations like the one I had with Aunt Susan continued throughout the memorial luncheon we held at Papa Luigi's Italian Restaurant. I invited people to sit, and Father Joe offered a blessing for the meal. I then invited people to the buffet table. "The fare is simple, but Mom's favorites. Mom loved pizza. She also loved cheeseburgers. Pretty much every time we went out to eat, unless it was some fancy, upscale restaurant, she ordered a good, old-fashioned cheeseburger. So today, in her honor, we're having salad, pizza, and cheeseburgers. She also loved chocolate cake, so be sure to grab a piece for dessert. After we have eaten, people can share thoughts or memories of Mom if they would like. Please help yourselves to some food."

Shelly tried to offer a tribute to Mom. She started to speak, started to cry, started to wail. I stepped up to her and put my hand on her back, offering support. She turned into my arms. I held her. Then I gently helped her back to her seat. I thought again of how she collapsed after the funeral service before the procession to the cemetery.

After the mourners left the church, the family stood in the vestibule. We watched reverently as the mortician and his assistant prepared to move the casket to the hearse. Dad looked at Shelly and made an unusual request, or so it seemed to me. After listening to Dad, the funeral home director nodded somberly—everything he did was somber, and I began to wonder if the guy ever smiled or if he laughed somberly, too. He asked his assistant to give the family a moment. When the assistant left, the director stepped to the casket. He unlatched the casket and lifted the lid. We gathered around and took one last look at Mom's body. To me, that's all it was—a body. It sort of looked like Mom, but it didn't project her essence, her spirit. To Shelly, it was Mom, and when the director closed the lid, it was as if the lid came down on Shelly, too. I could see an immense shadow darken her eyes.

Shelly continued to cry. We stepped away, and I wrapped my arm around Shelly, turning her toward the door. After a few unsteady steps with Shelly, I turned to offer my arm to Dad. At that moment Shelly just collapsed. She sank to the ground as if all the molecules of her body melted. Dad and I kneeled beside her. Dad swooped her in his arms and carried her to a pew, where he sat with her and drew her tight to him. He gently rocked her until she began gasping for air, and her body calmed, and the tears slowed. I sat in the pew behind her and rubbed her back. I couldn't tell if this was appropriate or if I was intruding on a special moment between Shelly and Dad.

Much later, as I reflected on this moment, I realized that though some guidelines exist for etiquette at funerals, almost all behavior is acceptable. You do what you need to do to get through it. As Mom said, people find the strength to survive these impossibly hard days.

After Shelly's attempt at a eulogy at the luncheon, Mom's youngest sister, Nancy, offered some words. She shared memories of growing up, of their childhood games, of their minor mischievous skirmishes, of their interests in boys, often the same boys. "My sister married the best one of the bunch. When I think about what a marriage should be, I think of their marriage." She looked at my dad and smiled. My aunt ended her eulogy with a poignant statement. "In every way she was her name—Grace."

Several others offered anecdotes or stories of praise. When I saw the last speaker approach the microphone, I fought to catch my breath. Amy stood before the mourners, and I wondered what my ex-wife would say about my mother.

From the first moment I introduced Amy to Mom, something clicked between them. Mom sat at the kitchen table as she often did, sipping a cup of tea. For her the kitchen was the living room. She felt most comfortable there. Sometimes she would read, sometimes she would write letters or notes to friends, always with NPR playing softly in the background. I once asked Mom about all these notes she wrote, and she said, "You have to work at friendships, just like you have to work at a marriage. It's like tending a garden. If you don't mind it regularly, weeds quickly take over. I don't let weeds grow in my friendships. Or my marriage." After introductions that evening, which occurred during the first week I started dating her, Amy sat down with Mom. They started chatting, and I became superfluous.

Amy began her eulogy with this anecdote. She left out the part about me being superfluous. "In Grace I found a kindred spirit. She and I understood each other. She treated me with respect, dignity, and love, qualities my own mother often found difficult to show. I began to turn to Grace for advice, counsel, support, and love. When I became engaged to Robb, she asked if I would feel comfortable calling her 'Mom.' I was ecstatic. She became my friend and my surrogate mother. Grace and I spoke almost every day. Even in recent years, she would call me or I her. 'Just checking in,' she would say. I never told her enough how good it made me feel that she checked in. I didn't tell Grace often enough how much I loved her. How could anyone ever adequately express how much they loved Grace?"

I knew Amy and Mom kept in touch after the divorce. I didn't know that they maintained such close contact. Neither ever spoke to me of their ongoing connection.

"Where others might have blamed me in some ways for things that happened in my life and the life of my family, Grace never imposed harsh judgment against me. She let me know that she would always treat me as her daughter, that she would love me unconditionally. Many people speak of unconditional love. Grace lived it. I will miss my friend, my mom, more than anybody can imagine. She watched over me for much of my life. Now God's best angels will watch over her."

Amy remained at the microphone. She dipped her head, and a solitary tear dropped to the podium. It became a solemn moment, as if she were saying goodbye to Mom. Then she slowly looked up and smiled, but it was a sad smile just the same. When she sat down, people started to applaud, a rarity from other eulogies I'd heard. Jessie and TJ hugged her, and she clung to our children as if she had just found them after thinking they were lost at Disney World.

After a few more people shared stories and memories about Mom, Dad approached the microphone. He hadn't performed a eulogy at the church, though he greeted all mourners at the funeral home and church with kindness and listened with rapt attention as they shared their experiences and love for his wife.

"Were my dear and loving wife here today, she would have appreciated the kind sentiments but privately would have thought it too much fuss. All your kind words and gestures captured the beauty and wonder that was Grace. She did so much good for people, but I know she never really thought she affected people's lives in so many positive ways. She showered people with kindness and love for only one reason: because that's how you should treat people. She never became upset when people didn't return that kindness. To Grace, that just signaled that they were having a bad day or a bad stretch, and they just needed a little bit more love."

Dad paused for a moment. It became a long moment. "Our dear Amy said recently that when Grace died, we lost a shining light. Amy was right. We did. The world will feel a bit darker now. But maybe, maybe, if we approach life as Grace always did, with as much kindness and love as we can muster, someday we will start to see the light again." Dad paused again, and I felt like I could actually see him committing himself to that cause, to kindness and love, not that Dad, in his own way, ever lacked in feeling those emotions, though he didn't always show them to the world.

"Our family thanks you for the gifts of your kindness in recent days. We appreciate you. We love you."

I stood as Dad finished, about to return to the mic—I felt like an emcee for this memorial luncheon—to express one final show of gratitude to our guests. Dad stepped up to me. He touched my cheek and kissed my forehead. I touched his cheek.

Following the luncheon, people offered their last condolences and trickled out. Later, I would reflect on some of the comments people made. Many offered heartfelt, emotional condolences. Others made comments that showed their awkwardness over talking about death. Some people offered baffling comments. One woman, who claimed to be a friend, left me shaking my head. She said, "It's a blessing your mother died. She's not suffering anymore." I certainly didn't think it a blessing that Mom died. It's not like she battled cancer as it ravaged her body or suffered from dementia and lost herself in a dark, never-ending cave. It's not like she wanted to die. After this immediate reaction, I brushed aside the comment and talked to a few other friends and family members.

Throughout the entire funeral ordeal, my best friend, Cam, stood nearby. Friends for as long as I could remember, Cam had held the honor of being my best friend. My mother became a second mother to Cam, too. During Mom's time in the hospital, Cam visited every day. On the day of Mom's death, I called Cam. He immediately came to the house. He hugged me and held me for a long bro hug. "I'm here for you, bud." And he was. Cam stayed near me throughout the funeral, watching me closely, searching for cues that I needed consolation from him or merely the comfort of someone standing beside me to lean on should I need the support. It made me feel stronger just knowing he hovered nearby.

As people started to leave the luncheon, I walked up to Cam and hugged him. "I love you, buddy," I said to him. He slapped my back twice, fist closed, again the bro hug.

Later, some close friends and family sat in the living room of the house and talked about Mom. We told stories, we reminisced, we talked about our favorite memories of her. The kids talked about Christmas. Mom loved Christmas. She came to life during the holiday season. She kicked off the Christmas season with her annual tree-trimming party, when she invited family and friends to help decorate the tree. The elders sat on couches and chairs and strung popcorn. Others hung ornaments. People drifted out of the living room and into the kitchen to graze at the splendor of the food table. With the tree decorated, everyone would gather in the living room to sing carols. When the guests filtered out, Mom gathered the family to usher them out with a spirited singing of "We Wish You a Merry Christmas."

TJ and Jessie also held special memories of Christmas. It became our tradition to spend Christmas Eve at Mom and Dad's and open our presents at their house on Christmas morning, the kids' eyes bulging as they entered the living room. Presents would cover the entire floor. As they dug their way through the pile of goods, they would fling wrapping paper like treasure hunters to reveal the buried gold.

For me, stating a favorite memory proved difficult. I couldn't distill a lifetime of memories of my mom into a single moment or event. I suspected I would spend the rest of my days remembering so many special moments with Mom. Picking just one memory to share would have been like spending a lifetime reading a book a week and, at the end, trying to name your favorite book. Everybody was sharing memories. I felt like I needed to throw some of mine into the air. "Shelly, I think you'll remember this. When we were kids, Mom read about a meteor shower that would streak the sky. The shower would be the best at about three in the morning. Mom woke us up. Do you remember this, Dad? You grumbled a little bit because you had to go to work the next morning. In the end, you said it was worth it."

"I definitely remember that. The Perseid. They happen every year in mid-August. The heavens were ablaze that night," Dad said.

I launched into a description of that night. "Streak after streak trailed across the sky. We walked to the park and lay down in the dew-streaked grass. We stayed there for probably forty-five minutes. Sometimes we would see seven or eight shooting stars a minute. You had to look up and take in the entire sky so as not to miss any. Finally, like when the final kernels pop sporadically in the microwave bag, the shooting stars faded. As we walked home, Mom put her arm around me. I said, 'Mom, that was really beautiful,' which was pretty emotive for a teenager. Mom looked at me, and then she looked at Shelly, who Dad was carrying in his arms. She said, 'You two are my shooting stars.'"

After I finished the story, the room grew quiet. Shelly wore a perplexed expression. "I don't remember that. Any of it. At all."

The stories and the chatter continued for a while. When it seemed appropriate, I excused myself and stepped into the backyard. I found myself looking into the heavens, hoping for a shooting star. Cloud cover prevented me from seeing anything. As I looked up, I found myself silently crying.

Sometime later, I realized someone stood behind me. Without turning, I could tell Amy had followed me outside. I didn't turn to face her. And I didn't say anything. Neither did she. Then she walked up behind me, slipped her arm around my waist, and held me. She gently touched my face with her fingers, then she cradled my head and gave me a gentle, lingering kiss on the cheek. She stepped away and left me to my solitude. For a long time I could feel the sweetness of that kiss on my cheek.

When I finally stepped back into the house, Amy and the kids had left, Shelly retreated to her room, and Dad sat in the living room. We talked for a bit, and I said good night. “I’ll see you tomorrow, Dad.”

“You bet, son.”

Before she died, Mom had asked me for three favors. I vowed to fulfill my promises to her.

When I promised to honor her last wishes, she said, “Good, good.”

The next day, I got busy immediately fulfilling the first promise. I was moving home.

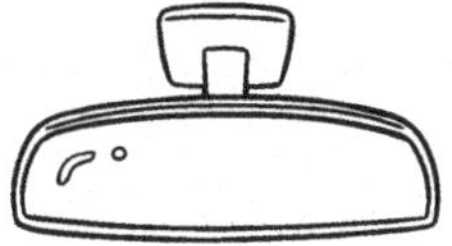

CHAPTER 3

Although I didn't officially move out until I went to college, I unofficially left home my senior year simply because I spent so little time at home that year. When I moved home after Mom's death, I found myself pondering how much my life changed the summer before my last year of high school. Senior year defined the high school experience for me. Something seemed to happen during the summer between junior and senior years. While I always had friends, I suddenly became popular.

You know your classmates through ten or eleven years of school, and suddenly they start to see you differently. Friendships change as you move into new cliques in high school. But really, who knows why that happens? Despite what Hollywood portrays, you can't just decide one day to be popular and then make it happen. But I've often pondered my own transformation. While I can speculate—people may have started listening to my witty quips; or they realized I was funny on a scale larger than as a jokester in the back of the classroom; or they also might have seen that I could carry my own in intellectual discussions in class—who really knows.

Throughout junior high and high school, music played a big part in my life. I participated in every band organization possible. I just enjoyed making music. Known as a school that excelled in the arts, my high school offered three concert bands, two jazz ensembles, and a marching band. During my senior year, I played in the top concert band, the wind ensemble, and the top jazz ensemble, the Gold Jazzers. I also participated in the marching band and had since seventh grade. Some of my closest friends throughout high school and beyond came about because of my marching band experiences. I met Cameron long before music grabbed me.

We remained friends, though he often felt he played second chair to my band experience and band friends.

That summer, when we were rising seniors, our marching band, which had always been good, became great. We won every field show competition we entered. At many high schools, students tag band members as geeks. Not at our school. We held status on par with the best athletes and the top scholars. With more than 200 members, 164 musicians, and a 42-person color guard, those who knew marching bands labeled us one of the best high school marching bands in the country. At that time, summer bands competed in events around the country, much like drum and bugle corps. Judges rated bands based on their concert performances, parade maneuvers, and field shows, which generally resemble what bands do at halftime of football games. But these field shows are much more sophisticated, more intricate, more difficult. While most high school marching bands stomp around the field, our band essentially performed the equivalent of twelve-minute Broadway musicals.

As we moved into that final summer, a group of seniors gathered. We vowed to provide the leadership that would make the summer band experience a winning campaign. We wanted to create a different experience from the previous summer, where it seemed we just went through the motions, like a football team with no energy or drive to win. We didn't win anything as juniors, and as juniors, we realized that the lackluster campaign happened because the seniors failed to provide any leadership. My friends and I all vowed to lead as best we could. That summer I became a vocal leader of the band, something I had never considered previously.

Before each competition, I made a motivational speech to the band. At the first competition, I told a story, a parable. People started to laugh when I opened with a statement about a wise, old man. "The wise, old man lived years ago in a small village. Everyone knew of his wisdom and frequently turned to him for answers to their problems, for insights into how to live their lives." When people started to laugh, one of my friends shouted, "Shut the fuck up, dudes! He's serious. Listen and learn, listen and learn."

I continued, imbued with renewed confidence that my audience would listen. "The wise, old man was always right. His advice always helped people find the correct path. A teenager decided he was going to trip up the wise, old man. He would hold a small bird in his hands behind his back and ask the wise, old man what he held in his hands behind his back. If the old man answered, 'a bird,' the teenager would then ask if the bird was alive or dead. If the old man said the bird was alive, the teenager would crush the bird to death. If the wise, old man said the bird was dead, the teenager would set it free to fly away. To the first question, the wise, old man answered correctly. When the teenager posed the second question, the old man wisely said, 'Whether the bird in your hands is alive or dead, the answer lies in your hands. The choice is yours.'"

To my bandmates, I said, "We can have a great season. Or we can be mediocre. It is in our hands. What are we going to do? We start answering those questions tonight. Let's make sure we answer correctly and wisely. Let's get out there tonight and show our competition how hard it is going to be for anyone to beat us this year. Are you ready?" I shouted. My bandmates started clapping. "Then Let's go! Let's go!" I shouted again.

The band let out a collective roar. If we had been preparing to play a football game for the conference championship against our biggest rival, we would have pulverized them. Our juices ran high. Only on some occasions since then have I experienced such an adrenaline rush. We went out and smashed the competition in the judged field show. I like to think my speech helped motivate us. After that, I gave the speech before every competition. Sometimes I delivered a purely motivational message. Sometimes I just spewed vitriol. Sometimes I just looked at my bandmates and said, "We're all friends here. Hell, we're all best friends. Let's do it tonight for each other." And we did. No matter what I said, it always seemed to work. The Trojan High School marching band won every competition that year, every field show, every parade, every concert. In many ways, at least within the band, next to the director and the drum major, I became the visual representation of the spirit of the band. Everyone looked to me. I really wasn't sure why this happened, but I had a blast.

I will never forget winning the Great Lakes Band Championship that year. We changed at the Elks Lodge, a block from the Memorial Stadium. We hosted the competition, so we got to change in a place nearest to the stadium. Other bands changed in schools and community centers farther away. We changed in the big banquet hall. The chaperones tried to create a human wall so that we couldn't see each other in our underwear. This happened every year. By the time we were seniors, we had stopped gaping, but it didn't mean we still didn't look. A rite of passage somehow.

Before we took the field that night, I again found all eyes on me, waiting for the motivational speech. They stared at me, and I said nothing for a long time. I seemed to possess the timing of a gospel minister. I held the silence until the breaking point, and then I launched in. "This is our crowd. This is our stadium. These are our families. These are our friends. The whole marching season has led to this point. Right now. Tonight. All that came before doesn't matter. What matters is right now. It's our night. Let's show these people what we can do for them. Let's give the competition another reason to fear us and who we are. And you all know who we are. We are the Trojans, the mighty mighty Trojans. They might fear us. They should fear us. Don't walk off that field wondering if you could have done better. Leave everything you have out there. We have nothing to save for. This is our night. This is our time. This. Is. Our. Time."

Then I started to shout to the mass of band members huddled together a block from the stadium. Here I really did resemble a minister as I engaged in call and response. "Are you proud of what we've done?"

"Yes," they responded in unison.

"Have we done enough?"

"No."

"What're we gonna do tonight?"

"Win."

"Just win? Is that going to be enough?"

"No."

"Should we pulverize? Demolish? Destroy?"

"Yes." A prolonged yes.

"This is our night. Now let's go and show 'em all. This is our time. Who are we?"

The band replied in unison, more than two hundred voices strong, "We are the Trojans, the mighty, mighty Trojans."

I shouted again. "This is our time!"

And it was.

Organizers always made a big show out of the distribution of awards after the competition. Each band paraded out onto the field. Close to two thousand kids in a panoply of band uniforms, guards with their drill rifles or a spectrum of colors in their flags marched onto the field, came to sharp attention, and then stood at parade rest throughout the ceremonies. First, the announcers called the category winners for the junior bands, culminating in best band on parade, best band in concert, and best band overall.

While this went on, we whispered conversations with our rank mates. Most of our conversations that night carried a tone of awe. "Holy shit. Every time I looked down ranks and files, I saw no one, I mean no one out of line."

Another person said, "Did you hear that fucking crowd? I know they're our people, but they screamed at everything we did. If it wasn't so fucking much fun on the field, I might have wanted to watch this one from the stands."

Yet another person piped in. "I've never been a part of anything so incredible. We won. Nobody could have beat us tonight."

Another trumpet player said, "Did any of you catch the guard? Those flags were sharp, crackling sharp. Every maneuver. And not a single person dropped a rifle."

A French horn player commented on the music. "I've never heard any marching band sound so good. We were musical tonight."

Another horn player gushed. "And we were fucking loud, too. Fucking A."

When the third person proclaimed our certain victory, I injected a word of caution: "We don't know that. Another band might have had the same kind of night. And if we don't win, no matter what, we will be gracious to the winners. Remember, we come to attention when they announce each of the other bands."

Then the announcers started calling the winners for the high school division. Tradition dictated that the announcer announced the results in reverse order from last place to first. Tension grew like a tsunami coming ashore as you waited to hear your band's name. Best band in concert: the Trojans marching band.

"Band, atten-shun!" called the assistant drum major. We snapped to attention while Jim, the drum major, collected the trophy. I mean, we snapped. I'd never seen a band come to attention with such force. You could feel the breeze from everyone moving abruptly and in complete unison.

Best band standing inspection: the Trojans marching band. "Band, atten-shun!"

Best color guard. Back to attention. Best drum major. Standing stiff at attention.

Best band on parade: the Trojans marching band. So far we had cleaned up in every category. We cared most about the field show competition.

Then the announcer started announcing the results of the field show competition in reverse order. Nine bands, the best in the Midwest that year, competed in the field show. "In third place, The Kilties of Racine, Wisconsin." Still waiting for our name to be called, we snapped to attention again to salute our competitors. The next call would determine the results. When the announcer named second place, the winner, too, would be clear.

I said in a loud voice so that all near me could hear: "Remember, respect to our competitors, no matter what!" Everybody stared straight ahead, eyes burning a hole in the head of the person in front of us.

"And in second place in tonight's Great Lakes Band Championship," and the announcer paused. He, too, understood the drama of this moment. In that pause, I found myself shaking with anticipation. "In second place with a score of 91.5, the Oregon Sound."

My friends and I screamed with delight. But we still popped to attention to show respect for our competitor. Then we went back to parade rest. Momentarily lost in the joy of the moment, I placed my hands on my knees and felt tears streaming down my cheeks. The moment slammed me. All of us had put in so much work to get to this point. I took a deep breath. Then I quickly straightened up.

The announcer finally called the first-place results. "And your Great Lakes Band Championship Champions, with a score of 93.5, the Trojans marching band."

"Band, atten-shun!" We snapped like we had never snapped to attention before. I don't think I will ever forget the crackle of our move to attention. Beside us, the Oregon Sound snapped to attention to salute our victory. I had a clear view of Jim collecting our trophy. He shook the hands of the presenters. Then he held the trophy aloft. The home crowd roared its approval.

Then he turned to us. He still held the trophy aloft and called out a command we had never heard before: "Band, celebrate!"

We stood stunned momentarily, but I quickly grabbed the person closest to me in a giant hug. That seemed to break the spell. Then everybody was hugging. I don't know that I have ever felt such pure joy as in that crazy moment of celebration. Tears streamed down my face. I quickly looked around at all of my fellow seniors, who were all crying. We had gone through so much together, including a dismal year as juniors, where we came in dead last at all field competitions. We did well in concert and always would. You knew all of the hours of summer toil through ninety-degree days at band camp, rehearsing music and marching for twelve hours a day, and after camp night practices four nights a week, swatting mosquitoes in the dusky light, marching two and three parades a day sometimes, competitions each weekend, success in other aspects of the summer band experience meant nothing if you failed on the field.

As the other bands paraded off the field, I broke ranks and started finding my fellow seniors. Drum cadences pounded as bands left the field. To this day, drum cadences always make me happy. I love the creativity and the driving beat of cadences. More than anything, they remind me of that night. To the beat of the other drummers, I hugged each senior. I worked through the band, back to front. At the front of the band, I worked my way through the color guard. I came to Amy, this girl who I had noticed and occasionally briefly chatted with and flirted with, especially on the last day of band camp. We hugged. I released her, but she grabbed me and hugged me again.

"I hope you're enjoying this. We certainly wouldn't have got this far without you," she said.

I smiled at her, very debonair. "Or without you." What a master of words. She smiled and hugged me again. Then I turned away from her, about to go grab Jim, the drum major and a good friend of mine. But I turned back and looked at Amy again. She was still looking at me. She smiled again. I felt my heart leap, like the announcer had just called out the results one more time in case anyone missed it. I ran toward Jim and lifted him high in the air. So much for decorum.

The Trojans marching band, as the host of the competition, earned the right to parade off the football field last. We were about to leave the field when I ran back up to Jim. He looked at me, surprised. "What's up? You need to be in your rank. They're about to call us to leave the field."

"I've got an idea!"

"Hurry up. We've got to go," Jim snapped.

"Let's do the show again!"

"What?"

"Christ, Jim. Look at those stands. Not a single person has left. They're dying for us to do it again. We'll never have this chance again."

Jim's eyes twinkled, and I knew I had him. "Get back to your spot."

"Band, atten-shun!" Jim called. "Two commands," he shouted. "Listen closely. Band, about-face."

Back in my spot, I shouted, "Yeah, baby!" People around me looked puzzled.

"March off the field. Reset field show start. Ready. Move!" We marched off the field to the sideline opposite the press box.

I heard the announcer say, "Something is up with the Trojans marching band. They don't appear ready to leave the field yet." His voice rose in pitch as his own hometown excitement took over.

We reset the field show start—an arrow. Jim smartly stepped to the center of the field at the point of the arrow. He turned to the stands, and the crowd screamed. The announcer quickly caught on as he saw the Trojans marching band standing at attention. "Folks, we are in for a special treat tonight, something we have never seen before at these championships." He paused again, milking the drama. "Is the Trojans marching band ready to take the field in exhibition?"

Jim counted off our quick step tempo. That year we had gone to a silent start. No commands, just the muffled clapping from Jim's gloved hands. After four counts, the arrow shot forward sixteen counts and stopped in unison. We quickly bowed our heads again in unison, and then the entire band came up in a military-style, right-handed salute. The crowd screamed and screamed.

Before we reprised our show, Jim pointed at me. I smiled.

"Trojans marching band," I shouted. "Just like before. This is our time!" And we once again performed a show that I will remember forever.

After we finished the drill, once again to a standing ovation, we marched off the field in our traditional style, by fours, with the color guard leading us off the field and the drummers taking up the rear. The drum major was always the last to leave the stadium. He stood at the corner of the end zone and high-fived each member of the band. When my rank near the front of the band marched by him, he grabbed me. I gave him a quizzical look.

"You're marching out with me tonight. We salute for the entire stands." Jim and I saluted the stands together. As we marched past the stands, I saw our director, Mr. Finch, standing there smiling. He gave us a pumped fist that he then touched to his heart. Jim and I did the same to him and then resumed our salute. We had broken protocol with the repeat of our show, but Mr. Finch seemed as enthused about it as we were. As we left Lakefront Stadium, he walked beside us on the outer edge of the cinder track. He smiled the entire way, shouting "Awesome" and "Unbelievable." Periodically, he would just break out in a solo of applause. Jim and I smiled all the way.

Jim and I walked out together, in salute, wearing the biggest smiles. One of those pictures made it into the yearbook. I don't need to see the photo to remember the moment, but it sure is nice to look at.

As soon as we left the stadium, Mr. Finch ran up to Jim and me and enveloped us. He lifted us both off the ground, sputtering with joy. Finally, he found a coherent sentence. "You boys, this band, tonight have given me something I will never forget. Never. Thank you!" Then he skipped ahead, grabbing random members of the band and enveloping them as well.

Just like we couldn't merely walk off the field after winning the show, we also couldn't just go back to the Elks and change and go home. The band that had earned first-place honors as best band in concert, best band on parade, best band at inspection, best drum major, best color guard, and best drum line band in field competition couldn't just go home. So we marched and played through the entire downtown.

People paraded with us. Cars followed us, honking their horns. It was a lot like winning the homecoming game. But it was more than that. It was like winning the conference, no the state championship. Eventually, we had a police escort. When we got back to the Elks Lodge, three hundred people surrounded us and demanded that we play our field show music again. After that, we finally changed out of our uniforms, and a big group of us went to Pizza Hut. A few seniors with good fake IDs were able to buy pitchers of beer. They generously shared the beer with some of the other seniors. Some of those seniors dribbled beer in the championship trophy. Each of us sipped out of the trophy cup, just like the victors of the Stanley Cup. I sipped a little beer, but I knew I didn't need the beer to enjoy this night. I also wanted to remember it all without having to recall fuzzy memories.

Standing in the parking lot at two o'clock in the morning, a group of us couldn't let the night end. We kept chatting, talking, laughing, and hugging each other. It seemed too magical, and because of that, it seemed like that euphoria should last forever. Beginning that night in the Pizza Hut parking lot throughout my entire senior year, that time passed as if I had been dipped in bliss.

The night that we stood around in the Pizza Hut parking lot happened more than twenty-five years ago, and I can picture it as if it happened yesterday. We talked with a tone of wonder, awe, pride, and silliness that winning and drinking, for many of the others, produces. "Can you believe this night?" people kept saying with wonder. At one point, I found myself standing next to Amy, remembering that hug during the awards ceremony from this cute girl who had just joined the color guard that year. I had never really interacted with her until that summer, first at our week of band camp and then in the subsequent weeks. We had started to chat at band camp, and I knew at some point I would ask her out. An incident happened at band camp that made that connection inevitable.

The camp had come to a close. We had just finished our last rehearsal. The chaperones made us clean out our rooms, and once the room passed their inspection, we brought our gear outside and started loading instruments, suitcases, and sleeping bags on the band truck. The buses were supposed to pick us up from St. John's Military Academy near Milwaukee at one o'clock for the hour-and-a-half ride home. But they were late. So we milled around in the commons, eating a last bowl of camp ice cream.

Some of us got bored, and we began to conspire. One by one, several of the seniors, including Brad, Phil, Steve, Jim, and I snuck off. Jim had saved a bag of balloons for just such an occasion. We created an arsenal of water balloons. We also filled bottles with icy water as the second prong of our attack. Then we snuck them outside, carrying them in pillowcases. Gradually, everybody came out of the commons to wait outside for the buses. On cue, I stood up and yelled, "Trojans forever!" and began hurling water balloons. I had positioned myself near Amy and the other girls from the color guard. Amy took the first two balloons. She started sputtering, then laughing as she swiped the water from her face. I quickly emptied my bag of balloons and retreated. After the shock of the attack, the girls showed their ingenuity. They found their own methods of dousing us. They ran to the commons and gathered plastic cups, which they quickly filled with water.

She used several guard members as a human shield. She snuck up with the stealth of a soldier about to ambush. She jumped out from behind her friends and dropped both cups of water over my head. It was my turn to sputter and laugh.

"Okay. Good show. I guess we're even," I said.

"Not even close," Amy said with sparkling eyes. I just stood there dumbfounded as her friends began handing her cups of water. She took each cup of water and poured it over my head.

After ten or twelve consecutive baths, I said, "Are we even now?"

She ran off with her friends, giggling. Meanwhile, the water fight raged. It swept up most of the band members. Puddles began forming on the ground. At first, the chaperones tried to make us stop, but Mr. Finch quickly called them off. Then he stood off to the side and laughed, offering a running commentary like a sports announcer.

In the midst of the melee, I pulled Phil and Brad aside, and they quickly agreed to my plan. We each took a bottle of water from our stash and snuck off to the side of the battle. Then we let out our war yelps and chased down Mr. Finch and thoroughly soaked him, which became the signal for about fifty other people to hit him with more water. If we had been the football team, it would have been Gatorade. He just roared with laughter. Some of the chaperones stood shaking their heads in disgust at our disrespect for our conductor.

I came to realize later how important that water fight was to our success as a band. It created an identity and cohesiveness. It made us a team. The band camp water fight would forever now link us. Mr. Finch later told me he knew this moved us closer to success than all of the hours of rehearsal at camp. While we buzzed about the water fight all summer, Mr. Finch never mentioned it. In fact, he never said a word about it until years later, after we had reestablished contact and became friends as adults.

For me, though, the best part of the water fight hadn't happened yet. Eventually, the battle fizzled out, like water out of a hose after you had turned off the spigot. Groups of kids stood in clusters, dripping wet, recounting the epic battle, and then breaking out into giggles.

I found myself grouped up with my guys and several of the senior girls.

Amy stood with this group. Then Amy said, "What do you say, girls?" In unison, they screamed, "Yeah!" and attacked. Amy took two steps toward me, pulled out a bottle of Johnson's Baby Oil, and poured it over my head. Before she could dump all of the contents over my head, I gently grabbed her wrists and made sure she caught some as well. We wrestled for a moment, laughing with glee. I glanced around the group and saw similar pairs in clutches. By the end of the summer, many of the people in that circle had paired up. On the bus ride home, I smelled Johnson's Baby Oil and smiled. I turned around and looked at Amy, sitting two rows behind me. She was looking at me. We smiled. I swooned. I swear to God, I swooned. Whenever I smell Johnson's Baby Oil, to this day, despite all that has happened, I think of Amy.

I was definitely planning on asking Amy out, but I wasn't the fastest mover when it came to affairs of the heart. I progressed with the speed of a glacier

But I liked her. Oh yeah, I liked her.

Throughout the summer, when we did talk, we talked easily. She laughed at my jokes. And she was so cute. The more I talked with her, the more beautiful she became.

With the wonder, awe, pride, silliness, and a seemingly unending supply of adrenaline coursing through my veins that night we won the championship, I pulled Amy aside, where a tricked-out van shielded us from the view of others in the parking lot.

"There's something I wanted to tell you," I said.

She looked at me, puzzled.

"This," I said. Stepping closer to Amy, I touched her face with my fingertips, leaned toward her, and gently kissed her. When the kiss broke, we looked at each other and slid into another kiss, and another, and another. Fifteen minutes later, we officially began our relationship when I kissed her goodbye in front of our friends. That kiss generated a round of catcalls and whistles.

A few weeks later, after competing at the Cheyenne Frontier Days in Cheyenne, Wyoming, Mr. Finch gathered the seniors in the gym before we boarded the bus for the long ride home. He looked serious. Word had spread quickly that he had caught three kids, all rising sophomores, getting high in the guest high school's shower room, and punishment was pending. We wondered if there would be more fallout. "I need to tell you guys something. And I wanted to tell you first because this is on you." He paused and looked at each of us, thirty-seven in all.

"Organizers of the event just informed me that the Trojans marching band won every award they offered this year, including The Frontier Champion Award, which they award to the group with the best character. Congratulations. The band has enjoyed great success this year. It started with you. This has been the best group I have ever worked with. And I thank you."

Rarely in life do you get to be the best. But that year, we were the best. Nobody can ever take that away from us. Even though the bus ride home lasted about eighteen hours, we smiled all the way. Amy and I probably smiled the most. The chaperones tried at first to keep the couples separated but finally gave up, knowing we were almost home, and their summer of supervision would end. Amy and I curled into each other and held hands most of the way back. We kissed occasionally, but mostly, we just wanted to feel connected to each other. Since that night outside of Pizza Hut, through the rest of the summer that constant touching became our pattern. We couldn't be near each other without touching in some way, often just fingertips pressed lightly together or a gentle connection at the hips. Everybody assumed we were doing it, but we weren't. We just wanted to always feel connected. Whenever I would see her and first touch her, I would feel a pleasant jolt. I found myself addicted to those light shocks and the pleasantness that followed.

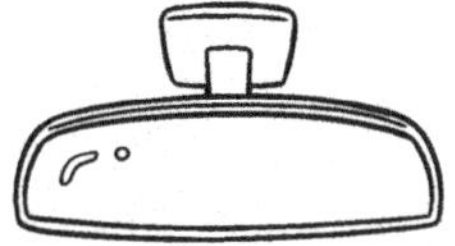

CHAPTER 4

I returned to work the day after Mom's funeral. I didn't really have to. Mom died on a Friday, and the funeral was the following Wednesday. The company gave us a week of bereavement, but I felt as if I wanted to get back to the office. It wasn't because I loved my job and couldn't bear to be away any longer. I needed to find a way to get some sense of normalcy back into my life. My plan made sense to me, but normalcy didn't really happen. As the saying goes, "Man plans, God laughs."

I arrived a little early and just sat in my cube, staring at the fabric-covered partition, thinking, *How strange. How absolutely strange. I've worked in this cube for seven years, and it seems as if I've never seen it before.* The strangeness unsettled me. Over time, I had covered some of the walls with personal items: the waterfall snapshots, pictures of the kids, still one of Amy, ticket stubs, a couple of Badger items, including a steel mug embossed with the motion W and a cheap aerial photo of the stadium from the Badgers first trip to Pasadena for the Rose Bowl. It felt as if I were looking at it for the first time. In that moment, my desire for normalcy seemed destined for failure.

I looked at the photos of waterfalls. I thought about our hobby of collecting waterfalls, one which Amy and I had pursued together, and how much pleasure it gave us. When we drove to northern Wisconsin or the mountains out East or West, we would always divert from the chosen path if we saw a sign for a waterfall.

Mom had given Shelly and me this hobby when we were kids. She loved waterfalls, and when new-age music came out, she scurried to find a tape of one. She could listen to it for hours. I could, too. When I would find her listening to the tape, I would see the smile spread gently on her face, like a little boy or girl running their tiny hands over your face, as if blind but experiencing your beauty anyway. When I saw that smile, I would know where Mom had gone. I went there, too, when I thought about waterfalls. So it seemed natural for me to introduce Amy to this hobby, and then we gave the hobby to our children. We never told other people that we collected waterfalls. We kept that our secret, though people knew we loved them. Our home contained several photos and paintings of waterfalls. We always hung a waterfall calendar in the kitchen. We could never get enough of them.

That day at my cubicle, when I looked at the waterfalls, I felt nothing but overwhelming sadness. No smile played with my face like the hands of a little child. All I could think of was Mom and how she would never again get to experience a waterfall. Immediately, I knew that this revelation would change the way I looked at waterfalls, and it could be a long time before I could enjoy one again.

As the witching hour approached, the other cubicle rats must have smelled the cheese because they started searching me out. They came and offered their condolences, which seemed heartfelt, but people struggle with something to say when great sadness touches your life. I don't know how many times in the past five days I had heard, "I'm sorry for your loss," or "My prayers are with you," or "My heart goes out to you." People mean well, but those words don't really say anything. They just represent empty platitudes.

As I stood in the visitation line with Shelly, the kids, and Amy, I lost track of the number of times well-wishing, earnest people said those exact words. I appreciated the sentiment. I just wished they would have found something real to say. People tend to fall back into what is safe, what they know everybody says. In the visitation line, I reveled when people would offer a personal story about Mom and how she had touched their lives. That meant something. It gave me something real to hang on to.

The cubicle rats, just like the well-wishers at the visitation, though, offered the same empty words designed to comfort but fell so far short. A couple of friends hugged me. The only real comments came from fellow travelers or members of the same club, those who had lost a parent. They knew what to say. They offered me real comfort. I noted another interesting phenomenon. Those who offered comfort most often made it about themselves. When people know someone who is grieving over the death of a loved one, it's almost as if they see it as permission to talk about their own grief, still so close to the surface. Instead of providing comfort to you, they comfort themselves by sharing what they went through and how much they miss their father, mother, best friend, first girlfriend, faithful dog. I found myself often giving them comfort, kind words, a hug, a pat on the shoulder. They leave, and you feel as if you have just taken a long drink of water yet remain parched.

Trev, who held the cube next to mine, said, "I know what you're going through, and it is going to be so hard. You will spend the next year emitting heavy sighs. Some people might think you are doing breathing exercises. But the smallest little thing is going to make you think of her, and it's going to make you sad, really sad. You will feel as if you are going along and doing okay, and suddenly the littlest thing or tiniest moment will trigger a memory and leave you weeping and aching with grief. And then you must work hard to get back to the point where you think you are okay." I could relate to that. Every thought connected somehow to Mom.

Another woman walked up to me with tears in her eyes. She gave me a long hug, touched my arm, and hugged me again. "That's from your mom." I started to cry.

Trev sat quietly while I cried myself out. "You will never stop missing your mom. But the good news is that you will get to the point where you go on. And honestly, that is what your mom would want you to do. Live your life. That is the best way to honor her memory."

About ten in the morning, just as I started thinking about sneaking out for my usual venti frappuccino from Starbucks, the boss, Jennifer, filled the entry to my cube. I could just feel the warmth, the love, the empathy, the humanity, the concern. Ha! "Welcome back, Robb. I'm glad you're back. Some of the people have been pitching in for you in your absence. But we've got a lot of ground to cover. The call sheet is long. So we're all probably going to have to work some extra hours to catch up. I'm authorizing up to two hours per day of overtime for the next week."

If I had given a shit, I would have reacted, perhaps scowled, or offered her some flippant remark. I didn't say anything, but then Jennifer placed the overtime authorization sheet on my desk. I guess that nudged me over the edge. When Jennifer turned to leave, I thought, *Wow, thanks for those meaningful, kind, sympathetic words about the loss of my mother. What a cold, heartless bitch.* She turned and looked at me.

Fuck. "What?"

"You really need to learn to control that mouth of yours," Jennifer said.

"Oh shit. Did I really just say that out loud again?" I gave her a contrite smile.

"This one is going in your file, too," Jennifer said before making the most dramatic exit you can make from a doorless cube. When I was certain she had left the room, I held my hand high and flipped her off. I marveled at how I really wasn't even mad. I guess when you have had your heart ripped out, and it's pretty obvious you will never again feel anything but sad, you just can't work up righteous anger.

Trev poked his head over the cube wall, looking like a groundhog

"There's your proof, man," Trev said.

"Yeah? Proof of what?"

"Proof that we don't work for a human being. We work for a cyborg, completely devoid of any human emotion, especially those who would reflect kindness and compassion."

I just nodded.

"Is she just talking, or do they really put that kind of stuff in our files?" Trev wondered.

"I don't know if any other bosses do, but I'm dead certain that Jennifer does. And Jennifer has probably replaced my manila folder with a four-inch thick, three-ring binder. She would love to fire me right now, but firing someone the day they return from burying their mother crosses every line imaginable. Bad form, even for Jennifer."

—x—x—x—

I swung by my apartment after work and filled a couple of suitcases with clothes. Without really looking too closely, I grabbed a stack of books and stuffed them in a duffle. Then I packed my new digital camera and my laptop into my computer bag. Finally, I pulled two photos off the wall, both montages of the family. Standing at the door, looking around, I couldn't think of another thing I had to take with me. In fact, for as much as the place meant to me, I could have just closed the door and never returned. The only decent memories occurred when the kids came to stay with me three to four days each week. Sometimes they came more often. Sometimes they would swing by for dinner. I had chosen the apartment because it was about a half mile from Amy's house, so the kids could do just that, stop by. It also wouldn't disrupt their lives as greatly if I lived on the same side of town.

Amy and I had agreed to stick with the same visitation schedule to limit the amount of disruption in the kids' lives. Our divorce proved amicable. We never hated each other. We never threw things at each other. We never snarled or attacked or belittled or cursed the other or name-called. Mostly, we were just sad that, for whatever reason, it didn't work. No matter how hard I tried, I could never envision Amy and me treating each other the way other divorcing couples we knew did when they seemed bent on destruction.

A guy at work ended up spending a night in jail once during his prolonged divorce. While waiting for the decree, he lived in a neighbor's basement to remain close to his children. One night he stopped by to visit and to pick up his toolbox to help his neighbor. He asked his estranged wife if she would get the toolbox from the basement. She refused. He asked again. She refused. Then he just pushed past her and walked into the house. She turned and started pummeling him in the back. He said he put his hands on her shoulders and pushed her away. Then she called the cops and told them he had assaulted her. When the cops arrived, she showed her chest, which appeared red and blotchy. She had gone to a tanning salon that day, but the cop believed her when she flat-out lied and said he had punched her in the chest. With his hands cuffed behind his back, the cops led him out of the house, past his two pre-teen sons watching in tears. Now that the divorce settlement finally ended the mess, he planned to make her life as miserable as possible. He wanted to manipulate the kids into declaring they hated their mother and wanted to live with him. He schemed to turn his kids against their mother as a matter of vengeance.

Another friend from work got to the point where he couldn't stand to talk to his soon-to-be ex-wife. They resorted to communication through text messages. As they tried to work out visitation for New Years, his soon-to-be ex texted him and said: "No more texts in the upcoming year unless they are happy or say you want to come home." He happily stopped sending her the text messages. They just never communicated.

One man I know from the old neighborhood left his wife for another woman whom he had impregnated. This man probably angers me the most. He abandoned his two kids from his first marriage. He said, "I've got a new family to worry about. They can fend for themselves." He hasn't seen his teenage sons for four years. It wouldn't surprise anyone to learn that these boys frequently get free rides home from friendly police officers.

All these thoughts cascaded through my mind as I took one last look around the apartment that day. I would be back to gather my other belongings. I would have to contact my buddy Fred and see if we could use his pickup truck to move some of the furniture. I couldn't call Cam to help. He would just laugh and say he couldn't be much help with anything unless it involved counseling others on how to have better sex. Anyway, most of the furniture would just go back to Goodwill, which is where I got it in the first place. What little I wanted to keep would go into a storage bin, much like my rat hole at work. I certainly wouldn't need any of it at Dad's.

It surprised me how quickly I stopped thinking of my childhood home as Mom and Dad's and now just crossed Mom off the list. A more cynical person might have said out of sight, and then I wondered how long I would keep Mom in my cell phone directory. These thoughts danced through my head. I felt guilty that they even swirled at all, but I couldn't keep them at bay. They happened randomly. I wondered if others who had lost parents faced the same kinds of issues. Although I felt an instant distance from Mom as soon as she died, I recognized that by moving home, I actually was drawing closer to her.

I would be giving up this apartment and moving into her former lair, where her presence remained strong. Intuitively, I knew that would be both good and bad. The apartment felt like a place I retreated to when I wasn't working or out. It wasn't home. I've had two homes in my life—one with Amy and one with my parents. Now I was returning to my first home, but it occurred to me that maybe it was not the home of my choice.

—x—x—x—

When I arrived at the home from my youth, I sat in the driveway for several minutes contemplating the notion of walking inside, going home. Thomas Wolfe said you can't go home again. Sometimes you just have to. Even after Amy and I split up, I never considered returning to my parents' home. For me, leaving for college marked a rite of passage. I believed, at that point, that I would live independently of my parents. And although I remained in close contact with them, I never held a latent desire to live at home again. I had made my own way in the world. Granted, I had moved from my parents' home to a dorm room and then a college apartment that truly defined squalor with its tired, rundown appearance, the mice darting over our feet, and the squirrels cavorting in the walls, to my two homes with Amy to my post-divorce apartment. And now here I was, sitting in my car in my parents' driveway, and I found myself wondering how far I had come or if I had gone anywhere with my life.

I let myself in the back door and shouted, "Hello, Dad. I'm home." I meant to say it with ironic humor, but it came out plaintive. No response came. I slowly walked through the house. Wondering where Dad could be, I scanned room after room. His car was in the driveway. When I went upstairs, I saw the light on in his bedroom. The house seemed deathly still.

The sheer quietness made my skin tingle. For at least a minute, I stood at the top of the stairs, staring at my parents' room. Light from the room cast a rectangle of brightness on the hallway carpeting. It seemed too quiet to me. Instead of calling out, I slowly shuffled toward the rectangle of light. How many times had I heard of a spouse dying immediately after burying their partner, dying of a broken heart? I dreaded entering Dad's room to find him dead on the chair, or bed, or floor. After taking a deep breath, I pushed open the door. I saw Dad sitting in the bedside chair, his eyes closed, one of Mom's scarves in his hands. He wore a slight smile.

I slipped away and quietly walked back downstairs. I glanced at the family photos that lined the walls of the stairwell. One photo of Mom caught my eye. Dad dabbled in photography, and he took this one. Mom and her sisters used to gather each year before Christmas and bake massive batches of cookies, definitely more than any of the families could eat during the holiday season. In honor of their heritage, they made Italian wedding cookies, where they would take the dough, roll it out into strands the size of a pencil. Then they would tie the dough in a knot and bake it, later glazing the baked cookies with pastel-shaded frostings. As a kid, I used to help with these marathon baking sessions, rolling and tying dough for hours.

While I had long since abandoned those sessions with Mom and my aunts, I found myself looking at the picture on the wall and longing for one more day where we would all sit in the kitchen, tell stories, laugh, and roll dough strands that we would tie into square knots. The photo showed Mom sitting before a huge bowl of dough. A tray of cookies sat near Mom's right elbow. She held a strand of dough in her hand. She looked at the camera and wore a winsome expression. I wondered what she was thinking. I had looked at that photo of a younger Mom countless times, but I saw something there now that I had never noticed before. Looking into her eyes, I felt like she was on the verge of revealing some great secret about life that rolling dough had helped her sift through. I didn't know her secret, and I found myself longing to know. I don't know how long I stared at that photo. At some point, I realized that I was crying again, but quietly because I didn't want to disturb Dad's moment upstairs.

A half hour later, Dad found me sitting in the kitchen. I held a cup of coffee, which I still hadn't brought to my lips. Dad sat down. "Can a guy get a cup of coffee?" he asked.

I popped up and grabbed a cup from the cupboard and filled it. Then we sat there together, silently holding our coffee cups, not drinking, but acting like we were.

"How you doing, Robb?"

"Okay," I quietly mumbled. "You?"

"Okay. Are you any better than before? I saw you in the hallway."

"You saw that?"

Dad nodded.

"I saw you in the bedroom. You had your eyes closed. You were smiling," I said to him. We were both busted.

He smiled again, the same distant smile he showed in the bedroom. "I don't know what made me do it, but I opened one of the drawers in your mother's dresser. She kept her scarves there. I pulled one out, and I realized it smelled like her, like the perfume she wore, the same our whole married life. I was just remembering. It's a good memory."

—x—x—x—

After finishing the Chinese we ordered for dinner, Dad and I sat in the family room, sunk deep in the two leather recliners, each sipping on a scotch. The television sat dark and silent, a notable change.

An enduring memory for me involved my dad retreating to this family room after dinner for a scotch or two as he watched television. It didn't much matter what he watched as long as he anesthetized himself with the amber scotch. He seemed to favor sitcoms, but he also locked onto certain sporting events, primarily college basketball and football and always the Badgers on Saturdays and the Packers on Sundays. While Mom would go over housing listings in the kitchen, Dad holed up in the family room. As kids, we considered it a rule that we would find Dad in the family room after dinner. I often watched television with him.

As I grew older, though, my forays into the family room became less frequent. When I wanted to talk with Dad about something, especially early on in high school, as I tried to navigate my way through the choppy waters and dangerous shoals of adolescence, I thought Dad might be able to offer me some meaningful advice. Those conversations usually ended as I slinked out of the family room, frustrated and often angry. He refused to turn down the volume on the television, and whenever I tried to talk to him, he seemed to only give me a fraction of his attention. Mostly he remained focused on the drivel of his television families and ignored the real issues in his real family.

"Dad, did you ever find yourself interested in a girl but didn't know how to approach her?" I asked him once. Although I hoped for an intimate conversation, I found myself shouting so Dad could hear me over the din of the television. He always kept it loud, and it seemed intentional. His demeanor indicated he just didn't want to be bothered. I stopped trying to talk with him. Shelly did, too. I always resented that. When I turned to him for compassion, understanding, or advice, he turned to the television. He remained unavailable.

For many years we steadfastly maintained a superficial relationship. When I needed advice, I turned to Mom, who always had time to listen. We would gather at the kitchen table. She would pour me a cup of tea, and we would talk. She listened. She posed questions. Rarely, though, did she lecture me or give explicit directions on how to act. Recognizing that I just needed to share what was going on, and I wasn't asking her what to do, she never tried to impart her wisdom to me. She knew I had to find my own way through whatever was blocking my path.

For years I used Mom as my confidante. When my marriage started to implode, though, I came over one day desperate for advice, and she wasn't home. Also because of her mother-daughter connection with Amy, I thought Dad would give me a more favorable audience. For several minutes, I stomped around the kitchen like a caged bear, wishing Mom would get home. But the Rolling Stones put it best: "You can't always get what you want, but if you try sometime, you'll find you get what you need." The blaring television announced Dad's permanent presence in the family room. My impatience overtook me. I went into the family room and saw Dad horizontal in his recliner.

"Dad," I nearly shouted to be heard over the inanity of the current television commercial. He barely acknowledged my presence. I tried again. "Dad!" Barely a flicker. Then I swooped over to his end table, grabbed the remote, and turned off the television. That got his attention.

"What the hell do you think you're doing?"

"Dad, I'm in bad shape. And I really need to talk to someone. Mom's gone. So you're it," I said. He glared at me.

"Well, we can talk over the television," he said.

"No, we can't. Believe me, I've tried."

"You've never tried to talk to me."

"Dad, goddammit. When I was in high school, I would come in here and want to talk to you, and you would never once turn down the fucking television. I stopped trying. But you have to listen to me now. I need to talk to someone. Please!" I pleaded.

He looked stunned. "Really? I keep the television loud because I have trouble hearing it. And I always thought that you and your sister didn't want to share anything with me, that you preferred to talk to your mother."

"Aw, Dad, Jesus. It's hard to carry on a conversation when you have to spend all of your time shouting to someone who is sitting five feet away."

He looked at me and offered a sad smile. He pointed at the couch. I sat down. He turned toward me. "What's going on, son?"

"Dad, God, this is hard," I said and paused.

"Take your time. And when you feel like you can say what you want, I'm listening. Just remember, we're both new at this conversation thing. But if you give me a chance, I think I can get the hang of it." He gave me a little smile.

Taking a deep breath, I plowed into an explanation of the mess I found myself in. "I think Amy and I are heading toward a divorce."

"Oh, no, Robb. God, that's terrible. I'm so sorry for you." Anguish made his voice sound garbled, and I knew he was holding back tears. He paused and stood up. He walked to the window and stared out. I watched him, fighting to keep my own emotions in check. After about a minute, he wiped his eyes and returned to his chair.

"I think I need to say something. But first, stand up," Dad commanded. All I could think was he was going to punch me. Still, I stood up. Dad stood, too. He walked toward me and stopped.

Then he spread his arms, took another step, and engulfed me. He literally engulfed me. He held me tightly, pulled close to him so that I could smell the remnants of his Old Spice aftershave. He held me long past the point of awareness of the smell. He held me long past the point where we both stopped crying.

Then he did something I will never forget. Never. He gently placed his hand on my cheek. That gesture was something he routinely did, but its true meaning never before registered with me. At that moment it did. It conveyed his unconditional love for me. He never said the words that night. He didn't have to. Then he pulled me to him and hugged me again. Hard. Then he released me and gave me a gentle shove back toward the couch. After we both settled in again, he finally spoke.

"Okay, I think I can talk now. How are you feeling?"

"Terrible. This is the last thing I want to happen, but Amy has decided that it's time to move on."

"I see. What made her decide this? Has she found someone else? Is she having an affair?"

"No, she's not the one having an affair." I paused. I opened the door, and if I wanted this conversation to go anywhere, I knew I would have to take the next step through that doorway. I did. "She didn't dad. I slipped up." He looked at me with an understanding look. As a man in his late sixties, the mistakes people made in married life had long stopped surprising him. They still surprised me, but then again, I was just living through my mistakes. When Dad nodded, I took that as an indication that I should continue with what was becoming my first significant confession of my transgressions.

"I was feeling, I don't know, like I was in this big rut, and I wasn't happy at home, at work, nowhere. So when this woman at work made some overtures to me, I succumbed. Like an idiot. It didn't mean anything."

"No, Robb. It may not have meant anything to you. It might have meant something to the woman. It certainly meant something to Amy."

It wasn't like Amy and I hadn't argued this point over and over. But when Dad said it, something clicked. His simple statement made me finally recognize that I had hurt Amy. Before that, I kidded myself. I justified the affair by claiming it was her fault for never wanting to have sex with me, and this conversation with Dad also settled that notion. Not that Dad and I covered this ground, but the thought hit me like a bullet train smacking a cow wandering onto the tracks—hard. Amy didn't just want to just have sex with me. She wanted it to be making love. The woman from the affair, that was sex. I realized so many things in that epiphany. The act of making love faltered as it does in so many marriages for all those silly, sad reasons. We stopped having sex because I felt lost in the marriage and stopped knowing how to love my wife. I turned to a mere acquaintance for sex. It most certainly meant something to Amy.

"Have you told your mother?" When I shook my head, he said, "This is going to kill her. She and Amy are so very close." He fell silent, and then he grimaced. "This is going to be hard on your kids, too."

I knew all of this, and I knew intuitively how he would respond. Somewhere deep inside, I found myself hoping that he would see it my way and offer me unconditional parental support, where no matter what, every day he would love me absolutely. When you disappoint others, though, life doesn't necessarily offer padding for the subsequent blows.

Several minutes passed as we both contemplated the havoc my thoughtlessness created.

"It's going to be pretty hard on all of us, including me," I finally agreed.

"Yes, son, including you. Any chance she could forgive you?" Dad asked. "Have you gone through counseling? It can help."

We tried all of that. The therapist, Mom's friend, Helen, though, seemed to believe that, realistically, we couldn't salvage the marriage, that we had let too many small things become big things, issues that we now couldn't even begin to address. Neither one of us knew how to do the hard work of easing the pain from all those big things. I didn't go into all of this with Dad, not that day.

"Dad, the weird thing is that Amy forgave me immediately."

"So, then why this move to divorce?"

"I think she just got tired of fighting for our marriage. A fight is never any fun if you're the only one fighting. She says I'm not happy, not even close to it, and until I am, the marriage and our lives will just end up being one giant disappointment. She has come to believe that divorce might be the only chance we all have of finding happiness."

"Robb, if you want her, fight for her."

"I don't know how. And she's made it pretty clear that she's not up for the fight anymore."

"And what about you?"

I shrugged. This moment would be one I would always remember because right then, I gave up. I gave up on my marriage. I gave up on my wife. I gave up on my kids. Most tragically, I gave up on myself.

"I guess I'm not either. It might be easier. It might be best just to move on. Declare victory and go home."

"But son, this is not a victory. This is a major defeat. If you do what you're talking about, you will have lost it all."

"I know. I know, Dad. I just don't have anything left." The conversation essentially ended then. That day I know I lost a batch of my father's respect for me.

Since then, though, Dad and I developed the ability to talk more easily to each other. We found that we could share. He even turned to me on occasions when he had some big topics to explore. Now we only had each other. We spent the next two hours talking about how difficult our day had been, the first day of the real, new reality of life without Mom. The TV remained off.

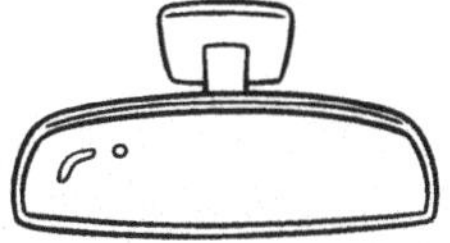

CHAPTER 5

As I drove over to Cam's house to pick him up before we headed out for a beer on the pretense that Cam would be conducting research for his next book, I found myself stepping back in time. It seemed like every moment pushed me back into the ethereal land of memory, where the edges tended to soften and, because of the space of time, the pictures enchanted. Recalling memories can be tricky. Because they may seem so enchanting with the distance of time, we tend to forget some of the harsher realities. If you don't force yourself to remember it all, you just might fall into the trap of thinking every moment you lived was coated in bliss.

Many of my memories centered on Mom, of course, but just as many focused on Amy, my best friend Cameron, and so many of my high school friends, especially my experiences from senior year. Even as I lived it, I knew that time held special qualities, but looking back, it seemed like the apex of my life. As I continuously scrolled through the memories of that year, I thought if I could step in close to focus on specifics and then step back to see the panoramic sweep of that year, I could figure out why the trajectory of my life took me to this point. Once I understood that, I could figure out where it would go next. Perhaps I could find that moving forward was better than looking back.

Cameron called me a stupid weenie in the first grade when I took his cookie during the morning snack break and ate it. Something about the way he said it drew me instantly to him. I felt bad enough about taking his cookie, so the next day, after enlisting Mom's help, I brought him a big baggie full of Chips Ahoy cookies. We bonded over cookies. Cam still swears that I brought him a bag of Oreos and not Chips Ahoy, but then I always ask him why he goes all gooey whenever he sees chocolate chip cookies anywhere. He swears that the chocolate chip cookies are what led him to his beautiful wife. They might have, but I really believe his affinity for chocolate chip cookies arose from my naive and apologetic act of kindness as a six-year-old. It gave him faith and a belief of the goodness possible in the world. He has forgotten that this act of goodness resulted from my wrongdoing. While I'm not so cynical as to believe that good never comes out of bad, it often does. My friendship came out of badness, but it was a good thing. I've cherished this friendship my entire life.

Cam was never my only friend, just my best friend. Sometimes he struggled with my many friendships, especially by the time we reached senior year, when I suddenly found myself on the edge of popularity and then actually squarely ensconced in it. Cam benefited from my newfound popularity, but he never wanted to admit it. If I started hanging around with the cool kids, Cam gleaned a little popularity just by association—the coattail effect that politicians crave. Cam often said, "The cool kids in high school were nice enough to let me stand near them."

While my rising star began with marching band, my status solidified because of football. As the school year approached and football practices started, we would finish our film sessions at about nine at night. After two-a-day practices where we ran x's and o's for up to six hours a day, three in the morning and three in the afternoon, and then two hours watching film, we would be not only exhausted but also famished.

I would head to McDonald's with Joey, T., Little John, Bug, and some other guys for burgers and fries. As the season got underway, we would arrive at McDonald's after Friday night games, usually as the conquering heroes. Those nights always proved interesting because we would recount the latest effort. Invariably, Bug and Bo, sometimes known as Mellon Belly—we were big on nicknames—would start attacking each other. Bug, our little scat back, would start abusing Bo. "Man, if you would only learn how to block, I might just be able to gain a yard or two once in a while." Bo would shove most of a burger in his mouth and just smile. After chewing a couple of times and swallowing, he would ask, "Refresh my memory. How many yards did you gain tonight?"

Bug would start to sputter. "That's irrelevant. If you blocked better, I might be able to gain more." Bug averaged one hundred fifty yards per game his senior year, and most of the time he ran right off Bo's hip. Bo earned all-state honors that year. So did Bug.

Only once that entire season did we forgo the victory lap at McDonald's.

We played City High in what turned out to be an epic battle. After regulation ended, we stood tied at twenty-eight each. That meant we would play overtime in a new format that high schools had moved to, the same format that high schools and colleges still use. Each team would get the ball at the twenty-five-yard line and have four plays to get a first down or score. A first down would generate another four plays. If both teams scored and made the extra or two-point conversions, they would play again. And if neither team scored, they would have another overtime.

We matched each other up through two overtimes. The score now stood at forty-two all. I scored one of the touchdowns by hauling in a sweet pass from Joey. In those days you didn't do anything flashy: no dances, no cartwheels, no mock autographs with a Sharpie, no distasteful mugging for the fans, no choreographed group dances. I just handed the ball to the ref and trotted off the field. I liked what Vince Lombardi always said: "Act like you've been there before." Our coach believed the same thing. City got the ball first in the third overtime and quickly scored and made its extra point. We scored on our fourth play when Sticks, our tall and skinny other wide receiver, caught a high pass just inside the end line. But Bo, who doubled as our kicker, missed the extra point as it just hooked wide of the right goalpost. We stood in that classic pose of dejection, shoulders slumped, hands on hips, heads down, unable to look reality in the eye, let alone our teammates or our opponents. Required to display good sportsmanship, we did congratulate the players from City High in the handshake line, but our handshakes were perfunctory. Although we still won the conference championship a week later, that loss kept us out of the state championship playoffs.

After the loss, we trudged off the field and across the parking lot that separated the stadium from the high school. The locker room door, situated at the back of the high school, gaped open. But nobody made a move to follow the coaches inside for the postgame team meeting. As a team, we all collapsed to the ground. Nobody said a word, but some of the guys were crying. Tears streamed down my face. I saw a few coaches peek out the door, wondering if the team was going to come in for the meeting. We didn't move. They left us alone. None of them said anything. Our head coach later said that moment made him realize he had truly turned around the program. We had only won three games the year before, so he might have become a believer as we notched win after win. He watched us suffer that loss so poignantly, and he knew that his Trojans would no longer, could no longer, accept losing. The next year, the Trojans won the state championship and then four out of the next five.

After about fifteen minutes, the snuffling had stopped, but still, no one had moved. No one had spoken a word. I grabbed my navy blue helmet with the red stripe and stood. "Let's call it a night, guys. Tomorrow's another day, and we've got practice at nine o'clock and a game to get ready for next week," I said. And just like that, the pall passed. Just like that, even though I wasn't a captain, the guys started looking at me as a leader.

When the football season ended, a couple of guys from the team invited me to join the school's Good Citizen Today Leaders for Tomorrow club, a ridiculous name, which students wisely shortened years before to Citizen's Club. It mainly consisted of jocks, a good portion of them from the football team, but it also included all of the starters on the basketball team and some of the big-time players in school. That invitation really opened my eyes. The cool kids.

While my school had multiple cliques, and I comfortably hopped between different groups, usually pulling Cam with me, this invitation marked a rite of passage. When Amy heard about the invitation, she kidded me. Hard. "Ooh, look who's arrived. Mr. Big Man on Campus." I wasn't so sure about that, but I wanted to be a part of this group. I realized that something dramatic had changed. I never imagined I would become a member of the Citizen's Club. I didn't think I would ever be cool enough to warrant an invitation. Once I had settled into the club, it took me three months to convince my brethren to invite Cam in. Eventually, they did. It didn't take long for the guys to really appreciate his sophomoric, tawdry sense of humor and his liberal use of sarcasm.

We went through the formal induction at the club's meeting on Monday, but then the real event that the guys called "initiation," but could best be described as "hazing," occurred the following Friday night. The initiation began with the ritual chugging of two beers, shotgun style. After that, you had a beer in your hands all night. Some of the clubs at that time remained gendered, and the Citizen's Club was all male. No girls were at the initiation, but many girls who were friends or girlfriends with guys in the club showed up for the post-initiation party. To pass this last set of tests, all of the initiates had to perform a series of feats, informally dubbed the Citizen's Olympics, which began with an obstacle course. Successful completion of a stage meant you "got" to chug a double shot of beer. I stopped chugging after the first and just sipped from then on. Two stations stood out. At one point we had to sit on a couch blindfolded, where we waited our turn for the next test. As we sat there, J.P. lifted the lid on a plastic garbage can and began fanning it over the top of the receptacle filled with manure. He wanted us to enjoy such a delightful smell. His rule was that you couldn't cover your nose. The smell gagged me, and I found my stomach spasming. My gag reflex kept threatening full-on puking. The whole time he shared this olfactory delight with us, he munched enthusiastically on a hot dog.

"You guys are going to love being in Citizen's," J.P. said, showing a mouthful of half-chewed hot dog and bun. "It's the greatest bunch of guys. And the parties are great. Like this one. Lots of beer and great eats." Then he took another hearty bite. I started fantasizing about puking, but I really wanted to finish the initiation and be part of the group.

The last stage involved plucking an olive off a block of ice and then carrying it across the finish line. Sounds easy enough, but the relay involved a trick. You had to drop your pants and squeeze the olive between your butt cheeks and then hobble twenty feet across the line. If you dropped the olive, you had to start again. On the other side of the line sat a cooler filled with ice-cold cans of beer. The beer became the goal.

I watched the four guys in front of me drop the olive again and again. I vowed to finish the task. So I clenched. Hard. I made it in one try. For the rest of the night the guys called me "Hoover." I'm glad the nickname didn't stick. Imagine explaining that over and over. I took several sips of beer to erase the memory of J.P. and his All-American snack from my mind. After the initiation ended, someone unlocked the front door and invited the girls in. They had been circling the house, trying to get a glimpse of what we were doing in the basement. Amy, already one of the cool kids, found me instantly, and I clutched her to me and didn't let go of her for the rest of the evening. I was afraid if I let go of her, my wobbly legs would leave me sprawled on the floor, where J.P. would bury me under a pile of manure. The best thing about Citizen's after that, though, was it provided an opportunity for me to maintain contact with my football buddies.

—x—x—x—

Cameron, of course, didn't play football. When it came to physical activity, he adhered to one simple rule: "I only run when being chased." Ironically, during elementary school, Cam ran for his life. Turns out he had some serious speed. He outran every bully who ever chased him. He never really understood my penchant for sports. So, while we quickly became best friends, and it was a friendship most people scratched their heads over, Cam occasionally came out to watch me play. Mostly he stayed behind, and we met up later. Until Cam discovered his true calling—sex—most people didn't quite get him.

Cam endured a socially awkward childhood. He could lacerate you with sarcasm so sharp that you often didn't see it coming until he removed the knife. He displayed haughtiness over everything except school, where he feigned ambivalence, but all of his teachers and I recognized his genius. He generally disdained his parents for ignoring him—they sent him to summer camp for the entire summer eight years in a row. His disdain didn't extend, however, to their wealth. He gleefully accepted every material possession they bestowed him. He believed these were his birthright and his parents' penance.

The judgmental types looked at our friendship and refused to understand that Cam could make me laugh. He read people with extraordinarily intense scrutiny, and he liked to share this talent with me. Over time I picked up on some of his abilities for astute observations of people. But I am strictly an amateur. Cam can know at a glance what will make someone laugh, cry, or fume with anger. He can tell instantly what someone craves, and he even claims general prescience on people's tastes—favorite foods, books, music, movies, sexual positions. Most people didn't get Cam because they didn't take the time to. But he remained my best friend. Moments like the one that occurred a couple of days after I returned to work following the funeral will always reinforce my deep friendship with him.

Cam called me that Friday at work and told me he would pick me up at seven thirty. He wanted to do some research and needed my help.

After I greeted Cam at the door, he ventured into the family room and sat down in the leather recliner beside my dad. Mom's reading chair. When she ventured into the family room, she would sit there and read while Dad watched TV, sound as loud as a Who concert. But when I asked Mom once how she could concentrate on the book she was reading with all that noise, she smiled and said, "What noise?" I must have given her a quizzical look. "Robbie, I just like being with your father. I always have."

Dad greeted Cam with an attempt at levity. "Robb tells me you're working tonight. What kinds of mating habits are we studying tonight? The lonely and desperate at strip clubs, or just the lonely intellectuals at a book reading at Barnes and Noble on a Friday night? Or are you going to the latest teen sexploitation flick at the Cineplex?"

"No, nothing so exciting, Bob. I asked Robb to come with me to a new sports bar that seems to be all the rage—a place called Sidelines. The latest place where all the cool twenty- and thirty-somethings are going. So I need to go there, too. Robb is my cover. It never looks good for a single man in his late thirties, ah, early forties, okay mid-forties, to be alone in a bar, reputed to be a pickup denizen. They might take me for a lech." Cam guffawed. So did Dad.

"I'm afraid that is exactly what you are, son. Don't ever apologize for it. It has made you a very successful man. Be proud of your lechery," Dad said.

"Thank you for the compliment, sir," Cam said, formally. "I can't tell you how proud that makes me. My father will be tickled to hear of the praise." Cam and Dad laughed some more because they both knew that Cam would tell his father to make him just a little more uncomfortable with his son's chosen career.

"Bob, how are the days going for you?"

Dad didn't say anything. He looked down at his hands that lay lifeless in his lap. The silence stretched beyond a minute. Cam, as a therapist, was an expert at waiting and silence.

"Can't really say they're easy. Actually, the days get long. With both of us retired, we spent pretty much all of our time together. Now I have no one to talk to until Robb gets home. All I do is sit here and think of Grace. I just find myself wishing I could talk to her, not even about the big stuff, just talk to her. You know?"

Cam nodded. Dad stood and paced back and forth, but just for a moment. Then Cam stood in front of Dad with his arms spread. Dad stepped into Cam's embrace, and Cam just held him until Dad broke contact.

Dad stared at Cam for a moment. Then he gently touched his cheek.

"You're a good kid, Cam." Then Dad hugged Cam again. When they broke this time, Dad said, "Tell your old man I said that, too."

Later, Cam and I sat perched at our tall table near the bar. The table had great sight lines so that Cam and I could each face the throngs of people and make our sundry observations. We just looked idly for a long time as we talked. Cam's psychological background came to the fore when he encouraged me to talk about my feelings. After he started studying this discipline in college, Cam became my own personal and free therapist. At first, I started out just to humor him, and the sessions continued that way for a long time, until Amy and I started having our troubles. Then I earnestly tried to get Cam to tell me the magical words that would save my marriage. When those never came, I tried to get him to reveal the magical words that would heal me. In those early days after the divorce, I felt completely lost. Cam's first response was to tell me simply, "Go out, Robbie, my friend, and get laid." Then he laughed. Though I sometimes followed his advice, I must have scowled a bit at him. Even though I had strayed during the marriage, as it crumbled around me, I found myself in a state of reformation, at least in terms of romantic relationships. Cam took a different view.

"Robb, truth is I'm not telling you to have sex. I'm telling you to lighten up. Laugh, for Christ's sake. That was funny. Ironic."

"Ha. Ha."

"Look, Robb, I'm no expert. Wait, yes, I am. I'm kind of a big deal. You seem to have taken a serious turn here. And I mean serious in all of its different meanings. What happened to the guy who used to find a way to make a joke out of everything?"

"I guess life just became more serious."

"Sure it did. But that doesn't mean that you should forget to laugh. If you lose your laugh, then you really have lost your way." At that moment I found it difficult to consider laughing at anything. My marriage was like the log that burns to ash in the fire pit. A good puff of wind had blown it all away. Frankly, I didn't know what I could laugh at. In time, though, I found that I could chuckle now and then. One night while I was sitting in my barren apartment watching the sitcom *Two and a Half Men*, I found myself guffawing at one of the ridiculous double entendres so common on the show. That moment was like placing a stick of dynamite into a thick slab of granite. It created the first cracks in the wall I had put up, and eventually, I discovered that I could laugh again. I started feeling better. Who knew? Cam was a psychological genius.

So as we sat at the bar, ogling and observing the adult mating rituals, I talked with Cam about the difficulties I was having with my mom's death. Only a little more than a week had passed. I realized I was only just getting through the days.

"Take it slow, Robb. Pretty soon it will get easier to get through the days. But grief is like water flowing downhill. It will take its natural course, and it's different for everyone."

"So you can't tell me how long this lasts? I was hoping for some of the special Cam voodoo."

"I'm afraid I don't have any magical words of wisdom. I know one thing. Be patient with yourself. Give it some time."

Those words would come back to me again and again. Eventually, I would realize how good the advice was when I struggled through so much, thinking ignorantly that I was handling it all well.

As we sat and sipped our beers, Cam's head pivoted on a swivel. He was working on another book. He had already written two psychological treatments on the human need for intimacy and relationships. He really was kind of a big deal. Others in the field considered him an expert, and he frequently made it onto the local news and periodically the national news to share his insights about intimacy. Again, no one in high school would have predicted this of the kid who couldn't get laid. He was like the pathetic kid in 1980s teen rom-coms. Now, though, he told everyone else how to achieve that feat. Cam scanned the crowd, seemingly making instant determinations about various patrons. His observations always struck me as interesting, but while the words might have seemed highly judgmental, the tone never did. If Cam met any of these people, he would instantly embrace them for who they were. I asked him once how he could do that when he could so clearly read their foibles.

"Who am I to judge? I mean, look at me. I know who I was, and I know how hard I had to work to remake myself. I also know how much those judgments hurt me before I remade myself. So I had a choice. I could be a negative, pompous, self-aggrandizing prick like my father, or I could embrace everyone for who they really were. It's much easier and much, much more pleasant my way. Trust me."

As we sipped our second beer, Cam started treating me to some of his observations of the various subspecies of barflies. Listening to Cam I flashed back to my intro to anthropology and psychology lectures from college. I almost felt as if I should be taking notes. I knew Cam would want to test me later.

"Ah, yes, let's begin with the most obvious pair—look at five o'clock." I glanced where Cam directed my gaze. "We have Maverick and Goose." Cam often connected his judgments to pop culture. Here he referred to *Top Gun*, a film that was hugely popular when we were in middle school—a propagandist tip of the hat to the U.S. fighter pilots. "If they find a free mike somewhere, I'm sure one of them will begin singing 'You've Lost That Lovin' Feeling.' They are obviously working the room together and have done it so often that they have a routine. The good-looking guy swoops in, and the other guy acts as his wingman to keep the conversation going, making Maverick look good. Look, they always try to separate a woman from the group. Two guys apparently lavishing her with attention will make her feel so good about herself that she will be drawn in. Once the move appears to be working, Goose will drop back. He always does."

"But why would Goose drop back? Doesn't he want to get laid, too?"

"Natural order of the universe. Mav's needs come first. Goose knows this. He gets his opportunities. Sometimes they will work on a couple of women so that Goose feels that he gets enough rewards for his efforts. But when Mav gets radar lock on a woman, Goose has to play along, or Mav will dump Goose and fly solo or find another wingman."

"Okay, enough with Mav and Goose. I'm getting tired of the *Top Gun* jargon. Let me pick the next couple." I scanned the bar, which had grown quite crowded. I saw a couple sitting at a table toward the back, farther away from the cacophony near the bar. I pointed them out to Cam. He nodded.

"First date." Then he started looking around the room for more targets.

"Wait. Explain. To me it looks like a couple that's in love. They've been dating for a long time. And you know that guy is thinking about asking her to marry him," I said.

"No, but that's a nice story. Look at their body language. He's leaning in, focusing all of his attention on her, listening to everything she says. Nodding at the appropriate moments, asking her more questions as any active listener would. He has positioned himself so he is looking at her and the wall behind her. That way he won't be distracted by any of the activity behind him, like all the games on the dozens of TVs. He especially won't be distracted by a pretty woman walking by. He wants this to go well. He has probably wanted to ask her out for a long time. This is his one big chance, and he doesn't want to blow it."

I took in all of the details that Cam had recited. I studied the guy, and none of the things Cam noted seemed obviously true. But still, I wondered.

"What about the woman? You didn't say anything about her."

"Okay, Robb. Look at the way she is sitting. While he has leaned forward, she is leaning back. It's almost as if he is pushing into her space, and she's a little unsure about that. Also, notice how she looks around as he is talking. She's taking in the crowd. She might be wishing she were here with her friends, getting drunk instead of carefully limiting herself to two drinks so she doesn't end up doing something that will make it difficult to extract herself from this guy. And there it is," Cam almost shouted. He bounced a little in his seat. "She just subtly checked her watch. For her, this date is over."

That news disappointed me. By this point, I was pulling for the guy. "So he has no hope?"

"I never said that. It may end up that they go for coffee after this, and he says something startling and true and beautiful. He just might give her an incredible good-night kiss. It could work. But it definitely is a first date, and right now he has some serious work to do if he wants to get to a second date."

"What does he need to do?" I asked, hoping Cam could get this all-important tip to the guy. It occurred to me that my romantic tendencies were taking over.

"Primarily, he needs to lighten up. He needs to stop being so careful and be himself. Make her laugh. Make her feel like he's going to be fun to be with, not just another drudge."

The waitress interrupted Cam's lecture and set down a plate of nachos that Cam had ordered. He liked to indulge when he was working. He said the more he got into the ambience of the occasion, the sharper his observations. We didn't talk for a few moments while we crunched through a couple of chips. I nibbled on the nachos and realized that this evening had distracted me somewhat, but not entirely, from my immense grief.

"Party girl just walked in. Look out." I immediately picked out his latest subject. She skipped into the bar, leading in four other women. She let out a woot and quickly found an opening at the bar. She wore a teal-colored summer dress and matching high heels, both of which emphasized her toned body. Her face radiated happiness, and her eyes seemed to sparkle, even across the bar.

"She does look like a party girl. It looks like she is expecting a good time."

"And she always has a good time," Cam said.

"You mean she's the kind of woman whose phone number gets written on bathroom stall walls?"

"No, you've confused the party girl with the town tramp. This woman likes to have fun. She gets laid as much as she wants, but she is more interested in the party, in having some drinks, in having fun, in making her friends feel good about being out, in dancing and laughing, in meeting people. And because she is fun, she is the party, and she meets a lot of people. You might think her friends would be jealous of her, but the truth is they absolutely love her because they always have fun with her, too."

"Down the road, what happens to party girl? Does she get to have a happy life?" Whenever I did this with Cam, I always found myself worrying about the people he observed.

"She may find the guy who meshes with her perfectly, and it's a little difficult to predict what kind of guy he is. It would have to be someone who likes the good time, too. Can't be a guy who would rather sit at home and cuddle or who is jealous. She is a woman on the go who needs to be doing something. She craves adventure. She wouldn't have patience for someone who wanted her to curtail her joy of living. If she finds the right guy, they will have the best wedding of all their friends. She also could end up being so attached to the party girl life that she never gives it up. In which case, she will become a sad caricature of who she is now."

We sat silently for a few moments watching party girl. "Well, I, for one, hope she finds happiness."

"It's all up to her."

"What about the mythical town tramp?" I asked.

"That is too easy," Cam said. "She will work the room so that by the end of the night, she is assured of going home with someone. She always does. Sadly, though, she is really looking for love. She just doesn't know how to go about finding it, so she demeans herself. You always hope that at some point she figures it out or she meets a guy who really does fall in love with her." Cam then eased out of his seat and excused himself before heading to the bathroom.

As I sat there idly scanning the crowd and not thinking about much, an image of my mother and father together popped into my head. Since Mom's death, I had been remembering moments from her life constantly. I found these memories both comforting and profoundly sad because I could never add to the library of memories.

The image didn't represent any moment of great significance; it was just an ordinary image of a tender caress when they thought no one would see them. We had gone up to their cottage in northern Wisconsin. Mom and Dad and our kids slept in the cottage, while Amy and I slept in a pop-up trailer I had purchased when I decided our family had to become campers. We turned out to be great campers. We used the pop-up camper once or twice a year when we went up to the cabin on Bogus Lake north of Antigo. When Amy and I divorced, and I needed cash, I sold the pop-up to some other guy who was sure that his family would love camping. After taking one long, lingering yet sideways look at his wife, wearing spiked heels and a diaphanous summer dress, I knew he would be selling the trailer, too, and soon. His wife didn't have the camping gene.

Amy, the kids, and I were inside making root beer floats, a long-standing tradition in our family. Whenever we went to the cottage as kids, we often ended the night with a root beer float. We slurped down our floats, feeling the brain freeze because we drank the cold concoction too quickly. The after-dinner treat marked the ending of another special day at the cottage. As an adult, root beer floats triggered memories, leading me to fondly recall the innocence, joy, and sense of fulfillment I found at the cottage.

Nowadays, I usually only ever have a root beer float at the cottage, and it tastes like childhood.

That night, after our floats, we all went to lie on the pier and look at the stars. The sky looked like black velvet sprinkled with powdered sugar. On this night, I knew that after the floats, we all would find our spot on the pier, a tradition my kids took to just like I had.

At sunset, Mom and Dad had slipped outside just before the float making. Not sure if they wanted to partake, I stepped out on the porch. About to shout my question, I stopped.

Mom and Dad sat side by side on the pier, their toes dragging across the surface of the water. They watched the sunset, which always stuck in my mind because God, the master painter, was showing off again. Yellow, orange, pink, red, purple, azure, cobalt, and indigo first appeared as distinct ribbons and then, like a watercolor painting, fused into a rainbow. It struck me that God had dipped his brush in splendor and dragged it across the sky. The image caused me to take a deep breath and give off a willowy sigh. Trips to the cottage always made me feel like I was one with nature, despite the fact that Mom always said I would never be one with nature. I was more of a two-with-nature kind of person, someone who didn't really get it or appreciate it the way she and Dad did. But at the cottage, I did appreciate it quietly. With those images locked in my memory, they became the places I would go when I wanted to escape from my dreary gray and maroon cubicle and the mind-numbing corporate world.

As I took in the sunset, I looked at Mom and Dad again. Mom took her hand and lightly traced her fingers along Dad's jawline. She smiled at him, and he beamed at her. Anybody with a pulse would have known that she just professed her love for him. Again. Then she laid her head on his shoulder. Quietly, I went back inside. We would just go ahead and make them a float, which they would gratefully accept.

—x—x—x—

Sitting in the bar, remembering that tender scene between Mom and Dad, I found my romantic feelings stirring. I glanced back at the young couple Cam determined were on their first date. Suddenly, I could no longer look at them dispassionately. I wanted the guy to succeed. It seemed like a way to honor Mom's memory. At just that moment, the woman stood up and grabbed her purse. I hoped she wasn't walking out on him. She turned toward the bathroom. Without a thought, I rose and quickly walked toward our guy, for that's the way I thought of him now. I slipped into the chair the woman had just left.

The guy looked at me with a curious look on his face.

"First date?" I said. He nodded.

"How's it going?" I asked and he shrugged.

"Not as well as I want it to. I like this woman so much. But I don't know what to do. Nothing seems to be working."

"Okay, well, we don't have much time, but I'm going to give you some quick advice. Ready?"

He nodded again.

"First, relax. You can't really make her like you. And she certainly won't like you if you're a bundle of tightly wrapped nerves. Stop being so careful and correct. Be yourself. Make her laugh. I've got a feeling you are a pretty entertaining guy. But before you do any of this, when she gets back to the table, let her know that you're nervous because you hoped the evening would go well enough that it could lead to a second date. But keep it light. So most importantly, one more time, be yourself. Got it?"

He swallowed.

"But what if that isn't good enough?"

"Then it isn't, and nothing you do will change that. But then you at least will know that truth. But it also might be just the ticket." I stood and gave his shoulder a guy's slap.

He swallowed again and nodded, then swallowed again. As I walked back to our table, I chuckled. Each of those swallows looked like someone trying to choke down a big mouthful of honey. Cam had already returned. He and the waitress laughed. Cam, no doubt, had made some joke about the musk in the air, which was getting stronger as the night wore on. Cam loved to bring sex out in the open.

After the waitress left, Cam arched an eyebrow. "You've been busy. Your interference is going to ruin my observational experiment, you know. Now I won't know for sure if I have made the correct assessment."

"What? What are you suggesting, Cam?" I said, playing the innocent.

"I'm suggesting I saw you talking with the guy when I left the bathroom."

"So, you'll leave that one out of your next book. I was remembering how much Mom and Dad loved each other. I just wanted our guy to get to a second and then a third date. Maybe they can have the kind of lifelong love my parents did."

"So, he's our guy now?"

"Yeah, Cam. I'm pulling for him. We're going to have to choke down another beer to monitor his progress."

Cam took a long pull on his beer and wiped the foam from his lip. "Being a scientist is such damned hard work."

We sat there for another hour. My gaze repeatedly returned to our guy. He was laughing now. So was our girl. My spirits soared. It gave me a little bit of hope.

Cam continued to evaluate the crowd.

"Shit! We are going to have some trouble," Cam suddenly said.

"We are?" I looked up, surprised. I had just taken my latest reading on our guy.

"See the bruiser over there?" Cam pointed across the bar near the entrance. You couldn't miss the guy. He wore a skintight t-shirt and tight jeans. Both showed his ripped body. The acne and the glazed, too-narrow eyes showed that the steroids were working. The malevolent sneer made it clear that he wanted to show off those muscles. It didn't take someone of Cam's psychological acumen to know this guy was here to pick a fight as quickly as possible.

"He is going to hit on a pretty woman, and he is going to make sure that she is with another guy. He's got his wingman, too, to back him up if the fight gets out of hand. We should probably go. I don't want to see the carnage," Cam said. What he was really worried about was getting sucked into a bully's sights. As a kid, Cam evaded countless beatings because of his speed, but to the bully he looked like easy pickings. The bruiser went to the bar. At just that moment our guy and our girl stood and then walked by us, the girl in front of the guy. The guy gave me a smile and then mouthed. "Thanks." I smiled back.

Cam and I had already eased off our stools, so we slipped in behind our guy and woman. As we walked past the bruiser, he spewed some misogynistic, homophobic shit. He said, "No way that woman should be with the gay accountant."

Our guy stopped and started to turn. I stepped up to him and gave him a gentle push forward. "Keep going. Don't ruin it." He nodded sagely. This guy now would have listened to anything I said. We all left the bar, and we all walked in the same direction. Cam and I did this instinctively because we knew the bruiser had spotted his prey and wanted our guy. So when the bruiser made it out of the bar, he saw this woman being escorted by three guys, even he didn't like the odds. He and his wingman went back inside.

Cam and I walked by our guy and woman, who stood beside his Nissan Rogue. I thought, *You're no rogue, my friend, but we can all dream. And maybe tonight is your night*. He opened her door, but before she got into the car, she turned to him. They stared into each other's eyes for a moment. Then our guy leaned forward. She stood up on her toes, and they kissed. It would be a first kiss that they would remember forever. I hoped so anyway.

We walked on. Cam draped his arm around my shoulder.

"Well, my friend, our work here is done."

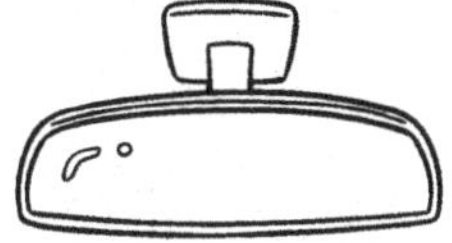

CHAPTER 6

Dad and I sat next to each other in companionable silence as I drove. He studied the countryside, which slowly transformed from farmland to cranberry bogs to deep pine forests. As we traveled north on Highway 51, Dad first told some stories of how he and Mom inherited the cottage on Bogus Lake shortly after they married. Dad's uncle died, and since he was childless himself, he passed the property to his nephew and niece, Dad and his sister, Mary, who didn't really want to have much to do with the cottage, especially the upkeep and the taxes. Dad still claimed she shared a stake in the property. Each summer she and her family would visit for a long weekend. That seemed to be enough to keep her share intact. Mom and Dad, though, loved the place. Like most newlyweds, they married poor, so when his uncle offered the cottage as a honeymoon shack, they quickly accepted. Somehow, in those first years, they managed to make the tax payments and provide enough upkeep to prevent the land from reclaiming the space.

Dad and Mom had spent a week at the cabin in late spring, about a week before she suffered her heart attack. Dad hadn't been back since. He asked me to go with him. He said he would have to cut the grass with a sickle, and he wasn't sure the neighbors would keep tabs on the place. They would, of course. They had for more than forty years. But Dad had to justify the trip in his mind. I quickly agreed to join him. Although Madison is a wonderful place in the summer, I always enjoyed spending time at the cottage. I took Friday off, so we left late Thursday afternoon. Our plan included performing the necessary maintenance on Friday, with a trip to Minocqua on Saturday.

We stopped at the Walmart in Merrill. For philosophical and personal reasons, I never shopped at Walmart except when I went to Antigo. Up north it seemed okay to shop there, but you almost had to because of the dearth of choices. We bought some basic provisions, which, to my surprise, included a case of Miller Genuine Draft. "I might need fortification," Dad said and shrugged.

I grabbed a second case off the shelf. "It's a long weekend," and then I shrugged. We both laughed. We then drove into Merrill and found a bait shop open, where we purchased fishing licenses and bait. Dad said he wanted to drop a line, if for no other reason than the memories. He also had learned long ago to never fish without a license. He shared a story I had heard many times.

"Your mother wanted to fish. It was evening, and we figured it wouldn't hurt to take a fish or two without a license. We also figured what were the odds that a DNR officer would be patrolling our small lake at just that moment when we were fishing without a license. Sometimes, the odds go against you. The DNR officer happened to be driving the road that circled the lake and looked over and saw us fishing. Because we didn't have life preservers in the canoe, we also got ticketed for lack of personal floatation devices, and this overzealous DNR officer wasn't even going to allow us to paddle back across that postage stamp of a lake. We got caught and had to pay a hefty fine. After that, Grace always insisted that we break out the cash for the license." Even though Dad and I each bought a license, it seemed like a frivolous purchase. I knew I wouldn't use it more than once that summer.

We turned off Highway 17 and started on the meandering back roads with blind sweeping curves. As a kid, I always drove these roads way too fast, sometimes taking the curves on two wheels. I had mellowed and drove more sedately. "You mind stopping the car for a minute?" Dad asked. It was only about three miles to the cabin, but Dad got out. I wondered why he would stop so close to the cottage. It seemed like part of his journey and part of his ritual, so I joined him.

He stood in front of a decaying one-room schoolhouse. The sign chiseled into the cement facade read "Forest School." Since we were on Forest Road, this made sense. Although decades had passed since this place had been used to educate the county's kids, you could tell that someone still cared for it because, on second inspection, it wasn't dilapidated at all. Someone routinely mowed the lawn. The trim on the school had recently received a new coat of dark green paint. As a joke, someone had stood an old suit of armor against the front door. It guarded not with menace but irony. You would think the elements would have turned the metal to rust. It gleamed. Then I began to wonder if someone lived there. I asked Dad.

"Don't know. Obviously, someone takes care of the place, though." Then he fell silent.

After a moment, I said, "Does this place hold special meaning for you? A place you and Mom once visited?"

"No. I love this old school. But it pisses me off. For years I have tried to get a decent photo of this place. I think I have taken photos of it every time I've come up here. Every picture is missing something. I have shot it from every angle in every season. It just always seems flat. I have never been able to figure it out, so I have never gotten the picture I want to hang on my wall at home, or even up here at the cottage." He stomped around for another minute, grabbed his camera, and snapped a quick photo, seemingly without even looking. Then he gave a final wave of disgust. With that, we got back in the car and made our final approach to the cottage.

I drove slowly. On the road's crest above the cottage, I slowed to a stop. From here you could see the cottage below and across the lake. Dad swallowed hard and just stared at the small building with the sage green siding. After several minutes, I continued driving. Finally, I pulled the car into the short drive. Dad didn't move.

"I'll open it up," I volunteered. I grabbed our bags and walked onto the porch. Dad had always taught me to inspect my property every time I approached it, so I took a glance around and then took a quick walk around the building. Everything looked fine, although the grass certainly needed cutting, which was one of my jobs for tomorrow. As I surveyed the property, I felt the stress oozing away. It was like coming home.

For several years, Amy and I took the kids to the cottage for a week during summer vacation. I wanted them to have this kind of experience in their lives. Because I had been to the cabin so often, I felt comfortable opening up the place. I knew the drill. Mom and Dad had taped opening and closing procedures to the side of the refrigerator. All guests, even sons, had to follow the procedures. After entering the cottage, I opened the drapes and then the windows. I flipped the circuit breaker to turn on the electricity. Then I stepped out the back door onto the deck and walked to the propane tanks in the corner. I opened the valve of the tank closest to the kitchen so we could use the stove. Then I took a look out over the lake. Standing for a moment, I absorbed the view from the deck, one of my favorite places in the world. It stood about five feet from the water's edge. The DNR would never allow this kind of structure now—too close to the water line—and so each time my parents rebuilt the deck, they had to keep one board from the old deck to convince the DNR that they were just enhancing the old structure.

I could sit on that deck through the long summer afternoons and never move. I would just lounge, read, watch the kids swim, and watch the loon pair swim by when the kids had left the water. Right there on the deck, I had all my needs, especially if the book was good. The only time I would move was when I joined the kids or needed a bathroom break. Amy could eventually find comfort on the deck with me, but it took her longer to slip into cabin mode, where idling for an entire afternoon seemed completely appropriate. That usually didn't happen for her until Thursday or Friday. For me, it happened instantly. It would take a few moments longer for me this time because I had to pull the lawn chairs out of the shed.

By this time, Dad had left the car and now stood out on the pier. Seeing him there, his shoulders heaving, I, too, felt the sadness so familiar. The sadness was like always wearing a heavy, uncomfortable winter coat you could never take off, even in warm weather.

I headed to the shed and pulled out a couple of chairs and placed them on the deck. I began unloading the rest of the gear from the car. I took my bike off the rack and wheeled it into the shed. Then I pulled the cooler inside and unpacked it.

Sitting on the deck a short while later, reading and sipping on a Genuine Draft, Dad finally joined me, his own beer clutched in his grasp.

"This is harder than I thought, Robb. All my memories here involve Grace, you and Shelly, Amy and the grandkids. I think I'm going to be crying a lot this weekend."

"Me, too, Dad. I guess we just have to get through it."

We sat and drank our beer silently. Later we built a campfire and stayed up late telling each other cabin stories. It seemed as if we would never run out of story material. By the time we called it a night and doused the fire, we had made a sizable dent into one of the cases of beer.

The next morning Dad felt lethargic. He was having problems with his blood sugar. "Of course, I shouldn't have been drinking beer last night. Not a good thing for a diabetic to do. Sometimes, though, you've just got to say, what the heck." Dad and I laughed at the old joke. Years earlier, we had watched *Risky Business* together. Dad could relate to the father. I wanted to be Tom Cruise, who got the girl in the end. This was before I began dating Amy. The father in the movie maintained, "Sometimes, you have to say,

'What the heck?'" Tom Cruise's character learned that sometimes you need to say, "What the fuck?"

—x—x—x—

When I started dating Amy, I became the guy in all the teenage movies who got the girl. My senior year in high school proved to be the watershed year of my life. None of it would have been as good without Amy, though. Our relationship and my love for her defined that year. When I think about the promise of our love, I find myself contemplating Dad and Mom because their relationship had that kind of promise—the kind of promise all new love offers. I wondered, though, why Mom and Dad and a few rare other couples could make that love flourish and grow when so many of us failed in our attempts. In high school, it seemed like the love I felt for Amy could never diminish.

School started at 8:10. By 7:45, the kids had started gathering in the commons. That year it seemed that seniors filled most of the space in the commons. My high school had three thousand students, and seniors in the commons would usually take up the majority of chairs, tables, benches, and wall space hanging out before school. Underclass students hung out in the hallways. Halfway through junior year, my football buddies started hanging out on the fringe of the commons, getting a feel for our upcoming turn as seniors. I have never experienced anything remotely like this since. We gathered each morning and just hung out. You would think we would run out of things to say, but that never happened, especially with so many people who could hold court.

When we became seniors, the word went out quickly: no cliques. We had to figure out how to make that happen, though. So about thirty of us, guys and girls, met in a park in early August before the football season started. It included different leaders, athletes, movers and shakers. Bo, T., and Joe-Joe invited me to join them. Bandmates Brad and Phil joined me. Of course, Amy came with her friends: Kathy, Mary, Jennifer, Pammy, and Sandy. All the big school leaders came together at Vilas Park.

We talked about what we wanted as seniors, how we wanted the year to go. The consensus was that we really wanted to come together as much as possible. We talked about what that would look like. We would all just enjoy each other's company. Two days later, our group of thirty invited everyone we knew to meet us at Westmorland Park. At least three hundred rising seniors showed up. So did the cops. They were certain we were holding a raging kegger. We weren't. In fact, no one drank anything. Seeing that all was quiet and no one was drinking, the cops left. That became one of our strongest traits. We weren't going to be a hard-partying class. Certainly, partying happened. It just wasn't a defining trait. We wanted to be remembered as a close group of friends. Although you saw distinct groups among the underclassmen, those divisions disappeared with our senior class. You could hang with anybody, any time. That picnic in the park before school started set the tone for the rest of the year.

I usually got to school first. After five or ten minutes of tall tales and bravado from my buddies, Amy would sidle up beside me, slip her hand in mine, and give me a quick kiss. That always gave me a great start to what would be another great day. How can you possibly have a bad day when the prettiest girl in school has just given you a good morning kiss? After a few more minutes, I would walk Amy to class. Although I wasn't the guy who made his girl late for class every day and then arrived late himself, I would linger as long as possible and make it to class just before the bell rang, sometimes having to sprint down the last hallway.

Our paths wouldn't cross until lunch. Although we usually had lunch at a table in the cafeteria with a group of friends, Amy and I always sat together and shared our lunch. On our three-month anniversary, I brought a white tablecloth, candles, grape juice, and a heart necklace. Other guys later tried to copy my romantic flair. They didn't succeed.

During football and track season, Amy and I would meet for five minutes after school before I had to leave for practice. Then we would get together at either her house or mine and study. When I would lean in to kiss Amy, she would push me away. "No, Robb. We have to study. We can make out later." I mostly wanted to make out with her, but she insisted that we at least do some studying. So she instituted the twenty-five and five study rewards program. If I let her study for twenty-five minutes without interrupting, we could make out for five minutes. Her rule stated that if I interrupted her, I would forfeit the five until the next half hour. Although we generally stuck to the plan for a couple of hours, sometimes we did push that five-minute limit. After we finished studying, we went off the clock. I sometimes marvel at how long we could just kiss. Certainly, I wanted more. What guy doesn't? Kissing brought its own form of contentment. I was kissing Amy. That was enough.

—x—x—x—

After my reverie about the beginning of the relationship with Amy, I didn't want the memory to end. I slowly came back to the present moment at the cabin. That morning, while I mowed the grass and completed some other cabin maintenance, Dad dipped into memories about Mom, and I became lost yet again in memories of Amy. We were both thinking about love lost. After I completed my chores, I went for a bike ride. Ever since we used to come up to the cabin during our summer vacations, I have biked these back roads. Riding the rolling hills lined by pine forests always gives me a sense of peace. I found myself riding past Forest School. Just as Dad had the day before, I stopped in front of the school. I pulled my phone out of my bike bag and snapped a few photos. I don't know if I had achieved any more success than Dad, but I knew that this would become as much my challenge as his.

After lunch, Dad pulled out his fishing pole and launched the canoe. He knew he wouldn't catch any fish in the middle of the day. "I've just got a hankerin' to wet a line. I should probably fish tonight when we get back or drop a line early tomorrow morning before we go to Minocqua."

"Dad, get back from where tonight? Are we going somewhere?"

"Yeah, I guess I didn't tell you. I've been thinking about it all morning. At the bait shop last night, I picked up a copy of the *North Woods Leader*. It lists all kinds of events in the Northwoods. Which is where we are." He winked and smiled, enjoying his moment of Dad humor. "I saw something that I thought might be interesting to take a look at."

"So where are we going tonight?"

"Down to Symco. It's a little more than an hour away. They're having their annual thresheree."

"Thresher what?" I said.

"Thresheree. It's a farming festival. They've been doing it for years. Your mother and I always talked about going. We just never made it. If I'm going to keep coming up to the cabin, I'm going to have to make some new memories, or I will just wallow in the memories Grace and I made up here."

I nodded in agreement. His observation didn't seem to require a comment.

"Anyway, it always looked interesting. I guess it's just the old farm boy in me."

"Dad, the family farm you always talk about was forty acres on the edge of town, where you didn't really do any farming."

"Not so fast. We raised chickens. Sold a couple of dozen eggs each morning. My mother raised the chickens. She worked the farm. Dad didn't have time. He had to work the railroad run of the Milwaukee Road from Madison to Milwaukee. I loved those years on the farm. I often wish we wouldn't have moved to the house in the city."

"I've never heard you talk so romantically about farming," I said, smiling.

"Well, I don't know. I just thought it would be fun to go to this thresheree. We should leave about two o'clock."

"All right. We'd better get busy. You fish. I'll try to square up the door to the shed. That big gap in the frame is letting in the mice." So we went off to our appointed rounds.

Before we left for Symco, I read about Unionville on my phone. Unionville stands on the fairgrounds at Symco. It sounded quaint, a collection of buildings simulating life in a farming community in the late 1800s. It contained a general store, blacksmith, harness shop, firehouse, church, and saloon. The replica of the sawmill looked intriguing because several hundred chainsaws hung from the ceiling. When we walked onto the grounds of Unionville, we saw a sight that made me smile. "I thought you said we were going to a thresheree. It looks like we have gone to *Petticoat Junction*," the old TV show I caught reruns of as a kid. A tall wooden water tower greeted guests beside the train depot and general store. Dad laughed. I think we both spent a minute thinking about that old, early 1960s television show where the women draped their petticoats over the edge of the water tower while they bathed inside.

The general store was closed, but we peered in the window. Although I didn't live through such times, Dad remembered elements of small-time life. He pointed out the soda fountain and the candy jars. At the back of the store, you could see the buckets of nails and screws, tar paper, and assorted hand tools. It looked real to me. I imagined at any moment that some slightly balding guy with slicked back strands of hair, wearing a black apron, would come scurrying up, apologizing about being late as he stuck the key in the door. I realized it must have been an image I picked up from TV.

We walked farther onto the fairgrounds, where we saw people eating ice cream cones and ears of corn. We also saw many guys carrying cardboard cases of Coors Light. It turns out that at the thresheree you could buy a thirty-pack for twenty dollars and carry that around the grounds. After the previous night's indulgences, though, Dad and I settled for freshly squeezed lemonade.

We saw a long arc of gleaming, refurbished tractors lining both sides of the walkway through the village. Whoever owned these tractors obviously spent hours restoring and maintaining them. It also was clear that these tractors never saw the fields anymore. They received the kind of pampering that gearheads gave to their restored hot rods. Those who farmed would have recognized the names of all the tractors we saw. All I could do was read their names and scratch my head, thinking, *Yeah, I might have heard of Case, or International Harvester, or John Deere.* I found myself snapping photo after photo of the old steam engine tractors with their massive steel wheels.

As we walked through the grounds, we followed the crowd and ended up at the tractor pull. Many of the tractors we had just walked by would compete. The farmer would hook his tractor up to this sled that contained a huge, heavy weight on a hydraulic pulley. The farmer would start pulling forward, and with the tractor's forward movement, the weight started moving. The idea was for the farmer to pull the tractor as far forward as possible before the weight reached the end of the sled closest to the tractor, rendering it unable to pull forward any more. Most of the farmers ended up somewhere around 200 to 230 feet. The winner went 257 feet. Dad and I watched, mesmerized. We had never watched such an event, which I'm sure these farmers considered as much a sport as NASCAR.

Dad sidled up to an older gentleman, who scrutinized the pulling tractors. "Quite an event you've got here," my dad said, leaning on the fence beside the gentleman.

"Yup. Forty-second year. Crowds down a little bit right now. Cuz of the rain earlier. Should get 'em back for the dance tonight, I s'pose."

"You ever pull that weight?" Dad asked.

"Years ago, when I was working the farm. I never placed higher than the middle of the pack. My tractor didn't have the power for this kind of thing. It was fine, though, for the work at home."

"Why'd you stop competing?" Dad wondered.

"Stopped farming. Sold the spread. None of the kids wanted to take her over. And the wife wanted an easier life. Been off the farm for seventeen years. The wife died about eight years ago. Every day I miss her. And every day I miss that farm." He laughed. "Sounds like a country song, don't it? Nah, more than anything, I miss my wife, but a lot of days I do find myself getting a little sentimental about the old spread."

Dad didn't say anything, so silence reigned for several minutes.

"So, tell me more about this thresheree and this village," Dad said. "I'm Bob, by the way," Dad said, offering his hand. He gestured at me. "This is my son, Robb."

The men shook. I nodded. Dad's new friend started laughing.

"I'm Bob, too. Around here everybody calls me Old Bob. Used to be a lot of us in the old days. Now you got names like Trentin and Justin and Silas and Trevor. Not so many Bobs anymore. Remember that whole Bob movement a couple of years ago? My daughter bought me one of those bracelets. Remember the whole What Would Jesus Do? campaign? My daughter bought me a 'What Would Bob Do?' bracelet. I wore it until it rotted off my wrist. Thought it was a damned good joke."

Dad laughed. "Did you hear that, Robb? Now you know what to get me for my birthday." We all laughed.

Eventually, Old Bob gave Dad the skinny on the village and the event, which they held every year to honor the farmers and the farming heritage.

"Back in the sixties, some far-sighted people started recognizing that the metaphorical end of the family farm was comin'. They wanted to mark it somehow. So they started gatherin' up all this stuff. Most all of it's found. The original organizers put out the word. They would take anything. Pretty much did, too. Did ya see all them chainsaws? Good example. Hundreds of 'em." He held up his hand and watched a tractor coming down the track, pulling the weight.

"This guy's gonna have a good run." When the distance, 244 feet, went up, Bob slapped his thighs. "That was a good one. That just might win it all. Have you been to the bar yet? Got to take a look at that. All that drinking stuff—beer signs and posters came from attics and junk piles. The bar itself came from a bar in Iola that was closing for good. We took it for our bar here. Look at the bar stools. Farmers donated all those tractor seats settin' atop the stools. Some farmers feel most comfortable sitting on a tractor seat. For my money, it's the best bar in the whole damn state. You'll see."

Bob's description made me curious, and suddenly a beer didn't sound so bad.

"Two of my favorites—that generator shed back yonder and the bridge."

"Old Bob, I thought you just said the bar was the best part of the village," Dad ribbed his new buddy.

"Ya got me there," Old Bob said, laughing. "I guess I just really like this whole place. I put in a lot of time and sweat equity into helping create and maintain this place. As a young farmer I thought it was a good way to connect to my farming heritage. Now when I come back for the thresheree, I take pride in knowing I helped build this. Anyway, about that generator and shed, small towns used to buy these generators for electricity. When they joined the grid, didn't need those generators anymore. We took 'em. I helped restore one myself. Still works. Every year we fire 'em up on Sunday. You wouldn't believe the racket."

Bob continued to regale us. "My favorite, though, Bob, is the bridge. We bought it as kind of a joke. It's a truss bridge. Down in Manawa, they wanted to get rid of it. The state was taking out that old metal truss bridge, putting up a concrete one. We bought the bridge for one dollar. Then on the appointed day, a bunch of us showed up with our tractors and wagons. We hired a crane, which loaded the bridge on the wagons. Then we started the damndest parade home. All kinds of farmers came out with their tractors, hoping they could help haul it. So we probably had a hunnert tractors trailing that bridge. Word got out to the sheriff. He stopped our little procession. Said we had to have permits. Took about three hours to get the proper paperwork. Then we finally could be on our way. Took most of the day to move it here. Eleven miles. Best damned road trip I ever took."

We stayed with Old Bob for a while at the tractor pull, and then he walked us over to the Unionville Bar, where we pulled up a tractor seat and listened to more of Bob's chatter.

I tried to get into the spirit of things with a Coors Light, which everybody seemed to be drinking. It didn't go down well, so I switched to the safer route. Still sluggish from our beers the night before, Dad and I opted for Diet Cokes, while Bob steadily drained the beers we bought for him. He seemed to be drinking with a purpose. For the next two hours, we listened to Old Bob tell stories about family, fights, homegrown food, and always about farming. Even though many of his stories carried the frivolity of youth and the wisdom of age, they also carried the sadness of loss. Dad and I seconded that emotion.

Dad and I later walked by the generators. A couple of them were the size of a locomotive engine. I could imagine the roar they would make. I also found myself thinking about the people who invented such contraptions more than a hundred years ago. They are the same kind of inventors who today are pushing the tech envelope and developing and enhancing everything digital—phones, watches, and tablets, along with all the apps to power them.

—x—x—x—

On the quiet drive home, where Dad and I slipped off into our own personal reveries, necessary after listening so long to someone else's, I realized that our new friend Old Bob drank to forget.

After spending this day with Dad, I knew later we would reminisce about this trip. We would talk about tractor pulls, a loud racket from generators, and Bob. We would laugh about thirty-packs of Coors Light.

Mostly, though, Dad and I would always acknowledge the importance of this cottage weekend in our father-son bond.

In Minocqua the next day, Dad and I drove over to Snag Lake and took a short walk on the path. We didn't get very far.

"Son, I think we're going to have to take a rest and then turn back." Dad slumped onto the bench beside the path. The way he dropped like dead weight made me realize that Dad had made the bench his goal.

"Are you okay?"

"My legs are cramping up. They do that more and more now."

"The diabetes?" I asked.

"Yeah, I'm starting to lose circulation in my legs, a common affliction for diabetics. I think part of the problem is that I haven't been exercising much, so I'm starting to lose strength. I need to try to walk more."

"Well, we'll have to develop a walking program," I said. "We can talk about it tomorrow on the drive home."

We grabbed lunch at Otto's Bar and Restaurant, each of us eating a signature brat. Our table faced the street. Dad took a sudden sharp breath.

"Son of a gun," Dad said, looking out the window at a couple perusing the posted menu near the front door.

"Know 'em?"

"Yup. Bill and Mary. Used to live up the street. He retired about seven, eight years ago, and they bought a retirement home on the Lac du Flambeau. I haven't seen them since they moved away." Just as Dad completed his explanation, the couple entered, and when they saw Dad, their faces brightened as if just lighted by the sun.

They came to the table, all smiles, arms outstretched. Dad stood and embraced his old neighbors.

"So, how's retirement life up north in a cottage by the lake?" Dad said, needling them with all the Northwoods clichés he could use. Bill and Mary told a few stories about their adventures on the lake.

"Driving home from dinner the other night, we were on the gravel road leading up to our house, and suddenly this black bear darted out of the woods and in front of the truck. I slowed down," Bill said. "Then the bear rose on its haunches and roared. Then it ambled off into the woods. We started driving. Then I looked out my side window. The bear had appeared again, and now it was running beside our car. Looked like it wanted the challenge of racing us. After about two hundred meters, it ran back into the woods."

"You never told me that," Mary said, acting like she didn't want to believe it.

“You were dozing. I didn’t want to scare you. I’ve been meaning to tell you that we should keep the dog pretty close to the house.” Mary put her hand on Bill’s forearm and squeezed.

After a few more minutes of chatter, Dad asked about the winters. “Don’t get me started on the winters,” Bill said. “Living up here is wonderful six months a year. The other six is where it gets hard. You feel your toughness when you make it through another winter.”

“That long drive to your house? Do you have someone plow it or do it yourself?” Dad asked. And then he followed up with several other meaningless questions.

The kind of chatter you engage in with people you haven’t seen for a long time tends to run out fairly quickly. The conversation sputters like a car running out of gas.

“Say,” Mary said, trying to revitalize the conversation, “where’s Grace? Is this a boys’ day out or something?”

Neither Dad nor I said anything for several moments. Dad looked at me, and I leaned forward and opened my mouth. I was about to answer when Dad put his hand on my forearm and squeezed.

“Grace passed a little more than a month ago,” Dad said, his voice barely above a whisper.

“Oh my God, Bob. No,” Mary said.

“We’re so sorry. We’re so sorry,” Bill said.

Then Dad had to explain everything that had happened. His voice grew more and more soft. It dawned on me that Dad hadn’t yet retold the entire story since the funeral, and it was taking a toll on him.

After another round of condolences from Bill and Mary, they hugged Dad and encouraged him to get in touch when he came north again. He promised he would.

“Whew,” Dad said. “That was hard.”

“Are you okay?” It was now my turn to squeeze someone’s arm.

“Yeah. I haven’t had to go through that yet. It was only a matter of time. Maybe it will get easier after this.”

“Maybe,” I said and thought, *Don’t count on it.*

—x—x—x—

Later in the afternoon, I took the canoe out for a solo paddle. Bogus Lake connected to Lake Charm through a fifty-yard, three-foot wide channel. Lake Charm held, well, charming memories for me. As a teenager, when

I started needing more of my own space, when I needed to escape the annoyance of pre-teen Shelly who was nowhere near as cool as I was, when I needed space from meddling parents, I would step into the canoe and paddle the tight channel into Lake Charm.

To me its charm came from its isolation. No roads connected to it. No one had built cabins or houses there. It seemed as if you quickly passed from the enticing escape from the city that attracted the weekend warriors from Madison and Milwaukee into the unexplored wilderness. For a brief time, I felt like an old-world explorer. That would last until you heard a car from a cabin on Bogus Lake turn over or heard the shouts from children cavorting in the lake. Sounds of people intruded on my wilderness escapes.

The paddle around the shoreline of Lake Charm took me away when the world at the cottage became too close for me. Mom could sense when I would need just such an escape. She would pack me a lunch. "Be home by five for dinner. Have fun!" I realized as an adult just how attuned Mom was to the needs of a teenage boy. Really, though, she was attuned to the needs of everyone.

"Did you enjoy your canoe trip?" She would ask upon my return. Sometimes we would talk about my afternoon escape. Sometimes not. She knew I enjoyed the outing when I would engage in chatter about ferns, the pattern of fallen leaves on the ground beneath the maples and oaks, the soft rustle of pine trees shushing in a gentle breeze, the spongy moss-covered ground that deadened the sound of footfalls, the plunge and swirl of the paddle pulling through the water. She would add her own descriptions of natural beauty. As she mentioned different elements of natural beauty, she was encouraging me to notice the beauty all around. Of course, I didn't understand that then. It just seemed like chatter. Years later, though, I realized how subtly she taught me to appreciate nature's bounty and beauty.

—x—x—x—

Those memories comforted me on my afternoon paddle. I found myself observing the different elements she encouraged me to notice as a teenage boy. I beached the canoe at a grassy opening, just as I had done so often years ago. I climbed a small hill to an opening overlooking the lake. Sipping from my water bottle, a new accessory that the world would have marveled at years ago when I used a metal canteen, I found myself thinking about then and now, thinking about here and gone, thinking about Mom and death.

Time had passed. Some things remained so much the same. Some things changed so much that the world seemed completely new and different. I thought about Dad, probably back at the cabin sitting on the deck, watching the pair of loons float by. He might have been wondering about the loons, which pair for life, wondering what happens when one of the loons dies or somehow disappears, wondering what becomes of the survivor. Dad and I were entertaining similar thoughts. We were trying to figure out how to paddle our way home when neither of us really knew what home meant anymore.

As I continued my slow, solo journey around Lake Charm, I found myself grateful that Dad and I were trying to redefine home together.

When I got back to the cabin, I joined Dad on the deck.

"How is Lake Charm?" Dad asked.

"Good. The same."

"That's good. Some things shouldn't change."

—x—x—x—

The next morning, I awoke to the smell of bacon and eggs frying. I lay in bed for a few minutes, enjoying the smell. Through the open window above my head, I could see the blue sky. It looked to be another beautiful day in the Northwoods. But I think Dad and I were ready to start making our way home.

When I stepped out of the room, Dad stood over the stove. He hadn't taken this kind of initiative since Mom died.

"Morning, Dad. Smells good."

"Yeah. I thought a good breakfast would help us get off to a good start."

"All right, I'm in."

"Your mom and I always did this before we left the cottage. Thought I'd keep up with the tradition."

As we ate, we filled the air with some idle chatter. After breakfast I volunteered to pack the lawn chairs, grill, and fishing gear into the shed. Dad and I dropped a line Saturday night. We fished off the pier. We didn't catch anything, but going through the motions seemed important. I unlocked the shed with the same code: 13-15-25. They hadn't ever changed the lock. It amazed me that the lock never rusted away or froze. As long as it worked, Dad didn't see any reason for changing it. I loaded the gear in the shed and relocked it. Then I turned off the gas. When I went back inside, Dad was just finishing up the dishes.

"Got everything packed?"

Dad nodded. "I put my suitcase by the door. I just need to finish up in here. I'm going to run the vacuum. Then I guess we can get started on down the road."

I grabbed the suitcases and the cooler and stuffed them in the back. Then I loaded my bike on the rack. I got in two good rides on the winding, hilly back county roads. Along the way, I had snapped a couple of pictures that looked pretty good on a small digital screen, but I wanted to load them on the computer and see how they looked after some refinements.

Dad stepped out of the cottage and walked out onto the pier. I gave him a few minutes and stepped back inside and checked to make sure I had all our gear. Then I pulled the shades, locked the back door, and stepped out the front, closing it behind me and checking to make sure it was locked. From the porch I took another look at the lake, and then I got behind the wheel.

After several more minutes on the pier, Dad slowly walked up the slight incline, took a lingering look at the cabin, and then got in the car. We sat for a minute in silence.

"Ready?"

"Yup."

I backed out and slowly pulled away. From the crest of the hill leading to Bogus Road, we both took one more look at the cottage below and across the lake. After the three miles of travel on Bogus Road, we turned onto Highway C. Dad stared out the window.

"Robb, stop the car!" Dad shouted after traveling about three miles through farm country toward Antigo.

I slammed on the brakes, looking around frantically for whatever I was about to hit, thinking deer? Bear? Skunk?

"What? What, Dad? Where?"

"Pull in this driveway."

I couldn't understand what had gotten into him. After stopping, we got out of the car. Dad walked toward the farmer standing near the barn.

"Howdy," Dad said. "Saw the sign out front. The puppies. Still got some available?"

"Yup. Interested?"

"I'd like to see what you've got. What kind of dogs are they?"

"Beagle-golden retriever mix."

"Nice mix," Dad said.

"The mom's the beagle, and the dad's the golden. Both pure. Somehow, they got mixed up with each other. Got their shots, microchips. They haven't been altered yet. I'll throw in a bag of dog food."

"How much?" Dad asked as we followed the farmer into the kitchen.

"A hundred dollars. Used to just give away the pups, but my wife says we need to get some money to cover the vet costs."

We could hear little yips from the puppies in the kennel. They all had tan coats, the general markings and color of the golden, but they appeared smaller than the typical golden. A few had multi-colored faces. We stood and watched the puppies for a few minutes. They rolled around and crawled over each other, their pliable little bodies undulating. We caught them in a moment of high play. They certainly hadn't noticed us, but Dad stood transfixed. He wore an almost beatific smile. I, too, enjoyed watching the puppies, but I didn't find as much enjoyment as he did. It became clear that he wasn't just enjoying the moment. The sight of the puppies had transported him to some cherished memory. I wondered what he was remembering. Dad kneeled and placed his hand inside the crate. The dogs continued their frolicking and hadn't yet noticed Dad, that is, all of the puppies except the obvious runt of the litter, which had been pushed aside.

This puppy came up to Dad and nuzzled his hand. It also began licking his fingers, probably hoping for some food. Dad sat on the floor, clearly willing to let this puppy try and lick away his skin.

Dad looked up at me.

"Robb, I think I've just found my exercise plan."

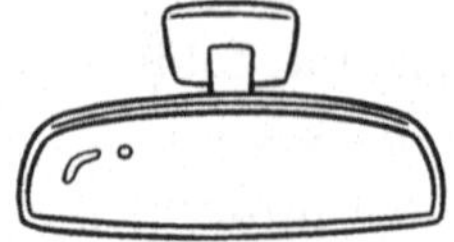

CHAPTER 7

The puppy quickly became a part of our household and took to us like peanut butter to jelly. When we left the farm, Dad sat in the back seat and cradled Ole Blue in his arms, talking calmly, gently petting her back. He had me pull into the Antigo Farm and Fleet to pick up pet supplies, which included a crate, puppy collar, leash, chew toys, padded bed, puppy gate, water and food dishes, puppy food, and the book *Raising Puppies for Dummies*. It took me forty-five minutes to find all of the items on Dad's shopping list.

While I shopped, he and Ole Blue bonded. The bonding continued as we began to move down the highway. He poured a little water from his water bottle into a dish, and the puppy quickly lapped it up. Then he ate a few biscuits from Dad's hand.

"I hope you're not in a hurry, Robb. This is probably going to be a fairly slow ride home. I think this little pup is going to be asking us to make a lot of stops, aren't ya little girl?" Dad kept cooing.

I shook my head, bemused.

"So, have you decided on a name for that little puppy?"

"Yup. Ole Blue," Dad said, smiling. Even a quick glance in the rearview mirror, and I wouldn't have been able to miss Dad's smile. This puppy tickled him to the bone. *What the hell*, I thought.

"Seeing as how the puppy is a nice creamy color, you're going to need to explain that."

"Sure. You might remember this when I tell you the story. Do you remember that Volkswagen van we had for a couple of years? It was bright orange. We took two family camping trips in that van."

"Yeah," I said, the memory coming back to me slowly. "Didn't the top pop up?"

"It did. And it also had a cooler and a little sink. The bed pulled out and could sleep two. And it was bright orange. We didn't actually sleep in the van unless it was raining. We pitched a tent and rolled out the sleeping bags. But it was a comfortable way for us to get down the road.

"Your mother and I used to laugh about that van. We thought we were so smart buying it. Of course, not a damned thing worked. The sink was a bust, and the cooler fridge worked more like an oven than a cooler. The canvas netting on the pop top ripped on our first camping trip."

I interrupted. "Dad, I'm not sure I see where the Ole Blue name comes from in relation to that van."

"Well, on that first camping trip, you kids had crawled into the tent and fallen asleep. Your mother and I sat by the fire, drinking straight from the bottle of wine we uncorked as soon as you kids were asleep. We got a little tipsy, drinking and snuggling by the fire. The van loomed behind us. Grace said, 'I'm sure glad we bought that van. I think it's going to be good for our family.' I agreed, saying, 'Ole Blue sure is a good girl.' Your mother gave me one of those arched-eyebrow looks. I said in response, 'I always wanted to have a horse and name it Ole Blue. I think that van is as close as I'm going to get.' Well, your mother just cackled. She giggled about Ole Blue through the rest of that bottle of wine. We also christened the pullout bed in Ole Blue that night."

I now gave Dad an arched-eyebrow look of my own. He just laughed, looking forward at me in the rearview mirror.

"Anyway, to quote your mother, 'I think Ole Blue is going to be good for our family.'"

As kids, Shelly and I begged our parents to get us a dog. Whenever we went to the little shopping mall on the near west side, we would go to Wilson's and fawn over the puppies they kept in cages near the back of the store. It wasn't much of a pet store, but to us, looking at those puppies each week filled us with longing. We had an aunt, one of mom's sisters, who had a Brittany spaniel. We fell in love with that dog. Eventually, we began to wear down Mom and Dad, and finally, they took us to a farm, where we picked out our puppy, a beautiful Brittany with a bright white coat and large, reddish-orange, round splotches. We called the dog Brandy.

Shelly didn't really have the focus to care for a dog, so I became the principal caretaker. I walked Brandy every night. I took him to obedience school and taught him to walk on a leash. I taught him to sit and a few other basic tricks. The family favorite came when I taught Brandy to shake. It got to the point where I would just hold out my hand, and Brandy would drape his paw over it. If I were lying on the couch with my arm hanging off the end, Brandy would drape his paw over my hand. When it was just us in the house, Brandy proved to be a great dog. He loved to wrestle and pull. He preened when we petted him, and he would sit near us for hours, hoping for more affection. When I would be sick and listless, he wouldn't leave my side.

This dog, though, had a huge downside, which began to wear down my parents. As a hunting dog, Brandy needed to work. He also needed to wear off the extra energy. To help him become calmer, I used to take him on runs with me. He kept pace with me throughout the run, no matter how long. When I got up to three miles, he never faltered. When we got home, he would drink bowls of water. But he usually would be calmer that night. He also showed tendencies of being a good watchdog. If someone rang the doorbell, Brandy would erupt into ferocious barking. Seemingly always excited when guests arrived, Brandy would bark incessantly and frequently begin humping the legs of the guests to our home. No matter what we did, we couldn't calm him down.

Brandy also proved to be an angry dog. When we left for work or school in the morning, we had to leave him home alone throughout the day. He didn't like this. It got to the point where we had to leave him locked in the basement because he became a malicious shitter. He would leave huge dumps at the front door, almost as if he were saying, "You leave me home alone all day, well then just take that." Dad ripped up a square of carpeting around the front door because Brandy had defiled it. Brandy also took to peeing on the furniture. We knew he could hold it. But he soiled the furniture because he didn't like being alone. Mom and Dad ended up throwing out two couches, both besotted with Brandy's pee.

Brandy also became a runner. If we opened the door and didn't block the opening with our bodies, Brandy would bolt. I spent many hours chasing down that damned dog. He seemed to love the chase. It became part game and part punishment for him. After a while, we stopped chasing. One morning, as Mom, Shelly, and I were leaving for the ride to school, Brandy bolted. "Let him run," Mom said. "We don't have time to chase him." Mom dropped us off at school. When I arrived home from school that day, the first to get there, I saw Brandy lying on the front porch. He was breathing ragged breaths. I tried to get him to move into the house. Then I tried to carry him inside, but he yelped in pain. It occurred to me that a car had probably hit him. I called Mom, terrified. She left work, and we brought Brandy to the vet, where he confirmed my suspicions. Brandy didn't run for a long time after that.

The final insult came, though, when Brandy shredded a quilt that Mom's aunt had made for her as a child. When Mom saw the damage, she went ballistic. She said she was going to find someone to take Brandy. No matter how much Shelly and I begged and pleaded, Mom refused to back down. I came home one day to find Brandy missing. I called Mom again at her realty office.

"Mom, Brandy's gone. I think he must have somehow gotten out and run away again," I reported.

"He didn't run away. I found a family with a nice big farm to adopt him. He will be happy there. He will have so much room to run." I missed Brandy, but the loneliness slowly ebbed away.

—x—x—x—

As Dad and I were riding home from the cabin with Ole Blue in the backseat, we reminisced about Brandy. On that ride, Dad revealed the truth.

"Son, you know what your mom told you about Brandy and the family with the big farm, the family that adopted Brandy." I nodded as I looked at him in the rearview mirror. "That's what all parents tell their kids when they take their dogs to the pound."

I looked up quickly and caught Dad's eyes in the rearview.

"So you had Brandy put down. Jesus Christ! Why am I just hearing this now? You really killed my dog?"

He just nodded. We drove in silence for several miles. "Your mother just got to the point where she didn't want the hassle anymore. When we saw how sad you were, we both regretted it, but once you take the dog to the pound, it's not like you can get it back. We agreed to keep that secret from you and Shelly. That was a mistake. You know what they say about hindsight. It's how you gain wisdom for the future." He nodded again and looked at Ole Blue curled asleep in his lap. Dad smiled again, wistfully.

—x—x—x—

Taking care of a puppy is a lot like taking care of a baby. It takes a lot of time and consistent effort. After that long, sleepless first night, where Dad and I took turns cuddling Ole Blue and taking her outside for potty breaks, she quickly settled into our family. As I would walk that sweet little pup through the neighborhood, I often found myself thinking of children, of babies. One night my thoughts turned to my first up-close encounter with parenthood, which came, ironically, at senior prom.

Prom happened in late May, but we spent a couple of months before the actual prom talking about it. I know now that expectations are usually far bigger than reality. But my buddies, who weren't in relationships, tried to decide who to ask. Those of us in relationships spent time with our partners plotting pre- and post-prom activities. Though many couples joined another couple, Amy and I knew we wanted to enjoy a nice dinner on our own. After the obligatory photos with our families, Amy and I went to dinner. Worried about missing anything, I made early reservations. We ate our dinner and then headed back to school for the big event. We arrived a few minutes after the doors opened, and we were the third couple inside. We milled around until people we knew started showing up. Bug made the biggest splash of the night. His entrance was big. It was memorable. It was pure entertainment. Years later, we still talk about it.

He arrived at prom sputtering like a teenager whose parents told him that no, he couldn't stay out past curfew just because other kids do. Whenever Bug appeared like this, we all gathered around because we knew it would end up being a good story. That night a bunch of guys from the football team encircled him. Most of us wore light blue tuxedos with a ruffled front and a light blue bow tie. Fashionistas! No, really! It was the style then. For nostalgic reasons, I often thought of buying one off eBay. They have countless kinds of suits available. At prom that night, I looked at the guys and thought, *Christ, we're still in uniform.*

Of course, the girls wore their own kind of uniform, each with a slight variation. Most girls wore peasant dresses and wrist corsages. When I first saw Amy, my breath caught. She looked stunning. The simplicity of the dress accented her beauty. In retrospect, even though prom really is about kids trying to behave like adults in the safety of their fleeting childhood, I think the dress accented her innocence. Amy's beauty could often make me lightheaded, but that night my knees literally knocked. A year earlier I never would have predicted that I would be going to prom with, in my mind, the most beautiful girl in the school. I wouldn't have felt qualified. It might sound cheesy, but I think our intense love for each other made us both more attractive and not just to each other. That night, as we stood first in the commons and later danced in the gym, no one doubted that we belonged together.

The pre-prom activities required that Amy and I make the requisite circuit for pictures. I picked her up at her house, where the evening began with photo opportunities. Then my house. Then her grandmother's. Finally, we headed off to dinner. I didn't even mind driving the Dodge Dart that night. With Amy by my side, it seemed like the swankiest car on the road, a limousine suitable for A-list celebrities, the kind of car everybody stared at and wondered who rode behind those tinted windows. I completely forgot it was just the most basic, cheapest Dodge Dart.

When we finally made it to the school, I looked around at the empty commons and gym. "Uh-oh," I said. "Wrong night." Amy laughed.

"No, just early. We probably could have had another glass or two of wine. since you spent so much on that fake ID just for prom. That must be what most of our friends are doing. And remember, they mostly went to Milwaukee. Let's go look at the gym and see how all of our decorating work turned out." Decorating the gym for prom became a group effort, much like float building did for homecoming. Clubs and organizations, teams, and musical groups all constructed and decorated homecoming floats, pulling rolls of toilet paper through chicken wire. Each night the guys from the Citizen's Club and the girls from Socials Club, a traditional girls' club throwback to the fifties, met at Diane's house to build our float. We usually also went to at least one other house to help another group with their float.

Decorating for prom proved to be a similar experience. A group of about seventy-five seniors built this elaborate castle. We had a drawbridge and even a moat filled with goldfish. We painted flats as if we were building a set for a musical, so an enchanted forest surrounded the castle. We made paper mache trees. We hung a disco ball and streamers and banners from the ceiling. We built and then decorated a stage for the band. The theme for prom was "An Enchanted Evening."

When Amy and I entered the gym, she stopped and held her hand to her mouth. "Oh my."

I looked around, panicked, fearing the disco ball had dropped into the moat.

Amy swept her arm across the vista. "It's so beautiful." Then she reached for my hand again. That's the thing about Amy and me. Our relationship began with us needing to touch each other. It continued to be something that defined us. Not in illicit or inappropriate ways. We held hands, entwined fingers, or wrapped our arms around each other's waists, or we just stood so that our hips connected. "Kiss me right now, in this enchanted place," Amy said. So I did.

We walked back out into the commons just in time for the Bug show.

Bug was our scat back on the football team. Coach nicknamed him. Said he moved so fast he looked like a bug skittering on the water. When Bug started telling this story, it was like a comic opera.

"Oh my God. You won't believe what happened," he almost shouted, pacing manically in the small circle surrounding him. "We had gone over to Milwaukee for dinner."

Bug continued. "After dinner, we were heading back here, and I saw that a state trooper had pulled over Bo. I slowed down, rolled down my window, gave Bo the finger, and called him a fat ass. Well, the cop thought I was referring to him. He jumped in his car and gave chase. I decided to try and outrun him. It didn't work. When the cop finally pulled me over, man was he pissed. He wrote me a ticket for everything he could imagine. I just lost twenty-three points. I won't be driving for a couple of years."

We all laughed and then laughed even harder when Bo arrived because Bug started sputtering again. Joe-Joe asked Bug where his date was. "Well, to put it mildly, she was pretty pissed at me. She broke up with me on the spot. Told me to drop her off at home. So here I am. Alone. At my senior prom. Fucking alone. Guys, watch out! I just might try to steal your date." Several guys shoved him at that comment. Some guys shared subtle and not-so-subtle threats.

As I walked away, I heard Patrick say, "Just stay the fuck away from my girlfriend." I laughed at that. I didn't have any concerns about Amy.

When I found Amy a few minutes later, I told the story. She laughed and then snuggled into my arms. "I'm really glad I'm dating you. You would never embarrass me like that. Another reason why I love you so much." She always found the best ways and the best times to tell me she loved me.

Later that night, as we waited in line for the promenade at midnight—we really did have an old-fashioned promenade where parents stayed up late and came to school at midnight to watch the spectacle—I stood talking with Andy. We'd been friends since sixth grade. He leaned in and whispered, "Guess what?" I had no idea. "I'm going to be a daddy." He smiled, but he certainly didn't look overjoyed.

"She's four months pregnant. So I get to graduate, and then I will get married. Two big parties in one summer. You're coming, right?"

"To your graduation party, sure."

He laughed. "Cool. Maybe you could drop by the wedding, too." We laughed. "You know I think I love Deb. It sure felt like it when we made this baby. So now I'm getting married, and instead of going to college at UW–Madison, I'm going to go to night school at the community college and work at Kohl's, maybe try to get a management position to make more money. It will be good. I'm really excited." Andy paused and looked up and down the line. Our dates stood a few feet in front of us, deep in conversation. "Sometimes I can't help feeling like I'm fucked. Totally fucked."

My jaw dropped. That proved to be quite a revelation, and it made me sweat a little bit. Amy and I had been doing it for a couple of months, and we'd already had a close call. But I didn't have any announcements to make about little Trojans.

But, hey, prom is supposed to be about memories.

That memory made me contemplate the first time Amy and I made love. The memory, one of pure joy over a rite of passage that was so monumental in my life, also became a bit tarnished. Like most memories, as we age, the shine of the memory tends to lose some of its luster. As our lives change, so does the memory. Many of my memories of senior year in high school with Amy now sadden me.

—x—x—x—

Always the first one out the door, I usually took Ole Blue for her first walk of the day. It wasn't so much a walk as a frolic. She was the baby who had just learned to crawl. She explored everything. She sniffed everything. It didn't matter if she had sniffed the same tree and telephone pole three times the day before. She had to take up the cause anew each day, checking to see who had been there since she had. The change in routine required that I awaken fifteen minutes earlier, but I quickly adapted. By seven, Blue and I were out the door. We usually didn't cover much ground in those fifteen minutes. Sometimes she got so busy that she forgot to do the duty. Before re-entering the house, I would stand patiently by the back door. Blue would dance around, twirl in circles, sniff a little more, dance up the steps, and then look quizzically at me. I would wait patiently, often encouraging her. Finally, she would get the idea and go into her trademark squat.

I quickly took to those early morning walks and found that I really enjoyed walking through the old neighborhood, watching it wake up. It reminded me of that year and a half when I delivered the paper. In eighth and ninth grade, I didn't like the morning constitutional so much, but I enjoyed the money. And just like that time when I delivered the newspaper, the morning walks made for a lovely start to the day. But it was summer, and I knew I would quickly come to abhor those walks when it was ten below zero and still dark, when I would be encouraging Blue to squat for Chrissakes.

I noticed the routines of the early risers. I noted the joggers and walkers, the other dog owners, those who sprinted from the house to the car, apparently already late for work. A couple of the neighbors liked to get out in their yards and do a little light gardening before the sun got up, which made sense to me. If I were ever a nut about my yard, I probably would have done the same thing. Even when I owned the house with Amy, she gardened. I mowed the lawn. Since I preferred to spend my time on other pursuits, Amy quickly realized that our yard would have no curb appeal if she left it to me. So she dug her hands in the soil, planted the flowers and bushes, trimmed, weeded, etc. When she wanted me to fertilize the yard or cut down a low-hanging or dying limb, I would. Otherwise, the beauty of the yard was her provenance.

One thing surprised me early on in my constitutionals with Blue. That little girl drew people to her, and she loved the attention. Strangers, who never would have talked to me before, suddenly dropped into a crouch to pet Blue. "What a pretty dog," they would say, and that would provide an opening for conversation. In a matter of a week, I had met more people from the neighborhood that I grew up in than I ever seem to remember knowing when I lived there as a kid. After the initial comments about Blue and the human contact that she adored, she would resume her exploration, leaving the humans to sort it out.

That's basically how I met Sara. I never would have known her without Blue. She approached us from the opposite side of the street, running at a quick pace. Her ponytail danced behind her. Sweat stained the front of her shirt, and her arms and legs glistened. Thoughts immediately turned to sex. My old friend Cameron would have sighed and said, "Of course they did. You're still a man." When she saw little Blue, she slowed her pace, jogged across the street, and went into the routine that I had become so familiar with recently.

"What a beautiful little puppy!" I must admit to being just a little bit of a cad because my thought was, *Right now, I love this dog because this would never happen without her*. She crouched and hugged Blue, who happily licked her face and then licked some more, obviously intrigued with the salty taste. Oh, to be a puppy, where that kind of behavior is acceptable. Then she nuzzled Blue to her chest. I sighed and repeated the thought.

We chatted a little bit. I gave her the basics about Blue. We introduced ourselves. "So, do you tend to walk her at the same time?" Sara asked.

"Yup." Very suave.

"So, I'll probably see you tomorrow," she said and then just like that ran out of my life. I fished in my pocket, hunkered down, and gave Blue a treat. "Good girl." She'd earned it.

The next morning, just like that, Sara ran right back into my life. And the next morning, and the next. And then she asked me out. I accepted.

In high school, I asked some girls out and always struggled with the timing of it. I only ever got it right with Amy. Later, after the divorce, I didn't really date. I generally slept with women I would pick up at bars. Obviously, not a serial monogamist. I would pick up women when I needed some human companionship or nurturing or just really wanted to get laid. The idea of dating didn't appeal to me, and the last thing I really wanted was another relationship.

For a long time I tried to heal my wounds from the split with Amy, which was amiable, don't get me wrong. I still felt sad about it. She was supposed to be my soul mate—forever—not just for twenty-four years, including that glorious senior year. Also, I didn't want to just jump into another relationship because I never wanted my kids to feel like I didn't love their mother. I'll say it again. We divorced because I screwed up. When it came time to do the heavy lifting in the marriage, I didn't think I had the strength for the job.

For three years, I lived on my own. I got used to it. Before Mom's death, I believed, or rather convinced myself, that I would be perfectly happy if I never had to deal with another romantic relationship in my life. As Mom was dying, and then after she died, I saw the depth of love she and Dad felt. I felt another layer of mourning weight settle on me. I mourned the loss of companionship. Again, I found myself wondering what I gave up by not trying harder to save the marriage with Amy. The longing for a shared life began to swell almost instantly in me.

When this beautiful, sexy woman, who ran in what essentially amounted to her underwear, asked me out, I accepted and found myself thinking more about relationship things than jumping between the sheets. Don't get me wrong. I thought about getting between the sheets, too. I am still a man. Trust me, Cam knows these things.

On our first date we went for a bike ride on the relatively flat Military Ridge State Trail that meandered through farm country southwest of Madison. After riding for more than an hour, we arrived at the Riley Tavern, whose backyard slopes down to the bike path. We parked the bikes, ordered a beer, and grabbed a picnic table.

Then it became just like any other first date: What kind of work do you do? What would you like to be doing? Dogs or cats? How many siblings?

Where did you grow up? What are your parents like? Do you like to travel? Where have you been? Where would you like to go? Favorite restaurant? Best pizza? What's your favorite flavor of ice cream? Ever married? Worst relationship? Worst breakup? (I declined to talk about the end of my marriage.) Best kiss? You ask these questions in search of commonalities, in search of topics to explore more deeply, in search of intrigue, in search of red flags.

Sara finally raised her hand and gave the universal sign for "halt." I felt a little bit like a character from *Hogan's Heroes* when Sergeant Schultz finally decided to do his job.

"What? Do I have a booger hanging from my nose?" I said and quickly rubbed my face.

"No, no boogers, Robb," Sara said and laughed. "But how many times have you done this first date bullshit?"

I shrugged because although many people in high school thought of me as a player, I'd only earned that reputation because I was the guy who ended up with Amy. I really hadn't done the first date thing much. I once had a friend who went on two or three first dates a week. When I asked him why he dated so much, he said, "Because I hope to get good at first dates so I can meet the right person."

His answer unsettled me. I never would have believed that you could get so good at first dates that it would lead you to the right person. In fact, if you get too good at the first date routine, then you become so slick and polished that you tend to hide your true self under the sheen. All you really get are first dates. I believe a good first date leads to a second date, not another first date. On the other hand, I felt that I should have practiced more. I had just wandered out into the dark woods at night and had no idea how to get home.

Sara, though, took my hand and guided me. "What would you most like to be doing right now?"

I didn't hesitate to answer, but when I heard the words, they surprised me. "I'd like to be talking to my mom. Just having a conversation with her, you know. She died two months ago, and I find myself wishing every day that I could talk with her. It wouldn't have to be any big, deep, revelatory conversation. Just chatter. When my mom was alive, I think I took her for granted. A week, sometimes two, would go by before I would call her. And now barely an hour goes by when I don't find myself just wanting to talk to her."

Sara squeezed my hand. "So, what would you tell her about today?"

"I'd tell her about this. About me sitting here, talking with you, just getting to know you, and liking what I'm discovering. She'd want to know what you look like."

"And?"

"Mom wouldn't want to know superficial things like your height or weight, or hair color, and the size of your feet."

"I think my feet are about average," Sara said, raising her foot. We laughed again.

"Maybe a little bigger than average," I said, holding back a giggle. "Big feet, big ... Oh yeah, that doesn't apply to women."

Sara gave me a flirtatious shove and laughed. "You were describing me to your mom."

I decided to be honest and stop trying to say the right things.

"You've got eyes and a smile that really complement each other. And when you smile, I think you could light up the room—you know, turn it from night to day. The smile doesn't always reach the eyes, which makes me think there seems to be an underlying sadness behind your eyes. I find myself wondering about that."

Sara shifted a little on the bench seat. Then she looked away.

"Does the sadness really show? I thought I'd finally figured out how to cover that up."

"It shows a little. A lot of people wouldn't notice it because you're so beautiful. But it's definitely there."

She picked up her beer, took a couple of swallows, and set the glass down again. "Thanks for the beautiful comment, but yeah, it's there. You're right. The sadness. Bad relationships, bad experiences, and a feeling of inescapable loneliness. It's all stuff I'm not really very good at talking about, but if you're patient with me, I think it will come out. But it might take some time if you're willing to give it to me."

At that moment, I liked the way that sounded. It was real. It was honest. It said let's keep going and see where this leads. What I heard her say was that she wanted to spend more time with me. I wanted that, too. "We've got nothing but time, Sara. This is a first date. We don't have to overturn every rock that has been in our path. When you're more comfortable with me, you might feel like you can tell me more."

She squeezed my hand again, and I felt my heart contract. That contact made me believe that this relationship would lead to good things. But later, after our return ride and a long, smoldering first kiss that led to a protracted make-out session on her couch like a couple of high school kids,

I lay on the bed of my childhood and reviewed the day's events. Still juiced from the adrenaline of making out with Sara, I could only think about the possibilities of hope. Just before I fell asleep, a frightening thought slipped in, and I quickly pushed it aside. *She is going to break my heart. She is going to grab it with both hands and squeeze the love and life out of it.* Much later, I realized that when she backed out of talking about those moments of sadness in her life, she had slowly and quietly closed and locked the door. She never did return to the topic to share what had caused that sadness. She always deflected. That realization didn't come until later.

—x—x—x—

"So, how's the sex?"

"Cameron, will you stop? I'm not one of your clients," I said, a little miffed. "I don't want to talk with you about sex with Sara. I want to talk about what might become a relationship. It's not all about sex."

"Robb, it is always about sex. If you tell me about the quality of the sex and the kinds of sex you have, I will be able to tell you if the relationship you secretly yearn for will amount to anything. My dear friend, I repeat, it is always about the sex."

"Cameron, this is not high school, where I'm going to give you prurient thrills by describing every in and out with you."

"Your high school stories did get me through a lot of lonesome nights," Cameron said, and he looked off into the distance, pulling up those memories. "Liked the 'in and out' pun, by the way."

"Cameron, you bastard, stop thinking about Amy. And what pun are you talking about? Oh, Christ, Cam. That was really juvenile."

"Okay, forget the pun. But it's hard to stop thinking about the girl I fantasized about since the first time I saw her kissing my best friend, and oh, how I wanted to be you. I was more than just a bit jealous."

"I know," I said. "I guess that's why I shared some details with you. You know, like a gift from one friend to another."

"If I've never thanked you for sharing those stories, I really should. So thank you."

"You've thanked me probably a thousand times. It led you to your great success in life."

"Yeah, true. Hearing you talk about making out and love and, finally, sex made me realize how much I loved listening to others talk about sex. Almost as much as I like having sex. I really liked listening to people talk about relationships. I searched for a legitimate career where I could listen to people talk about sex and relationships. I became a sex therapist. And God, I love my fucking job so much. So, for fuck's sake, please, tell me about sex with Sara," Cameron said, smiling with anticipation.

"Fuck you, Cameron."

His smile instantly disappeared. "I'm hurt."

"You'll get over it. So, now really, can I talk to you about the relationship or what looks like could become one, because I'm really confused. Really out-of-my-league confused."

"So, the guy from high school who got voted most likely to succeed at everything just because he was banging Amy is finding the dating and relationship scene confusing? The irony is so rich. If only all of our classmates could witness this conversation."

Cameron seemed to be relishing this too much. But I would give him this. I know he was just stating how some would obviously feel. Cameron has been a lifelong friend and stood by me through all of it. Many of those high school classmates would probably gloat. While I enjoyed a wealth of friendships in high school, I also know that many of my classmates wanted to see me crash and burn, ala Maverick from *Top Gun*. They thought I had it too easy, too good, too perfect. Certainly, I had a good senior year. Lately I've wondered if that's all you get: one good year. Okay, that might be too melodramatic. Many of those years of my marriage when Amy and I were feeling our way but so rapturously in love, and those years when the kids were born and the joys of our family kept growing were good years. Those years when we established our sense of family and traditions, and those years when we faced relationship problems with determination and confidence and moved forward in positive ways were really good years. I found myself hoping to get a bit of that goodness back. Maybe, though, I used up all my karma and have now gone into a deficit.

"Okay, Robb. I'm not kidding here. What's so difficult about this? You were the guy in high school who ended up dating and marrying Amy, the girl that every guy and more than a few girls dreamed of. No matter how wonderful this woman Sara may seem, do you really see her as being in Amy's league?"

"I don't know, Cam. I don't know if you really can compare your high school sweetheart with a woman in her late thirties who has some steamer trunk-sized baggage. I just don't know how heavy it is, how long she's been carrying it, and how that burden has affected her. The thing is, Cam, I don't know how much of an issue her past is with her now."

"Robb, be easy on the judgments. You're doing your own heavy lifting with your own baggage."

"I know. There's a lot of stuff. But lately, well, since Mom died, I've felt like I want to be in a relationship again. I miss having someone in my life like that. My dad claims to be getting on fine since Mom's death, but he's not. You know ..."

"Your mom was his best friend and constant companion for almost fifty years. And suddenly she's gone. Between you and me, a dog is not really enough to fill the hole in his life," Cameron said. "Ole Blue is a cute distraction for your dear dad. The best thing about the dog is that it might end up getting you laid more with Sara or with the next woman who can't resist the man with the cute puppy."

"It always comes back to sex with you, doesn't it, Cam?" I laughed because with Cam, life really did exist in the stark ranges of black and white. Either you were having sex with someone, or you weren't. Most people didn't live in such absolutes, but for Cameron, it worked. He had lived his life obsessively pursuing the one thing that life denied him for a beat too long. He focused all of his energy on thinking of, talking about, and pursuing sex. It made him happy, but the reality for most people, including me, was that sex played a role in life. A fulfilling life, though, involved more than sex. Much more. The intricacies and difficulties and rewards of human connection with another person, the complete and full involvement in another person's life, included sex, but it didn't define life. It enriched life.

"Robb, I'm just saying that you really won't know about how deep a connection you can ever have with Sara until you begin to know her intimately. I'm not just making this shit up. You know I have devoted myself to the pursuit of carnal knowledge, and I have studied the theoretical and psychological applications of sex. I've looked at sex from every possible position ..." Cameron stopped talking to allow me to finish laughing. He really was quite good at dropping in sexual double entendres. "Yes, thank you for catching my little pun. Most people wouldn't have gleaned the extra meaning, Robb. Sexual intimacy adds another layer to the relationship."

"True. I will give you that, Cam. But it also complicates things. I've found that the physical act can often cloud rational thought where a clear head is paramount to avoid making stupid mistakes. Don't forget that sex ruined my marriage."

"No, Robb. Don't blame the end of your marriage on sex. Your marriage ended because you lost sight of the hard work and commitment it takes to make a marriage work. You acted in an irrational way. You essentially used indiscriminate sex outside your marriage to inflict punishment on your wife because you couldn't figure out how to love her anymore. It wasn't just your fault, either. Amy was to blame, too. She knows it. She's told me that she feels like she pushed you away."

"You and Amy have talked about this? I've never heard this before."

"Robb, Amy and I have been friends for a long time, too. Don't forget that during high school, she gave me legitimacy, just like you did. She was dating you, but I got some residuals because of my friendship with you. She became my friend. If I could be friends with both you and Amy, well, then I must have possessed my own level of coolness. Certainly much, much less than both of you, but still a smidge.

"Amy came to me before you ever slept with someone else. She wanted advice on how to rekindle that flame. She knew things had changed. The relationship became hard. Those good moments where you would just look at each other and smile, or sing together to songs on the car radio, or merely always be touching because that's how you connected, those little moments that defined your relationship together never seemed to happen anymore. I'm not very good at my job, though, because I couldn't figure out how to save your marriage. Don't tell my clients and the paying customers who buy my books, or I will go flat broke."

"So, what did you tell Amy?"

"The same thing I told you—don't give up on it. Keep trying. Be romantic. Be attentive. Be empathetic. Be kind when you find it most difficult. Be present in the marriage, especially when you can't figure out why. Stick with it, and time will bring you back to each other."

"That's really good advice, with sound psychological principles behind it," I said. "You really may know something about human relationships that goes beyond sex. I just wish it would have worked."

"Don't forget," Cameron said, "that I also told both of you to fuck more."

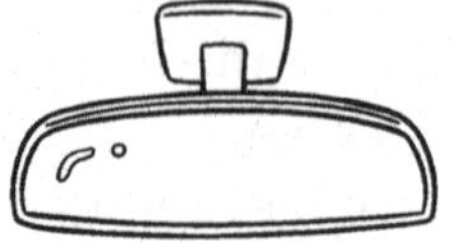

CHAPTER 8

It often amazes me how many parallels exist between my high school experiences and those of my children. Some things just seem to be universal components of growing up. If you looked and compared—and you really didn't have to look that closely—you could spot the similarities. Sadly, one of those similarities from my experiences became a part of my son's life.

Will Charles, the kid with two first names, always had the witty quip when we were in junior high. He could light up the classroom with his running commentary. He would sometimes whisper his comments that would leave his targets sliced and bleeding before they ever felt any pain. He could deliver sarcastic jabs, but his true forte lay with wit. Everyone considered him the class clown, but most people didn't really know about his sharp edge. He covered it up with his impeccable timing. Most of the time, teachers loved him because he lightened up the class, and he knew how to deliver without disrupting or publicly embarrassing the teacher.

By sophomore year, he had a firmly established reputation. His charismatic character drew people to him. Will always said that you can't hurt steel. He frequently got the entire class to repeat this absurd claim. He discovered, though, that you actually can hurt steel. Will craved attention, and gradually, when he stopped attracting the positive attention he needed, he started connecting with those kids who would give him his kudos, often for less-than-respectable actions. All he had to do was change his act and his actions to correspond more closely with what they said and did.

By the time we became juniors, though, we started drifting apart. I no longer felt comfortable hanging out with Will. We'd been buddies since fifth grade when he made a sexual comment about Lori, who always sat at the desk in front of me. He thought she might have started showing a little development in the chest area. Of course, it was rude and insensitive, but to a boy about to enter adolescence, fairly standard stuff. As Will thought about Lori, he said he would like to have sex with her. None of us really knew what that meant exactly. The gathered boys laughed, knowingly, all trying to hide our cluelessness. It made me laugh for real, mostly because he used the f-word, something that seemed dangerous and risky. My mom once made me sit in the chair for an hour repeating the word *bastard* because I had shouted, "Take that, you bastard," while stomping on a june bug. So saying the word *fuck*, especially about a girl, seemed like a very dangerous thing to do.

But when Will started hanging out with the guys who got high all the time, I realized I wanted no part of that. He wasn't the only one. At that time, it seemed like everyone in school was getting high. If you didn't, you were unusual. Will's hair grew stringy. He started speaking like a stoner. The quips in class stopped, and Will started talking about how blazed he got the night before. As soon as he left class, he would head out the door, spark a joint, and refresh his buzz. Will grabbed a few jobs, but he quickly lost them. He still needed money to pay for the weed. He started committing petty thefts.

Word quickly spread through school one Monday morning. It went like this: "Did you hear about Will, dude?" No, what happened? "He got arrested for theft. His old lady turned him in." What kind of mother would do that to their own son? "I don't know, but she's fucked up. He stole a stack of lumber from a construction site and was storing it in the garage until he could find a buyer." Why'd the mother do it? "She needed a place to park the car."

Will ended up spending nine months at a juvenile detention center. I was not a straight arrow to that point because I did drink a couple of beers occasionally, but that incident alone kept me from smoking weed. The cool kids were getting stoned. I wasn't a cool kid yet, so I never partook. And after Will got arrested, I never wanted to.

—x—x—x—

When I moved in with Dad, it meant that my kids now also spent three to four days a week at the house. Jessie adhered to the custody agreement. TJ showed up sometimes, and sometimes he didn't. He usually called to tell me that he would be staying with friends. I was never quite sure who those friends were or where exactly he stayed. I wondered. I worried. I walked a tightrope of trying to be a good father and just trying to connect with my children.

Because of the custody agreement, I didn't get to be a constant fixture in the kids' lives. I often chose not to push things. The divorce ripped the family apart. While Amy and I didn't dissolve into screaming fights and breaking dishes, the kids felt the tension every day. It affected them. Smiles in our household became rare events. I sometimes thought we should note on a calendar each time someone smiled because a smile became such a momentous moment, like spotting a near-extinct species. To avoid conflict, I let some things go. I took the easy way out and hoped that we would all find our way relatively unscathed. Jessie, wise like her mother, chipped away at my studied ambivalence and made me face reality.

Jessie and I sat in the living room. I was reading a book. She was sitting on the floor, playing with Old Blue. At one point, she and Blue were growling at each other as each pulled on one end of a rubber pull toy. "Oh, you think you're so tough, don't you. Well, you're not. You're just a little puppy, and I own this toy," Jessie said, providing a running commentary. After a while, the tug-of-war died down when Jessie cradled Blue in her arms.

"You seem to really like that little puppy, don't you, Jess?"

"Yeah, she's cute. She reminds me of Patches when she was little. I think it's cool that you and Grandpa got a puppy. It will give you something to do and keep both of you out of trouble," she said, smiling.

"Hey, that's my line," I protested. As a parent I gave that retort as a standard reply when my kids protested about the chores and responsibilities I assigned.

"Well, I do really think it's good for both of you. I sometimes wonder, though, what you do when we're at Mom's. I wonder the same thing about her when we're with you. Neither of you ever really give a straight answer about how you fill your time."

"What do you think we do?" I asked. This topic of conversation was new. I slid down on the floor and began petting Old Blue with her.

"I'm pretty sure that you partied a lot before you moved in with Grandpa."

I didn't respond to this statement. To affirm or deny would essentially verify her guess.

"Now I think you and Grandpa sit and watch television and fall asleep by nine o'clock, just like Ole Blue here."

"That sounds about right. What does your mom do when you're with me?"

"She sits around the house and reads. Sometimes she gets together with Emily. I know that she doesn't date."

Although I had never heard of Amy dating anyone, it made me sad to think that such a wonderful woman had no companionship other than her friend Emily, whom she had known since she was two years old. I became friends with Emily when Amy and I started dating. We even made a failed—no, disastrous—attempt to set her up with Cameron. The double date with them was an immense failure. Even though they each had a mutual friend sitting at the table, they could find nothing to talk about, in large part because Cam still hadn't learned how to talk with women. Long silences ruled the night, which lasted sixty-seven minutes, just as long as it took to order and eat pizza at Pizza Hut. Oddly, as our relationship grew and developed into our eventual marriage, Cam and Emily did become good friends. Emily became a dear friend of mine, too. But that friendship became a casualty of the divorce. I became Emily's enemy because I had hurt her best friend. I understood that.

"Does it bother you that I date?"

"No, it seems inevitable. You're much more discreet than some of my friends' parents, who see boyfriends and girlfriends at their house at all hours of the night and morning and in various stages of undress. I wish you and Mom could both find someone that would make you both happy."

"I wish that, too, Jessie, and not just for me. I want your mom to be happy, too. She is a wonderful woman and a great mother. She deserves to have someone she can share her life with."

"Yeah, I know you do, Dad. I know you and Mom tried, and your marriage couldn't last. I wish it could have. I mean, I'm used to the way things are now, the divorce and all, and changing houses on a regular basis. I'm used to the new routines. Things are definitely calm and almost serene now. It got pretty rough the last year or two."

Jessie paused, looked at Ole Blue, and gently stroked her back. The puppy had slipped into a slumber, the perfect image of that calmness that Jessie noted. I knew the serenity Jessie talked about, though, lacked the sweet innocence of puppy slumber. It was a serenity that comes more from emptiness than fulsome goodness.

Jessie and I had broached this topic before. When she chose to or needed to talk about the divorce, I encouraged her reflection. I knew she needed to find perspective as much as Amy and I did. We needed to find ways to accept what our family had become. I acknowledged Jessie's anger and sadness, which nowadays usually came out as sadness. I never put words in her mouth, so it took her some time to articulate her emotions.

When Amy and I divorced, we broke the family compact. Perhaps more important than any other part of parenthood is the promise that parents make to their children, the promise of family. When couples separate or divorce, they break that promise. It leads to a range of emotions in their children. It can lead to behaviors that are antithetical to how their children might have always acted before. They might lash out in anger. They might break things intentionally, as intentionally as their parents broke their sacred promise. They might face all-consuming sadness. They might hide in their room. They might become the model students, hoping no one will notice the all-consuming sadness they confront each day. They might say hurtful things again and again. All of this could happen as they try to understand why their parents would let something as perfectly formed, at least in their mind, as a snowflake just slip away with a good gust of wind. They try to understand how something so perfect could so quickly and completely disappear.

Jessie was trying to think her way through this while also trying to figure out her identity and future place in the world. TJ took a different approach. He chose to run away from familial strife and find his way with a cadre of friends. I had begun to question his choices regarding those friendships. Before the divorce, Amy and I found joy in watching TJ and his friends play any sports, organized or otherwise. When they weren't chasing a round ball in real life, they bonded by playing video games. The parents smiled as TJ and his friends tried to find music that spoke to them, such an important step for all teenagers. All of that quickly slipped out of TJ's life after the divorce. He left his old friendships and turned to hanging out with kids Amy and I didn't know. We worried about TJ and tried to help him make good choices. When Amy and I talked about our children, we expressed concern about TJ. We knew Jessie, though, was working through things and moving in a positive direction.

—x—x—x—

Jessie continued sharing her thoughts with me. "I think you and Mom are both in a better place now. Maybe that's because you aren't always in a fight. You both smile more and even laugh. I know you are feeling better about things because you again think you're being funny with your obnoxious dad jokes." She thoughtfully and lovingly caressed Ole Blue.

"Little puppy, I'll tell you he really isn't that funny. He thinks he is, so we sometimes humor him." Ole Blue stirred a little, sinking just a bit deeper into Jessie's embrace.

"I still wish that you and Mom could have found that happiness together. I liked our family. No, I loved our family. So, sometimes I still get sad that we aren't a family anymore. You and Mom have helped me understand better what happened."

She became quiet again. I crawled on the floor to sit beside her. I put my arm around her shoulder and pulled her into a hug. We sat quietly for several minutes, a father and daughter sharing a tender moment.

That tender moment ended when Ole Blue, drowsing in puppy bliss, oozed out a silent dog fart that reached Jessie and me simultaneously. We both gagged and coughed and made feeble attempts to cover our noses.

"She sure does produce some pretty potent stink bombs. They kind of remind me of you," Jessie said. We both laughed. "I'm still glad you've got her. She gives me a friend to play with when I visit you, which is kind of nice since TJ usually doesn't come by anymore."

Jessie was talkative tonight. Sometimes she could sit through an entire evening plugged in and listening to her music on her phone, avoiding all conversation. Sometimes, she would kid and joke the entire evening. And sometimes, like tonight, she wanted to talk and get into some serious topics. She was working up to something specific about TJ, but I had learned long ago not to push her. If I pushed her, she would close down. She spoke when she was ready to. I let her talk without interrupting. The conversation didn't really interest Blue, whose eyes remained closed, and he seemed to be in puppy heaven with two people caressing him.

"Does it bother you that TJ doesn't come by that much? I mean, do you miss him or anything?" she asked.

I could sense we were getting closer to her topic. It seemed she wanted to talk about her brother, but at this point, I still didn't know about what specifically. One of my philosophical mainstays as a parent required that I would never lie to my kids about the important stuff. You naturally tell some lies as parents. You lie about things like Santa Claus and the Easter Bunny. You lie about how certain foods will do certain things for you, either good or bad. You lie about how long it will take to get from point A to B. But when my kids asked me about certain topics, I always answered them truthfully.

"Yeah, Jess. I miss TJ. A lot. I've tried to stay in touch with him. Even when he does grace me with his presence, he is still mostly absent. He is still very angry with me about the divorce, so I'm trying not to force him into acting like he wants to be with me. I hope someday that he will feel more comfortable with me."

"Dad, the divorce has been hard on me, too, but I still want to see you and Mom."

"TJ is a couple of years older than you. Part of this is also that he is trying to find his way toward more independence. All kids start doing that in their last couple of years of high school."

"Dad, do you remember what you and Mom used to say when TJ and I wanted to have a later curfew?"

"Yeah, sure."

"You used to say that after nine or ten or eleven, whatever the curfew was, staying out past a certain point only led to trouble. You wouldn't have anything to do and would just start looking for some excitement," Jessie said.

I nodded. I had repeated over and over those words to my children, just like my mom and dad had said them to me.

"Well, here's the thing, Dad. TJ is getting into trouble. And you and Mom both seem to be ignoring this fact."

"What kind of trouble is TJ in?"

"Dad, I'm not trying to get him into trouble. I'm not tattling on him. I'm just worried about him."

"I know, Jess. But if you're really worried about him, can you help me out by giving me some more information?"

"Dad, he's staying out until two and three and four o'clock in the morning. What do you think he's doing? You know he is not making good choices. You always said, 'Show me who your friends are, and I will know who you are.' You might want to find out more about TJ's friends. All I'm saying is that maybe you should have a talk with him. Even if he will hate you for it."

As Jessie sat there cuddling Blue, I still could see the little girl in her, the girl who loved to crawl into my lap and snuggle until she fell asleep, or the girl who liked nothing more than for me to read her stories, or the girl who would come running up to me and leap into my arms when I came home from work, smiling and giggling with absolute joy, the kind of emotion that made life wonderful. I also could see the young woman she was becoming, the fourteen-year-old girl with a growing understanding of how the world worked. I could see her intense concern for her brother.

"Just talk to him, Dad."

"Okay, I will," making a promise I intended to keep, but at the same time, feeling like a colossal failure as a parent.

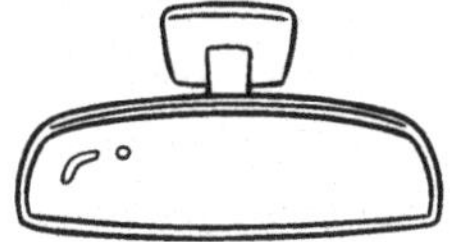

CHAPTER 9

Sara slept beside me, breathing easily and slowly, a far cry from the desperate panting for air an hour ago. She was breathing so hard I thought I might have killed her. After cuddling for fifteen minutes, Sara, in a drowsy afterglow, slipped off to sleep. I still needed more time to come down. Tonight marked the third time we had been together. I couldn't call it making love because it wasn't that yet, and to call it something else, as Cameron might, seemed crude. But after the tameness of the first time, where we didn't want to offend, and the second time, where we still were tentative, we let our inhibitions go tonight. I guess the results showed in Sara's reaction.

It's funny how we can become timid about sex as we grow older. It certainly wasn't like that when Amy and I consummated our relationship. Passion consumed us. It took months for us to build up to the big climax. Yeah, I know, a cheap double entendre. The night after we won the band championship in what I've come to think of as "my summer of love," Amy and I went to a movie. We watched the first fifteen minutes. Then we started making out. We came up for air when the movie ended. Then we went down to a park on the shore of Lake Mendota. I found a secluded parking spot—one I had previously scoped out—and made out for another two hours. When I brought her home, we made out for another fifteen minutes until her father flashed the lights.

I'm sure they were wondering about this boy who had suddenly entered their daughter's life. I had met them earlier when I went to pick up Amy. I stood nervously in the foyer and made small talk with her mother and father. "That was quite a show last night," Amy's father said. "I never really took much interest in marching bands before this summer. I thought they were just what you saw at parades and when the football team needed a rest. I didn't know there was so much to them. It was pretty amazing last night."

I was still feeling the euphoria of the night before. I'm sure the grin plastered on my face was due in large part to the band's grand success, but a large part of it was also due to the lovely vision of Amy coming into the room. To her father, I said, "Thank you, sir. It really was a magical night. I hope to have a lot more nights like that in my life."

He smiled. "I'm sure you will. Cherish those moments of happiness. I hope you have many of them in your life. I can sense that you have some special qualities. I think life will be good for you. Have fun tonight. We want Amy home by eleven thirty."

I murmured another thanks before Amy dragged me out the door. Throughout the night, we mashed our lips together for hours. The next day my jaw seemed locked, and my tongue rubbed raw. I had kissed other girls. But it never felt as good as kissing Amy.

Amy and I became a couple instantly. For many of my classmates, we were "the" couple of senior year. When summer band ended, we still had two weeks before football practice started. We went to the beach and hung out with friends. One weekend, Mom and Dad took us up to the cabin. This surprised me, but they both instantly took to Amy. Who wouldn't? At the cabin, Amy had the second bedroom. I slept on the old pullout couch. We spent three glorious days together. We hiked in the woods, where we would dawdle and make out. The first time we prepared for a hike, I heard Dad say to Mom, "Grace, are you sure we should let them go off alone? I mean, it's almost like we are daring them to have intercourse."

"Bob, relax. Have you noticed yet how much time they are spending together? If they want to do it, they've had plenty of opportunities. They're both seventeen. We have to trust them. But we also have to recognize that they are in the throes of love, and them having sex just might be something that we have to deal with." Mom said these words toward the open window. She knew we were listening. Dad ignored that possibility. Mom had pulled Amy and me aside the day before we left for the cottage, and she had the sex talk with us. She didn't pull any punches.

"Before we go north, we need to talk about this," she said. I fidgeted because I could sense where this was going. Amy seemed completely at ease. "I don't know if you two have done it yet, or at what stage of physical intimacy you are at, but I don't want to be an instant grandmother. There need to be certain steps."

Amy interrupted her. "Mrs. Cesario, to set your mind at ease, Robb and I aren't having sex yet."

"Good. I'm happy to hear that. I can see, though, that you two have instantly become a couple. It always looks like you are joined at the hip, and when two people are joined at the hip, sex naturally follows. Always remember this: I don't want to be an instant grandmother. There are steps. You date as you like and pursue what my parents called courtship. You get engaged and have a glorious wedding, a beautiful honeymoon, and then the baby can come. You both need to keep zipped up. If you don't keep zipped up, then use protection. Robb, put some of these in the car, put some in your room, put one in your wallet." She handed me a box of condoms. My absolute shock showed on my face. "I don't, I repeat, I don't want to be an instant grandmother."

I sat there turning red, wishing I was getting pummeled on the football field. It would have been more fun. Amy laughed. "We get it, Mrs. Cesario. I like the way you have framed the message—straightforward, forthright. My mom can't even say the word *sex*. She whispers it." Amy laughed again, this time almost going into hysterics. Mom quickly joined in the laughter, too.

When the giggling slowed, Mom said, "The word does carry a certain weight. But Amy and Robb, when the time comes when you will be having sex, please take precautions. You have all kinds of options now. We didn't have those options when I was a kid. Remember, I don't want to be an instant grandmother. Steps: dating, kissing, fondling, long engagement, marriage, grandkids. In that order. No surprises, okay? We can talk any time about this, and if you have any questions, please ask me."

"We promise, Mrs. Cesario, and you can bet I'll be coming to you again with some questions," Amy said. I groaned. I had come to know Amy well enough to know that she would indeed ask my mom—yes, my mom—questions about sex, and my mom would give answers to her about how to have sex with her son.

"And when you do finally have sex, make it special," Mom said. "Please don't do it in the back seat of the family car. That's so cliché. And besides, then we will all know immediately what has happened."

I continued to blush. Amy continued to smile. Later, when we spent time fumbling and groping, breathing hard behind fogged windows in various stages of undress, when we got closer and closer to consummating, Amy always reminded me, "Not here. This isn't our place." When I would persist, overcome with desire for her, Amy would gently slow down our groping, just as if she were easing the foot off the throttle. So we would stop. I would go home and find the need for a long shower.

At the cabin when we went hiking in the woods, sure, we made out passionately. We had started lightly groping each other, too. I loved the feel of her body against mine. But we didn't even consider going for it. Like most boys, I could engage in locker room talk about sex. I could do the double entendres with the best of them, almost as good as Cam. Fantasies about sex pummeled me like punches from an Olympic boxer, and I would take the ongoing assault like a punch-drunk boxer. In truth, even though I wanted nothing more than to make love with Amy, I didn't really think I was ready. Clearly, I knew what the act of sex entailed. I just didn't know what it would mean for my relationship with her. I really, really liked this girl. I didn't want to end any chance of a relationship by having sex with her before it seemed right. Because you see, I wanted it to be special, too. It's not like Amy kept her feelings bottled up. We talked about sex. A lot. She clearly told me she wasn't ready for the whole smash. She wanted to have sex with me. She just wanted it to be the right time.

"But how will we know?" I would wail plaintively, shaking in the back seat of the car, acting, not really acting, a little desperate.

"Believe me, we'll know," Amy replied.

Before all of this happened later, Amy and I reveled in that first summer outing at the cottage. When we went to the Northwoods, we hit one of those perfect weekends. The temperature hovered in the low eighties, and the humidity was low. Puffy clouds floated by. A breeze blew continually, strong enough to push away the blackflies and mosquitoes. To this day, when I'm at the cabin, I think of what Dad said on each of the three days that weekend as we sat on the deck, luxuriating in cabin mode, where time slides by unnoticed, like leaves on the surface of a slow-moving river. "I wonder what the poor folks are doing?" We would all smile.

In the afternoon, Amy and I typically would don suits and swim out to the neighbor's raft. We lay on the raft, arms spread out, fingertips touching, drying in the sun. When we became too warm, we would slide into the water on the far side of the raft, hidden from Dad's prying eyes. We would hold each other and kiss for a few moments. Then we would climb out of the water and flop back on the raft. After these quick dips, I usually had to lie on my stomach.

I would lay my head on my arms and stare at Amy until she said, "Robb, quit staring. You're giving me a complex."

I would reply, "I can't help it. When you discover the most beautiful vision in the world, you just want to keep looking at her."

To which she would reply, "Okay, since you put it like that," and she would smile, and our fingertips would find each other again.

Our passions, though, kept building, and eventually things started popping. By Christmas, we were going pretty far, but not all the way. We came close, sitting in front of her Christmas tree on Christmas Eve after midnight Mass and her family's quick retreat to bed. Amy finally stopped me. "Oh, Robb, it wouldn't be right tonight. Let's not do it tonight. It's Christmas, and it doesn't seem right to me."

I never argued with Amy over this. She reassured me over and over that we would have sex—when the time was right. "But how will we know?" I asked over and over.

"We will. We just will," she said. Although her answer perplexed me, I trusted her intuition and went home to the new ritual, the nightly shower. I did agree with her about consummating on Christmas. She had convinced me about the correctness on that one, too.

I knew for certain that if I badgered Amy to have sex, it would tarnish our relationship. We were moving toward it, circling in smaller spirals. Eventually, we would get there. Amy seemed to have to go through adjustments and phases in our intimacy. After she passed through a green light, she proceeded with caution to the next intersection. I just wanted to get there. I trusted her to lead us on the journey. I let her determine the speed and the route.

We finally reached our destination on an innocuous night. It wasn't a special occasion. We had gone to a movie at the Retroplex, a name the town used to identify the theater that played old movies and gave audiences another chance to see the classics on the big screen. *The Princess Bride*, a movie gave audiences the story of "Twuu wuv," true love. We went back to my house that night. Shelly was staying over at a friend's. When we arrived, Mom and Dad were going out with some friends to a piano bar. As we got older, they started going out more on Saturday nights to late movies, or going out to hear music, sometimes going out to dance. It was like they were dating and rediscovering their lost youth. Long before it became fashionable among the hip and trendy married couples, Mom and Dad called these outings "date nights."

"Don't wait up," Mom said, and she kissed both of us. She and Amy had become friends. I often came home from work and found Amy and Mom in deep conversation. After the football season ended, I started grilling steaks at Ponderosa, a steakhouse chain. The restaurant was on the near west side. Several of my friends worked there. I would usually get home between eight and ten, depending on when they cleared me. I would walk in smelling like grilled steak. Amy always made the same joke. She would look behind me and say, "Did any dogs follow you in?" And then she would giggle. I did, too, though I didn't find it particularly funny. I was a little self-conscious about always smelling like someone's dinner. But Amy said it, and everything from Amy's mouth was delicious, like those steaks I used to love before working at Ponderosa. Grilling steaks every night and then scouring the grease and grime off the grill made the whole idea of a juicy steak much less appealing. I grew to detest the smell I carried with me after a shift of work. I always showered. I lived with the smell of charred meat seared into my olfactory senses. Even now I prefer pasta or a salad to a steak.

Often, when I got home from work, I would find Mom and Amy sitting in the kitchen, each clutching a cup of coffee, talking quietly, leaning in toward each other. For a long time, I thought they were talking about me. That's just vanity. They quickly moved beyond talking about me and delved into far deeper topics.

On that ordinary night, Amy and I sat in the kitchen and drank a soda, chatting with Mom and Dad momentarily before they left. Then we chatted together for a few minutes. Amy stood, reached out and grabbed my hand, and kissed me passionately. Then again. I smiled through the second kiss. I knew that we would spend an indeterminate amount of time groping each other. She broke off the kiss. She grabbed my hand, turned, and led me out of the kitchen. I thought we were moving toward the comfort of the living room or the family room. But when she reached the hallway separating the kitchen and the living room, she turned and led me upstairs. This, I have to say, took me by surprise. Then she took me to the bedroom.

"Robb," she said after a long, breathless, passionate kiss, "I love you. Do you love me?"

"Amy, you know I love you."

"Say it then."

"Amy, I love you. I love you so much. When I see you, when I think of you, I always smile. People probably think I'm some sort of idiot. But I can't help it. Thinking of you, seeing you, being with you, makes me so happy. I think about you all of the time. Clearly, I'm happy, and I'm smiling all of the time. If that's not love, I don't know what is."

We kissed again.

"Then, let's make love. It's time," Amy said.

And we did.

—x—x—x—

Once Sara and I got over our initial excessive politeness in bed, we began to enjoy the sex. Besides the bedroom, we spent a lot of time together. We became a couple and did "couple" things.

In Madison, during the summer, that meant going to the Farmers' Market on Saturdays, strolling around the square, looking at every farmer's goods, buying a bunch or bag or two of vegetables or fruit, a cup of coffee, a scone or donut. Then we continued our stroll.

In Madison, being a couple also meant going to the Terrace on the college campus, sitting on the shore of Lake Mendota, to hear bands or drink a pitcher of beer and engage in Terrace speak. The topics never really matter. Typically, you aren't talking about serious issues. Mostly you spiral from one topic to the next. You talk for a bit and then stop to watch sunbathing college students jump off the pier into Lake Mendota to cool down. You might watch a sailboarder try to lift the sail out of the water. You watch the sailboats glide by with the grace of a ballet dancer. Out in the middle of the lake you might watch water skiers. Behind the cover of your sunglasses you might scan the crowd, eyes constantly moving from one college student to the next, noting with a sense of whimsy and jealousy that people, young men and women, never looked so good when you were in college. On Monday nights you might go to the Terrace to watch a movie, which was not always a crowd-pleaser. Not everyone in a crowd of two to three thousand people is going to like *The Blues Brothers, The Hangover*, Hitchcock's *The Birds*, or *Crazy Rich Asians*. On Friday nights you might go listen to a smokin' hot band.

Being a couple in Madison might mean that you drag your lawn chairs or blankets to hear Opera in the Park or Concerts on the Square, where you go to socialize instead of really listening to the music.

Being a couple also meant going for a bike ride on one of the many bike trails or taking in one of the many festivals happening all over the area.

Sara and I sampled the many different joys of summer life in Madison. When not sampling Madison's many options, Sara really loved to garden. I didn't, but she cajoled me into helping her work in her garden on several Saturday afternoons. My tasks involved simple obligations like pulling weeds. She took special pleasure in the richness of her flower garden. She seemed to calm and find a different center with her hands in the dirt. On a primal level, it seemed to fulfill her. With my hands grimy with dirt from pulling weeds, I would look at Sara kneeling in the dirt, tending to the flowers with gentle caresses. She typically wore a blissful smile. I paused to take in that look. Amy used to get the same look on her face when she worked in the garden. I never bothered to understand it with Amy. I decided to try with Sara.

I started asking her questions about her garden. "What kind of flower is that?" She would patiently answer my questions, but she became a little exasperated when I first posed that question because I was pointing at a weed.

"That, Robb, is a weed. Really, you didn't know that?"

"Sara, your best bet here is to assume that I don't know anything about gardening. Because I don't. This is your chance to mold me and impart all of your gardening knowledge. Go on, hit me. I've got a half hour to figure out this gardening stuff and then we've got to get ready for our dinner reservations."

She rolled her eyes. She then tossed a handful of dirt at me. "That is dirt," she said, smiling. "That is what flowers grow in. Am I going too fast for you?"

"No, Vince Lombardi, you're not going too fast." Anybody who grew up in Wisconsin and followed the Packers would get that reference.

Then Sara started naming different flowers. After she finished naming five, she would make me point and recite the names. I found her method allowed me to start recognizing different flowers and putting names to them.

"Sara, you obviously know your flowers. And you are apparently good at gardening because even I can see that this is a really nice garden. What do you like so much about it?"

She paused for a while. Then she stood, brushed off her hands, grabbed my hand, and led me to a bench on her patio, where we sat side by side. The bench faced her yard, her garden. "What do you see?"

"A garden," I said. She punched my arm.

"No, what do you see?"

"I see a bunch of flowers. But whatever I see, I'm not going to see what you see. So what do you see?" I played a little naive, trying to get her to open up like a blooming flower. In fact, I could appreciate the beauty of the garden's design.

In college I studied graphic design. My intention had been to become a graphic artist. When I was in high school, I wanted a car. My parents gave me a computer. Even though computers were in the earliest stages, I saw their great potential. My plan coming out of high school and going to college was to get an education that would allow me to ride the technological wave I saw bearing down on the world. I was going to ride that sucker like a Hawaiian surf bum. I was going to use my computer skills to enter the burgeoning field of graphic design by creating digital art, most likely for marketing. It was a good plan. Like all of my plans coming out of high school, this one also failed to bear fruit. After graduation, those jobs just weren't available. I needed a job. Amy and I were getting married. All my grand designs of life ended up being mere puffs of smoke that I tried to grasp but could never hold.

—x—x—x—

I did know something about art. I did recognize that Sara's meticulous work showed her attention to color, values, tone, and texture.

"Look at all the colors. With each garden I grow, I am painting a picture. A living picture. My plants are my paints. These," and she held up her hands, "are my brushes. Throughout the spring, summer, and fall, I keep applying layers of paint, and the picture keeps changing. But each day it becomes more beautiful, more full of depth. I am an artist who works in a temporary medium."

"So, you see yourself as an artist?"

"I do. In the winter I try to create acrylic paintings of my gardens from the photographs I take. But they never come close to what I can paint during the spring, summer, and fall."

We sat silently for several minutes, admiring her brushstrokes.

"I should probably warn you, Robb, that these gardens of mine are the only beautiful things I have ever created in my life." She said this lightly and then laughed. "But even this beauty is fleeting, a sunset, a burst of lightning, an illusion, a moment. And then it's gone." She gave me a half smile, which quickly disappeared, to be replaced by the sadness in her eyes.

Sara's face lit up when she smiled. Behind that smile, sadness always lurked, like the guest who never leaves Gatsby's mansion. She laughed. She sparkled. She told humorous anecdotes. She entertained everybody around. People liked being with her. At parties everyone wanted to sit near Sara.

At dinner parties that I suddenly found myself going to with her, her array of friends always treated Sara as the guest of honor. Sara worked as a news producer for Wisconsin Public Television. She racked up unique experiences. She also had detailed knowledge about so many different things. Politics. Business. The media. Madison area history. Quirky and interesting people. At dinner parties she shined.

I found myself a detached bystander listening to Sara and her friends talk emphatically about politics. I didn't follow politics. Politics meant nothing to me. I listened and tried to engage in some discussions to show an interest in another of Sara's passions.

Since I'd started dating Sara, though, I started following the news more. I started reading stories about politics. I thought I should make this effort to connect more with her world. In the past I only read the sports page and the comics, in that order. Now I found myself reading op-ed pieces and letters to the editor. To keep up with Sara and to try to offer meaningful conversation, I grudgingly started educating myself about politics.

When Sara and I first started dating, and she shared her political viewpoints with me, I said, "I thought journalists weren't supposed to have political opinions. That you were supposed to be unbiased or something. You know, for credibility." With this question, I was reaching all the way back to a basic journalism class I took as a high school junior, a class I didn't take very seriously and managed to get a "C," a class and a topic I hadn't given much thought to since.

"Good question. Here's what all journalists know. We all hold opinions, especially in regard to politics and social issues. The good journalists know, though, that they keep their opinions out of the news reports. They report facts and let the audience decide what to believe." Sara worked hard to educate me and to convert me into a political junkie. I humored her and engaged in these discussions, though after a diligent effort to engage in a political discussion I usually found a way to successfully bring them to a screeching halt. Often all it took was a question like this:

"So, given all of that, you want to have sex?"

Sara would laugh. "Too much?"

I'd nod.

"Okay, let's have sex," she said. She appreciated that I tried. She also appreciated that I moved our interactions in a direction we both would enjoy. My friend Cameron would have been proud.

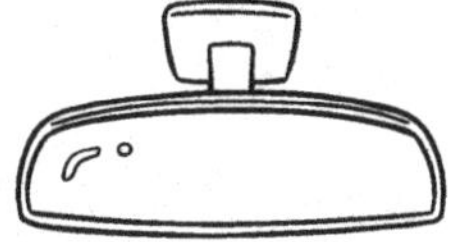

CHAPTER 10

"We've got to go to the funeral to show our respects," Cam said with a force I hadn't heard much from him unless he was talking about sex.

"Cam, why? It's been twenty-five years since we sat in this guy's economics class. His classes were so boring. I mean pictures of his class would have been the perfect illustration of boredom."

I didn't tell Cam the real reason for wanting to avoid funeral homes and churches. This would be the first funeral I attended since Mom's death. It would force me all over again to relive that horribly sad day. I didn't need to keep reliving it. I needed to move forward from it. In some ways, I wanted to leapfrog ahead in time so that the funeral became a distant memory, one that I kept carefully tucked away. Sadly, it didn't work that way. I thought about Mom's death every day. Granted, some days it was less of an oppressive weight, but I always carried it. No matter how much I wanted to, I couldn't set that weight down.

I didn't tell Cam all of this. Society gives you, at most, a couple of weeks to grieve. Then you have to move on, at least publicly. Everyone else has moved on, and they're tired of listening to your sad tales of woe. Even Cam. He was better than most. At times he would ask me how I was doing. He would let me talk for a few minutes. Then he would tell me how to deal with my sadness and that life goes on, so get living. Rather than go into all of these macabre thoughts, I tried to deflect the funeral issue by attacking the dead.

"Careful there, Robb. The man was a genius when it came to economics and U.S. history."

"If he was such a genius, why did I get a "C" in Econ 101 at the U?"

"Simple answer. You never studied, and you never paid attention to him in class. You were too focused on making gooey eyes at Amy sitting across the room."

"Wait! Are you, the love doctor, giving me a hard time about being caught in the vise-like grip of young love? You, who always says that when the possibility of love presents itself, you've got to throw yourself at it like it was a wall of Velcro and hope you stick? You who—"

"Yes, me. Now stop trying to distract me on this. I'm going to the funeral. I want you to go with me. I've also asked Amy, and she said she will go," Cam said.

Cam just played his ace. He knew I wouldn't refuse if I heard Amy was going. Even with all the bad that had happened, or perhaps because of it, I didn't want to disappoint her.

"That's not fair, Cam."

"What? What did I do?" Cam protested.

"You know what you did. You played the Amy card, the queen of hearts. You know I can't and won't refuse when Amy is involved."

"I know," Cam said with a smug smile on his face. "The funeral visitation begins tomorrow at three in the afternoon. I'll pick you up about then. A funeral is just like a college frat party: you don't want to be the first one there."

The next day, when Cam pulled into the driveway, Amy sat beside him in the front seat. I stood on the front porch steps and mused a moment before walking down the steps toward the car. This moment, and the rest of the day to follow, would represent an odd sort of symmetry.

The family tried to make the funeral service about the man. They decorated the funeral home with artifacts from his life. The children had put together a few poster boards of pictures. The man liked to make pens on his wood lathe. They had set up a little display of his pens. On a side table stood a sheaf of papers. I looked closely at it and saw that it was an unpublished manuscript: *On Economics, A Treatise,* by Cliff Stevenson. *That has to be a page-turner*, I thought. As I looked at the display, meager to paltry, it seemed sad. This little bit represented this man's life. The entirety of a life could fit on a few poster boards and a couple of small side tables.

Then I looked toward the front of the parlor, where I saw Stevenson's wife, two middle-aged children, and five grandchildren greeting the mourners and paying respects. They smiled at the stories people told. They shook hands and shared hugs. They treated all the mourners with respect, grateful for the kind words they said about their husband, father, grandfather. My smarmy, superior attitude soured. The man had people in his life who loved him, people who would miss him terribly. Who knows? Maybe the man wasn't as boring as July Fourth without fireworks when he was with his family. Maybe he lived a life that fulfilled him. Who was I to judge his life just because I thought his class was boring when I was a know-everything/know-nothing seventeen-year-old?

I watched the receiving line for another moment, my head tilted in contemplation. Cam gently called me to the photo display. "Look, there's a picture of Mr. Stevenson teaching a class. It looks like it was after we graduated, judging by the hairstyles."

"Yup, that class looks about the way I remember our class—totally engaged, totally absorbing all he said. Learning." I said it without sarcasm because I was starting to think that I might have completely misread that man twenty-five years ago. Cam assumed he heard sarcasm and scoffed.

Under his breath, he said, "Show respect. You're at the man's funeral."

We joined the receiving line, and Cam and Amy were just in front of me. We slowly worked toward the front of the room and the casket. I typically refuse to look into the casket. I cringe at the custom of viewing the dead body. I know the viewing allows mourners to see an image of the loved person one more time, at peace, pain free, looking better in death than they most likely looked in their last days or moments or possibly even years of life.

The viewing also creates a moment of stark realization. The person really has died. No one is playing a horrible practical joke. There's a body in the box. Uncle Joe really did die. Aunt Sara finally succumbed to the cancer, and lying there in the casket she looks grateful that the ordeal has ended. Granny, at eighty-seven, finally lost the will to thrive. Funerals for children make me feel the worst. This young life full of possibilities, this young sprout of a flower, will never bloom.

It all makes me feel sad, which is part of the point. We should mourn the loss of life, the end of a story. No new chapters will be written. No more new moments will occur with this person. The end has come with finality. Funerals connect us to the starkness of our own mortality. They also make me think that we should do all we can to make each chapter as full and rich as possible. If only we all lived life recognizing that the novel would end, and no matter the life we lived, it often would end sooner than we would have liked.

We all die. I'm just uncomfortable with the possibility that I could die soon. That says something about the way my life has turned out. If I were to die right now, I would feel grossly cheated. My life didn't turn out the way I would have wanted, and I would be pissed to die now before I have a chance to fix things, to enact a do-over of sorts, to try to make my life mean more than it has to this point. These strains of thought—and they do stress me—haunt me after attending a funeral visitation. All of the trappings of a funeral conjure these uncomfortable thoughts about my own mortality. The image of the dead body always stays with me for days, haunting me. I vow not to look. Somehow, though, I always end up looking. It leads to waking nightmares. I find myself asking, *What if?* I would entertain these thoughts at any funeral, but they seemed more intense at the first funeral since Mom died.

I watched Cam gush to the family about how wonderful Mr. Stevenson was, how his teaching meant so much to Cam, how he would call his senior economics teacher one of the most influential people in his life. Amy offered gracious and heartfelt condolences to the family. Her sincerity touched me. Again, as always, I felt inspired by Amy's wisdom, grace, and compassion. She naturally acted most appropriately in every situation. When she smiled at the grandchildren, they smiled back at her. When she spoke to the children, just a few years younger than us, they leaned into her, wanting her words to soothe. I could see they did. Again, I marveled.

I offered polite condolences to the grandchildren. To the children and the wife, speaking to them as a group, I surprised myself with the words that flowed naturally.

"I was a student years ago in Mr. Stevenson's economics class. He taught me many things, lessons that continue to have an impact on me to this day," I said, thinking of how this funeral was evidence that he had lived a good life. "He lived a meaningful life. Through his work, he touched many lives. I am grateful that I could learn so much from him. He was a good man. He made his corner of the world a better place." The children shook my hand. Mrs. Stevenson hugged me and thanked me for sharing my comments.

As I stepped away from the family, I glanced at the coffin and nodded a silent thanks at Mr. Stevenson. Memories of the visitation for my mom bombarded me. I remembered the people who said something truly meaningful. Those thoughtful comments added to my understanding of how my mom touched the lives of others. Some mourners could only shake my hand or give me a comforting hug. Knowing, though, that my mom's life meant enough to them that they had to offer their condolences in person gave me great comfort.

I also thought about how the family would get through this day and then collapse from emotional exhaustion. The mourners see us holding up, holding on. They don't see the collapse. That comes later and in private. The lingering sadness seeps in like a bone-chilling cold that never seems to leave you.

In that moment, after my brief words to the family, I felt an overwhelming sadness for what was to come for them. For a time, it would seem as if everything would remind them of Mr. Stevenson. Tears would flow. Then they would get to the point where they would think they were doing fine, only to find themselves crying because something triggered a memory. They would have to endure a cycle of holidays, anniversaries, and birthdays that would torment them through the first year. I brushed away a tear that wet my cheek.

Cam and Amy stood a few feet away. Cam pointed his finger at me and gave me a small nod, a reassuring smile. Amy and I stared at each other, and she shared a sad smile. I wondered what thoughts lay behind that smile. I didn't have to wonder too much. I surmised I caused the sadness. I also want to think that her smile showed an understanding of how difficult this funeral was for me. It occurred to me that Amy was also thinking of my mom and feeling a similar level of sadness. I walked up to her and gave her a brief hug. I also shared a hard embrace with Cam.

During the service, the three of us sat together near the back of the parlor, Amy between Cam and me. We noticed some other former students. You could tell by their ages, by their conversations. We also saw some former teachers, reconnecting during the visitation and sitting together during the prayers and eulogies. Two grandchildren and both children offered remarks, filling out the picture of the life of their grandfather, their father.

After the family members spoke, the minister returned to the podium. "Would anyone from the audience like to share remarks about Cliff Stevenson?"

The room remained silent. No one moved. No one said anything. On impulse, I repeated Mr. Stevenson's standard reply to the silence that would greet his questions. "Anyone? Anyone?" I didn't intend to say it out loud and certainly not as loudly as I did. But it seemed like everyone in the room heard. A generous round of laughter followed, led by former students and colleagues. The minister even chuckled. He obviously knew Mr. Stevenson.

Though she laughed, Amy elbowed me.

"Following the service, please join the family for a celebration of Cliff Stevenson's life," the minister said. "A reception will follow at the Infusino's Pizzeria on University. Cliff loved his pizza." Everybody laughed. Another nugget that many wouldn't have known had they not attended the funeral.

As we stood to file out, I scanned the crowd and saw Jim Finch, my old band director. He smiled at me and pointed outside.

I came down the steps and extended my hand toward him. Mr. Finch pushed aside my hand. "Not good enough, Robb. Give me a hug." We embraced.

"Mr. Finch, it is so good to see you," I gushed.

"Robb, I think we're way beyond the courtesy titles. Call me Jim."

That didn't seem likely. To me it would have been a sign of disrespect. "I'll certainly try, Mr. Finch." He laughed and nodded. He didn't push me. Like Amy, he always acted in the most appropriate way. We chatted a bit. The conversation held two awkward moments.

"And how are the two of you doing?" He asked Amy. Finch had attended our wedding. Amy and I thought it only appropriate to invite the man who gave us the opportunity to meet. He didn't know, though, that we had divorced. I explained the situation as delicately and quickly as possible. It seemed almost easier to explain to him that my mom had died just a few months earlier.

After we parted, Cam and Amy talked to a couple of other former students just a few years younger than we were. I stood aside and watched Finch walk away. *A great man*, I thought. He played such a tremendous role in influencing my life. When I studied music with him as a sax player, it seemed like life offered endless possibilities. I felt confident that I would attain all that I wanted. Then I looked toward Amy again. For a while it seemed like I had. Sadness washed over me. I almost wept, but the sound of laughter, genuine and robust, was the next thing to wash over me. I moved toward Cam and Amy, drawn by their laughter.

The three of us stood together. Sometimes funerals generate the feeling of hopelessness. For the three of us, though, we seemed to get a different vibe—hope.

"It's five thirty," I said. "Let's grab a bite to eat." Amy nodded.

"What is it with you and funerals?" Cam asked. "You always have to get something to eat after a funeral."

I nodded and smiled. A few years before Mom died, I asked her the same question. We always went out to eat after a funeral. Always.

"You don't bring death home with you," she had said. Then I understood. The act of eating, of talking, of sharing memories of the person who had died, helped you move away from the sadness of their death and funeral back into the realm of living. I shared this with Cam, who nodded.

"Infusino's then?" Cam asked.

"No. I'm in the mood for pizza, but not from Infusino's," I said. Cam smiled. He knew what I was going to suggest.

"Pizza Hut," I shouted and Cam laughed.

"Oh, God," Amy sighed with the gusto of a first-year drama student.

—x—x—x—

Some things really don't change. Years can pass, and you can still find everything pretty much as you left it so long ago. As we headed to our booth, that thought, and the company, gave a surge of pleasure. I experience this familiarity of the past when I go to the cottage. Until Mom died, I felt it when I returned to the home of my youth. But the house feels different now, expectant and sad at the same time. We expect Mom, as always, to come through the door at any minute. She never does. The house sighs and settles in, like a dog taking its spot in the corner for an afternoon nap but always casting an eye when someone enters the room.

I feel this familiarity when I drive the streets of my hometown. Of course, I feel it when I return to the home Amy and I made. And, perhaps oddly, I feel it at Pizza Hut.

All these years later, Pizza Hut looked exactly the same. It even appeared the high school waitresses still wore the same polyester uniforms, black pants, black aprons with the Pizza Hut logo sewn on the pocket, and a red Pizza Hut polo with the same logo sewn on the chest. The owner of this store, holding down a location with high traffic, apparently saw no reason to remodel. The dough kept flowing in and out. You could smell and see the success of this operation in the amount of dough it made. He did keep up, though, with the Pizza Hut innovations regarding different kinds of pizzas. He didn't keep up with the move toward serving patrons good beers. Although I found myself craving a good scotch ale, we settled on a pitcher of Miller High Life.

After the waitress walked away, Amy groaned. "God, how I hated those uniforms. So completely unflattering. No matter what I did, I always felt like I looked like a giant piece of polyester had attacked me and swallowed me whole. And then once you guys started coming in, I always thought I was going to get fired for giving you free beer and pizza."

"God, we had quite a thing going on then, didn't we? Why did you ever quit? Free beer and pizza for life. Anyway, from my perspective, Amy," Cameron said, "you looked perfectly wonderful and beautiful."

I smiled and nodded. Long ago I forfeited complimenting Amy, and she stopped taking them seriously anyway. But I never stopped seeing her as the most beautiful woman in the room.

"Cam, you don't have to flatter. I will always be your friend." Then Amy looked at me.

"That's right, Cam. I think we have proved we will always be your friends. Despite not thinking of Mr. Stevenson once since high school, didn't we go to this funeral today? That sure seems like proof to me," I said.

My tone might have been a little harsh. I didn't mean to be snarky about the funeral. Amy sensed my tone, and as always, wanting to both protect me and avoid confrontation, she steered the conversation in a different direction.

"Cam, obviously Mr. Stevenson meant a lot to you. I never knew that. We were in the same AP Government class together senior year. Sure, I learned some things, mostly facts. He was big on facts."

"Anyone? Anyone?" I interjected. I couldn't resist. They laughed.

"When Stevenson taught me economics junior year," Cam said, "he gave me incredible insights into how the business of business works. I really came to understand different economic systems and how governments take most steps, unless they are attacking social agendas, to fuel the economy. Then during senior year, when both of you only had eyes for each other, Stevenson saw that I had been left behind."

"Cam, we always included you. Didn't we do all kinds of things together, the three of us?" I asked.

"A couple of my friends used to joke and ask me how my boyfriends were doing," Amy said. "And when I wasn't with Robb, you and I did things together, too."

"True. All of that is true. And you guys were really great because you did include me in a lot of things. But when I say you left me behind, you were in love, and I was alone. Stevenson noticed. Our class was right before lunch. Stevenson asked me to stay behind one day, and he simply asked me how I was doing. I mumbled something. But the man gently got me to talk about my loneliness. And he encouraged me. He told me something that meant a lot, and I have never forgotten it. He said, 'Your friends have this great relationship going. Be happy for them. Someday you're going to have the same thing. Cam, this isn't your time. But your time is coming. And your life will be amazing. Not everybody strikes gold in high school. I often think the people who have to wait a little longer for the riches to start pouring in live better lives. Hang in there. Keep doing what you're doing. Your time is coming.'

"So yeah, Stevenson always asked these dreadful, factual questions as a way to engage the class, to get some sort of discussion going. He could have found a better way to get us to talk, like by maybe asking us to apply the facts to our world. But he knew what to say to me. After that, I didn't stop being completely jealous of you two. But life got better. I ended up marrying an incredible woman, who helps me find joy every single day. Stevenson was right. I really did strike it rich, and I have so far lived an amazing life. Yes, high school truly sucked. But it has been pretty damned good since. Mr. Stevenson gave me the encouragement I needed to be patient. So, yeah, I will always hold Mr. Stevenson in high esteem."

Amy did what she always did in the moment. She made the perfect gesture. She didn't have to say anything. She took Cam's hand and squeezed it, then continued to hold his hand gently. Cam smiled. You could visibly see stress and sadness leaving his body. Amy had that effect on everyone.

A comfortable quiet settled over our booth. We all disappeared in our own memories. I found myself thinking about Cam and senior year. At first, it seemed like he was with us all the time. That wasn't true at all. Sure, we included Cam. But Amy and I always ended the night together, while Cam always ended his alone. I wanted nothing more at the end of the night than to hold Amy and kiss her until my jaw ached. It didn't seem like we flaunted our romance in front of Cam. He wasn't the fourth leg on a stool that only needed three to function perfectly. On most nights, Cam drove because he was the only one who had his own car. When Amy and I first started dating, he would drop Amy off at home first, thinking I would be next. I always got out at Amy's, though, and would walk home hours later. When he dropped us at my house, I would walk Amy home later. I never thought about what those drop-offs must have been like for Cam.

Romance swept Amy and me up in its tide, and we rode the crest of ever-moving waves. To Cam it must have seemed like we had left him behind on the beach, watching us drift ever farther away from him. Occasionally, Amy and I talked about Cam. She worried about him. At one point she even suggested that we try to find someone for him to date. I couldn't imagine who would want to date Cam, which was shortsighted on my part. In retrospect, I can also see that it was selfish. Part of me didn't want to have to double date with Cam, and part of me wanted him to always be the devoted friend to me, supporting me in every way, even going so far as to think that he should feel privileged that we would deign to allow him to hang out with us. Selfish, you're damned right it was. So, I would deflect Amy's concerns about Cam.

"He's fine," I would say. "He's different. I don't think he wants what we have."

"Robb, look more closely at your friend. He always looks so sad."

"That's just the way he's made. He's one of those people who has been blessed with a hangdog face. Now kiss me." She would comply. She reveled in our time together as much as I did. By the time we broke from the first kiss we had forgotten all about Cam's existence.

As our deep-dish pan pizza came, Cam asked Amy, "Who was your favorite teacher in high school?"

"Mr. Finch," Amy said without hesitation.

"You, too? What was it about the guy that everyone seemed to love so much? I don't get it. I wasn't a band guy. But, Amy, you weren't either. You were just in the color guard, and yet you call him your favorite teacher."

Amy and I had discussed this one often. She saw in Mr. Finch the same qualities I did. I knew how she would answer. "He was so genuine. He always showed compassion for all his students, even the ones who showed so much disrespect by their immature actions. He demanded excellence. He also knew how to have fun. He used to tell us 'If it isn't fun, what's the point?' Like you turned to Mr. Stevenson for advice, you could always go to Mr. Finch to talk. You could share problems with him. He didn't judge. He didn't tell you what to do. He just listened. Even though I never had him for band, I went to him a couple of times. He showed such great understanding and respect."

"Robb says the same things. I wish I could have had him for a teacher. Okay, so your favorite teacher was easy. Who was the worst teacher you ever had?"

"That's easy. Mr. Hawke," I shouted. Cam and Amy both sat back, startled by my aggressiveness.

"That's just because you hate math," Cam said.

"No way, man. Hawke used to make you go to the board to solve problems," I started to say, but Cam interrupted me.

"Christ, that's what you do in a math class."

"I know, but it was the way he did it. You had to stand at the board until you could solve the problem. As if standing there would make you suddenly know how to solve it. I was a senior with a bunch of sophomores. Cuz, you know, math and I didn't exactly get along. Girls used to stand at the board the entire hour, just sobbing, and Hawke wouldn't let them sit down. That is no exaggeration."

"How often did you stand there and cry?" Cam wondered.

"Once I felt like it, but that's the last thing I would do in high school. Now I'm just an old softy."

Amy rolled her eyes and smirked. "Tell me about it. Tears all the time. Just an old crybaby." She smirked again, so I knew she intended no malice. Make no mistake. I shed enough tears as an adult to fill more than my share of beer mugs.

"No, I broke Hawke's code. He made me go to the board one day. I could only get so far in the problem. I stood there, getting more and more frustrated. Pissed, really.

"Hawke kept prodding me. 'Solve the problem.'

"Finally, I snapped. 'Look,' I almost shouted. 'Obviously I don't know how to solve the problem. You're the teacher. Help me figure out what to do.' So he did. He came to the board, stood beside me, and explained, gently and quietly, step by step, what to do to solve the problem.

"When we finished, he said, 'Do you see it now?'"

"That sounds like an example of a pretty good teacher, there, old friend," Cam said. "He taught you how to solve the problem."

"He did. I saw how to solve the problem, but I saw something else. 'Why won't you help the other students like you just helped me?' I asked Hawke.

"'All they have to do is ask.' At that moment I realized that he would help anytime. All I had to do was ask for help. But he wasn't going to volunteer his help. I never understood that.

"'The other kids are terrified of you.' I said, bluntly.

"'I know. But I need them to ask for my help.'"

"My classmates either got it or they didn't. They were too terrified of him to ask for help. So if they didn't get it, they lost a whole year of mathematics instruction. I always thought Hawke could have been a phenomenal, much-loved teacher. Instead, students reviled him."

The table went silent for a minute. Cam and I took another slug of our Miller High Life. "It just seems like a teacher should be willing to just help," I said.

"Another math teacher told me to cheat on a test. I had missed class that day because of an appointment. The math teacher told me to take it at lunch in the cafeteria. He strongly suggested I sit by a friend who was acing his class. He said ask my friend to help with any questions I had. Then he winked. Without actually saying so, he told me to cheat that day. I hated him. That teacher took something from me that day."

Cam and Amy then told some of their horror stories about bad teachers—the racist, sexist teacher who called the girls fat pigs; the history teacher who always fell asleep during movies, which was about every other day; the English teacher who never graded essays; the wood shop teacher who used to make boys grab keys to the supply closet from his pants pocket, the same guy who was later fired for sexual molestation of boys; the gay man who was so furious about the hardships of life as a gay man that he tormented his students with unrealistic homework demands and shockingly low grades on essays and tests.

We had no trouble recalling stories about teachers. They played a big role in our lives. They could be godlike and heinous villains. With just about everybody I talked with from my high school days, they could quickly recount high school memories about the experiences and many of the players from that time in their lives.

When we finished reminiscing about teachers, other memories filled our conversation.

"I will never forget the M&M sucks senior year," Amy said. "How crazy was that? Seeing how many M&M's you could hoover into your mouth in one big suck. It got so big that it seemed to define our senior year. We even put it on the yearbook cover. When we were discussing possible cover ideas, I quickly suggested a train of M&M's. It seemed to define us."

"Yeah, oh man, we would hold suck-offs during lunch," I added, laughing. "We had emcees doing play-by-play of the round-robin sucking competitions."

"What you didn't know about those championships," Cam said to Amy, "is that the boys were scouting out the girls who seemed to have the greatest capacity for sucking."

Amy and I both groaned. If we closed our eyes and imagined just a tiny bit, we would have found ourselves right back in high school, senior year, listening to Cam and his double entendres.

"You always have to go to sex, don't you, Cam?" I said, chuckling.

"Hey, it's hanging in the air, like a big slow softball pitch. Someone has to take the swing. Remember, freshman English, when someone let out this hellaciously smelly fart. We're all covering our noses, trying not to breathe, damn near suffocating."

I started chuckling. "We were all casting suspicious glances. Then Mrs. Scarpelli spoke up. 'That was me. Sorry. I didn't think it would be this bad.' And then she started laughing. And then the whole class started laughing. Tears were rolling down everyone's cheeks."

Everyone laughed. Amy wondered, "Cam, how do you know this story?"

"I had Wheeler fourth hour. He told us everything, especially if it had anything to do with sex. He had a lot of stories to share. And kids, of course, were often the topic. Like right after prom, kids were all buzzing about one group's post-prom party at a local campground. Everybody sat around the campfire, but one couple retired to their tent and had very loud, first-time sex. Everyone sat around listening in awkward silence. I'm not saying anybody else in that group had sex that night, but if they did, they did so quietly. The next morning one of the boys in the group started laughing, which, of course, became contagious. Soon, everyone was roaring with laughter. One of the boys told the couple what they heard the night before. The girl was mortified. The boy sort of preened."

"That whole thing is so sad," Amy said. "Not only does that become their memory of prom, but it also becomes how everyone will remember this couple. At their reunions, even though no one probably said anything publicly, they were thinking, 'That's the couple who got it on after prom.'" Amy gave me a sad, wistful smile. I know she was remembering our prom.

The stories from high school continued. Just like we did in high school, we talked and we laughed. We kept calling for pitcher refills. The difference was that the hangover would last longer now than it did in high school. At the end of the night, Cam drove us all home. He dropped me off first, Amy last.

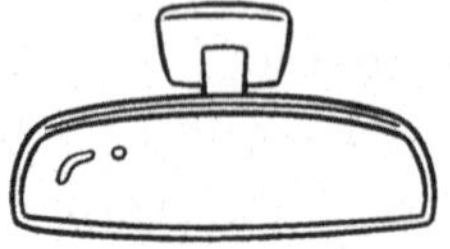

CHAPTER 11

"Shotgun!" The crowd yelled in anticipation as Brad punched a hole in the bottom of the beer can. Then he puckered up to the can and flipped the pop top. The beer cascaded into his open mouth like water coming out of a firehose. He downed the entire can in about three seconds. The crowd roared. He wiped his chin, took an unbalanced step away from the sink, clutching his next beer.

People drank beer. They drank wine. They drank from plastic cups that they dipped into a metal tub to fill their glass with what the host called "wapitui," a mix of several different kinds of hard liquor and cut with Hawaiian Punch, a deceptively sweet drink that packed an amazing wallop. Aerosmith wailed in the background. Bodies writhed in the living room. Amy and I cuddled on the couch, watching the party unfold. We each held a glass of wap, sipping slowly and quietly.

"It is quite a scene," I observed.

"Kind of unbelievable," Amy said. She pointed at one of my football teammates who was doing a waterfall, where he held three cups of beer in both hands over his open mouth. He slowly tipped the cups up, and the beer cascaded from the bottom cup into his mouth, and beer from the above cups flowed into each successive cup, creating a waterfall effect.

"God, look at Happy Jack. That's incredible and disgusting. He's going to be so drunk. I'm glad you're not like that," she said and snuggled in tighter to me. I didn't think it was the right time to confess to teaching the waterfall to Happy Jack at one of our football victory parties. Happy Jack had been my friend since grade school.

This was just another Friday night party. Some of our friends were going at it hard, but not for any special reason besides it being Friday night. Most of us in our senior year didn't really drink hard. Often, though, there were parties to mark the end of the week. We didn't really think about it too much. It was just what high school kids did. After the football season, partying picked up for many of us seniors. What we did wasn't so far removed from my parents going out for a steak dinner at the Green Mill and having three brandy old fashioneds before dinner. While I did drink sometimes before I met Amy, I never spun out of control. I seemed adept at handling my drinking. I often became the person who made sure that no one did something hurtful or so outrageous to draw the cops. We were fairly responsible and did designate drivers and key masters. Some of my friends still drove drunk. The teenage gods must have watched over us because no one ever had a serious accident. I also kept a watchful eye and didn't let someone drive if they were too drunk.

I don't want this to seem like I am some sort of saint. I'm not. Mom raised me to uphold certain principles. Years later, I realized that much of what she taught me and what she expected of me was to treat people with respect. She also expected me to make sure those around me did the same. Some people would describe that as the golden rule. I know for certain it was Mom's golden rule. "People will do stupid and hurtful things. Don't you be one of those people. You will make mistakes as you go. Don't compound those mistakes by thinking you are better than other people."

As I was entering high school, Mom sat me down at the kitchen table for what she called perhaps our most important talk. Over the years, we had many of those "most important talks," so it was hard to determine which really was the most important. This one, though, ranks up there. She laid out several photos of Shelly, as if she were dealing out a deck of cards. "You will always, always, always treat women with respect. You will never inflict any physical harm on a woman. If you are involved in any kind of sexual activity (shock must have registered on my face)—yes, we are talking about sex. If a girl or woman says 'No,' you stop whatever you are doing immediately. Immediately. In every instance, no means absolutely no, and stop. If you ever need reminders of this message, think of someone refusing to stop with your sister. You are to always respect and protect women."

I did my best to adhere to Mom's message. It wasn't always easy. I acted as protector and social conscience during my senior year. I kept an eye on the girls at parties. I broke up a couple of potential sexual assaults by stepping in to protect the girl. In one case, one of my football teammates took a swing at me. He was so pissed. The following Monday at practice, he laid some ferocious licks on me. After driving me to the ground and punching his knee into my back, he leaned toward me and hissed, "That's for keeping me from getting laid, fucker." The very next play, I took him down in the same way. I leaned toward him and hissed, "No, motherfucker. I kept you from getting arrested for rape. Dumb fuck. If you're not going to think and treat women with respect, then I will do your thinking for you." And I shoved him away.

"We're not done with this motherfucker!" The teammate in question was Happy Jack. He snarled, looking anything but happy.

"No," I shouted back. "We're completely done." At that moment, our friendship since sixth grade ended. Then the coach blew the whistle and ordered us to run it again.

Sometimes we did drink on special occasions. Like most high schoolers, you found ways to push the boundaries, to experiment, to see what you might like to do and what you would never want to experience again. Many of my peers drank. The numbers grew the deeper we got into the school year. A large subset of them also smoked weed. Some just smoked weed. Some slipped into harder drugs. Some turned to criminal behavior. Most, though, did the safe, the accepted, the expected—they drank.

Our senior party was a drinking event, too. No surprise there. We had the senior party at the Elks Lodge. A week away from graduation, we drank heavily. Many people arrived loaded and a number of people snuck in booze in flasks or water bottles. At one point, a bunch of guys from Citizen's Club re-enacted our kickline performance from the variety show in the spring. Immediately following that, the entire senior class of football players took to the dance floor and did a line dance. Then the rest of the class joined us. Alcohol fueled that event and dropped our inhibitions.

We have a drinking culture. Many people begin their lifelong affair with alcohol during high school. Nowadays, accepting parents will throw keggers for their children, thinking it better to be involved in their children's exploration with alcohol, insisting that no one drives home drunk because they collect keys from everyone, or requiring everyone to sleep over. Kids, though, drink a whole lot more often than just at big parties. Even the national merit 4.0 students drink. Vodka in the water bottle is a real thing. Kids never seem to find any difficulty obtaining alcohol.

As an adult, it never surprised me to hear parents talking about their kids' experimentation with alcohol. Many parents bemoan these developments, acting like booze is the latest in boutique drugs. Adults often become the biggest hypocrites, refusing to take even the briefest glance at reality. One college acquaintance recently spent two hours in a drunken rant about a drinking and hazing scandal that had rocked a campus group he had been involved in. "The advisor has lost control. He shouldn't be allowing those kids to drink like he does. It's a disgrace." As he tried to make these statements of disgust, he kept drinking, finishing another four beers during the ongoing diatribe.

After trying to turn the conversation into a rational debate, I gave up. "You're such an ass," I said. "You're arguing against the drinking culture, and yet you're making the argument while you're so drunk you probably won't even remember this tomorrow. And don't ever forget, you stupid ass, that you helped create that drinking culture. So get off your sanctimonious pedestal. The more you talk, the more ignorant you sound." That didn't shut him up. He must have thought that he was making cogent arguments. He wasn't. Finally, another friend, who was hosting the party, shouted at the acquaintance: "Get the fuck out of my house. I'm tired of listening to your shit." The guy slumped down into the folds of the couch and passed out. It wasn't the first party he ruined because of his drinking.

A high school buddy, who regularly drank in high school, said to me recently, "My son is drinking. That's just wrong. He shouldn't be drinking. We raised him to be a Christian, and that is not Christian behavior."

I worked to stifle my laughter. "Oh, stop. You certainly drank more than your share in high school."

"I did. I freely admit it," he said. "We raised him to be better than that."

And your parents didn't? I didn't say it, but I wanted to.

His response, though, made me pause. Seeing his son drink made him feel as if he had failed as a parent. I knew I would have to face those same demons with my own children. I just didn't expect to face them as soon as I did.

—x—x—x—

The kids were staying with me for the weekend. After dinner, TJ pushed himself back from the table and said, "I'm going out with the guys tonight. Don't wait up."

"I'll be waiting up," I said. "You know your curfew is midnight. I expect you to be home by then."

"Yeah, right," he said, smirked, and left the kitchen. I wasn't looking at him, but in the reflection of the kitchen window, I saw him give me the finger.

A few years back, at a neighborhood party, one of the dads got a similar reaction from his son. After the dad offered his son a compliment, the son glared at him and returned the compliment with a surly, snarling response. “Like that means anything to me.”

After the son stomped away, the father turned to me and shrugged. “At some point I guess it is natural for all sons to hate their fathers. I’m just not sure what I did to deserve such intense hatred. Maybe I should have been a Bears fan instead of a Packers fan.” The dad tried to pass off the family tension with a joke, but that didn’t cover up the hurt in his eyes or the quaver in his voice. The cute boy, who had loved his father so much that he would leap into his arms after soccer games, had somehow turned into a hating, hulking monster. The dad clearly wondered how that could have happened.

I didn’t have to wonder. I knew why my son hated me. I just kept wishing that, at some point, he would get tired of expending the energy it required to hang onto so much hate. Dad used to always offer this old bit of wisdom: “Wish into one hand, shit into the other, and see which hand fills up faster.” At some point wishing turns into hoping. Same results.

I believe in hope. It gives us a reason to keep going. We hope for a better life, for fewer problems to face, for just a bit more happiness, for fulfilling love, or at least a little less hate. Hope gives me a reason to get up in the morning because I hope today will be better than yesterday. Even though I have been disappointed for a long string of days now, I still wake up every morning and think, *Maybe today*. I used to call myself an optimist. After all of these lesser days, though, I have become more of a realist. Now I have added to my daily hope mantra: *Maybe today, but probably not*. Even though I may slowly be in the process of giving up on myself, I won’t give up on my son.

“You know he’s going out drinking tonight, don’t you?” Jessie asked me.

“Jess, we don’t know that. He’s going out with his friends. He may be going to a movie. He may be playing video games,” I said, hoping.

“Or he may be getting high or drunk. Don’t keep fooling yourself, Dad. TJ may not be all grown up, but he also is not the cute little boy who used to crawl into your lap for his bedtime story.”

My daughter was more of a realist than me. Much more. High school kids lose their idealism much more quickly now. The innocence flees quickly, and that makes me sad. I want to believe in better possibilities for TJ. Or maybe Jess has just seen too much of the reality of TJ’s life to think that things could get better for him. Reality had dictated harsh conditions too often for Jessie. A major part of that reality came from my failures that ripped apart our family. I wanted to cry and knew that I would later in the quiet darkness of my bedroom, the same room I occupied as a teenage boy, so full of questions about the world and so full of hope. Now with so many of the questions answered and so many disappointments to add to the mix, hope was fading away, like the images of now aging rockers forever frozen in the vitality of youth on some of the posters still hanging on my bedroom walls.

Jessie leaned over and gave me a hard hug. "It's okay, Dad. TJ is rebelling. But I hear all teenagers do it. Grandpa says even you did." She hugged me again.

"You wash. I'll dry," Jessie said, tapping me on the shoulder. Someone always called drying in our family. It was the easiest job in the kitchen. Amy and I would sometimes intercede and dictate jobs, but we usually let the kids determine the chores themselves. We were just grateful that they had learned our lessons about shared responsibility in the household. Our kids, while not obsessed with cleanliness, kept the house and their rooms presentable. We had a dishwasher and used it, but Amy and I believed in the power of washing and drying dishes side by side. When you worked in such close proximity, you tended to talk to each other. Amy and I always relished kitchen cleanup. It presented another opportunity for us to hang together. Jess was finally getting into the routine of conversation while we worked.

"No, I cooked. You wash. How'd you get so wise?" I said as I picked up a dish towel and waited for her to slide the first plate into the drying rack.

"I come from pretty smart parents, even though they made such a mess of things," she said and gave me a stern look. Then she smiled. "Just kidding, Dad. You know I don't blame you for the divorce. At least not so much anymore. When I look at my friends' parents, it would be weird if you and Mom were still married."

"Are that many parents divorced?"

"You know the statistics. One in two. And that's pretty much true among my friends," Jessie said, pulling a handful of soapy silverware out of the suds and holding it under the running faucet for a rinse.

"It doesn't seem like the stat should be that high. I mean, I see a lot of couples at soccer games and concerts. Marriage must be working for a lot of people," I said.

"Second marriages, Dad. That will be you and Mom someday, married a second time and much happier."

"I have heard that a lot of people find more happiness in a second marriage," I said.

"Of course they do. The second time they go into marriage with a more realistic idea of what they are getting into. They are not blinded by notions of love and romance," Jessie said while putting another dish in the drying rack. "They're not Romeo and Juliet, naive to the realities of the world. God, how I found those two idiots annoying."

Jessie had been complaining about Romeo and Juliet for a month now, ever since her freshman English class finished reading the play.

She continued with her Ted Talk on love, marriage, divorce, rinse and repeat.

"The second time around they are looking for someone who will be their partner, someone they actually may love but someone they certainly like," Jessie said, her head bent down as she scrubbed the frying pan.

I didn't respond to her statement. It seemed to carry a lot of truth.

"Stop wondering how I got so smart," Jessie said, looking at me, smiling. "Let's just agree that I'm pretty damned smart. Even though you and Mom messed up, you had some pretty good genes and pretty good intentions. Talking to Uncle Cameron has certainly helped, too. Now he's smart. Probably a genius." Jessie giggled. "He told me to say that."

The silliness out of the way, Jessie and I discussed the important stuff, the strengths and weaknesses of her freshman volleyball team, and how she wished some boy would ask her to homecoming but how she knew that wouldn't happen with only a week until the dance.

Later that night, I sat in the den long after Jessie had gone to bed. Although I did intend to wait up for TJ to come home, I found myself immersed in a book. Sara said that I needed enlightenment, especially if we were going to keep hanging out together. She gave me two books to read. As I sat in the den, I compared the heft of both books. She gave me *Peril* by Costa and Woodward and a slightly older book, *How to Win a Fight With a Conservative* by Daniel Kurtzman. The Kurtzman book had more physical heft to it, but Woodward and Costa detailed the less-than-peaceful transfer of power from Trump to Biden. I chose Kurtzman's satire on conservatives.

As I read his mockery of all things conservative, I thought of Sara and how she would have taken the book. She would have been cheering because of the rightness of the observations. Since I really didn't have the passion either way, I just found it funny. But I can only read satire for so long. I set it down about eleven o'clock and thought I would tune in to *The Tonight*

Show.

Instead, I picked up *Peril* and found myself adrift. I never considered myself a reader, and certainly not someone who reads political arguments. But Woodward and Costa hooked me as they carefully presented details of the end of one presidential era and the shaky transition into the next. As I read, I found myself again thinking of Sara. Political players on both sides exhibited intense passion for their beliefs. Sara seemed to burn brightly with her political passions. Her passions motivated and inspired her. I found myself wondering if I had any great passions in my life now that I was no longer with Amy.

I lost awareness of time and lightly dozed. My son's loud return home at one thirty startled me. He made no effort to hide his entrance. I sensed the way he came into the house as a challenge. I walked from the den into the kitchen to find him walking across the kitchen toward the refrigerator. To call what he was doing walking is overkind. He lurched and stumbled, walking sideways. In his gait, I recognized every drunk I had ever seen. For the briefest moment, I mused, *My sixteen-year-old son is drunk.* Anger quickly replaced the musing. He didn't even recognize that I watched him stagger past me.

He lifted the lid from the pizza box, pulled out two slices of leftover pizza, and stumbled away from the open door.

Seeing his brazen drunkenness, I became every cliched father. "You're late. And you're drunk," I said in a quiet voice that seethed with anger.

"Yup," TJ said as he collapsed into a chair. He immediately stuffed a third of one piece into his mouth. As he chewed with a wide-open mouth, reverting to the most childish forms of challenge, he slurred his next statement. "Whatcha gonna do 'bout it?" He glared at me, anger and hatred the clearest emotions I could read on his face.

When I saw that face, I recalled a nearly identical scene with my own father, at least the drunk part. I don't think I ever glared at him with such open contempt. At least I hope not. As I considered TJ's question, I also remembered how my wise father dealt with my own high school drunkenness.

"We will talk about this in the morning. For now, finish your pizza and go to bed," I said. TJ looked disappointed. In his addled state, I'm sure he was looking forward to a fight. I quickly realized my father's own wisdom. It's not like my son could rationally consider anything I might say. At worst, this would escalate into a major blowout. To what end?

TJ opened his mouth, closed it, shrugged, took another bite of pizza, and mumbled the one-word teenage phrase of derision. “Whatever!”

I walked back to the den and sank into the recliner. Even though I realized I would have to face this as a parent, I didn’t expect to face it tonight. The shock of seeing not just the sullenness of my sweet little boy but also the staggering drunkenness is something no parent is really equipped to handle the first time they encounter it.

I heard TJ’s heavy steps as he walked upstairs. It was almost as if he intentionally drove his feet down with as much force as possible to emphasize his intoxicated state. It also seemed like he wanted to wake up the entire house but also send me a deliberate message about how much he hated me.

A swirl of thoughts pummeled me for hours until I staggered to bed, almost as if I were drunk myself. I thought I would go to bed when I had a plan for dealing with TJ. The plan never developed, but I did wallow for a long time in a guilt-ridden personal attack.

I woke up the next morning shortly after seven, having slept for about three hours. I still had no plan. In the kitchen I found Dad pouring his first cup of coffee. Dad didn’t say anything until he handed me what some might have called a pail of coffee.

“From what I heard last night, I’m guessing you need this.” He gestured with his head toward the den. “Let’s go have a quiet talk.” When he reached the den, he took his recliner, and I sat on the couch. Momentarily, I flashed back to when I was in high school, and Dad would commence to lecture me. He tried to soften the blow of the routine lectures by saying, “You don’t have to do what I say. I just want you to listen.” Then he would smile and launch into his latest round of “advice.” It took me years to realize that he was full of shit. He wasn’t giving me advice and allowing me to make my own choices. He wanted me to do exactly what he was saying, all the while appearing the forgiving and sage father. When I finally told him I was on to his game, he just laughed. Today I sensed that he really wouldn’t be giving me advice at the time when I most wanted him to tell me what to do. I know I would have listened carefully and followed his advice.

We sat in companionable silence and sipped our coffee. The house mimicked our silence, all the normal creaks and groans fading away. The couch afforded me a view of the backyard. I could still see the fall perennials in full bloom. Mom’s handiwork. For as long as I could remember, she tended the garden. She loved to dig her hands into the rich, dark loam, to plant, to weed, to pick for display. Mom didn’t have a garden that matched the beautiful panoply of Sara’s garden, but the yard was always pretty. She planted some annuals, flowers that grew quickly and bloomed often. Over the years she had also planted perennials that seemed to rotate into beauty with the turn of calendar pages. The gold and orange mums had taken over the back fence line. They would soon match the colorful fall coats the trees would wear shortly before giving up to winter gray overcoats, more focused on practicality than beauty. The sullen grays of winter would have better matched my mood.

"TJ was falling down drunk last night," I said and saw Dad nod. TJ made enough noise so that everyone on the block probably knew he was drunk. Dad wasn't surprised. "It's all my fault, you know. He wouldn't be doing this if I had been a better husband and father. If I hadn't screwed up the marriage, Amy and I could have worked through this together."

I slumped back in the chair, feeling more defeated than I had ever been. We sat in silence. It felt like a judgmental silence, and I was the one doing the judging. "You remember that movie *Ferris Bueller's Day Off*? I asked Dad. He nodded. "Boy, I could sure use a day off." Dad gave me a slight smile.

"Sorry, son, but I don't think you get to take a day off on this one," Dad said.

I continued my judgmental pity party. "If I had been a better husband to Amy and a better father to the kids, we wouldn't be facing these issues. We would have been the right influence on him. We would have kept him from being friends with destructive people. He would have been surrounded by love and never would have felt the need to get drunk."

Dad let me have at it with my intense pity party. Eventually, I stopped talking. Silence reigned king again. Dad was going to let me keep working on this on my own.

"At least I didn't start yelling at him last night." I gave Dad a rundown of some of my stunned observations from the night before. After talking for about fifteen minutes, I said, "I just feel so lost. I feel like I felt when Amy told me she had to divorce me. I don't know what to do. You and Mom always seemed to know what to do," I said in desperation.

Dad finally spoke. "Bullshit," he said.

I gave him a sharp look.

"That is a whole lot of bullshit, Robb. All of it. Especially the part about your mom and me always knowing what to do. No, son, the truth is we were as lost as you are right now. Your mom always seemed to ultimately find the right solution. I don't know how many times she talked me down off the ledge. I would listen to myself talk to you and be amazed at what I was saying." He paused and smiled.

"No, I was clueless. I was just repeating what she suggested I say to you kids. She made it seem sometimes like I had the wisdom of Solomon. In truth, I was more like Barney from Mayberry."

"Mom was pretty amazing," I agreed. "What do you think she would have to say about this?"

"She would say the same thing to you that she said to me when you came home drunk for the first time—that we knew of—when you were a junior. Deliver some punishment, be firm, but do it with love."

We slipped into another stretch of silence. These silences with Dad had become comfortable. Neither of us felt the need to break them. "Could you use a refill on the coffee?"

"God, yes. Here, let me get it," I said, pushing myself up from the couch. Dad was already standing.

"Nah, I'll get it. The doc said I need to walk as much as possible. Otherwise, the diabetes will cause neuropathy." He grabbed my cup. At the door, he turned to look at me. "Robb, another thing your mother would have said: 'Follow your heart. Always.' I agree with her. You've got a good one. Let it be your guide."

Four hours later TJ shuffled into the kitchen. I sat at the table where I had remained since ending my chat with Dad. I lay in wait. When TJ came into the kitchen, he glared at me again, a look I was becoming accustomed to. "What?" he growled.

I remained silent. After standing I walked to him and pulled him into a hard hug. At first, he fought and tried to pull away. I wouldn't let go. Then he collapsed into the hug. I held him in my arms for a long time, longer than I had held him since the divorce. I gently touched his face with my hand. I didn't say anything, but I could feel him softly weeping.

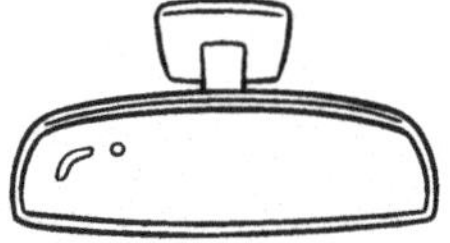

CHAPTER 12

Now that I'm older I drive sensible cars that get pretty good mileage and are reliable. If the car gets me to and from, I don't necessarily worry about how it looks or the impression it might make on others. In high school the car mattered a whole lot more. Some of my buddies drove souped-up muscle cars. I worked at Ponderosa with them. They grilled steaks so they could afford to spend batches of money to trick out their rides. Chrome wheels, racing slicks, spoilers, four-barrel carbs, fancy paint jobs. The works. When we would go cruising, they would prowl up and down East Washington, where other cats with the fast cars would go.

Cam rarely joined us on Friday nights out. By the time I was a junior, though, I craved more social interaction than video games with Cam could provide. He never joined us during junior year and only came out a little more often during senior year. Even though I always did all I could to make him feel welcome, he told me that he felt like he didn't fit in. On those occasions when he did join us, he stood off to the side and looked on in what I always felt was harsh judgment. Cam denied it, though he later acknowledged that his observations in high school helped him decide that he wanted to counsel people on how to achieve better relationships. After watching Friday night rituals, Cam always said he knew he could make a living offering advice to the clueless.

So I spent a lot of Friday nights with my marching band buddies, Brad, Phil, and Steve. When Brad, Phil, or Steve saw another challenger, they would slide up next to them and gun the engine. When the other driver looked up and smiled, Brad—usually Brad because he probably liked to race the most—would nod at the driver and yell over me in the shotgun seat,

"Let's go! On the green." Then he would give a thumbs up, gun his engine, and roar through the gears as soon as the light changed. My stomach would lurch as if I were experiencing maximum g-force on a NASA liftoff. I didn't race for two reasons. I didn't have a car, and when I could get the car from my parents for a Friday night, I was stuck driving the blue Dodge Dart that could reach sixty miles per hour in about three hours.

My football buddies trained, partied, or played other sports. They didn't have time for jobs or interest in cars. Mostly they bummed rides, drove their parents' cars, or drove junkers passed down from sibling to sibling. On the rare occasions when Mom and Dad would let me drive, I got behind the wheel of the old Dodge Dart, a functional car that never impressed anyone. Point A to point B. Not fast, not in style, but you got there.

One time, after grabbing some beers at the White Hen corner grocery store, Steve flipped me the keys. I caught them and looked at him quizzically. "You drive," he said, as he pulled out a beer and opened it. "I feel like having a beer." No one really thought much about drinking and driving then. Societal concerns about that came later. Drinking and driving created some opportunities for routine teenage antics. We pulled off numerous five-alarm car fire drills at stoplights. When we pulled up to a red light, the driver would throw the car in park or neutral, everyone would leap out of the car, race around it, and climb back in, always in a different spot. The only one who reclaimed his original position would be the driver.

Once a carload of girls stopped beside us at a red light. We pointed and laughed. Brad yelled, "Fire drill." The girls picked up on our intentions immediately. We ran around both cars. All the boys crawled in the girls' car, and all the girls leaped in the boys' car. We laughed hysterically at our impromptu variation of the traditional activity.

Many times, a car would pull up alongside us, and you would see a bare ass or two hanging in the window. You or the driver in your car would honk in appreciation. Mooning became a big thing. Mostly guys would hang their asses. We always counted our blessings when girls would show us their best assets. You never knew when someone would honk and show.

Two of the best moonings occurred when I was on the bus for track meets. After returning from a Tuesday night track meet, one of the pole vaulters decided to moon the car behind us. He dropped trow not once but three times. When we got back to school, the driver of the car pulled the kid off the bus and suspended him from the team. The boy had been mooning one of the assistant coaches.

Another time we rode back into town on a Saturday afternoon after a long invitational meet. After one of my teammates urged a passenger in the car behind us to lift her top, which she did, exposing her breasts. The seven or eight boys at the back roared their approval. Instantly all the boys leaped to the back of the bus. She flashed us again and again. Her boyfriend, the driver, just laughed at her brazen behavior.

The driving and cruising culture, and the antics we enjoyed, constituted a big part of our activities on Friday and Saturday nights during the school year and most summer nights. Innocent. Harmless. Fun.

So when Steve flipped me his keys, I slipped into the driver's seat of his cherry red Camaro, which possessed more guts under the hood than Brad's Dodge Charger. Driving Steve's car always thrilled me because it allowed me to imagine that someday I could drive something else besides the safe but unimaginative Dodge Dart. I asked Steve once why he didn't ever race. "Don't really like to, especially against my friends. Brad takes this so seriously. It wouldn't be worth it to beat him. Which I would." He knew he didn't have to prove anything about his car or his racing abilities. But he also admitted to me that sometimes he would find himself sneaking off to Broadway Avenue, where he would pick up the occasional race, just to reassure himself that he could beat pretty much anything and anyone on the road.

As we left the White Hen Pantry and started driving up Speedway, Brad pulled up beside me and gunned his engine. It sounded like Gasoline Alley before the start of the Indy 500. I looked at Steve. He took a slow sip of his beer. "Take him," he said.

I punched the accelerator and the Camaro shot off. Even with the automatic transmission we quickly shot past Brad. He pulled even for a moment, but I goosed the Camaro and got a little more juice out of it. Then I glanced at the speedometer. We were going ninety-five miles an hour. And I came to my senses and immediately let up on the gas. Speedway is a small, four-lane city street. Whenever I remember that night, I shake my head in amazement. So stupid, so dangerous. Even when I had the opportunity, I never raced again.

Cars played a big part in our lives. On Friday nights it seemed everyone hit the streets for some cruising or racing. The only kids who didn't cruise were the freshmen and sophomores, who hadn't gotten their driver's licenses yet. They showed up early at McDonald's on their bikes. As an upperclassman, you didn't mock the underclassmen because you remembered the humility of wanting to be part of something so bad that you would ride your older brother's Schwinn Varsity ten-speed down to

McDonald's on a Friday night. Mind you this wasn't the 1950s, but unless someone threw a party, the school held a dance, or one of the school's teams had a game that night, you cruised.

Everybody followed the same basic routine. Cruise for a while, then head to McDonald's, where you would hang out with everybody from your class. As long as some people in the group ate food or drank beverages, McDonald's would let you loiter in the parking lot for about thirty minutes, and then a cop would slowly cruise through. Everyone would hop in their cars for another half hour of cruising, and then we would head back to McDonald's. We ate in shifts. That way, if a few people held food in their hands, the McDonald's management wouldn't harass us.

By that point I had become somewhat of a clique hopper. Cam remained my best friend, but after marching band that summer when I was a rising senior, I started hanging around a lot with Brad, Phil, and Steve. I also hung around with my buddies from the football team. I spent time with guys from the chess team, the ski team, the track team, Citizen's Club, and the yearbook. I really just liked the people from my school and wanted to get to know as many of them as possible.

Amy was always there throughout senior year.

After football games, when we won, I would show up at McDonald's with the guys from the team. We swaggered in like conquering heroes. That year we only lost twice. After road games we would get back too late for the victory lap through McDonald's. After home games, though, we would arrive to different levels of applause, depending on the time and the closeness of the game—the more intense the victory, the more raucous the applause.

A particular memory will always stay in my mind, and it involved Brad, celebrating after another one of his racing victories. The football team was holding court, too. I had heard replays and commentaries of almost the entire game twice now. I wanted to see what Brad had to say. Rightly, I predicted smugness. Brad rarely disappointed. "Yeah, so what do you have under the hood—a 150? It took you so long to get off the line, I thought I was going to graduate before you got started." To the victor go the spoils, and to the loser go the jabs.

Brad continued the attack for a few more minutes, but then he let his opponent up off the mat. Although he was gloating a bit, he also avoided being a bad winner. If he developed that reputation, no one would want to race him anymore. Brad needed the races. They gave him status.

A crowd of about thirty kids had gathered around now. Some of these folks held unofficial membership in the unofficial, local, gear head group. A few girls always hung around because of all the guys in the circle. Because of the tight bond from the summer, a handful of friends from marching band loitered, too, laughing at Brad. He played to the audience so smoothly. It made sense that later in life Brad would become a marketing exec. He also could have been a talk show host or comedian on the circuit.

Amy stood talking to Jenna, one of her friends from the band color guard. When she saw me, she smiled and waved. My heart soared like it always did. Earlier she had leaped into my arms after the game as I was walking off the field. I was headed back to the school locker room. She held me tightly. "Hey stud!" she whispered into my ear. "Ooh, what's that smell?" She didn't say it with disgust. Her tone of voice made me think I was wearing the most exotic fragrance of cologne known to man.

"That," I said, giving her a kiss, "is the smell of victory." I knew I smelled awful. I'd been in a full sweat for two hours. Amy was being playful.

"You know you were the star of the game again, don't you?"

"Not me. I just caught a couple of passes. Joe-Joe was the star. He had to get the ball to me," I said.

"Okay, Mr. Humble. He got the ball to you, and then you eluded tacklers and, with those couple of catches, scored a couple of touchdowns. It's okay for you to acknowledge, at least to me, that you're feeling pretty good right now."

Amy read me perfectly, but Mom had always taught me to accept my successes with humility and to take compliments with grace. "Thanks, Ames. I was happy to contribute. It was a great team win, and I do feel pretty good about that." After she kissed me again, I spouted the coach's mantra, something he had to say to us more than he ever had before. "Enjoy the win tonight. Tomorrow, we get back to work." We hadn't become jaded with winning. It was a new, exotic taste, and we wanted to keep tasting until we got our fill.

After Amy kissed me yet again, she said, "Well, then we are most definitely going to enjoy tonight." Then her tongue snaked so far down my throat that I thought she was scrubbing my intestines. That kiss caused an immediate state of discomfort. Throughout my senior year I seemed to always be standing with my hands clasped in front of me, smiling, looking relaxed, but really not.

—x—x—x—

At McDonald's, Amy and Jenna sauntered over to my side of the circle, laughing. They had known each other from being in some of the same classes, but as new members of the color guard, they naturally gravitated toward each other. They roomed together at band camp and on the road trip and were becoming lifelong friends. I liked Jenna. She was really cute and really smart. We also had several classes together. After our senior year, at the yearbook dance we sought out each other. "Will you write something in my yearbook?" Jenna asked.

I sat there for a moment with my pen poised over the book. Then I looked up at her. "I don't know what to write."

"Here, write this down," she said, and then she began reciting. "To the smartest, funniest, most beautiful girl in the senior class. I couldn't imagine a better friend, a friend for always. Now sign your name." She giggled.

Then I passed her my yearbook.

She asked, "What should I write in your yearbook?"

"The same thing," I said. We both laughed. We have essentially identical messages in our yearbooks. And we were great friends for a long while. I lost her in the divorce, though.

That night at McDonald's after saying hello to me, Jenna sidled up to Brad. She had developed a bit of a crush on him through the summer. I knew that Brad really liked her, too. What happened next, though, ruined any chance Brad could ever have of dating Jenna. Brad continued pontificating about the joys of driving fast, and Jenna offered a perfectly delightful comment.

"Driving fast is even better when it's summer, the windows are down, you have the right music, and the right company in the passenger seat." A perfect sentiment to add to the conversation. She looked at Brad and gave him a sweet and inviting smile, hoping he would acknowledge her invitation. She was hoping for an invitation to Brad's passenger seat.

"Don't talk, Jenna. Just stand there and look beautiful." Jenna smiled and laughed. Then she quietly slipped away from the group. Amy and I both saw the hurt through the veneer.

"God, Brad can be such an ass," Amy growled. "I'm glad you're not like that. I'm going to go talk to Jenna."

I gave her hand a squeeze. Jenna instantly cooled toward Brad, who later wondered what had happened. It took him a few months to seek my advice on how he could get closer to Jenna again. When I told him why he never would get close to her because Jenna understood human nature and understood Brad would hurt her again and again, Brad said, "Robbie, you know me. I was just joking. And I did say she was beautiful."

"Brad, Jenna was hurt by your joke. You humiliated her in front of a bunch of people. Sometimes you need to think about what you say before you blurt something out for a few laughs."

"Do you think I can get her back?"

"You know as well as I do she's with Brian. They like each other and have fun together."

"But it won't go anywhere. He's going to Harvard. She's going to Macalester."

"This is high school, Brad. None of these relationships are going anywhere." When I said it, I knew it was childish, but I held my hand behind my back and crossed my fingers. I really believed that my relationship with Amy was going the distance. We almost made it. Brad never did any better than he could have with Jenna. He has now been divorced three times, but his wallet still holds a picture of his hot rod from high school.

—x—x—x—

"I'm worried, Robb. TJ's driving now, and it terrifies me to think he might drive when he's as drunk as you describe. We have to agree on how we're going to deal with this."

Amy needed to talk. She needed to work through things. I learned long ago to let her process things in her own way. Periodically, I would offer assent or throw in a question. Amy didn't want discussion, nor did she want me to solve things. We stumbled into some of our biggest fights when I stepped in to fix things. She always reached a point where she would seek my advice, and then we could discuss options. Until we reached that point, though, she needed to think out loud. Amy and I worked well together as parents. We always had. We agreed before TJ was born that we would be parents who would always discuss before acting, at least in some fashion. We wanted to avoid sending mixed messages, and we wanted to avoid contradicting each other. Our kids also knew that they couldn't play one parent off the other. We acted in accord.

"I think we have to agree on where and when he gets to drive. That way we can maybe keep him from driving when he's drunk. Oh, God. That sounds so bad. I just admitted that TJ drinks. That he will continue to drink. That he will get drunk."

Amy put her face in her hands and rubbed her temples with her index fingers. She never made this gesture when we were young. And she didn't do it all the time, but she did it now when she faced stress, when she felt anxious, and when she struggled to understand something.

"Where is our sweet little boy? I want him back. Part of me wants to say that we have failed TJ as parents. Have we? Really, Robb. I need to know if we've failed our son."

"Amy, we didn't fail TJ. If anyone failed him, it was me. I failed him. We don't need to rehash everything that happened. But part of what he's doing feels like a rebellion—against me and against having to be labeled as a child of divorce. We need to remember, too, that part of what he is doing is part of growing up. He's a junior in high school. Kids drink in high school. It's part of growing up. We did. And you turned out great."

"Thank you," Amy said, looking down. She remained quiet for a moment, pondering. "Except for getting lost for a while a few years back, you turned out great, too. We don't have to blame ourselves or each other. We just need to figure out how to deal with our sixteen-year-old son, who now drinks. Once we figure that one out, then I can start working on how to deal with the issues at work."

"What's going on at work?"

"Just stuff. Never mind."

"Work stuff or colleague stuff?"

"It's colleague stuff. One of my supervisors. Well, he has done some things that seem to cross boundaries. Oh, never mind. I'll deal with that later. Right now, we have to deal with TJ. We have to figure out how to help him get through this without life-altering consequences."

"Okay, so how do we ensure that he doesn't drink and drive and hurt himself or someone else?" I asked. "What ideas do you have for that? Because of the situation and swapping households every three days, we've got to be clear and consistent."

"Right. We've always been consistent," Amy agreed. "I think we can let him drive during the day, but if we ask him to, he's got to check in with us. That's why he has a cell phone."

"And if he doesn't?"

"Then he loses driving privileges. And the loss of privileges has to be significant," Amy said. "Two weeks. If he does it again, he loses his cell phone. Maybe that should be his first punishment. You know he's tied to that damned thing. It's his lifeline, his oxygen tent."

"I'm willing to make it the first line of punishment. I think that's a good idea. So, agreed on that. What about riding around at night with his friends? How do we monitor that situation?"

"We can ask him to call and check in. But he won't. That's part of what this rebellion is all about, right?"

"Right," I said. "But we can strictly enforce curfews. If he doesn't get home by curfew, then he's grounded. Two weeks again. And we take away his phone for that, too. Let's make that the standard punishment. But if he drinks and ends up stranded someplace, we have to allow him to call us so that we can go and pick him up."

"And if he keeps coming home drunk, which I haven't noticed on my end?" Amy said.

"I don't think he is reserving that behavior for me. If he was as drunk as he was the other night, then he's not only drinking when he's with me on the weekends. Unless we see him partying during the day, I don't think we have to view him as having a problem."

"No, but I don't think we can just condone him going out and drinking either. We saw enough of this with some of our friends in high school. The problems they faced later in life were predictable because of how tied they were to partying in high school," Amy said.

"I agree. Let's keep talking about choices. We want him to make good choices. Safe choices. We don't want him to get hurt, and we certainly don't want him to hurt others. Good choices. Bad choices, and he will have to suffer consequences."

Then, as if on cue, Amy and I both simultaneously said, "Two weeks." We laughed, and I felt a warm glow. For the next five minutes we sat in contented silence, wrapping our hands around cooling coffee cups. I knew I was trying to think through possible scenarios and consequences. Mom's mantra about choices and consequences stood as a lesson I always returned to. She would say, "You get to make choices in life. Just always remember that with those choices come consequences. Always choose wisely."

Of course, no one ever chooses wisely all the time. They have to deal with the consequences. Sometimes that's when the best learning occurs. I knew I wanted TJ to learn that he had to make better choices. I wanted him to learn that lesson by mitigating potential consequences. I knew Amy and I would have to go all in to help our son.

I overheard Mom and Dad talking once when I was a junior in high school. I know I had disappointed them, but the details are fuzzy, probably because they were talking about me and drinking in high school. Dad said then, "My dad told me that as a parent, you either have to put the work in when the kids are young, or you put the work in when the kids are teenagers. But I think he was wrong. You always have to put the work in with your kids. You don't get to take any time off until they are good and well-grown.

Then, and only then can you enjoy the fruits of your labors."

Mom was wise. Dad was wise, too. As I pondered this, I knew that while Amy and I didn't take time off with TJ, maybe we had become less focused than we should have been. Now we had to refocus. Our son needed us.

Then the chatter resumed, and we spent the next hour catching up, talking about jobs. Amy revealed that her boss had asked her out. He also subtly tied his romantic interest in her to her future success at the company. Amy said she politely declined his date request. I said I hoped that would be enough.

In my view as an avid watcher of legal-based television shows, this clearly constituted sexual harassment. Amy could pursue those charges. It would end the situation at work. She wanted to avoid making it a big issue. He seemed to take her rejection of the date well enough, she said. Then she did something so charming that all I could do was smile. She held up her hand and crossed her fingers. We also talked about Mom and how we both missed her, how Dad was holding up, the kids. I never mentioned Sara and my developing relationship with her. I didn't want that to intrude on what seemed like a perfect Saturday morning, just like so many of those days we had enjoyed in the past. In retrospect, I certainly should have recognized that as a sign. Maybe I didn't see the relationship with Sara as having legs to really go the distance. While the thought was just fleeting, it didn't really disturb me.

—x—x—x—

The following Friday I got the phone call from Amy. "Robb, he's okay. Don't worry. He's okay, but they're going to keep him in the hospital overnight. Oh, God. I'm so relieved, but he's okay." Then she began to sob.

It took me a moment to catch up. The call at three o'clock in the morning jolted me out of a dead sleep. I saw "Amy" come up on the caller ID on my cell screen and immediately became hyper-alert as I took the call.

"Amy. Amy! What's going on? TJ? You're talking about TJ?"

"Yes, and he's okay."

"Good. Now tell me what happened and where he's at."

"He was in a car accident. He wasn't driving. His friend Christof was driving. He was drunk. They all were. He took a turn too fast, and the car hit a telephone pole. TJ was in the passenger seat. He banged his head and probably has a concussion. He also slammed his elbow into the dash. And they are x-raying that right now."

"When did this happen?"

"About an hour ago. They took them all to Mercy. Christof is probably in the worst condition. He probably has a concussion, too, and he might need surgery for internal bleeding."

"Ames, are you at the hospital yet?" I asked.

"No, I just got the call and called you as soon as I hung up."

"Okay, I'll swing by and pick you up on my way. We'll go to the hospital together. I'll see you in five."

I had started dressing as we talked. When I walked downstairs, I found Dad sitting at the kitchen table.

"I heard your phone ring. Something's wrong."

I explained about TJ. "I'm going to the hospital now. I'll call you in the morning to let you know how he is. Jess is sleeping. Can you let her know what's up when she wakes in the morning?"

"Call me as soon as you can. I won't be going back to sleep." He shrugged. "Old age."

I walked up to him and gave him a hard hug. Dad always said he didn't like to hug, but he'd grown into a hugger. In the past he would stand stiffly while I hugged him. His arms at his side as if standing at attention. Now he wrapped his arms around me and held me tight.

He looked at me with a question on his face.

"Call me when you know something."

I nodded and quickly left.

Amy paced in the driveway when I approached. I jumped out of the car. She ran up to me and folded herself into my arms and stayed there. I held her without saying anything. At the hospital we occupied one of the institutional loveseats in the waiting room. These loveseats encourage anything but love. Amy sat close to me, our shoulders touching. We sat in anxious silence. After a few minutes, she held my hand.

In my mind, I identified this as muscle memory. This closeness with Amy, the touching, the need to be with each other, without the need to talk to each other, the knowledge that everything was right with the world as long as we were together, enveloped me and transported me back to those days of high school, when Amy and I could have led fulfilled lives in any context as long as we were together, as long as we could always reach out and touch. Guilt assaulted me again. Despair throttled me. As Amy and I sat in the darkened waiting room, waiting for daylight, waiting for TJ to come back to us, I started to cry, silent sobs that wracked my body. Amy didn't say anything. She just continued to hold my hand.

When I could speak again, I said, "I'm sorry."

"I know."

Then time passed.

The nurse at the station said we could see TJ when he awoke. They let us know that he was stirring at about nine. We went to his room. I stood silently at the foot of his bed. Amy pulled a chair beside him and took his hand. Slowly TJ came back to us.

When he opened his eyes and saw us, he draped his arm over his eyes, and groaned. The doctor came through a half hour later, gave TJ a cursory examination, and signed the discharge papers. We led him to the car. Beyond some basic questions about how he felt, none of us really said anything. TJ had a headache, and his arm was throbbing, the kind of dull, intense throb that painkillers can't reach. He had fractured his elbow and would have to wear a soft cast. He wanted something to eat, so we hit the McDonald's drive-through.

TJ nibbled at his food. Once he smelled it, he realized that eating required more attention than he could muster at that point. The smell also made him nauseous, probably the painkillers working against his desire to eat. I drove to Amy's house, our house in another lifetime, and we settled TJ on the couch. He fell asleep almost immediately, showing only marginal interest in the Badgers football game on the TV.

I muted the announcers and watched without noticing, a rarity for me. I have to cop to being more than a bit of a fan when it comes to Badgers football. But today, the athletes and the x's and o's strategies and actual plays didn't interest me much. Amy spent time with Jess. Dad had brought her over shortly after we arrived. He was busy in the kitchen preparing a pot of chili. Amy sat with Jess, assuring her that everything would be okay. Jess listened, but as she looked at her brother, doubt shadowed her expression. The expression she wore could have summarized what Amy and I felt but were too afraid to acknowledge. They left the house to shop for dinner.

TJ awoke in mid-afternoon. This time he really was hungry and ate everything I placed before him that he could eat with one hand.

"I guess I screwed up again."

"We all screw up, son. But you need to find a way to screw up that doesn't have the potential to get you dead. Drinking and driving, or riding with someone who has been drinking can get you killed. You came close to that reality last night."

TJ nodded. "If you're up to it, we need to talk about some things." TJ nodded again. We talked through the afternoon. He knew that things could have been a lot worse. I didn't fool myself into thinking that his wild behavior would end here.

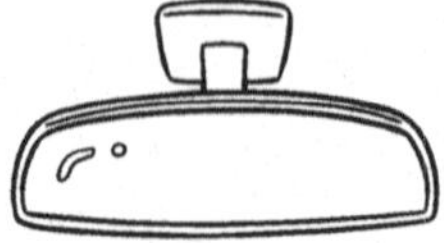

CHAPTER 13

Dad walked slowly from the place where we parked the car about ten blocks away, directly across the street from my old high school. I had always parked at this spot and walked to Camp Randall, too cheap to spend thirty dollars or more for the privilege of parking on someone's front lawn. In years past, Dad and I walked at a normal pace, keeping up with the crowd, moving with determination toward Babylon. The closer we got to the stadium, the more it seemed like a descent into depravity.

A college girl leaned under a garden hose hanging from a second-floor balcony.

"Good heavens, what's she doing?" Dad wondered.

"Beer bong. Gravity increases the flow of the beer. She'll suck hard until she can't take any more. She will either finish the beer in the tank, or the beer will soak her."

"Why on earth would anybody do something like that?" Dad said.

"You get drunk really fast."

"And this is what college kids do nowadays?"

"That's what college kids have always done. Get drunk fast. Are you going to tell me you never chugged a beer in college, Dad?"

"Got me there. But we only chugged one at a time. If you suckle that hose long enough, it looks like you could inhale several beers."

"At least two, maybe three beers before you have to come up for air," I agreed. We moved on.

Everyone wore red or white t-shirts. Most of the college students and most of the adults we saw held a can, bottle, or red Solo cup full of beer. In each front yard college students played different drinking games. Many played the bean bag toss, corn hole, and if you knocked someone's bean bag off the board, they had to chug a beer. Losers always had to chug. Winners drank because they could. Others had moved old ping pong tables into front yards and played beer pong. Adults who had bought parking in someone's front yard laid out card tables and tailgate spreads. Smoke and the scent of charred meat filled the air as many people grilled. The more sophisticated—yes, even some Badgers fans have sophistication—laid out spreads of smoked salmon, various cheeses, and bottles of wine. A festive atmosphere filled the air. Everyone looked forward to Badger football Saturdays, the occasion of seeing and being seen, the joy of cheering for your alma mater, even if you never once stepped foot on campus or matriculated in any way.

The game started at eleven o'clock, so all this tailgating took place at nine thirty. By six o'clock, many of the college students would be sleeping off the fumes, trying to sober up to begin some more serious partying later in the evening. I could speak from experience.

As we approached the stadium, we started seeing vendors. Different food stands filled the corner directly in front of the stadium. Most sold brats and hot dogs. Some sold deep-fried cheese curds, some sold barbecued pork sandwiches. Money freely changed hands. Dad and I always stopped at the Kiwanis stand and had a brat. I paid. I owned a pair of season tickets, so attending a football game together had become a tradition for Dad and me. I called it the father-son weekend. Football had always been something we could connect over. Throughout my entire life, we have watched Badgers games together on Saturdays and Packers games on Sundays. Then when I went to UW and joined the marching band, Dad and Mom would come to the games to watch the spectacle of the band, which all Badgers fans considered the best in all the land.

"Your mom and I always got our brats here from the Kiwanian brothers," Dad said, squeezing some mustard on his brat. "I was only a member of the club for about ten years, but I always liked the work they did. I happily give them my patronage." Every father-son weekend Dad said this. To me it represented part of the ritual.

As we ate our brats, Dad said, "So do you think your plan for well-defined punishment will work for TJ?"

I pondered Dad's question and looked at all the activity of a BadgerBadgers football Saturday. In the past I had always enjoyed the carnival atmosphere, especially when I was in college and for a few years after graduation. When the kids were old enough Amy and I would bring them to games. They always said they enjoyed the spectacle. Just as I always visited the Kiwanis brat stand with Dad, we always brought the kids to the same spot, aware that we were trying to build traditions. One of the beliefs marching band experiences instilled in me was the value of traditions.

"Honestly, Dad, I don't know. It seems we have reached an impasse. I know the car accident scared him. I also know that he is now only starting to feel better physically. The same seems to be true with his friends."

"I think the accident was a pretty serious warning call. We have to make sure we heed the warning," Dad said.

"We?"

"Yes, we." You are now living in with me. TJ also spends half of each week with us. So yes. We. We are all in this together."

Hearing that from Dad gave me a dose of comfort. I trusted him. With Dad involved I knew we would find a way to help TJ get through this time with as little damage as possible.

"Thanks, Dad. That means a lot to me. I know it will affect Amy the same way."

Dad nodded and wiped a smear of mustard off his chin. "Let's go cheer on the good guys," Dad said. We walked slowly to our seats. As I watched the marching band and then the game, some memories of my college experiences snuck in. When I watched the band perform at pregame, halftime, and in the Fifth Quarter, I recalled the long hours of practice leading up to game days. I remembered the partying that would take place after games. Amy joined me at those parties. My band friends became her band friends.

Just as I did in high school, in college I enjoyed varied friend groups in college. In high school and college, you have the natural environment to enjoy these many different friendships. Opportunities abound. Everybody is in the same place, relatively speaking. You live in the same space, you are generally the same age, and have the same opportunities. Many options exist for cultural and social entertainment.

Later in life I found it sad to experience shrinking friendship circles. You tend to do less with fewer people. As adults you might have couples friends before kids, then you tended to socialize with neighbors and parents of kids on the same soccer or baseball teams or Girl Scouts or similar activities. Then if you happen to get divorced, your friendship circles may shrink again by half, depending on how friends line up after the divorce.

After college I remained in close contact with my band friends until the divorce. The good friends made it clear they supported both Amy and me.

Eventually I withdrew from contact with the marching band friends from both high school and college. I felt like everyone was judging me, though I know I was just projecting that sentiment as an excuse to avoid seeing those people.

Life sometimes presents opportunities, both good and bad, that could allow for the renewal of things precious, occasions for connection that would allow you to resume friendships you put on hold.

That moment came about a year after the divorce. It was late January. I had fixed dinner, and because I hated eating alone, I sat in front of the TV and watched the nightly news. My attention shifted as I cut a piece from a chicken breast. I looked up when I heard that a former Madison cop had been killed in the line of duty in Florida. Cops were serving an arrest warrant on a man who turned it into a raging gunfight. The newscaster paused and said, "Former Madison Police Officer and Middleton native," I felt my chest heave when I saw Tommy's picture. "Oh, no!" I said. The headshot showed him with his usual big smile. Tears immediately started to flow.

I couldn't believe that Tommy had been killed. As the story continued it became clear that he died while trying to save the life of a fellow officer, who had been wounded in the gunfight. Tom ran forward to pull his friend out of the line of fire. After the news story concluded, I quickly logged into Facebook. It lit up with band friends sharing their grief. That represented one of the few moments when I saw any real value to social media. Most people at first shared their stunned disbelief over his death. The following day people began posting memories of Tommy. The stories were rich, funny, poignant, and they all shed light on his character. Because Amy had been part of the group that socialized together, I called to let her know.

She expressed her own shock, disbelief, and grief, as you would expect. "Will you let me know what the funeral arrangements are?" I said I would. I knew she would go.

At the funeral friends and family delivered eulogies. I hardly listened, so wrapped up in memories. His supervising officer delivered a brief eulogy and ended it by stating Tom's time of death. "2:36 p.m." Then he paused and said, "End of watch."

Immediately after the funeral one of Tommy's brothers found a few band friends and invited us to the Village Terrace to hoist a few in memory of Tommy. More than one hundred band friends filled the bar. I know I want a band wake when I die. I want people to celebrate, laugh, tell stories, and remember the joyful moments we all shared.

Amy and I chatted with old friends, many of whom we hadn't seen for years. We had to share the awkward news of our divorce.

One of our college "friends," Hal, who drank way too much and lost all tact when drunk, approached us. We stood next to each other and were enjoying another story about Tommy. Hal, with a beer in each hand, looked at Amy sideways. "I didn't expect to see you here, given the divorce and all." I face palmed and was about to light into Hal.

Amy gently put her hand on my forearm, smiled sadly at Hal, and said, "Someone in the family died. Where else would I be?"

—x—x—x—

I remembered all of this while I sat with Dad at the game shortly after TJ's accident. Dad and I talked some during the game. We cheered at the right times. We were both distracted by memories of our families. As I sat at the game and feigned interest, I lingered over the memories of Amy. I enjoyed some great times, some wonderful moments of happiness in my life. For most of the big events in my life, always there was Amy. I kept remembering the poignant sentiment she expressed when we had attended Tommy's funeral and she said someone in the family died. It made me think of our own family.

Though I found myself inadvertently recalling past times, those memories couldn't push aside worries for my son.

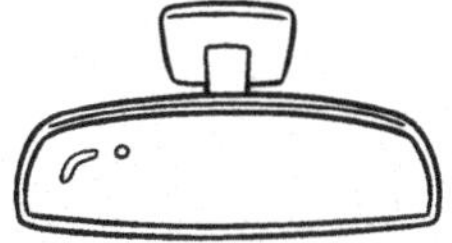

CHAPTER 14

Hitting milestones always leads to transitions. Some transitions prove easy. Some more difficult. Some raise big questions. Some answer them. Learning to ride a bike and going to school for the first time are both significant transitions. I moved fairly easily into both of those new phases of my life. It didn't take me long to find my balance without the training wheels. That ease of movement from one phase of my life to the next was like Michael Jordan on the basketball court. Okay, maybe not that smooth, but I really did seem to float forward from one phase of life to the next.

It took me much longer to find my balance after my divorce from Amy.

—x—x—x—

From the start, though, from kindergarten forward, school happened with ease. I could do school, in part, because teachers and other kids liked me. I have always known that I connected well with other people. If such a thing really exists, I emerged as a leader in kindergarten. When bullying erupted, I stopped it. At least that's what Mom always told me. She got regular reports from my teacher, a friend who lived nearby. Apparently, I encouraged kids to share everything—crayons, balls, books, food. My benevolence really appealed to one of my classmates. We went to school in the afternoon. Each day at the end of our session, I took Diane behind the piano and gave her a nice kiss goodbye. I guess I also always possessed at least some charm with the ladies.

In part I'm sure I did well because I always liked school. I liked books. I liked to read. No, I loved to read. From the moment I entered the world, as Mom used to say, I loved stories, which led to the love of reading. She started me off right away with books. She always read me stories before bed. When the letters on the page started to separate into individual blocks, and then those blocks became decipherable as words, the world opened up to me. Words, stories, books whisked me away to other places, other times, other people. Long before I understood the nuances of characters, symbols, or themes, I sensed that a good story led me to more, more knowledge, more understanding, more confusion, more happiness, more emotion, more wonder, more of myself. The stories fascinated me. I couldn't wait to finish one story and read the next.

A moment of panic set in when I graduated from picture books to my first chapter book. Each Saturday we went to the library, and Mom would let us check out as many books as we wanted. With picture books, I always checked one out for each day of the week. The first time I checked out the chapter books, I checked out one for each day of the week, as usual. Mom didn't say anything. She just raised an eyebrow. As soon as we got home, I started reading the book for Saturday. I experienced a moment of panic almost as soon as I started reading.

"Mom, Mom, what do I do? I've read to here," I said, pointing to the bottom of the page. "How do I keep reading? I know there's more story, but what do I do?" Mom calmly reached over from her spot at the kitchen table where she was reading *Good Housekeeping*. She licked her index finger and calmly turned the page. That simple gesture changed my life. I've been turning pages ever since.

I loved everything about school, and it came easily to me, so I found success in all aspects of school.

The transition from elementary to middle school brought two challenges, both of which I aptly solved on the first day. I worried about unlocking the lock on my locker. Mom patiently helped me learn the requirements of unlocking the combination padlock. The other challenge was the schedule. Instead of staying in the same classroom all day, we had to change classes every hour, moving down the halls from one room to the next, hugging the lockers to avoid the older students, holding the books and notebooks tightly in our arms to prevent older boys from dumping our books to the ground by shoving them out of our arms. Once I got through that first day, opening my locker and moving from class to class, I knew middle school would be fine. My aptitude and ability earned me spots in the top learning groups and, eventually, the honors classes. I earned good grades. Mom stressed the importance of school. I knew school would bring me more opportunities. By the time I went to high school, I knew I would go to college.

Learning to drive was another major transition. Every sophomore seemingly longs for that time when they start driving. My first driving experience, though, came when I was about fourteen when Dad initiated me into the wonderful world of driving. Dad and I went to the cottage for a long weekend. He wanted to finish prep work and then start painting the cabin. We had five days. Dad figured that would be enough time. He gave me no choice but to help him with this chore.

"But Dad, when will I get to fish?" I had entered that phase where all I wanted to do at the cabin was take out the boat and dip a line. Part of that desire to fish came from a desire as a teenager to find my own space. Part of that desire also came from really enjoying the act of fishing. Although I hardly ever fish anymore, on a primitive level I still enjoy it and know that when I get old it will be an activity I resume.

"You could always wake up early and drop a line. I hear the fish bite the best in the morning and in the evening. You'll have plenty of time. We'll paint from about eight to five, just like a regular workday." And that's just what we did. When we painted, we didn't talk much. I plugged in my radio, and we listened to the local FM station. It didn't have much to offer me, though Dad seemed to like it. Generally, you heard Whitney Houston, David Bowie, Prince, Springsteen. Occasionally, they played Boston, Aerosmith, or Queen tunes. Generally, they leaned more toward softer rock. Funny how I now crave music by those artists.

This FM station was okay to paint to, better than silence anyway, though I think Dad probably would have preferred silence. Dad painted the boards on the bottom, while I hung from the ladder and painted the upper ridge. First, we scraped. Then we sanded. Then we filled in cracks with putty and then cleaned the wood. Eventually, we primed. Finally, we painted. Dad explained each part of the process and gave me careful instructions as we completed each task.

"Do everything with the grain, son. You don't ever want to go against the grain. Going against the grain just invites problems. That's it. With the grain." In many ways Dad's instructions gave me insights into how to complete certain jobs I would find myself doing as an adult. The instructions also served as primers for how to live life. Going against the grain can feel wild, reckless, rebellious, fun. Eventually, though, you most likely will have to go back and fix your mistakes. At about three in the afternoon the first day, Dad set down his scraper and waved me over.

"We need to go into town to get some supplies and some food. We'll grab dinner in town tonight, and then you can do some fishing."

In town we spent about an hour at Benson's True Value hardware store. Dad knew these guys. When we got in the car, he said, "I really like those guys. Salt of the earth. Good, decent, honest men. Well, how about grabbing some food at Billy Timbers?" Years later when I would engage in conversations with tradesmen at the house or waitresses and other people in service jobs, or people on the bus, or at the mall, I found myself easily talking with these "salt-of-the-earth" people.

Dad showed me that I should always embrace everyone and enjoy what they offered the world because they offered so much. Dad taught me humility and kindness and a celebration of life. It took me a long time to understand many of these lessons from Dad because he never said, "This is what you should do. This is how you should act." He just did it. Later, when I became more reflective, I put those lessons into play. Often, I wish I would have understood his lessons before I self-detonated an grenade into my life and my family.

"Billy Timbers! God, that sounds great. I'm starving." Dad knew folks at the restaurant, too. He talked mostly to them, which was fine with me. We got along okay, but as a rule, we didn't talk much at that stage.

After we left the restaurant and walked toward the car, Dad called, "Robb!" I turned and looked at him. He tossed the car keys at me. "You drive. I had a couple of beers and probably shouldn't."

"What are you talking about? I've never driven before. I don't have the first clue how to do this."

"I'll coach you. You really need to do this. We're up here by ourselves. If something happens to me, you might have to drive into town to get help. So, let's call this your first driving lesson."

"Dad, I'm not old enough to drive. I'm only fourteen." Had I been able to admit the truth, I would have told him the thought of driving terrified me. I sensed, though, that he wasn't going to listen to any excuses. So I climbed behind the wheel.

"Now adjust your seat. Fasten your seatbelt. Set your mirrors."

"How do I know if they are set up right?"

Dad explained the mirrors and then every button, knob, and gauge on the dash. "Son, you've got to know yourself. Know your machine. Hey, now that I think about it, that's pretty good advice for life. Know yourself. Know your machine. You have no idea how often that advice will serve you well." Eventually, we pulled out of the parking lot at Billy Timbers.

At that time, he didn't believe in automatic transmissions, so Dad gave me a rudimentary lesson in shifting. He drove a Fiat, which in those days was a pretty good car. "Watch the tach. You want to shift when you get to three thousand rpms. When you shift, depress the clutch, shift smoothly to the next gear, and then slowly release the clutch until you hit the pressure point." The meticulous lesson continued on and on. I stalled the engine six times trying to get out of the parking lot.

Life, too, is full of those pressure points. You have to get through the pressure point to move forward. Finally, we rode one block on the highway and immediately turned onto the back roads that led to the cabin. I stalled the car several more times. We would lurch and buck like a bull out of the chute, the engine would die, and I would have to start everything all over again. "You're doing fine, son. Just remember to find the pressure point. It is a matter of feel. Once you gain the feel of it, you will never again have any problems driving a manual transmission." Dad spoke with patience, never getting upset with the bucking bronco ride.

By the time we reached the cabin, I had pitted out my t-shirt, and my shorts were clammy from constantly drying my sweaty palms on them. As I got out of the car, my legs quivered. By the end, though, I was starting to figure out how to shift gears.

"Good job, son. You're a natural driver. We'll practice some more before we finish painting. Now, grab your pole and catch us some fish. I'd really like to have a fish fry for dinner tomorrow night." I just nodded. I pulled the boat out into the middle of the lake and relived my first driving experience. I knew I had just experienced a major shift in my life. I wondered how it would affect me. It boosted my confidence.

After that, every time we went to the cabin, Dad made sure I drove when appropriate and safe. These lessons occurred long before the age of enlightenment regarding sound parenting, but once I got my license, Dad made sure I understood one thing. If I ever needed a ride because of drinking or drugs, he would come and get me—no questions or judgment. I never took him up on that because of my driving. Certainly, I probably drove on some occasions under the influence—stupidly—and I most definitely rode shotgun when Steve, Brad, or Phil had been imbibing. You do stupid things when you're young. Truth is you do stupid things throughout your life and just hope you can stay one step ahead of too stupid, where real damage can happen.

Drinking in high school was another one of those milestones. When we started experimenting more with drinking during our junior year, I experimented cautiously. I had my reasons. I didn't want to be one of those people who drank and became someone else, someone out of control. I'd seen enough of it from friends during high school. So I learned how to get a buzz and not stumble completely out of control. I never wanted to be that guy who walked sideways. That came later—in college. Some of my friends started shotgunning beer for the cheers of the crowd. I watched it and laughed, sipping my beer. On some occasions, I let it go a little further.

One time, Cam, Brad, Steve, and I were drinking in Brad's basement. We killed several PBRs each. I finally shotgunned a beer. The entire can emptied in three swallows. My eyes watered, and a huge belch followed. Brad shotgunned three beers, working for that fast buzz. Cam always laughed with giddy glee when he drank. His laugh verged on hysterical. It sometimes opened him up to ridicule from other guys. These friends, though, generally just accepted Cam. He was my friend. That made him okay.

"Let's drink some more beers and then cruise for women. Mothers and fathers, lock up your daughters," Cam shouted. Steve chortled. I just smiled. I knew Brad wouldn't let it go.

"Yeehaw!" Brad shouted. "Let's get on it. Cam, you're our lead tonight. We'll be your wingmen. You get the first pick. Just make sure you leave something for the rest of us."

Cam pointed his beer can at Brad. "You got it, buckeroo." Then he chugged the rest of his beer. I took a few more sips of beer. Brad and Cam each chugged another.

When Brad announced, "Let's cruise," we immediately headed out. Over the two hours we had cloistered ourselves in the basement, about three more inches of snow had fallen on top of the four inches that had fallen throughout the afternoon. Most smart drivers had made it home and settled in for the night. Not us.

We started cruising, mostly looking for action. We drove through the McDonald's parking lot, but it was deserted. We drove by Jenna's house. She was supposed to have some of her friends over. All the lights were off. She must have called it off. Then we drove by Amy's. I just wanted to be near her, even if it meant a quick drive-by. As we drove, we continued to sip our beers. After about forty-five minutes, we found ourselves in the school parking lot. Brad did a few donuts, which is always fun in the snow. Then he parked the car.

"I gotta piss," he said and slid out of the car. We all crawled out of his muscle car and stepped away to relieve ourselves.

Suddenly we stood awash in flashing red and blue lights. A cop shined a spotlight on Brad's car.

"What the hell are you guys doing?" The cop shouted.

"Uh, just relieving ourselves, officer," Brad said, sounding completely sober.

"Get back in the car and go home. These roads aren't safe," he chuckled as he rolled up his squad window. That was the extent of my run-ins with the law in high school. Not all of my buddies escaped high school unscathed. I'll never forget going to a dance in February and watching a cop walk Brian into school, cuffed and looking resigned to the reality of an arrest. He had been drinking in the school parking lot. Stupid. Stupid. Stupid. That incident made me quit drinking until late May, just before graduation.

—x—x—x—

We managed to get through our initiations into drinking relatively unscathed. I realized that TJ needed help getting through this transition because it already seemed like he had moved beyond experimentation into the realm of a problem.

They kept TJ in the hospital for another day after the accident and planned to release him the next day. When I returned home, I found Dad sitting at the kitchen table, reading a book and waiting for me. It's funny how quickly living with Dad became home, whereas I never had considered my apartment home.

"How's TJ?" Dad said, not attempting to hide his grave concern for his grandson.

"He's lucky. He's definitely in some pain right now, and he's doing some soul-searching. But for now, he's okay. But this was a wake-up. I don't know, though. How many kids his age really understand how great the risks are? And they seem to get bigger every year for kids."

"That's probably not true, Robb. I think they just have different toys—much different. You're right, though. TJ might not figure out things. At least not without some serious parental intervention."

"I don't know if I'm the right guy for the job. You know how much I screwed everything up."

Dad didn't say anything. He got up and went to the fridge, pulled out two beers, and grabbed a plate of brownies from the kitchen counter. He set them on the kitchen table.

"Dad, I really don't feel like drinking right now. I don't know if I will ever again."

"Beers are for me. Brownies are for you. I've never known you to turn away from brownies, especially if they are homemade. And I made these this afternoon. Dig in because we've got some serious things to talk about." He slid the plate of brownies toward me.

I grabbed the biggest one I could see on the plate. Dad always sliced the brownies big. He realized bite-sized morsels satisfied no one. I took a bite and started chewing, already eyeing up my second brownie. Dad popped the top on his can of Miller Lite.

"First things first. It's time to let yourself up off the mat."

"I'm not sure I follow," I said. "I thought we were going to talk about TJ."

"We are. And part of talking about TJ means we must talk about you and the way you've been treating yourself. And quite honestly, you've been treating yourself like a piece of shit. Time to let that go."

"I don't think I can. All of this is happening because of how I fucked up," I said, repeating a common refrain.

"I'm not absolving you of what you did. Your actions had consequences. You've been living with them daily. Now you have reached a crossroads. Your son needs you. All of you. He doesn't need a father so overrun with guilt that he can't provide any clarity or guidance. He needs you to be fully present in his life, not constantly belittling yourself for what you did in yours."

"This isn't at all what I expected to be talking about right now," I said a little defensively. I didn't want to get into this. My guilt and shame had become a defining issue for me. If I chose to be completely honest, I would also say that it became a natural excuse for anything bad that happened. Bad things happened in my life because I was a bad person. I had to take no responsibility for anything beyond saying I got what I deserved. It was so much easier that way. In essence, it absolved me from responsibility because I essentially convinced myself I held responsibility for everything. Now Dad was saying I had to give up what had become a big part of my current identity. I didn't know if I could or if I even wanted to.

"No, probably not. But it's what you need to do. It's time now to lay that burden down. You are a wonderful person, Robb, and a great father. You just won't let yourself believe that those qualities actually do define you. You've got to get out of your own way and start living up to your potential. That's when you will really start helping TJ."

"I don't think I know how to do all of that."

"Well, that's what we're going to figure out. You, me, and we're going to bring Amy in on this, too. I've invited her to dinner tomorrow night, and we're going to have a family meeting."

—x—x—x—

Dad asked me to help with the dinner preparations. I made two different kinds of salads. Dad baked a pecan pie. Somewhere along the way, he became quite a baker. And he grilled steaks wrapped in bacon, the candy of meats. While he tended the grill, Amy and I made the final preparations in the kitchen. The kitchen was always where our family gathered, where both the special and common times occurred that bound us together as a family. We would sit at the kitchen table, where we could settle in comfortably for a long discussion. It was the place where we always gathered, where our family throughout my life tended to define itself.

Some of my favorite memories involve Mom hovering over the stove while she participated in whatever conversations simmered around her. Occasionally, as the act of eating moved closer, Mom would start shouting instructions about clearing and setting the table. "Set it for five tonight. We don't know yet if Shelly will be here in time to eat with us, but set a place anyway. No, not the fancy dishes. Who do you think we are, the Rockefellers?" And just as we sat down to eat, Shelly would come running in to join us, dashing home from her play practice. Mom held the family dinner hour as sacred, and through most of my life in that home, we all ate together.

After Amy and I started going out, we never questioned if she would join us. If she was in our house, she would eat with us. Mom loved to cook. She believed that children should experience rich food aromas in their home. They should have ingrained in their head the smell of fresh bread coming out of the oven. They should be able to smell chocolate chip cookies when they come home from school, knowing they would be in for a treat. They should know vast varieties of smells that indicate a new treat or an old favorite would arrive on the table for dinner. Mom said these smells created memories. I couldn't smell fresh bread or steaming hot cookies without thinking of her. In the months since her death, I found myself tearing up in bakeries and coffee shops.

It felt comfortable working with Amy in the kitchen. We knew this space as well as we knew our own kitchen. We had prepared many meals here, starting with frozen pizzas when we were in high school and eventually moving into more complicated culinary creations as our tastes became more sophisticated. I still find myself salivating over a good plate of spaghetti and meat sauce, and I frequently whip up this simple dish exactly as Mom taught me.

With the table set, Amy and I waited for Dad to come in with the steaks.

We had been chattering about nothing specific, but we lapsed into silence. For the first time in years, the silence felt comfortable. Dad came in with the steaks, and my mouth involuntarily opened. The smell of charred meat appeals to me in a visceral way. It took a couple of years for the revulsion of the smells to leave me after my high school job. But once I digested that disgust, I found myself again drawn to specific smells and tastes. Like spaghetti, mashed potatoes, and pumpkin pie, grilled meats again came to represent comfort food to me.

"Okay, who's hungry? These steaks look good. Let's dig in," said Dad. We all filled our plates, and for several minutes we didn't speak other than to share compliments on the food. It was just the three of us. Jess was catering to TJ's needs at Amy's house. She wanted to take care of her brother.

"All right," Dad said, interrupting our grazing. "We got a family problem that we've got to figure out. TJ is in trouble, and he needs our help. So the three of us are going to figure this out."

Dad had decided to run this meeting. He looked intensely at Amy and me, sitting next to each other and across from him. We quickly glanced at each other. She nodded at Dad.

"Okay," Amy said, "but I'm out of ideas."

"Robb, how 'bout you? What ideas do you have?"

"Not really anything. Whatever we've tried obviously hasn't been working. So it seems like we need to go in a different direction. Do you have any ideas?"

"A few. Some are pretty straightforward. One might appear pretty radical. First, when TJ screws up, we need to hold him accountable."

"We?" I asked.

"Yes, we. Robb, Amy, and yes, me. I'm in this, too. You know the phrase: it takes a village. Well, I'm part of this village."

"Okay, so how are we going to hold him accountable? He doesn't do what we ask, and if we try to punish him, he just gives that taunting laugh and leaves," Amy said.

"Robb, I've talked to you about this, but we start taking things away from him. We make him participate in the life of the family. He's going to start doing chores again. If he won't do chores, we take away all privileges. When the family gathers, he will be a part of it. No more of this going off on his own. He has tangled himself up in a really destructive group of friends.

"Your mother always said, 'Show me who your friends are, and I will know pretty much everything I need to know about you.'

"Well, she was right. Right now, he has settled for essentially the lowest common denominator of friend groups. It is easy to be friends when everyone just wants to party. We must find a way for him to realize he has to aim higher. But we can't tell him that he can't be with this particular group of friends. He would just resist that wholeheartedly. He has to figure it out himself. That's partly where we come in. We're going to make it more difficult for him to be with his friends."

"How are we going to do that?" I wondered.

"I have two ideas. Like I said, the first is conventional; the second is radical. Ready?" Amy and I nodded. "First, he is going to get a job."

"Not sure he will agree to that," I said.

"We're not giving him a choice," Dad replied. "He has shown us that we can't trust the choices he makes. Only when he rebuilds our trust will he start to get choices back."

"Boy, where have we heard that before?" Amy said. "You always have choices ..."

"You just have to recognize that those choices come with consequences," Amy and I said together. We had heard it from Mom many times. We both chuckled a little bit. We delivered the same message to our kids when they were younger. TJ started disdaining the consequences as he entered high school.

"TJ has started to act entitled, like he doesn't have to work. He just asks for money, and he plays off Amy and me. Right, Ames?" Amy nodded at me, her eyes solemn. "He has learned to play the guilt card effectively. To assuage my guilt, I just open up the wallet."

"Robb's right. He is pretty good at that. He has never once mentioned getting a job. Why would he need to if we just keep giving him money?" Amy wondered.

"Okay. As of now, we are done giving him money. The bank is closed. So if he wants to buy a candy bar or a pack of gum, he better have his own money to pay up. We aren't going to just hand him cash anymore. In terms of a job, we're not going to give him a choice. Because of the way he has been acting, we are going to start limiting his opportunities for choices."

"Okay, so what kind of jobs are you thinking about? McDonald's, Taco Bell, Target, that kind of thing?" Amy asked. "I really think TJ believes he's above that kind of work."

"I've already made arrangements for a couple of things. I think he should be working two jobs—one during the week and one on the weekends."

"Dad, that's a lot of time. What about his schoolwork? He's got to make sure he keeps up with that."

"How are his grades? He has always seemed to do well in school," Dad wondered.

"He's got a 3.67," Amy quickly noted.

"My God, is that all? What the hell! Doesn't he work at all in school?"

"I get it, Dad. Sarcasm, right?" I said, smiling at him. Even when we were dealing with a difficult subject, Dad could always inject humor.

"Right. Either he gets two jobs, or he goes out for a sport. He needs something that will take up big chunks of his time. School is obviously important to him, so it is unlikely that he will let that slide, especially if we keep track of how he is doing."

"He doesn't have that much interest in sports. He never really has," I said.

"I always see him doodling. Does he like to draw?" Dad wondered.

"He does anime a lot. He has a definite style to what he does. I've also seen him scribbling stories to go along with his doodles. Maybe he has an interest there that we should pursue," I added, starting to feel some enthusiasm, something I hadn't felt for a very long time in any area of my life. "Maybe we could find a way for him to connect with some artistic types. That might be something he would take to."

Amy looked skeptical.

I looked at her and shrugged. She paused for a moment, collecting her thoughts. "Given where TJ is right now, I don't think we can really push him in any direction. I'm not saying I don't like these ideas, and I also really like the positive energy. But if we push, he is going to rebel even more. He's a little lost, and he's hanging with the wrong bunch of kids. If we tell him this is what he is going to do, we're going to lose him."

"What do we do, Ames? Nothing seems to be working right now. I see what Dad's getting at. We have to limit his choices and his options. I think we have to lay down some very hard boundaries. Some behaviors are unacceptable. No debate. No negotiation," I said.

"I agree with that, Robb. And I think he should get a job. I don't want to tell him what job to get or what activity to join," Amy said.

Always the negotiator, peacemaker, and problem solver, Dad said, "How about if we have a family meeting and we tell him that he will get a job, and he will join at least one activity at school. Non-negotiable. What he does is up to him."

I gave a small nod. I really liked the idea of pushing him into something like anime, but I saw Amy's point. We had to present a united front to

TJ. That didn't mean I couldn't find some ways to make some subtle suggestions to him at some point.

"Dad," Amy said, and I looked up immediately. It didn't really register until that moment that she had never stopped calling him Dad. Probably a force of habit. "You said you had two very specific suggestions. We've come to an agreement on one. What's the other?"

"TJ needs to move in with us and spend the majority of time here."

I must have physically flinched, but none of us spoke.

"Amy, you've been carrying the load alone with TJ. We're going to start pulling the wagon now. It's our turn. And it will be a little bit easier with the two of us here. It doesn't have to be a permanent situation. But you need a break. And to be quite honest, so does Jessie. She's watching her brother make these bad choices, and it really hurts her. She feels helpless, and she's very sad."

"What about them as brother and sister? Are we disavowing that relationship?" I asked with a little bit of defensiveness in my tone.

"No, not at all. We're going to strengthen it," Dad said.

"How's that going to happen if they aren't together?" I asked.

"Family dinners. All of us. Every night at six. I'll cook. I've got nothing better to do, and I've been hankering for a legitimate reason to get back in the kitchen."

"It seems like you've got this all worked out," Amy said.

"I've given it a little thought," Dad said with a shrug.

"What if TJ has to work? We did say that he had to get a job." I wondered.

"He does. But he won't be working every night. On those nights when he works, we'll still have the family dinners together, and I will keep food warm in the oven for him."

Amy and I spent several minutes absorbing this information. We both stared at the kitchen table, boring holes in the grain. I wondered if TJ would agree to this or succumb to this, or if he would rebel even more, or if he would dive deeper into illicit substances or run away, or, or, or ...

Amy wondered what would happen to these dinners if we had to work late, or if Jessie wanted to have dinner with friends, or, or, or ...

Dad sagely responded. "You can come up with a lot of reasons not to do this. We have to make this something that becomes ritual, something that none of us are inclined to miss. Working late is an excuse that can fly once in a while. But if either of you starts missing dinner often, why would TJ think that this was something he had to adhere to?"

"Why do you think," I interjected, "that these family dinners are going to become so appealing?"

Dad didn't say anything immediately. He took a sip of coffee and looked out the window for a long moment at the rose bushes in the backyard. Then his gaze returned to the kitchen. "Because your mother asked me to do this before she died. She said it was important for me, for you, for us, to have a family. And she always knew what was best for the family. I made a promise to her to do this. And I have been waiting for the right moment to make the proposal."

Silence ensued as we pondered Dad's reason for reinstating family dinners. Mom wanted this to happen.

"Don't you think it might feel awkward, forced?" Amy asked.

"Absolutely. At first. We just have to keep working through it until it stops feeling awkward and then starts to feel like something we should be doing, until it starts to feel like a given that we have a family meal together every day, and then until it feels like something none of us want to miss."

"No offense to Mom, but what if this doesn't work?" I asked. Failure of the family dinner loomed as a real possibility.

"We're all thoughtful, compassionate, loving people. We'll make it work. If at some point the endeavor really seems doomed to failure, we'll reassess. Think it over. And then let's decide."

"When do you want us to decide? It seems like Amy and I might want to talk this over ourselves first."

"Tonight. You can talk as much as you want right now. I'll go watch some television while you chat." Dad pulled himself out of the chair and slowly shuffled out of the kitchen.

Amy and I looked at each other and shrugged. Then silence fell while we digested the idea of a daily family meal. I know Amy was thinking the same thing as me. We weren't a family. Not really. We hadn't been for several years. Why would this work now? The silence pushed forward. It didn't feel awkward. Each of us had to consider the angles and possibilities.

We pondered all of this as if we were contemplating how to cook the most important seven-course meal in the history of families. What would we select as the main dish, side dishes, desserts? What if those selections led to nothing but indigestion or, worse, food poisoning? Only this would be worse than food poisoning. It would be family poisoning, the kind of malady from which all of us might never recover.

"Does this seem kind of crazy?" I asked.

"Yes and no. I think Dad is right. We need to shake things up. We need to do something to pull TJ back to us, and we need to pay attention to

Jessie, too. I don't want her to become collateral damage. If you're willing to have TJ live here and put in the daily hard work and monitoring, I'm willing to give it a try."

"Ames, you know I'm willing to do that. Through it all I never stopped loving our children or being a father to them. But there's more at play here. You and I are going to have to spend time together every day. We are going to have to be kind and thoughtful not only to our children but also to each other. And, well, even though time has passed, our divorce remains a sad thing."

"True, but not really contentious, just an ending. And those are usually sad. We didn't scream and yell at each other. We didn't fling dishes. And we didn't have cops intervening in our screaming matches because we didn't have those kinds of fights. Make no mistake, our marriage ending made me sad, so very sad. Time has passed. Sadness tends to pass, too. Whatever happened between us, we will have to put aside. And I think we have already done that. We're friends. And in truth, Robb, even at the worst of it, I've always considered you a friend. My best friend. Spending time with you to help our children isn't something that will make me uncomfortable."

She paused. That sentiment hung in the air. I just looked at her. I didn't know what that comment meant. I didn't know if we were now supposed to also make that another layer of this conversation. I decided to move the conversation back to the topic of TJ.

"Do you think TJ will agree to this? Or is all of this just mental masturbation? Talking, talking, talking, as if we know what we're doing. Three people grasping at air. Throwing plastic at a Velcro wall and hoping it sticks. Spending a lot of time thinking about the problem and possible solutions when we really don't have a clue. Should we maybe be doing something else?"

"Robb, you are a great father. I think this could be something good for our son. And I think it's worth a try. But is having TJ move in going to crimp your lifestyle?"

"What lifestyle?" I asked a little defensively.

"Going out with people. Cam, others. Perhaps dating. The single man lifestyle."

She didn't say anything about any specific woman, but the subtle accusation existed. I dated. She didn't. It had been relatively easy to pick up women or enter casual relationships built mostly around sex because I didn't have the kids with me all the time. I entered those casual relationships mostly out of boredom and loneliness. None of the pickups had ever materialized into anything.

My fledgling relationship with Sara loomed as a possibility, but if she meant that much to me, why hadn't I called her in six days? For that matter, why hadn't she called me? I texted her to let her know that I had some family stuff to address. She gave me the briefest acknowledgment possible. She texted back: "OK." That was it. Nothing else since, either. As I sat in my dad's kitchen across from my ex-wife and we contemplated resuming family relations in some form, I wondered what this would mean for any possible relationship with Sara and how she would deal with that. I didn't know her well enough to predict any kind of reaction. I pushed those thoughts aside and said to Amy, "What matters here is our son. I will do whatever I can for him. I will make whatever sacrifices I need to make to take care of him."

"Good. I know you will. I just wanted to hear you say it," Amy said. "Saying it makes it a commitment."

Her last comment made me think about the sanctity of our wedding vows. I had said those, too. I didn't carry through on the commitment.

"Okay, what about these family dinners?" I asked.

"Dad seems pretty focused on the concept," Amy said. "Jessie will think it's fun. TJ might go along grudgingly, but I don't really think he's going to buy into the whole Walton family togetherness fantasy."

"You remember that old TV show, too." I laughed. I shared a memory with Amy. "When we were young kids, we watched reruns of *The Waltons*."

"Yeah, our family did, too. It was good, wholesome family television," Amy said.

"Well, you know how it always ended—people in the family saying good night to each other. Good night, John Boy. Good night, Mary Ellen. Good night, Momma. We did that once, calling good night from room to room. Mom let us go through two rounds, and then she said, 'Shut your damn mouths and go to sleep. Good. Night!' But you could hear the laughter in her voice. We all busted out laughing, all of us in our separate bedrooms. We laughed ourselves to sleep. It was a special family moment. From that point on, whenever we said good night more than once, Mom would pull out her old line: 'Shut your damn mouth and go to sleep.' It always made us feel happy going to sleep."

I smiled at the memory. Amy let me linger in that memory. Then she pulled us back to the moment at hand.

"So back to our wayward son. We have to approach this like I think

Dad wants us to. We have to look at this like the government bailouts a few years ago. We have to look at it as too big to fail and make sure we do everything we can to keep failure from happening."

"Wow. Did you just make a political analogy? I have never heard you do that before," I said.

Amy paused and looked out at the rose bushes. "I like the analogy. We can't let this endeavor fail, or we are putting our children's lives on the line. Both of them."

Another silence ensued. After fifteen minutes, Dad walked back into the kitchen and sat down. He just looked at both of us. The stare-down lasted for about five minutes. Amy broke the silence.

"I'm in. Family dinners and all," she said.

I nodded in agreement.

"Okay. We start tomorrow. Dinner is at six. I'll do burgers on the grill," Dad said with finality.

I wasn't so sure about all this, but I tried to show some enthusiasm. "Good, good," I said.

Both Amy and Dad gave me gentle smiles.

—x—x—x—

TJ didn't speak during dinner. Not a word. He also barely ate. It was like watching a boy push peas around his plate because he couldn't stand to eat them. The rest of us tried to talk, but efforts at conversation stalled. Everything seemed forced. Jessie probably injected the most life into the conversation when she talked about the latest antics of her history teacher. He wanted the students to get the point of civil disobedience as opposed to violence and destruction.

"He pumped music from his phone to his Bluetooth speakers, blasting the metal as loud as it would go. He did this while we were writing the quiz that he just passed out.

"'Ahem, Mr. Clausen,' one of my classmates shouted to be heard over the music, 'we're trying to write your quiz here.'"

"'What, you don't like my music?'" The student nodded. Mr. Clausen nodded. Then he leaned over and turned the music up to full blast. We must have given him this dumbfounded look. He slouched back in his chair and flipped us all off. Then he said, 'What if I told you I can do whatever I want.'

"Then students leaped into the discussion, arguing all kinds of points, most saying that our freedoms ended when they harmed other people. It was like everyone had something to say. It was really quite impressive. He got us to think. It was outrageous. He does that kind of thing all the time. Everybody loves his methods. He is so funny. I saw him this one time talking with another teacher in the hallway. Clausen has a goatee. This other guy was trying out a soul patch. As I walked by, I saw Clausen point at himself and say, 'worldly,' indicating his sophistication, and then he pointed to the other dude and said, 'unsophisticated.' I busted out laughing. Both of them did, too."

We all listened to Jessie's story with rapt attention. I found myself thinking about old Joe Anderson, who I had for con law in high school. We studied some of the seminal historical cases involving constitutional law. He was a lawyer and knew what he was talking about. But he taught in a very different way, much more soft-spoken. He never would have blared music like that. But he got us to think. He told us, "Don't ever be afraid to sit on a stump and think. More people should give it a try." One of our more exuberant classmates while talking about Howard Hughes, said, "He had money coming out of his ass."

Old Joe gave a sardonic reply: "Well, I'm not sure he kept it there," and then he went on to make his point. He didn't preach, but he imparted wisdom.

—x—x—x—

I wish I could have summoned some of his wisdom as we explained the changes to Jess and TJ. Revelation of the plan went over like George Bush's plan to invade Iraq after 9/11. It was going to take a lot of convincing. I had picked up TJ and brought him back to Dad's. That conversation proved awkward.

"TJ, your mother and I look at this most recent incident as a warning sign. You are in trouble," I said.

Then Amy joined in. We had discussed our strategy before I picked him up. "TJ, your behavior really seems like a cry for help. We're telling you that we have heard you, and that we are going to respond, which means that from here on out, we make some changes."

TJ didn't say anything. He also didn't look at us. He either stared at his shoes or at the darkness beyond the kitchen window. Dad sat at the table, saying little but nodding at Amy and me, showing his support. We were a team.

"First," I continued, "you are going to start living here with Gramps and me."

TJ started to protest.

"Nope. That is the first of three non-negotiables. You don't get a choice here. This is the way it will be."

"Second, you will get a job, actually two jobs—one during the week, one on the weekend," Amy said.

TJ laughed.

"Hush," Amy continued. "Third, we will have a family dinner together every night. These three are non-negotiable. No debate."

TJ stood up. He was feeling strong enough to rebel. "Fuck this! I'm outta here."

"Put your ass back in that chair, son," Dad said with force. "Now!" TJ looked at his grandfather as if he had just lost his best childhood friend. His grandfather had been the one who taught him to ride a bike, to bait a hook and land a fish, to build model cars, to understand certain football plays. He always looked at his grandfather as a friend. The pictures of them when TJ was young are the kind that would look great as covers for Hallmark Father's Day cards.

TJ sat and worked hard to affect indifference. He couldn't do it. His grandfather had stunned him, shocked him.

"I have a friend who owns a law office. He said he needs someone to help with filing. You could do that work after school for two to three hours," Dad said. Then he continued, "I also have a friend who owns a brew pub. He hires high school students to work, bussing tables, hosting, cleaning. He is looking for someone right now to work weekends. You can contact either of them. Or you can find a job on your own. Your choice. We expect you to report each night on your progress in finding a job."

Throughout all of this, TJ silently and continuously shook his head.

"Remember, TJ, these are non-negotiable," Dad said. "You have no choice. I will be picking you up after school to take you to your job, and then one of the three of us will pick you up after work. You go to school. You go to work. You come home. Period. And when you're home, you will be an engaged member of this family."

"You can't hold me fucking hostage!" TJ shouted.

"Language, please, TJ. You know your grandmother and I don't approve of that kind of language," Dad said, apparently slipping.

"Grammy's dead," TJ retorted.

"Son, do you think I don't know that?" Dad paused for several beats. "She is physically dead, but in this house, she is very much alive. You would do well to remember," Dad said. I nodded at the sentiment. I felt her presence every day.

TJ stood up abruptly, sending his chair crashing into the wall. "Like I said before, fuck this."

"And like I said before, put your ass back in that chair. NOW!" Dad stood up, affecting a menacing look. I remember seeing that look on a couple of occasions. TJ sat down.

Some shouting and more profanity ensued from our son. Gradually, he calmed down. The conversation lurched like when Dad first taught me to drive stick at the cottage. As TJ realized we were serious, he started to accept the situation. Then we moved into a phase where we talked, sort of.

At one point, I asked TJ why he had become so rebellious, and he glared at me. "Well, let's see. You treated Mom and the rest of us like we were disposable—threw away our family. I'm just doing what troubled kids do when their parents divorce. I'm rebelling. I'm drinking. I'm doing drugs. I'm getting into trouble. You know, fitting the stereotype."

I sat silent, gut-punched. The silence grew. Time stretched out. Slowly, tears started to flow. I didn't wipe them away. After ten minutes, I looked at Amy first, then Dad, and then TJ.

"I'm sorry."

TJ just nodded. "Yeah, right. I've heard that before."

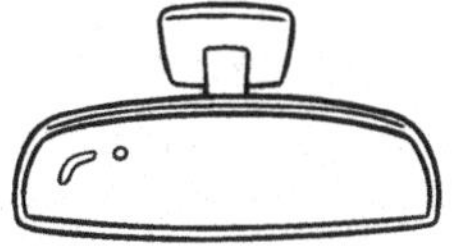

CHAPTER 15

I had arrived. You know when they happen. Some moments mark a rite of passage, and at that moment, you realize your life will never be the same again. You have entered a new realm of possibility. One of those moments occurred for me during my freshman year of high school. Somehow, and I have never really figured out how, I snagged an invite to a cool kids' party. I didn't so much snag it as it fell in my lap. Sandy came up to me after English class. We were walking to our next classes. Sandy was on the elite dance squad. I was a mediocre football player. I still lacked coordination. I hadn't grown through the six-inch spurt that moved my body out of the chubby, lineman range and into the wide receiver category.

Sandy and I had been friends since sixth grade, or I might have been surprised that she was talking to me. The conversation didn't last long. It was long enough, though

"I'm having a party Friday night," Sandy said. "Why don't you come?" She handed me an invitation. I held it with absolute care, as if she had just handed me the original copy of the Declaration of Independence.

My life would change with this momentous Friday night. But the change really came the moment Sandy bestowed the invite.

This represented new territory for me. I didn't really lead a sheltered life, but I hadn't really made it into the high school social scene. Freshmen didn't really have many options. Cam and I usually got together on Friday nights. We would play some ball, play video games, eat all kinds of junk food, watch movies, and talk knowingly, but really unknowingly, about girls. Our Friday nights had been the same since we hit junior high. They were about to change. Sandy didn't say anything about inviting Cam. I just assumed he would join me. I invited him. He declined saying he had no desire to go. I have to admit that I was a little bit relieved. Cam was my best friend. I knew, though, that Cam wouldn't fit in. I didn't know if I would fit in either. I wanted to try. Cam knew he didn't.

Mom wasn't so sure about my entry into the social party scene. She had her rules. Generally, Shelly and I adhered to her rules without much drama. We had a curfew. Violating a curfew was never an issue. We really didn't have opportunities yet, until Sandy gave me the invitation. "I will let you go—under these conditions," Mom said. My curfew would remain at ten thirty. Mom didn't care that the invitation said the party would end at midnight. She would drive me because she was going to meet Sandy's parents and make sure they chaperoned the event. She would pick me up at ten thirty, and I was to be waiting at the door when she arrived.

I put up a little resistance to these conditions. They didn't seem excessive, but I had heard other kids talking. I knew they didn't have to worry about things like a curfew. When I made that argument to Mom, she simply said, "They're not my children. You are. No good comes from being out past ten thirty. You will follow my rules, or you will stay home on Friday night and miss this big party." I quickly backed down. Going to this party seemed too important. Later, senior year, I learned that some good things could happen later at night. Those were things I learned from Amy.

As with most planned events, the anticipation usually holds more significance than the actual event. I didn't really know how to fit in at the party. The music was loud, and though I knew most of the kids, I hadn't really learned yet how to talk to them in a social setting. I stood near the food table in the basement, a paper plate with some snacks in my hands. I laughed when the others laughed. I carefully observed how they interacted. I watched body language. My friend Stevie seemed most comfortable with the scene, so I focused on his demeanor.

Sandy, a great host, made me feel welcome. I'm sure she did the same for everyone else, but I only noticed her attention to me. At one point as I sat on the couch, watching a couple of guys play ping pong, Melissa sat next to me. I knew Melissa from band. She played clarinet. We started talking. Then we started laughing about our band director and how exasperated he got with Brad, our friend who played last chair trumpet, never practiced, and only cracked jokes nonstop. Because he didn't care, Brad would often read off my first chair alto sax part. Melissa and I giggled. We chatted. We giggled some more. At different times she leaned against me. On some level I understood she was flirting with me. A few times she put her hand on my forearm.

The music shifted to a love song. The room became quiet. Melissa slipped her left hand into my right hand. She looked at me. She gave me a slight smile. At this point, it seemed as if I stopped breathing. I know I consciously thought, *I am about to have my first kiss.* Excitement and terror coursed through me. I wondered if I had bad breath. I could feel the sweat under my arms. As if on a roller coaster, my stomach dropped to my shoes. What if I'm a bad kisser? In an instant all this coursed through my thoughts. Then I thought again, *I am about to have my first kiss.* I felt this incredible anticipation and excitement. I also felt completely ready. Melissa leaned in. Our lips met, softly. It became clear that she had kissed before. She kissed me again. By the third kiss I settled in and thought, *This is pretty cool.* We kissed for a while. Time disappeared. So did all the other partygoers. All that mattered was what was happening with Melissa. When we paused in our experimentation, I looked around. It seemed almost everyone else had partnered up and were engaged in various forms of making out. Those without a partner stood awkwardly around the food table, trying to act like they didn't notice all the making out going on in the room.

At one point, someone yelled, "Switch!" Many of the couples disentangled and found a new partner and started making out with them. I looked at Melissa, confused and dumbfounded. "Do we have to switch? I want to keep making out with you," I said.

"Good answer because that's what I want, too." Melissa and I kissed for another hour.

Somehow, I remained peripherally aware of the time. At 10:20, I told her I had to get ready to go because my mom was picking me up at 10:30. "I'll walk you out," she said. At the door as I waited for Mom to arrive, Melissa and I held each other.

"Can I call you?" I asked.

"You better!" She whispered in my ear.

A car pulled up. "My mom," I said, gesturing at the car. Melissa gave me a chaste kiss good night. I walked out wiping my mouth.

As I settled in the car, Mom asked, "Well, how was your first party?"

"Good. It was good." That was all I said. I knew I would have to think about things. It took me a while to get to sleep that night. I kept thinking about kissing Melissa. The next night I called her, and we talked for an hour on the phone. Somewhere in that conversation I asked her out. Suddenly, I had a girlfriend.

My first.

Melissa and I talked at school. I walked her to classes, which often meant I was sprinting down the halls to get to my next class on time. We talked every night on the phone. We went to movies and school sporting events together. I spent a lot of time at her house, and she spent a lot of time at mine. Dad and Mom both liked Melissa.

It turns out Mom liked every girl and woman I ever dated. She never liked anyone as much as she liked Amy. She loved Amy. But Amy wasn't in my life at fifteen. Melissa was. The process of discovering this new, incredible life offering, enraptured me. I suspected it resembled what it must be like to be a one-year-old who somehow suddenly recognized the exponential growth of their world. With Melissa my world both expanded and contracted. Our budding puppy love and progressive physical contact expanded my world beyond anything I ever expected. Because I wanted to have so much more of that physical contact, it also meant my world contracted. Contentment and excitement unsettled me whenever I spent time with Melissa. I wanted to spend as much time as possible pursuing those physical contacts. We kissed. A lot.

Everyone knew we were boyfriend and girlfriend. I didn't think about other girls. She was my first girlfriend, though I certainly didn't think about marrying her. For Chrissake, I was fifteen. Thoroughly blinded by first love, though, I didn't think I could find someone I would want to be with more. While I remained fully focused on Melissa, it turned out Melissa didn't feel quite as committed. Another party six months down the road brought an end to my first love, rending my heart in a pile of savagely torn little pieces.

I had already made plans to spend that Friday night with Cam. He asked me to come over to play some video games. I agreed before Melissa invited me to another cool kid party happening. When I told Melissa I planned to spend the night with Cam, she responded harshly. "Oh my God. What! He's so weird. Why do you want to spend time with him when we could be together all night long?"

"Melissa, we've talked about this. I love spending time with you, but I am also going to spend time with Cam. He's my best friend. You're my girlfriend. This is not a competition. At the end of the night you're the one I want to be kissing."

Melissa laughed at that and gave me a great kiss. When she pulled away, I must have looked a little startled. "Don't ever forget what you just said." She smiled and then she leaned in and gave me another softer, gentler, more loving kiss.

Cam and I played video games. Melissa went to her party. This one, though, ended up being different. The parents left once the party got started, and the kids started drinking beer the parents had left discreetly in the basement in a metal tub covered by a towel. Melissa got hammered. It was her first time getting drunk, she told me later, through the tears of regret. "And then I was talking to Billy about how much I was missing you. He started comforting me. And then he kissed me. I kissed him. And we started making out. He wants to go out with me," Melissa told me the next afternoon.

Confused, angry, and hurt, I stood there, awkwardly silent. I didn't know what to say.

Melissa ended the awkward silence. "I guess I want to go out with him."

"What does this mean for us?" I said, stupidly, not realizing I was getting dumped. I couldn't fathom that she was breaking up with me because while she was hammered, she had swapped spit with another boy and liked his spit better.

Melissa sat there quietly for a moment. Then she said, "It means there is no more of us." She got up and walked out of my life without ever looking back. I didn't know life could be so cruel. Nothing I had experienced could have prepared me for this hurt. I sat on the park bench—someone told her to break up with me in a public place, so she chose Neumann Park near my house. Probably forty-five minutes later, I got up and started walking. I don't know where I walked. I just know I kept shuffling along, one foot in front of the other. Two hours later I finally staggered into the house. My legs ached but not as much as my heart.

"Hi, honey. How was your date with Melissa?" Mom asked.

"Um, not so good. She broke up with me," I said and collapsed into a chair. Mom turned off the stove and sat down at the kitchen table beside me.

"Do you want to talk about it?" Mom asked.

"I really don't know what to say. It seems so strange. Everything was great two days ago. Today I am just the guy Melissa broke up with," I said, my voice quaking like it had two years ago when puberty hit.

Mom sat with me in silence for a half hour. Neither of us said anything. She didn't try to tell me things would get better, I would get over this, there would be other girls, I would love again. None of that. Mom wisely just sat with me. She knew I didn't need to have her platitudes. She just knew that, more than anything, I needed her to sit by me.

She knew.

Mom always knew.

I spent the rest of that Saturday night in pain, sharing some of it with Cam in a long phone call, where I bared my soul to him. Cam just listened. And then finally he said, "Boy, if we were sexually active, I would just tell you to go out and get laid. I hear that's a good solution to heartbreak. But what do I know." Then he started laughing hysterically. I laughed, too.

"Cam, can I be honest? You don't know a fucking thing. But then again, neither do I."

Back at school Monday I felt confused and lost. I had to create new routines. When I walked down the hall to my locker, I saw Melissa down the hall at her locker making out with Billy. I abruptly turned around and walked away. I abandoned plans to go to my locker before first hour and drop off my coat and pick up my books. I went to class without the books and wore my coat until lunch. I altered every route before and after classes to avoid seeing Melissa. By Wednesday I had carved out new pathways. By Friday I was talking to other girls in my classes again.

At that age life swirls fast. What was monumental and life-changing the day before would be passé tomorrow. You feel passionate about everything, but your passions redirect as quickly as fallen leaves dancing in a strong wind. I quickly redirected my passions, putting more effort into training for football, more time into practicing music for band. I started talking to kids in other friend circles, extending my friendships toward them and away from Melissa and her coterie of cool kids.

I dated other girls after Melissa and realized that I really liked spending time with them. I really liked dating. Post Melissa, though, I exercised more caution, more restraint. One girl accused me of being aloof. She wanted me to proclaim to the world that she was my girlfriend. I didn't want to anoint her to that status because I knew I really didn't want her as a girlfriend. I guarded my heart. I dabbled in romance. I dipped a toe in the water. I didn't dive in. Melissa hurt me, so I insulated myself and my heart from more heartache. The breakup hardened me. I wasn't going to give my heart to just anyone. At times I told myself maybe I would never love again. Love hurts too much.

Then Amy.

A love story for the ages. A love story they make movies about. A love story that would make men and women weep. A love story that nothing could put asunder.

And I shit the bed.

—x—x—x—

Post-Amy and post-divorce I seemed to go through my wild partying period. I started drinking more often. Many times I got drunk, numbing myself against the sadness. I also spent time with various women. I didn't so much date other women as I tried to sleep with as many as possible to avoid confronting my emotions. Sex with random women put distance between me and the only woman who ever mattered.

If I did enough walks of shame, I believed I would finally stop hating myself so much for destroying the best thing that ever happened to me. Even when I was destroying my marriage, I knew I would never find a better person than Amy. Never. The only problem with my plan is that it didn't work. Sleeping with different women didn't help me get over the loss of Amy. It only made me feel terrible and absolutely hate myself.

Mom's death filled me with a sadness that pushed aside the shame and self-hatred. I suppose that allowed some emotional room for Sara to make an entrance into my life.

I had enjoyed spending time with Sara. I wondered if it could grow into something more. Something, though, held me back from fully committing to the relationship idea. This reticence came from doubts about myself, but it also came from that sadness I often saw in Sara.

We did typical Madison things on dates. We experimented with what Madison offered in the summer. Several times in the fall we took in the uniquely Madison ritual of Badger football Saturdays. I had held season tickets for decades. I first went to games with Amy. Then we started bringing our kids. For the past couple of years, I took different friends to the games with me. I had one condition: Here's a free ticket. Go to the game with me, and all I ask is that we see the band perform in its pregame show, halftime, and Fifth Quarter, a unique Badgers tradition of celebration. The fifth quarter, a rambunctious free-for-all put on by the band after every home game, allowed fans, who for decades had been disappointed with the team's mediocrity, to find joy in the band. The band celebrated whether the team won or lost. The message was this: We are lucky to be Badgers. We're going to celebrate that. And you damned well better believe that we are always going to have fun.

Sara and I would take in the UW–Madison marching band concert in a festive pregame performance, then saunter to the stadium, walking with people all dressed in cardinal and white. It was like watching a school of fish swimming upriver. Everybody was moving in the same direction, essentially at the same speed, with the same purpose.

Sara, a Badger alum, like me, enjoyed the spectacle of Badger football games. We had both suffered through horrible years of losing football teams. The marching band, though, always delivered. As a former football player, I loved watching the games and could relate to the ebb and flow of the game's action. The real joy for me, though, came from watching the marching band.

Even though I would sit there beside Sara, watching the team and the band, I always found my thoughts drifting to Amy

Sara also really liked to hike. We took several trips to Devil's Lake State Park to hike the bluffs. We hiked through Parfrey's Glen. When we didn't want to drive, we would just go for a walk at the UW Arboretum. On a Sunday just after Halloween, Sara invited me to join her for a stroll at the arb.

We parked in the lot and started a slow stroll over the well-tended paths. Even though it was a nature preserve, you could still see human fingerprints everywhere. In the distance, at the horizon, just past the skeletal trees now braced for winter, you could see cars flying by on the Beltline. Leaves crunched underfoot as we walked, first in an amiable silence, giving a cadence to our stroll. It was a slow drumbeat, each step carrying weight.

I looked around and still saw signs of the just past fall splendor. It wasn't hard to imagine the panoply of beautiful colors. As we started strolling in silence I contemplated the cycles of life. The beauty of fall prepared us for the stark harshness of winter approaching. The landscape had turned to browns and grays, the color of winter coats, as if those dark tones would soak up heat and retain the warmth to help us get through the cold white months of winter. I soaked in the ambience, thoroughly enjoying the beauty surrounding me, a beauty that included Sara. The silence made me think Sara was lost in similar reflections. We enjoyed an easy camaraderie with no drama and no fights.

I assumed Sara also enjoyed the silence of our walk as much as I did. She didn't.

"I don't know, Sara. I just have always really appreciated the changing seasons, especially the transitions. Each season, each change, brings us something new to appreciate, and it also allows us to ease out of those joys of the previous season."

"I suppose so," Sara said.

We walked on.

I paused to study a spider web stitched betwixt two low branches of a tree. The low light of the afternoon illuminated it against the golden-brown backdrop.

"Wow," I said, gesturing at the spider web, thinking Sara would come in for a closer look. She didn't.

"Nice," was all she said.

We walked on.

I tried one more time. "Though I like the changing seasons, it is always difficult to face that first really cold weather. That brittle slap in the face means that we will be embalmed in the cold for the next three to four months, minimum," I said.

"The cold sucks."

That was all. We walked on.

"Everything sucks. The cold. The emptiness of fall. The season of dying, getting us ready for the season of death," Sara said. "Give me spring and summer. Give me colors. Give me hope. Everything, and I mean everything, seems hopeless now." She said this and gave me an intense, piercing look.

My gait faltered. *That sounded ominous*, I thought.

"That sounds ominous," I said, smiling, trying to lighten the mood.

Sara stopped walking. She turned away from me.

"We need to talk," she said. Then she fell quiet. Of course, every person who has ever been in a relationship and heard those words, knows they spell doom. If this were a movie, the soundtrack would soften but vibrate with the key change.

I stood a few feet away from her, waiting for her to start the conversation. She didn't. She just looked off toward the Beltline, breathing with a serious focus. Each breath let out an angry puff of condensation. I could have given her an easy entry by asking her what was bothering her. This was her show, though, and I decided to let her direct the scene. I prepared for the obvious, though I didn't know why it should happen here and now.

Eventually, Sara started to talk. "Things aren't working for me here."

"Does 'here' mean with you and me, or does here mean the arboretum?" Again, I hoped a little humor could warm the day up and blow away the chill that surrounded us.

"Us, of course! What the hell else would I be talking about?" She snapped. It became clear I shouldn't attempt any more jokes.

"I just don't like to assume, Sara. Assumptions always get me into trouble. So I am going to ask you to be as direct as possible."

She looked at me with an expression that to me seemed to be saying, *What the hell kind of moron are you?* I just shrugged. Clearly, I was some kind of moron, but she needed to tell me exactly what kind.

"We're supposed to be in some sort of relationship here, and this is the first time we have seen each other in two weeks. You spend more time with your ex-wife than with your girlfriend. You eat dinner with her every night. You wash dishes with her. You sit on the couch and watch TV with her. And I sit at home. Alone."

She was right about all of that. She had spliced different conversations together. But she had spliced correctly. I had told her that Amy and I did all of those things together.

"A few things going on with my family right now, Sara. I've told you all of that. I've told you that I, we, are trying to save my son's life, literally, and so yes, I am spending time with my ex-wife. Saving my son's life has to be the most important thing in my life right now."

As I spoke, I acknowledged the truth of what I was saying. I accepted I would never back away from that responsibility. I also recognized that it clearly threatened Sara. It made her jealous.

Sara rolled her eyes. She literally rolled her eyes, looked away, and let out a sarcastic laugh full of bitterness.

"Please! Do you really think you are the only parent to ever have a teenage child who rebelled by drinking and doing drugs? Let's not be so melodramatic thinking you are saving his life. Kids do that. Christ, I was a major partier in high school, and by junior year of college I almost never drank again."

"Well, Sara, I don't want to be one of those parents who has to go through life saying, 'I wish I would have done more' while they stare at a photo of the mantle of the child who will never age. I think my son's life is on the line. I am for damn sure going to do all I can to help him get through this. And if it is only a phase, well that's wonderful. But helping him get through this phase will surely bring us closer together. It already has."

"I'm glad it's brought you, him, and your ex-wife closer together. It certainly hasn't brought us closer together." She turned and slowly walked away, ten feet, twenty feet. She stopped, facing away from me, staring down the trail until it curved out of sight.

She turned back toward me, and from twenty feet away, she said, "I need to be in a relationship with someone who is there for me. Who does all they can to spend time with me. Who makes me the most important person in their life. And that is not happening with us."

"What do you want to do, Sara?" If she wanted a breakup, she was going to have to do it.

"You fucking idiot. I'm breaking up with you." She threw some more choice epithets at me, told me she was done with me, and then stalked off back toward the parking lot. The sudden breakup stunned me. It made me sad in a way I hadn't anticipated. I stood there for a few minutes before tracing her path to the parking lot. I needed to steel myself for the silent and certainly awkward ride home.

When I got to the parking lot, I looked for Sara's car. She had clearly left without me. If I would have known she was going to break up with me, I would have insisted on separate cars. She had left me stranded at the arboretum.

I did what made the most sense and started walking down the road that would drop me on Seminole Highway. I figured the walk, close to three miles, would take me at least an hour. Walking is thinking time. I do my best thinking when I walk. I replayed the relationship with Sara and remembered that I predicted Sara would smash my heart into shattered glass. I felt sad, but not sad like I had felt after my first breakup with Melissa and not sad like when my marriage ended. Still sad, though.

By the time I arrived home, I realized that my heart didn't feel shattered. I felt a little sad about the end, but by no means did this breakup overwhelm me. I didn't have that much emotion invested in Sara. Sure, I enjoyed spending time with her. If I was being truly honest with myself, and I finally arrived at that point on the walk home, I knew from the first date that I was not getting into a relationship that would go the distance. Sara's reluctance to fully engage and be honest sent tremors, the kind you feel before an earthquake. More than anything, Sara was a placeholder. It gave me a chance to have someone I could go to dinner and movies with, and maybe enjoy some fun recreational sex.

My walking route took me past Sara's house, which remained dark. She might have been home. I guessed she probably had latched on to one of her friends. By that point, now just blocks from home, I didn't even feel a little bit sad or angry or whimsical over the loss. Tomorrow I would start walking Blue on a different route.

When I turned onto my street and saw Dad's house before me, I smiled. I was going home to the family that waited for me.

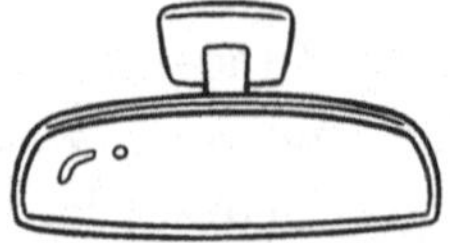

CHAPTER 16

As TJ started contemplating different job options, he suggested a possibility that unearthed a pleasant memory that would suffer some damage because of TJ's subsequent action. When we were seniors in high school Amy wanted us to do something different, so on a Saturday night in February, she brought me back to her middle school haunt, trying to recapture the feeling she had when she was thirteen, and life seemed like one big dance party—on roller skates.

"Wear something polyester. And shiny," she said before our date at Red's Roller Rink.

"I will, if you will."

"Oh, believe me, I have my entire outfit planned. You will be astonished by what I wear, and you will be thinking, who is this gorgeous eighth grader," Amy said, giggling.

"Those kinds of thoughts can get an eighteen-year-old into some serious trouble," I replied.

"Robby, since we are doubling with Steve and Julia, tell Steve to dress appropriately, too."

"Ames, no matter what, Steve is going to wear jeans and a flannel shirt. That will never change. Maybe you could exert some influence, but Steve will just flip me off." I laughed because I knew that was exactly what Steve would do. He didn't disappoint.

"Luigi's before we go to the rink for a good sausage and pepperoni pizza?" Amy said.

"Better make it Pizza Hut. Steve is going to insist on having some beers if he is going to get out there and dance on roller skates," I said. Truthfully,

I knew I would want beer beforehand to give me a dose of courage, and I knew because Amy's friends worked there, they wouldn't scrutinize Steve's fake ID too closely. If I was going to look as ridiculous as I expected I would, I had to have something that would make me less self-conscious.

Steve and Julia had just started dating, getting comfortable with each other, in that stage of being in the fog. The fog in the beginning of a relationship softened all of the edges and made the new partner look absolutely amazing. When the fog cleared and you could see the person more clearly, then you could decide if you realistically saw a future with them. We were all in marching band together that summer before our senior year. We all celebrated together the night we won the band championships. Amy and Julia became instant friends that summer. Steve and I had been friends since middle school. I knew we all would have fun together. Roller skating would allow Steve many opportunities for his sarcastic observations.

After some pizza and a pitcher of beer, we made our way to Red's. Since Amy wanted to do this one, I allowed her to pay the entrance and skate rental fees. We approached the rental counter, and I immediately crinkled my nose. The stench of sweaty feet produced a quick wave of nausea.

"Whoa, that is ripe," I said.

"Yeah, I'm so glad I get to put my feet into someone else's foot sweat," Steve said. I watched the counter attendant skating back and forth, grabbing skates for different patrons. I wondered if everyone who worked here completed their entire shift on skates. I looked at the concession stand, where it appeared that even the two people working over there wore skates.

"Oh, guys, they spray each skate with disinfectant," Julia said. "Grab a pair, strap 'em on, and let's dance." I looked at her. She was bouncing a little, like a little girl hosting a tea party. I looked at Amy. She wore a smile that matched Julia's.

Steve looked at me and rolled his eyes.

"The things we do to humiliate ourselves, just for the girls we like. Right, Robby?" Steve said. He gave me his signature laugh.

I would have to say that I was the stereotypical first-time roller skater. I clung to the rail. My skates slipped out from under me. I pulled myself back up. My feet slipped apart, and I almost completed the splits. *That's going to hurt*, I thought. When I let go of the rail, I fell over and over. After fifteen minutes, I was already sorer than I had been from any football games that fall.

Amy wore a look of distress. "Oh my God, Robby. You're awful. What did

I get you into? I'm so sorry. You look miserable," she said as she looked down at me. I was lying flat on my back after my last fall. She looked concerned but also like she was going to break out into peals of laughter.

I just moaned. I played it up a bit, but not actually that much. I knew the sympathy would be good for some extra passion at the end of the night, if I could move.

"Help me up, Ames, and I'll just grab a seat over by the concession stand. I'll watch you dance the night away. And apparently, I get to watch Julia and Steve, too." Amy and I both watched as Steve and Julia skated by, sashaying to music from *Saturday Night Live*.

I sat down. Amy made like she was going to sit with me. "No way!" I scolded. "You need to get out there and skate. You've been wanting to relive your middle school highlights for some time now. So go out there and skate."

"Are you sure?" Amy asked.

"I am. Have fun. Just don't get crushes on any cute middle school boys. I will try to join you later."

I hobbled to the concession stand and bought a Coke. Then I sat and watched all the skaters. As I watched, I started to figure out some of the mechanics. I was just about ready to give it another try when Amy skated over to the concession area. She joined me and took a sip from my soda.

"Whew, I need a break," she said. A line of perspiration had broken out along her hairline. She was skating mostly for the memories, but she looked like she was having a blast. She had worn a light blue dress that cascaded and flipped with her moves. The sequins, which I know she had sewn onto the dress when she was an eighth grader, flashed under the disco ball. At one point she skated up to one of the guards, who was skating backward. She grabbed his hand and gave him a twirl. Then she was gone, pushing hard around the rink like she was preparing to leap into an axel jump. And then she did leap into a salchow, a skating jump She skated with a huge smile, as if she were skating to impress judges. She impressed me.

"This is fun," she enthused. "I always loved skating. It made me feel so free. I think I should do more of it."

"Okay, but next time, can I forgo the pretense of renting skates and just sit here and watch you grace the rink?" I said.

"You wouldn't have to come again, but I do love it when you watch me," Amy said.

"I've been watching, and I think I am starting to figure out some of the mechanics. I also started putting together some of the things Dad told me before we went out tonight. Did I ever tell you that he worked as a roller rink guard when he was in high school?"

"No way!" Amy said.

"Yeah, for real. And he loved it. When he was in school, he said a lot of his friends hit the rink on Fridays or Saturdays. It was a real social event for him. He got really excited when he heard that we were coming to Red's. And get this. He suggested that he and Mom double date with us sometime at the roller rink."

"Get out!" Amy squealed. "Let's. That would be so much fun." She jumped up and clapped her hands.

Then she pulled me to my feet. "If we're going to double with them, then you have to learn how to skate, mister." Then she gave me my first proper lesson. When I made it around the rink for the first time, I whooped and gave a big fist pump. Then I promptly fell.

—x—x—x—

Amy and I remained skeptical about TJ's sudden acquiescence to the reformation plan. He accepted Dad's offer to work in the law office after school. We made sure that TJ had to log in to the company computer, which their tech person rigged so that we would get a notice on our cell phones. And true to his word, he reported to his job and worked two hours a day, from three thirty to five thirty. Then one of us picked him up.

His weekend job seemed curious to us. He took a job as a skating rink attendant. I didn't know skating rinks still existed. He remembered that his grandfather held such a job when he was in high school. If it was good enough for his grandfather, he could do the same.

He took a job at Red's Roller Rink, our old stomping, er, falling ground. Amy and I drove him on his first Friday night. We dropped him off at the door, and then were about to leave when Amy said, "Pull in over there and park for a minute. Do you remember our first date at Red's halfway through senior year?"

"Of course," I said. "I was in traction for a week."

"Yeah, you were awful at roller skating. It was so funny to watch you fall," Amy said, giving off a pure laugh at the memory.

"Funny for you. Painful for me," I said, smiling. We spent a couple of minutes recounting some of my spectacular falls. Then we became silent as we remembered why we were now sitting in the parking lot at Red's.

"So, what do you think?" Amy asked.

"This job seems so far out of the realm of reality that I just don't know.

Almost like he is trying to prove in a 1950s sort of way that he is listening to his parents. A Beaver Cleaver moment."

"Don't say that to him. He won't have a clue what you're talking about. I agree about this job, but what do you think about how things are going? Is it possible that TJ has heard us and is turning over a new leaf, getting back to the respectful and good son we always knew?" Amy wondered.

"No."

Amy looked instantly sad.

"Too soon. People don't change instantly. If they do, it doesn't take. Believe me, I know something about this," I said.

"So what is going on?"

"He is doing what he thinks we want to see. Then we will slack off, and he will get back to doing what he has been doing, which is fucking off."

"That's an awfully cynical view," Amy said.

"No, just realistic. Remember, he is his father's son. But one thing I do like is having him at home and seeing him start to talk a little bit at the family dinners and watching TV with him after he finishes his homework."

"The family dinners are nice, sort of," Amy said. I raised an eyebrow. "Well, it is forced family time. It doesn't exactly feel natural yet."

"True. Right now we are all just feeling out the situation. We need to give it some time. And trust Dad—"

"Oh, shit!" Amy said and grabbed my arm. "Look!"

TJ had just walked out the front door of Red's Roller Rink. He pulled his hoodie over his head and continued walking, looking at the ground like he was trying to avoid attention, like he had just robbed a bank or something.

"That little shit." I opened the car door.

Amy grabbed my arm. "Wait. I hate to say it, but we have to let him go and see a bit of what he's up to. Follow him, but make sure to leave some distance."

"God, this is like *Law and Order*," I said, starting the car.

"No lights," Amy ordered.

"That's pretty dangerous, babe," I said, and an awkward silence hung in the air. "Sorry, old habit." Amy waved it off.

"Look, he's making a call. I could have sworn we took his phone from him," Amy said.

"We did. That little shit bought a burner phone." Amy stared at me again. "Sorry, old habit." We both busted out laughing. "Okay, enough of this, Ames. Let's just confront him now. Have the scene and take him home."

"You're probably right. It's been kind of fun, though, acting like we were on a stakeout. Even if it was only for a few minutes."

I turned to her, and we fist bumped. "I think we probably will have the chance to do this again."

The confrontation went as we suspected. We heard a lot of profanity, he refused to get in the car, more profanity, him stalking off, us following. Then another car showed up, pulled up slowly beside TJ, who shook his head and angrily gestured at us following him. The car drove off. Then we pulled up beside him, and after more profanity and determined stomping forward, he got in the car, and we drove home. You would think it would have been a silent ride. You would be wrong. TJ screamed at us the entire way.

We both also predicted what followed. Complete radio silence followed. Our son refused to speak with us. He only grunted when his grandfather spoke to him. The silence lasted for three weeks. In that time the "friends" stopped calling. It didn't take them long to move on, showing the true depth of their connection. Eventually, TJ started talking to us again. Ironically, about a second job.

"Can I try to get that second job now?" TJ asked us at dinner. It took a minute before we all looked up. I think I must have had a dumbfounded look on my face. "What?"

"Sorry, it's just that I think I forgot what your voice sounded like," I said.

"Yeah, I was giving you the silent treatment."

"So we gathered," Amy said.

Dad just sat and watched carefully, taking it all in as he always did.

"You all showed remarkable commitment to the cause. I've known for a week that none of you were going to break, not even you, Jessie. And if you want to know the truth, that sort of killed me. You and I have always talked, and it was like you were telling me to fuck off. I know, I know, not at the dinner table. But behind the fuck off, there was another message. It took me a while to figure that one out." He paused.

"And what was that message?" Dad asked.

"You know. You tell them," TJ said.

"That none of us were giving up on you, and we could wait for you to figure that out," Dad said.

TJ nodded.

A prolonged silence followed. It took TJ to break the silence again.

"Look, we've all been quiet long enough. Can we start talking again? I'll try real hard not to be such a dick. I mean asshole. I mean jerk." Jessie started laughing first. Then we all joined in. It was a cleansing laughter.

We laughed for a long time, and I saw at one point that we all were brushing away tears from laughing so hard. My tears came from relief. So did Amy's.

The next night at dinner we started talking about the second job.

"Are you sure you can handle that second job?" Dad asked.

"That was the plan all along, right?" TJ asked. "If you originally thought I could handle it, nothing's really changed."

"Well, actually, there was the violation of our trust," Amy said. "Your intention was to use the excuse of the second job to get drunk or high with your friends. You taught us not to be so naive. You have violated our trust for a long time. It is going to take you some time to earn that back."

Amy didn't say this with cruelty. If you can say something like this with love, she did. She used a firm voice, but all of us could see the love in her eyes. She made it clear that we still planned to keep TJ on a tight lead, as tight a lead as he would need.

"I know. I get that. I'm not just saying what you want to hear. I needed you to do what you have done. I guess on some level I wanted to see if you would do something like this."

"Why?" I blurted out. "Was it some sort of cry for help?"

"To see if we loved him," Dad said with his own quality of gentleness.

"Yeah, those things. And I'm not going to lie. It was a lot of fun to only worry about the next party. But even I know that is not sustainable. Eventually, the bottom falls out of the wet paper bag."

"Okay, TJ, go back to what you just brought up," Amy said. "If you liked the party, how do we know that you won't just go right back to it? It has only been a month since you've been on lockdown."

"Truthfully, those friends stopped calling, I guess. I mean, I don't really know because you have my phone. But I'm pretty sure they have moved on. There is always someone else who is happy to join the party, someone else to take my place."

"And they would be happy enough to welcome you back if you wanted to rejoin the party," Amy said.

"That's just the thing. I really don't want to. I'm not saying I'll never drink or smoke weed again. But it was getting old. I have enjoyed having a clear head again."

We all sat there in silence for several minutes. I remained skeptical. TJ was my son. If he inherited my bad qualities, he would continue to fuck up, just like I had. He was also Amy's son. Maybe those better qualities were showing dominance. I looked around the table, my eyes finally resting on Dad. He sat there with a bemused expression. History repeats itself.

Though as a kid I didn't really get into much trouble, he had participated in this kind of conversation before, especially when I sabotaged my family. He had seen a lot more rebellion from my sister Shelly. He knew that the tentative detente could fall apart in an instant.

Strangely enough, TJ got a job at the roller rink. He said that after thinking about it, the job intrigued him and sounded fun. Amy and I just shrugged. If he was working somewhere and avoiding trouble, it was going to be fine with us. We did another stakeout on his first real night on the job. The next night, the whole family went to skate at the rink, relieved to see TJ trying to stay upright behind the skate rental counter.

We slipped into a routine. Time passed. After Sara broke up with me, I realized I didn't really miss her. My family took all of my focus and energy. TJ's troubles shifted my priorities. One change occurred with minimal effort. I called Alex, a woman I had met just before Mom died. She ran her own business, Shenk and Company. She remembered me, our conversation, and the brief time we spent together, brief being a one-nighter. I wondered if she had any openings. It turned out they were looking for someone at essentially an entry-level position to do computer graphics. There would be good opportunities for advancement. When she offered me a position I leaped at the opportunity. The salary would be fine for now. Most importantly, it got me out of the cubicle farm, which immediately changed my attitude about work. I went in early and ate lunch at my desk so I could be sure to be home for the family dinner. I couldn't afford to fritter away this time with my family. I had work to do. A promise to fulfill for Dad.

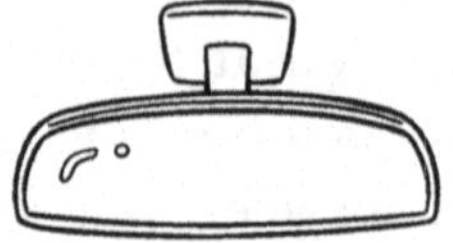

CHAPTER 17

I took his class because I liked to write. It played into my creative side. Mom thought it would help set me up for college. The school called the course College Prep for the College Bound. Definitely pretentious. School officials could have come up with a better name. All of us in the college track took the course. Some took the class because they thought it gave them higher status. Look at me. I'm taking one of the hardest classes the school offers. I must be a pretty big deal. Some of us took it because we really did believe it would help us do better at college. We didn't know what it would entail, but we knew that it would be a lot of work. We would be studying a wide variety of writing strategies, facing intense grammar demands, and writing essays almost weekly.

My sophomore English teacher really pushed us on grammar. We spent almost the entire first semester learning all the grammar rules. I knew the rules, and I could identify the grammatical parts of a sentence and how the grammar functioned. I could diagram sentences. Big deal. That knowledge didn't really help me become a better writer. I knew you could learn to be a better writer. In the second semester, the class gave me more writing strategies to incorporate into my writing. I wrote well. I would have been just fine without the college prep class. I liked to write, though, and I figured it would be fun to have a writing class. I should have taken creative writing instead.

You know how some teachers make a positive impression on the first day? They say something that makes everyone excited about the class. Perhaps they just seem like they will be really nice. Or funny. Or tell good stories. As students, we all liked the jokesters and the storytellers. They made the class entertaining. Ron Decker didn't. He looked like a middle-aged man who had long ago stopped trying. Polyester from the neck down. A soup-stained tie. A bowl cut. And unbelievable arrogance. He looked like an insurance salesman from that era. At some point early in his career, someone tabbed him as an up-and-coming star of the English department. He did know his discipline. That's not all that matters, though, in a high school class. As Mom would say, "He thought he was God's gift to mankind." He also thought he was God's gift to womankind.

"This will be the best semester you have ever had as a student. It will be the best semester to this point, and no other semester afterward will ever compare to this one. You may be wondering what will make this such a special semester. It is quite simple. It will be the best semester for one simple reason: you have the unique opportunity of having me as your teacher." Then he gave us a Richard Nixon-like smile.

Some people can pull off that kind of commentary if they make it with an ironic smile or a sarcastic tone. His demeanor showed he really meant it. The words offended most of us. The actions behind obvious hubris heightened the awkwardness. Every guy in the room knew that he was looking down girls' shirts. When class ended, most teachers would shuffle papers and prepare for the next class. They might go to the door and wish students a good day as they left. He leaned against the window and watched everyone leave. You knew he was checking out the girls' asses.

Amy and I were in his class together. Because of the seating chart, we sat on opposite sides of the room. We could catch each other's glances. Sometimes we made googly eyes. Sometimes we rolled them at what he said. As we walked out together after the first day of class, I said to Amy, "Well, what do you think?"

"He's kind of a weird dude," Amy said. The conversation didn't go any further as we stopped to talk with a couple of band friends. However, we would spend a great deal of time talking about him throughout the semester.

He tended to make everyone uncomfortable. His smarmy way made most of the girls squirm with discomfort. His smarmy ways made the guys want to punch him.

He leered. He made inappropriate comments. He routinely made double entendres. He always tried to find ways to talk about sex. When we would read pieces of literature, he always made a big deal of having us search for phallic symbols and references to female sexuality. When we did an analysis of short stories and poems, we knew we could score a higher grade by basing the analysis on sexual imagery.

When we would do in-class writing exercises, he usually found a way to incorporate sex into the topic. Once he said to us, "Studies have shown that high school students think about sex every fifteen seconds." Then he looked at a girl sitting beside me and said, "Stephanie, you just smiled. You must have been thinking about sex." The class laughed. It was early in the semester, and it still seemed risqué to talk about sex. Stephanie, though, blushed and looked down. After class that day, Amy was furious.

"That man is such a pig," Amy said. "He should be called out for how he embarrassed Stephanie. And we all know that she could have been thinking about anything. He embarrassed her just so he could make a joke at her expense." Then Amy walked away from me without saying goodbye.

On Fridays we would have an author's chair. Students could share something they wrote during the week. All of us had to share at least twice per semester. Lauren wrote about the dressage competition she participated in the previous weekend. Everyone knew she loved to ride her horse. She took the competitions seriously and trained hard to perform well. Amy told me she had a shelf full of trophies in her room. She placed second in the competition that weekend and felt good about her effort. It was like a warmup to a statewide championship that would be happening the next weekend. As Lauren read, we all could see her puffed up with excitement and pride.

After the classmates applauded, Decker made a comment that was like a Mike Tyson punch to the jaw. "Thanks, Lauren. But I think we're all wondering how it felt to have that big, sweaty, throbbing piece of meat between your legs." A few people laughed. It was a nervous laugh.

The statement shocked me. It incensed Amy.

"That man is an absolute, fucking pig. He should be fired for something like that," Amy said after class.

"I completely agree. That was so far out of line. I think we should tell the principal. He needs to face some consequences. That is sexual harassment," I said. I meant it, too.

Amy glared at me and strode away, which happened more and more often coming out of Decker's class.

Dumbfounded, I watched her walk away.

We talked at lunch, and I told her I was on her side but wondered what I had done to her.

She looked at me sweetly, took my hand, and said, "I'm sorry. I shouldn't react like that, and I really don't want to lump all men together, but when I see something like that, I can't help but think all men are just fuckers." I knew enough not to say anything. It was generally a quiet lunch.

Later in the semester, after the football season had ended, I chatted with friends in the commons area for quite a while after school. This was one of those days when my buddies were joking around. It was too much fun to walk away from, so the after-school chatter lasted almost half an hour instead of the usual ten minutes. As so often happened with our senior class, about forty-five seniors clustered together. A big group, as usual. We really did thrive on interacting with each other. When the cluster finally dissolved, I walked Amy to her car about two blocks away. We climbed in and chatted for a couple of minutes, and then we made out for several more minutes.

"Babe, I've got to go. You know I've got to get to work at five," Amy said.

"Yeah, and I really should get back and hit the weight room." Still, we kissed for a few more minutes. I finally dragged myself away and jogged back to school.

In the locker room, I quickly changed into workout clothes and jogged to the weight room. As I was about to enter the facility, I pulled up short. One of my classmates was blocking the door. It was Patty. She didn't go into the weight room, and she certainly wasn't dressed for it. I heard her call out, "Mr. Decker, can I talk to you for a minute?"

I had to wait for Patty to move out of the doorway. She finally stepped aside, and Decker stormed through the open door. Patty said, "I really need to talk to you."

He snarled at Patty. "I told you not to talk to me at school. You know how this has to work." Then Decker saw me standing ten feet away.

"God dammit," he said, mostly under his breath. "Let's go over here," he said to Patty. I walked into the weight room and shook my head. I had seen enough. I had seen too much.

In the middle of the second semester, Decker took an administrative leave of absence. He never returned to school. Everyone knew what had transpired. The district made an embarrassing situation go away. Decker never taught again. Ironically, he became an insurance salesman.

When Amy heard the news, all she said was, "Good. The bastard got what he deserved." Sexual harassment incensed Amy.

—x—x—x—

Years later, the topic of sexual harassment again became an important topic. "Should we get another pitcher?" Cam asked when the waitress approached our booth. Not at Pizza Hut this time, and not drinking Miller

Lite, I knew we would go for a pitcher of Porter.

"Absolutely. Bring it," Amy said.

I didn't expect Amy to agree to another pitcher so quickly. I suspected she was feeling relaxed and comfortable, but I wasn't certain of that. A couple of times she seemed to lose track of the conversation.

Cam, as always, was in a storytelling mood. And as always, his stories had to do with the sex lives of his clients. He didn't violate client-patient confidentiality because he was careful to leave out identifying characteristics.

"You know how I've always said people would rather talk about their financial affairs or their feelings than talk about their sex lives?" he asked before taking another long sip of a freshly poured beer. "Oh, that is good. Too good. I can almost see us going for a third pitcher tonight, just like we used to at Pizza Hut in high school."

"Easy, big shooter. In high school we were drinking brews with three and a half percent alcohol content. This one is pushing seven percent," I said, sipping from my own mug. "We'll stagger out of here like sailors battling a hurricane."

Amy took a big gulp. "Absolutely. Bring it." We all laughed. The first pitcher affected us. The bar crowd roared. We all turned toward one of the many TV screens in the place. Even though this wasn't a sports bar, it had that vibe whenever any Badgers team played, and tonight everyone was watching the women's volleyball team decimate Penn State en route to a Big Ten title. While we were enjoying each other's company, we all also kept one eye on the Badgers action, even Cam, who generally didn't care much for sports. Cam came with me to Badger games of different sports teams, but he came to people-watch. It was a pastime for both of us.

"So anyway, back to my clients. Not all clients have trouble talking about sex. This couple always seemed to be talking about sex. I think they were bragging. These clients are old, in their mid to late seventies. The husband was telling me that he has prostate cancer, and the doctor wants him to undergo surgery. The time has come to remove the tumor. He tells me he's ready to have it done. But then the wife chimes in and makes her feelings known. 'Absolutely not, dearie. The doctor told you it would mean a hiatus from sex for several months. You go several months without sex, and that means I go several months without sex. That's not happening.'

"So the husband gives the doctor this pleading look, a look that seems to be saying, 'Doc, please! I need a break.'

"The wife doubled down. She said, 'Who knows how much more time

I have on this earth. Either you have sex with me, or I find someone who will.' The husband is telling me this and his wife is just sitting there looking proud and fiery and determined.

"Her husband and I exchanged looks. I'm sure I wore the same dumbfounded expression as he did. Her sex life is more important than her husband's life. The issues in sex therapy are becoming more and more complicated. I wish I could go back to the days when I could just tell people to fuck more."

Cam regaled us with more stories. Then we chatted about TJ's progress. He had known TJ all his life.

"Whew! That is good to hear. That kid has caused me some sleepless nights." Now Amy and I both wore dumbfounded looks and then started laughing.

"What? Can't I be concerned about the kid? I love TJ. You guys know that. Really, I have been worried about him. I can't tell you how relieved I am to hear that he might have turned a corner."

"I know, Cam. We're just giving you a hard time," I said. "I give Dad all the credit for having the foresight to propose this 'all in for the family' arrangement. He seemed to know how this would go."

"Mr. Cesario is a wise man. And don't ever forget that he and your mom somehow had to figure out how to raise you and Shelly. Your parents deserve medals for the work they did, especially with you."

"Ha. Ha. Very funny, Mr. Sex Therapist."

"I'm going to have a medal made for your dad. It will read, 'Father of the Century.'

"You know my dad would love that. You also know my dad would make sure to show it to your dad," I said.

"That would be great. Maybe my dad would finally realize what a colossal fuck up of a father he was. But I doubt it."

"But seriously, Dad was right. We had to come together as a family to help TJ. I think TJ realizes that we are making the moves on his behalf, that we are making our own sacrifices for him," I said.

"Yeah, I think we got a little complacent. We all did," Amy said. Another roar from the crowd drew our attention back to the TV. But instead of looking at the TV, Amy looked at me. She gently put her hand on my forearm. She said quietly and under the hum of the bar crowd, "We all did."

I gave Amy a slight nod. She was offering her own apology to me. She had told me before that she knew she had stopped trying with us. I was never willing to accept that we both were responsible for what was lacking in our marriage. In this moment I realized that Amy, dear, wise Amy, knew all this long before I could have ever realized it. She had always been willing to shoulder her responsibility for what happened in our marriage. I was never willing to acknowledge that it wasn't all my fault. At this moment, I felt some weight come off my shoulders.

Cam, observant, knowing Cam, had watched what was subtly happening before him. A slight smile came to his lips. He gave his own small nod.

Another roar from the bar crowd forced all conversation to pause. He raised his beer glass. "Cheers to sports and what it can do for people," he said with absolutely no irony.

By the time we had downed the second pitcher, the Badgers had won, securing the conference championship. Maybe this year we would win the whole thing, the national championship. Bar crowds tend to thin out quickly when the game ends. The norm repeated itself, and soon the cavernous space felt more like an intimate neighborhood corner tap as small groups continued their conversations.

Cam had asked me how we would spend our first Christmas without Mom. As I told him how much I was dreading it already, and how sad the prospect made me, Amy sat quietly beside me. "We'll try to maintain some of the traditions, of course. We have to, but we may try to find some new traditions to carry us forward," I said.

"Go for it. Do whatever feels right this year. When you repeat it again next year, you've got the makings of a tradition," Cam said. "What kinds of things are you thinking about doing? Include us if you think it can be a group thing. What do you say, Amy?"

"What? Oh, sure. We'll have some new traditions, if I make it to Christmas," Amy said softly.

Cam and I instantly turned to her, our questioning looks saying everything.

"What's going on, Amy?" Cam said.

"What do you mean, Ames?" I said at the same time as Cam.

"Nothing. Forget I said anything," Amy said, looking a little scared.

"No, we're not going to work that way anymore, Amy. We talk things out," I said.

There was a long silence. Cam stared into a neutral space beside Amy. I stared into Amy's eyes.

"Oh, shit. Well, just a lot of stress at work, you know."

"No, judging from your comment, this is more than just regular work stress. Talk to us," Cam said.

"Robb, do you remember a while back when I told you I was having some problems with my supervisor at work?"

I nodded. I had asked Amy about it a few times, and she basically waved it off. Obviously, it was more than a little issue.

"He's become much more blatant about his advances. He has promised me promotions, if I just, you know."

Cam and I nodded. We knew. Cam listened with laser focus.

"In crowded spaces, he has blatantly groped me twice now and then apologized as if the cramped quarters caused it. I've been so stressed about this that it started feeling like I was having heart palpitations. Or more like my heart was skipping beats. So I went to my doctor last week, who assured me I was experiencing PVCs induced by stress."

"PVCs?"

"Premature ventricular contractions," Cam interjected before Amy answered.

Amy nodded. "Nothing to worry about, the doctor assured me. They will just go away at some point, probably when the stress ends."

"Shit, Amy. I'm sorry. I wish I had asked you for more information. Has anything happened recently?" I asked.

"At work or with my heart?"

"Both," I said, lightly touching my hand to her forearm.

"I'm still having the PVCs. No new harassment incidents, though." Tears now streamed down her face. I gave her a hug. Cam would have, too, if he were on the same side of the table.

"I just don't know what to do."

She softly cried for another minute. I gave her another hug. Cam and I brushed away some of our own tears.

"Amy, we're going to help you get through this," Cam said. "First, have you said in a voice loud enough for anyone near you to hear that he isn't allowed to ever again touch you like that? If not, do so whenever he touches you. Then there is another step you need to take. I'm going to give you the name of a colleague, someone you can talk through this with. Obviously, I can't be your therapist. Can I offer a suggestion for you to pursue?"

"Of course, Cam. You know I will take your advice on anything." Amy reached across the table and held his hand. The three of us, all for one, one for all. The three musketeers.

"This may not be an easy thing to do, Amy, but it is a step you need to take, for your own health and safety. You need to create a statement documenting all of the incidents of sexual harassment. Where, when, details of the incident. Include in that document how each incident made you feel. Create a list of demands. Number one should be that the harassment stops immediately. Identify what your next steps will be if the company doesn't meet these demands. The first step, if they don't, is filing a complaint with the city's human rights department. They will then initiate legal steps."

Amy blanched as Cam spoke.

"I don't know if I can do that, Cam. People get fired for making that kind of accusation, proof or not. Won't that put me at risk?"

"It might, certainly. You need to formally document that this has happened. If something further happens, this will make other legal strategies up to arrest and prosecution necessary to pursue. Every day you allow this to continue allows him to validate, in his mind, what he is doing. Abusers must be stopped, or the abuse will continue. Amy, you need to acknowledge something: if you take this step, things might get worse before they get better. But they will get better. If you do nothing, they most certainly will get worse."

At this point, silence surrounded the table like a winter night after a fresh snow.

We sat there for another ten minutes, the third pitcher barely touched.

When we stood beside our cars on the chilly November night, thinking about the weight of what we had talked about throughout the night, we struggled to find the words for goodbye.

"No matter what, Amy, know that you can count on us for anything. Right, Robb?"

I nodded. Cam hugged Amy and whispered something in her ear. Then he drove away.

I hugged Amy. I now whispered into her ear, "For anything!"

Turns out Cam and I delivered the same message.

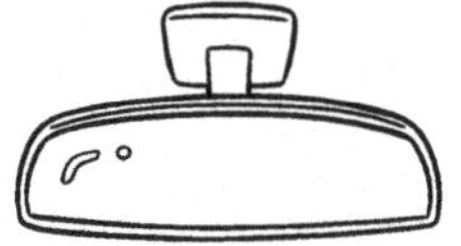

CHAPTER 18

Continuation of one of Mom's Christmas traditions almost undid all of us. Mom had held the tree-trimming party for more than forty years. It began when I was twelve, and Mom invited her best friend, Shug, over for dinner and asked her to stay and help us put up the tree. Shug's husband had died suddenly nine months before. Mom knew she was struggling to get through the Christmas season. Prior to that we had always decorated our tree on the first Saturday in December, but it had just been our family. Dad didn't mind the inclusion of Shug. Neither of them made a big deal out of it, so then neither did Shelly or me.

Mom made lasagna, a family favorite, for dinner. After we finished eating, Dad and I went into the living room and began stringing the lights. He used to take care of this duty, but a few years earlier, he invited me to help him. That invitation sparked another tradition that never ended. Shelly sat in front of cardboard boxes, pulling tissue-wrapped ornaments out and unfurling the tissue paper. She created piles of ornaments. Then Mom and Shug joined us, and we started hanging them. Mom liked a tree full of ornaments. It took almost two hours to hang all the ornaments. Then Dad hoisted Shelly up so she could top the tree with the angel.

The next year the tree-trimming party grew. "I like the idea of having other people help us decorate," Mom said to Dad, who merely shrugged. He generally accepted whatever Mom proposed.

"Invite whomever you like," Dad said. The party grew to twenty people. She invited some colleagues and her two sisters and their families. With that second party, the tree-trimming party became ritualized. So that everyone would feel as if they contributed to the decorating, Mom popped a big bowl of popcorn and invited everyone to string it. When the strands were long enough, they became garlands. As guests left the party, Mom and Dad sang, "We Wish You a Merry Christmas."

Shug continued to attend the tree-trimming parties. The next year she asked if she could invite her sister, her sister's husband, and their two children. She and her family never missed. "How could I miss the kickoff of the Christmas season?" Shug said. That's how the party swelled until, in Mom's last years, more than sixty people came. Once they came for the first time, they never wanted to miss it.

People felt the warm embrace of the Christmas season. Everyone who came to that party felt like family. It also offered a big dose of nostalgia. It was living out a live version of a Norman Rockwell painting, where the world seemed simpler, at least in the moment. People could forget about their struggles and enjoy the simple pleasure of celebrating a holiday with as much joy as they could muster. I don't think anyone ever had a bad time tree trimming.

Throughout the night, people laughed, talked, sang, hugged each other, and flashed smiles of happiness. Most of them, I know, when they reflect on their lives at different points, would look at those tree-trimming parties as moments of happiness. I know I did.

Mom always said tree trimming "feels like a good way to kick off the Christmas season."

Major family events centered around tree trimming. Shelly brought her first boyfriend, and much later her future husband, to tree trimming, where she introduced them to the family. As a senior, after Amy and I had started dating, I asked her before Halloween if she would come to the tree-trimming party with me. She was the most important person in my life. She had to come to the party. I wanted a firm commitment long before the event, so I could savor the anticipation, which always made it better. "We will probably start with lasagna for dinner," I told Amy, and then I filled her in on the rest of the party.

"There will be all of this great food. Mom will have been baking Christmas cookies for more than two weeks leading up to it. At some point we will sing Christmas carols. We run through them all. The singing always ends with a heartfelt offering of "Silent Night." After everyone is gone, we spend time as a family cleaning up. And then we just sit in front of the tree, enraptured by its beauty. Somewhere in there, Mom always says, 'It's the best Christmas tree ever.' And it always is. It's always the first Saturday in December. So, what do you think, Amy? Will you come with me, for dinner and everything? The whole smash?"

"I don't know. I might be busy," Amy said with a slight smile on her lips. My shoulders slumped.

"Oh, Robb. Sorry. I was just teasing. Of course I will come to the party. From the way you described it, I wouldn't want to be anywhere else. And if that's where you're going to be, I wouldn't be anywhere else, anyway."

Mom loved Amy instantly, but I always felt that having her at tree trimming solidified the genuine love between the two. At dinner Mom served Amy a piece of steaming hot lasagna and began to pass the plate back to her. "Wait a minute, Mrs. Cesario. You forgot the good stuff." Mom looked perplexed. "All that sauce and cheese and meat that didn't make it onto the spatula. I want it all." Mom looked at me and smiled. That smile told me she thought I had found the good stuff. I smiled because I knew it, too.

Mom brought Amy's plate back over the pan of lasagna, scooped the remnants of Amy's piece onto her plate, and passed it to Amy. "This looks beyond delicious."

"Good, good," Mom said.

From that moment on, all of us asked for the good stuff.

Later that night after all the guests had left, Amy and I cuddled on the couch, Mom and Dad sat in their respective chairs. Shelly lay on the floor. Bing Crosby Christmas music played softly in the background. It was another Norman Rockwell painting of the happy family at Christmas. That image remains in my mind as one of the happiest of my life. When I start remembering other happy moments, almost all the images include Amy.

Another of those life-defining images came when I proposed to Amy. That big moment came our first Christmas after completing college. I did so in front of the newly decorated tree on the night of tree trimming. People had gone into the kitchen to reload on snacks and drinks. I dropped to one knee, pulled the ring out of my pocket, and proposed. "Amy, you are the most important person in my life, and I can't imagine living my life without you." She reached out and gently touched my face, staring into my eyes the entire time. "I love you and will never stop loving you. I am so much better because I have you in my life. I will love you forever. Will you marry me?" She said yes and professed her own deep love for me. After a long, deep kiss, we looked up and saw Mom standing in the doorway.

"I thought something like this might be happening tonight," Mom said. She walked up to us and embraced us both at the same time. Then we rushed into the kitchen, where Amy shouted out the news. "We just got engaged! Robb asked me to marry him."

—x—x—x—

On several occasions that fall after Mom's death, I had opened the door and stared at the closet full of Christmas decorations. Though no one in the family talked about it, the unspoken agreement seemed to indicate that no decorations would go up this year. The reminders of Mom would hurt too much.

The adjustment of the experimental living arrangements continued with major disruptions to peace and serenity occurring about every other day. During long conversations that Amy and I had with TJ about the new and unusual living arrangements, he seemed to appreciate the effort. It didn't take much, though, for his anger to surface and the rebellions to ensue. Thanksgiving, the mother of all awkward holidays, resulted in all of us wishing that the pilgrims had crashed on Plymouth Rock instead of landing there successfully. Most of that awkwardness emerged because we missed Mom—wife, mother, grandmother, dear friend. The day stretched on and on with awkward silences and stilted conversations.

TJ and Jessie rarely bickered. Like many siblings they seemed to believe life was better if they stuck together. That attitude continued through TJ's darkest days. But on Thanksgiving they fought over who washed and who dried, something they had given up years earlier.

"Why the hell do you always get to wash?" TJ said, his tone far too harsh over something so insignificant.

"Because I'm better at it than you," Jessie said and smirked. She turned on the hot water tap. TJ reached in and turned it off.

"I'm washing," TJ said.

"The hell you are," Jessie said.

"Move away from the sink," TJ said. "I'm washing."

"Given the way you've treated this family," Jessie said, "you don't get to order anybody around."

Amy heard the wind of the storm bearing down like an approaching tornado. She quickly moved into the kitchen.

"Enough," Amy said loudly, so she could be heard. "Out. I'm washing. You both get out of here. Go sit with your grandfather, who might crave the comfort of his loving grandchildren on this sad day when all anyone can do is remember Gram, who isn't here with us. And maybe since you both are obviously feeling the same sadness, maybe you can be a little nicer to each other. That's what Gram would have expected of you. Do better."

I had heard the tornado winds beating on the house, too, and rushed toward the kitchen. As the kids walked out of the kitchen and moved toward the den, I walked into the kitchen. Suds rose above the sink. I reached in and turned down the faucet. I picked up a dish towel and started drying the dishes Amy had already washed.

We continued this daily chore in silence, in some ways drawing comfort from this familiar kitchen dance step. When you cook a Thanksgiving meal for five, a relatively small gathering, you still face a pile of dirty dishes. We would be at it for a while.

After ten minutes, I said simply, "Thanks."

Amy smiled. "We're all missing Mom. I just identified the rhinoceros in the room."

"According to the cliché, isn't it an elephant?" I asked.

"I was just trying to be original," Amy said.

"Oh, you are definitely original," I said, chuckling.

"I know you are, but what am I?"

The silliness of parroting a statement from a six-year-old made me guffaw. Amy and I then started riffing by repeating statements our kids said when they were little, statements that made us laugh so much harder as the memories came back, but laughter no one else would understand.

The pile of dirty dishes dwindled.

When we finished, Amy and I sat at the kitchen table. "It felt good to laugh," I said. "I didn't realize this day would be so hard without Mom."

"I have a feeling the next month is going to be really hard," Amy said. "I guess we have to steel ourselves and try to get through Mom's favorite season without her."

"I know. I'm dreading it," I agreed. We chatted a bit more about Mom and the holidays.

"We'll just have to help each other get through it," Amy said. I gave a slow nod of agreement. Later in the evening, Amy left and went home, which had started to seem strange.

While no one spoke of it, no one really wanted to bring negative feelings into a cherished Christmas memory and tradition—tree trimming. *Maybe*, I thought, *it would be best to allow the tree-trimming party to exist only as a memory.*

So when Dad mentioned decorating the house for Christmas, I said, "I don't really see much point in that."

"No, I generally agree, but your mother would have been disappointed if we didn't do anything. You know how much Christmas meant to her,"

Dad said. And then we fell silent, remembering. Mom seemed to come to life at Christmas. Over the years she had created and maintained so many traditions that it seemed as if every decoration and occasion carried special meaning. Sometimes it seemed hard to keep up, especially when Mom would say, "Well, you remember we always do it this way ..." If I didn't remember, I acted as if I did. Funny thing: Now that she died, I seemed to remember everything. Every memory hurt. "Robb, we have to keep the rituals alive, even if your mom isn't here to help us. We have a lot of family traditions. Most of them start with your mother. If we carry on those traditions, we carry her forward with us," Dad said. "All of the rituals began with tree trimming."

As I thought about Dad's desire to continue this tradition, I realized how much I wanted it to continue, too.

"Dad, this party was so important to Mom. It is going to be really hard to do this. I don't think it will be much fun. But I'll help if you want to do it."

"Good, good," Dad said and offered a sad smile.

"Robb, I don't expect it will be much fun. I actually think it will be awkward and painful and sad. It will feel a lot like going through the motions. People will come, though, because we are trying. Then next year it will be easier. And maybe we can get back to the point where it's really fun and people won't want to miss it because it's so much fun. So let's get going."

The next day we started calling around to invite guests. All our family and friends basically gave the same response: "I wouldn't miss it."

Amy and Jessie spent days baking cookies. The house always smelled like a bakery. It smelled like Mom. They made sugar cookies, haystacks, icaboxa cookies (rolled dough that you would freeze and bake at any time you wanted fresh baked cookies, officially named icebox but icaboxa in our family), M&M cookies, Hershey's kiss drops, Italian Christmas cookies. Every time I walked through the kitchen, I snatched a cookie and quickly stuffed it in my mouth. "Robb, leave some for the guests," Amy would say and swat at me with the spatula. I dodged, weaved, and grabbed another cookie.

It felt familiar. Good.

On the day of the party, Dad and I pulled out the decorations and then began cooking the main dishes. The heavy rich scent of lasagna filled the air. Steam covered the windows. We both knew Mom's recipe for sauce. We could make sauce no other way. Christmas music played loudly. Everyone sang along, even TJ. We didn't need conversation, and didn't want it. We wanted the festive sound to crowd out the sadness that lurked around the edges. When the guests started to arrive, we turned down the music.

Everyone tried on a festive demeanor.

Everyone knew Mom was gone.

Still, we re-enacted old traditions of a lifetime of tree trimming, my lifetime anyway. We invited our guests to eat. We made sure they got their fill. Then I moved people to different staging stations. The guests, though, only had one task. Needle in hand, they had to string popcorn. Some of the more industrious made long strings, occasionally joining in on the conversation, and some did all the talking.

Mom always gathered the strings and tied the ends together, creating the garland for the tree. While she did that, Dad and I hung the lights. He believed that a tree should shine brightly with many varicolored lights. Sometimes the room seemed so bright you could safely land planes in the backyard. Mom believed branches should sag with multiple ornaments, as many as each branch would take. Between the two of them and the guests, who could start hanging ornaments after the lights went on, we created these gaudy, beautiful displays. We created trees no department store or garden store would ever display. But we loved them.

When Amy and I married, I made sure that we continued that tradition with our family. So we bought any ornaments that appealed to us. We filled shelves in our basement with boxes of Christmas ornaments. I knew our kids would do the same when they started decorating their own trees. After the divorce, separated from my family and living in a shitty apartment, I felt the malaise so many experience around the holidays. I put up a small tree so the kids would feel a little cheer when they visited. Amy always invited me over to partake in the gift-opening extravaganza on Christmas morning. I feigned happiness for the kids. I knew I was an interloper in the scene.

That night, as we began decorating, I stood behind the tree, placing an ornament just so. Mom always insisted we decorate the entire tree, which sat nestled in the bay picture window. "The neighbors need to see the beauty, too."

TJ sidled up to me and hung an ornament, an old-fashioned plastic red ball, simple but beautiful. I recognized it as one of Mom's favorites. She kept twelve ornaments from her and Dad's first Christmas tree. That was all they had to decorate that tree. Over time they collected more and more precious ornaments. She stored those precious ornaments in a velvet lined box that Dad made her after their second Christmas. Even though they quickly began filling up the tree, and it likely resembled trees from previous years, Mom always said that first tree was her favorite. Rituals. Traditions.

TJ stayed relatively close to me throughout the party.

With the tree decorated in a coat of splendor, people offered admiring comments, saying how beautiful it looked, knowing only one thing was missing.

I heard Dad quote Mom to Shug: "It's the best Christmas tree ever." His voice caught, and Shug gave him a long, hard hug.

As the final guests left, gently ushered out as we softly crooned, "We Wish You a Merry Christmas," TJ stood beside me again. He leaned against me, something he had always done as a little boy, something he hadn't done for probably five years.

"I miss Gram," he said quietly. I gave him a one-armed hug.

"Me, too."

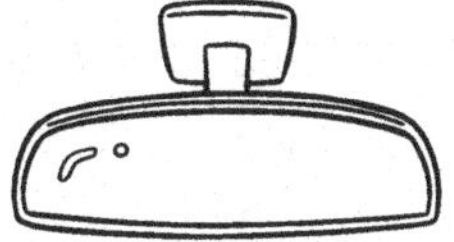

CHAPTER 19

Every high school student knew what to do in certain situations. When you would see trouble in the hallways, you would assess the threat and walk by quickly or back out and take the long way around. I was never that person who loved to watch a fight. It made me uneasy. The sound of fists slamming into flesh turned my stomach. On occasion I would try to be the peacemaker. I would get between two guys who were posturing. Many times, with guys, they did a lot of sizing each other up, trying to decide if a fight was really going to happen. Most guys usually didn't want to fight. If a crowd gathered, it became a different story. Pride often dictated when guys fought. They had to consider their reputation. They couldn't be the wimp who walked away from a fight. It could escalate quickly, too. A guy might throw a sucker punch to get in the first good lick. Guys, though, generally tended to follow some rules. Even though the fights were barbaric, you knew once the punches started to fly, it would be a fair fight, a mix between a boxing, cage fighting and a wrestling match. Rarely did anyone draw a weapon. Fists served as the weapon of choice. If they got into the zone, they might have wanted to kill, but fists usually wouldn't result in life-or-death injuries.

If I walked into a fight, like I said, I went into threat assessment mode.

If I knew one or both guys, I would try to distract them and get them to move on to class before any teachers or principals got involved. "Hey, guys, come on. Let's not do this here. I've got to get to class to expand my ability to critically think about U.S. history." Or I might say, "Hey, dude, let me through. I've got to take advantage of my free education." If I got a laugh or a smirk, I knew the fight wouldn't happen. We would laugh, I would high five the pugilists, and we would all move on, the fight averted for the moment.

If the dudes were already throwing punches, I scurried away.

If two girls were about to fight, I cleared out as fast as possible. Girls fought and rules didn't apply. You could tell when a girl fight happened at school. You might see hunks of hair scattered on the floor. Blood droplets leaving a trail that would allow you to follow the trajectory of the fight, like the scene in *The Princess Bride*. Ripped pieces of clothing. Contents of backpacks scattered up and down the hallway. Screaming and crying from onlookers. When I happened on a girl fight, I ran as fast as I could the other way.

Boys liked to think they fought about honor. Pride. Dignity. Reputation. Girls usually fought about those things, too, which often connected to some boy. All of it was just stupid.

Once as I left English a couple minutes late following a quick chat with my teacher about an upcoming essay, I rushed to band second hour. The band room was on the opposite side of the building. I knew the talk with my teacher would likely make me late, especially if I ran into any roadblocks in the hallway. Unfortunately, I didn't notice the signs and plowed into chaos. I inadvertently walked into a brawl. This was an incident that featured several combatants on the fight bill. You had three pockets of boys throwing knockout punches. You had another four or five girls trying to destroy each other. It seemed like half the school surrounded the fight, taunting, yelling, screaming insults, encouraging the brawlers to continue.

I saw tufts of hair floating in the air. You could almost see the blood splatter. The melee had been going on for a while. The crowd surged and morphed like a living entity. In an instant it encircled me, trapping me. I tried to slip through, but I couldn't move. "Excuse me, excuse me," I softly implored. Nobody moved. Nobody heard. People screamed at the fighters, trapped in their own blood lust. It was a mob. This frightening energy exploded around me.

"Kill him. Kick him in the balls." "Rip that bitch's hair out." "Teach that fucker not to mess with you!" I looked at those doing the shouting, seeing rage and mob hatred on their faces. I was shocked to see these facial expressions on some people I thought I knew so well. Now they looked like aliens. Now they looked capable of doing unthinkable things, capable of hate.

The blood lust ended when the police arrived, running into the fray, shouting and swinging batons. They forcefully threw two boys against the lockers. One officer tackled another boy. I noticed that they broke up the boys first. Once they subdued the boys, they began the dangerous process of separating the girls. Three cops got punched by girls, so enraged and in tunnel vision that they never looked at who they were punching, enhancing whatever charges were coming against them.

The cops broke apart the main players. The fight ended quickly after that. The officers quickly cuffed the major assailants. Administrators worked to disperse gawking students and get everyone to class. I was already ten minutes late to band. I knew I would be walking in without a pass, getting a disdainful look from Finch. I would explain my lateness to him after class but knew not to expect sympathy. He tolerated a lot, but he drew the line at tardiness. Every rehearsal minute was as precious as rare metals. You couldn't approach perfection if you didn't put in the hard work of practice.

As I hustled to class, dashing through the commons, I looked out the window and saw the flashing lights atop the cop cruisers. They already had dragged one student to the cop car, holding their head so they wouldn't bang it crawling into the back seat. That image seemed so stark; it drew me up short.

I paused and looked out of the windows. That scene always stayed with me. On those occasions when I saw the police arrest someone, I watched the swirling red and blue lights. I saw the officers taking the cuffed suspect to the squad car, getting ready to take them to the jail. I knew that moment could bring about a major change in someone's life, altering it forever. The moments that led up to it, however many moments there were, and the long stretch of time following the incident and the arrest would have long-lasting and profound impacts. Lives would change, and usually not for the better. An arrest played out as a major scene in the misery of human drama.

—x—x—x—

A few days after tree trimming, as I approached home, I slowed because of a swirl of red and blue lights. I approached the squad car clearly blocking the road. I stopped. I quickly opened my door and was about to start to run home, when a cop boxed me in the driver's seat.

"Sir, we have a situation ahead. For your safety, I need you to get back in your car and find an alternate route."

"Your situation ahead involves my wife, now. Now please get out of my way. She is in danger," I yelled, adrenaline shooting through me like rainwater sluicing out of a drainpipe. Only later would I realize I identified

Amy as my wife.

"What is your address, sir?" I gave it to him. The cop turned away from me and spoke into his shoulder mike. He turned back to me. "I've been instructed to keep you here until I get the all clear. It should just be a minute or two. Then I will bring you to the house."

"Can you tell me if my wife is still being threatened?"

"Your wife is being treated by paramedics. We need you to wait here until we take away the suspect." The cop continued to block my way out of the car. I contemplated starting the car and making a dash for the house, but I knew that would just get me arrested. That wouldn't be productive. My family needed me. I sat there and nervously tapped my hands on the steering wheel, staring straight ahead trying to see any signs that would give me hope.

Another car pulled up behind me and parked. I couldn't see anything because of the blinding headlights, but an old man walked toward my car. He shuffled quickly, or what now passed for quickly with him, walking with a slight stoop. *Funny, how I had never noticed the stoop before*, I thought. I knew now that I would always see it. Somehow along the way Dad had gotten old. When did that happen? Would it happen to me that quickly?

The cop stopped him, too.

"It's all right, officer. That's my son in the car there. I'll just sit with him." Dad climbed in the passenger side.

"I'm glad the cops got here in a hurry," Dad said.

"I just hope they weren't too late. The paramedics are treating Amy," I said, telling Dad all I knew, which wasn't much.

He had called me ten minutes ago, right after he called the cops. "Amy's in trouble," he had said. "We were talking on the phone as she got home, and then she screamed and screamed. It became clear someone was threatening to assault her. I could hear a man's voice in the background, threatening her. Amy just kept screaming. She pleaded with me to get to the house as quickly as possible. I just called the cops."

With that warning, Dad and I both rushed to the house, arriving almost simultaneously. Now we waited. Neither of us talked. What could we say? As I continued to fidget, Dad calmly reached over and put his left hand on top of mine. It calmed me instantly, and the fidgeting stopped. It never ceases to amaze me how calming a parent's touch can be, no matter what your stage of life. I remembered Mom holding my hand in the hospital, shortly after her heart attack. I think she knew she was dying. If I am honest with myself, I would say I knew it, too. Her gentle touch calmed me.

Dad's touch, though different, produced the same effect.

We waited. One minute turned into five. Ten. Twenty. After a half hour the cop waved at us to follow, and he stepped back in his squad car. He swung it around and drove toward the house. Two squads remained on the scene. A cop was talking to Amy, who looked panicked. I ran toward her. She stepped into my arms and almost collapsed. I had to hold her up because she could no longer support herself.

"Thank God you're okay," I said into her ear.

"I'll be okay, but right now we've got to worry about TJ," Amy said.

"TJ? What's going on with TJ?"

"Ma'am, we've got a few more questions for you, and then you can follow the ambulance to the hospital," another cop said, and now I almost collapsed, feeling like I couldn't bear any more weight, Amy's or mine.

Amy shook her head. "I will answer any other questions you have at the hospital. We need to be there now for our son." I heeded Amy's cue and walked toward my car.

As I opened the door and turned to her, Amy put her hand on my chest and looked into my eyes. "Is he okay?" I asked.

"He will be, too. But he is going to hurt for a while. I will explain everything. Um, listen, can you ask Dad to pick up Jess at school? Her glee club rehearsal will be over soon, and someone should tell her what is going on." It barely registered that Amy had referred to Jess's show choir rehearsal as glee club. That had been my dad joke when Jess first joined. Jess, and thus Amy, thought it disrespectful.

"What is going on?" I asked.

"Just have Dad tell her that there was an incident at home, and TJ saved my life." She looked me in the eyes and slowly nodded. I did collapse then. I just fell to the ground and, on my hands and knees, started crying. I don't know if the tears were fear, terror, anger, or relief. Amy kneeled in front of me and lifted me into another hug. She started to cry, too. Then we felt Dad kneel beside us. He had stood back about ten feet while Amy talked with me. Then his parental instinct kicked in when I collapsed. He rushed to us. We encircled him in the hug. Our tears seemed to mingle. I don't know how long we kneeled in that hug. One minute. Five. Ten. Twenty. Thirty.

"We'll be okay," Amy murmured. "We'll all be okay."

—x—x—x—

An hour later we all sat in the waiting room, waiting for an update on TJ, who was being treated out of sight in the emergency room. We had been here before. The stakes were high after the car accident. They seemed to have risen exponentially now.

We barely talked. If we started talking, there might be too much to say, too much to deal with, too much weight to carry, and that weight would squash us all like a falling boulder.

As Amy later gave a detailed statement to the police, I stood nearby, listening with clenched fists, wanting to spend five minutes alone with the guy they took away in the second ambulance.

"You know the man who assaulted you?" the cop asked.

Amy nodded. "I worked with him."

"Do you know what might have caused this assault?"

Amy nodded again and without any more prompting, she told the story. She had been sitting in one of the chairs in the waiting area. But as soon as she started to speak, she stood and began pacing a little, slowly walking three or four feet, pausing, slowly retracing her steps.

They worked in the same office, though they didn't work together, per se. He was her boss. The man started trying to engage in friendly conversations, and then he asked Amy out on a date. She declined, saying she didn't date people she worked with. The guy kept pressuring her to join him for a drink. He promised her things, pay raises, promotions. She declined all of his advances. This had been going on for months. Amy had filed a complaint with her boss's supervisor, she told the cop.

As I listened, I realized this was the guy Amy talked about with Cam and me, the guy who scared her. We thought we had given her good advice and the harassment ended. Obviously, we should have taken her fears more seriously. This guy almost destroyed an entire family.

She started avoiding him at work, she told the police officer, because he made her uncomfortable. But he was her boss. She couldn't avoid him completely. After each rejection, he treated her harshly, criticizing her work, demanding she do more, work overtime, do it again, do it better. In those encounters he would threaten to fire her if she didn't do better work.

"What happened today?" the officer asked.

"I came home, let myself in, set my things down on the kitchen counter, and turned around to close the door." Amy paused as a tremor worked down her body. "He was standing just inside the door. I didn't hear him come in. I must have been in that daze you get into at the end of the day, where you are tired and relieved that you can start to wind down."

She continued to tell the story. "'Hi, Amy,'" he said. "'How about that drink now?'"

"He closed the door, slammed it, actually, and turned the deadbolt. I went from calm to terror in an instant.

"I am going to ask you once to leave, right now. And then I am calling the police," Amy told the investigating officers. "I pulled out my phone and was about to dial 911, when he slapped the phone out of my hands with a forehand punch. Then he slapped my face with the backhand rebound. As I leaned on the kitchen table in pain and terror, he grabbed me, spun me around, slapped me again, and tossed me against the wall."

The cop continued writing. I continued clenching my fists.

"My shoulder banged into the wall," Amy said. She flexed and rolled her shoulder. Then she grimaced. "That is going to hurt."

"Do you need to see a doctor?" I asked.

"Let's worry about TJ first," Amy said.

"Ma'am, then what happened?" the officer prodded.

"He held me against the wall and pinned my hands at my side. He pushed his leg between my legs. It was clear he was going to rape me." She paused. She shuddered again at stating the obvious intentions of this depraved pervert.

"He said, 'You treated me badly. When I asked you out, you mocked me. You belittled me. You made me feel like a little boy, not good enough for Miss High and Mighty, you fuckin' bitch.' Then he punched me in the stomach. I tried to scream again, but he had knocked the air out of me.

"'Well, you're going out with me now. Only we're not going out, if you catch my meaning.' He snarled this in my face. The whole time I was struggling against the vice grip he had around my wrists. I couldn't get any leverage." Amy stopped again and subconsciously rubbed her wrists. You could see the dark, circular bruises that had formed around her wrists.

Amy had been telling the story almost in a trance up to this point, revealing details with little inflection in her voice. Her pacing had stopped, though. She had seemed strong and committed to telling the police all that had happened. In the pause, her resolve seemed to weaken. Her shoulders started to hunch over and then shake.

I stepped up to her and wrapped my arms around her. She turned into my hug and buried her face in my chest. I held her tight until the sobbing slowed and then stopped. Time passed. One minute. Five. Ten ...

When she collected herself, she sat down. The officer had remained in the waiting area, looking at his phone, which he used to record her story. He waited until the victim was ready to continue retelling the story.

She resumed her account. "'Now, you will do what I tell you to, and you will like it,' he commanded. Then he backhanded me again.

"That's when TJ came in the kitchen door. Because of his yelling and the adrenaline, the man didn't hear him unlock the deadbolt. TJ stood there for a moment, eyes wide in terror. He quickly assessed the situation, and he charged across the kitchen, screaming, 'Nooooo!'

"TJ leaped in the air and attempted to tackle the man. The force of his leap pushed the man into me, which knocked the wind out of me again. He let me go, and I slid down the wall, desperately trying to breathe, knowing this monster would kill my son. He was stronger than TJ, but I saw TJ pummeling his head with punches.

"The man roared and flipped TJ off him and punched him several times in the face and the stomach. At one point TJ's head snapped back and banged into the overhanging cupboard. TJ slumped to the floor. The man reached into the knife rack and pulled out a butcher knife. This man, who seemed like nothing more than an office drone at work, every person who had ever been over-promoted, had attempted to rape me, and now he was going to kill my son. I knew I had to stop him from plunging that knife into TJ. I pulled a rolling pin out of the caddy on the counter beside the stove. I leaped, swinging the rolling pin as hard as I could. I aimed for his head.

"I know I connected. I felt the vibrations in my wrist. It was his turn to slump to the floor. I hit him again in the head, dropped the rolling pin, and rushed over to TJ, who was unconscious, as near as I could tell. I held him a moment and kissed his face. The man started to stir, so I gave him another shot with the rolling pin. Then I reached into the junk drawer, grabbed an extension cord, and wrapped it around his hands and legs as tightly as I could. Then I tied him as tightly as I could to the refrigerator door.

"TJ started moaning. I crawled back to him and helped him stumble out of the house and sat him against a tree, ran back in the house, and called Dad, then 911. You guys arrived quickly after that."

She sat quietly for a minute, breathing slowly and deeply.

The officer let her recenter. "I'll file my report and then the DA will decide how to proceed."

Amy looked at the officer. "Will I be arrested?"

"My God. For what?" I practically shouted at Amy, and the officer shook his head, seeming to agree with me. "You protected yourself and your son."

"I tried to," Amy said. "I also tried to kill that sonofabitch!"

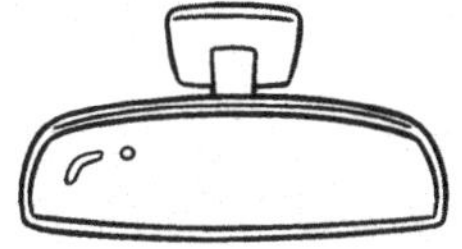

CHAPTER 20

I was restless, anxious, unsettled. High school would officially end the next day. I would officially graduate in two days. I prowled around the house, opening the refrigerator, kitchen cupboards. Aimlessly, I walked downstairs and took a survey of all the detritus of life discarded, items no longer useful to the family.

I walked upstairs to my bedroom and looked at the posters on my walls, the requisite images of rock bands and beautiful women. A UW pennant hung over the bed. Good thing I chose to go to college there. I had a few trophies from Pop Warner football, a bookshelf filled with Scholastic books Mom always let me order throughout junior high. I wondered how long Mom and Dad would leave them up after I left for college. It was a typical boys' room. I would be a high school graduate. It seemed time to leave the things of boyhood behind. I just didn't know what I would replace them with.

I took the dog outside three or four times for quick walks around the block. When I tried to take him out again at about ten thirty, he gave me a baleful look and laid his head back down again. I walked through the dining room, where Mom sat at the table as she often did through the evening if nothing on the television interested her. She would write notes to friends or read a book in the dining room because it gave her close enough access to the family room and the kitchen. She could monitor her family's activities.

"Honey, you're pacing around like a caged polar bear. Why don't you go into the family room and watch some TV." Mom turned back to the magazine article she was reading, essentially dismissing me.

I continued to pace. I wandered into my bedroom, took a long look around, again studied the posters that hung on the walls, and in some cases wondered what possessed me to hang things like AC/DC posters, images from the Packers' glory days, and even one picture of fluffy puppies, which Amy had tacked up as a joke.

I realized the AC/DC poster and other acid rock band concert shots were probably leftovers from Shelly. She and I pulled a room switch when I got to high school. I wanted her room because it was farthest from Mom and Dad's bedroom. It also suited my needs when I wanted to sneak out. I could open the window and step onto the roof of the back porch, grab a nearby tree limb, and let myself to the ground.

I used this escape hatch many times. It even afforded easy re-entry. I just had to carefully step onto the small chest full of garden tools Mom kept by the back porch. I grabbed the same branch, pulled myself onto the roof, and crawled back in through my window. As I stood looking at the posters, I paused and remembered some of those excursions into the night, where Cam and I got into minor troubles, nothing serious or significant, but enough to make us believe we were badasses. A couple of times cops hit the flashing lights on the squad to scare us. We ran, darting through backyards.

Once I started dating girls in high school, I would use the escape hatch to go see girls. I snuck out often to see Amy. We would walk the dark streets, holding hands, thinking ourselves utter romantics, who loved the nightlife. Sometimes we would walk down to the park, sit on a park bench and make out, kissing long past the point where we derived any joy from it but smart enough and scared enough not to go much further. No matter who I spent time with when I snuck out of the house, it just felt daring and rebellious, to creep away from home knowing I was violating all of my parents' dictates, and knowing that if I got caught, I would have some consequences to face. I never got caught.

Mom always said if you're out late, you're only looking for trouble. She was right. The whole point of sneaking out was to see if you could find some trouble.

With Amy, my reasons for sneaking out took on new meaning. I didn't sneak out to find trouble. I snuck out for one reason: to find Amy. If I could spend time with her, even if it meant violating house rules, I didn't care. I was going to do it.

It turns out Mom knew what I was doing. Shortly after Amy and I married, Mom said to me, "Well, now that you two are officially living together, you won't have to sneak out the bedroom window anymore to see her."

"You knew about that?" I asked, incredulous.

"That and all those times you snuck out to create mischief with Cam and your little girlfriends."

"How did you know? I thought I was always so careful and quiet," I said.

"The footprints on top of my garden chest were the first indicator. Then I checked the window and saw no dust around it. Your father regularly tended all the windows of the house. But I asked him to leave your window alone. I wanted to hear when you left. It made just enough of a scraping sound that in a quiet house, I could hear it from our bedroom. So I would hear you when you left. I would also hear when you returned. In between I dozed. When you were in for the night, I finally fell into deep sleep."

I looked down, embarrassed. "Wow, Mom. I'm sorry that I put you through that. Why didn't you ever say something to make me stop?"

"Kids need to rebel against their parents some. We knew you weren't getting into serious trouble. So until you did, we loosened the grip on the leash."

She was right about my late-night escapes to see Amy. That night before high school ended, as I ran out of places to prowl to at home, I knew I had to see Amy. I decided to use my escape hatch. Just because. I wanted to have that feeling one more time of sneaking out of the house. Both Mom and Dad were still up. Who knew about Shelly? Even though I was legally an adult, I was still in high school. One thing I learned later in life, though I knew intuitively at the time, no activity is ever as much fun if you don't have to sneak around to do it. The risk of getting caught heightens the thrill. When I could legally drink, it never seemed quite as bold. So I eased up the bedroom window, stepped onto the porch below, swung to the ground, and began jogging toward Amy's house.

Some lights still shined inside the house. Someone was up. I couldn't ring the doorbell, though. Her parents didn't appreciate late-night visits. Late night for them meant anything after eight o'clock. I snuck around to the back, grabbed the sill seven feet up, and pulled myself up to her window. I gave it three light taps, our signal. It was almost eleven thirty. She opened the window immediately. I pulled my head above the sill. "Hey," she whispered, smiling. She leaned out and kissed me. No doubt coming to Amy's was the right antidote for my restlessness.

"Go for a walk with me!" I implored.

"Kind of late," she said, teasing. I knew she would join me. She knew it, too.

My arms were starting to quiver. I was losing my grip. So I pulled myself up again, kissed her with deep passion, and just said, “Please!”

“Let me put on some shoes. I’ll be right back.”

A few minutes later we walked down the darkened city streets, holding hands, not talking. Without saying anything, our route took us toward the high school. She lived a half mile from school. We paused when we realized we were standing in front of our soon-to-be alma mater. We stared at the front edifice, three floors of classrooms, each highlighted by tall windows. The main entrance consisted of an arched doorway. Directly above the doorway, and three floors up, a cupola centered the building. Except for a light over the main doorway, the building squatted amidst the deep night shadows.

“So tomorrow we will be high school graduates,” Amy said. “It seems surreal. I mean, I’m ready. I’m ready to be done with high school, I’m ready to start college. And after the senior party last weekend, it seems like we are already done, just going through the motions right now.”

“The senior party was something else, wasn’t it?” I said joining the small talk. We were both circling. Sometimes it took us a few minutes of warm-up before we really delved into a topic.

“I don’t think I will ever forget seeing all of you hulking football players doing a kickline together. It reminded me of the variety show. Did you guys practice that recently? You looked almost as good as you did the night of the variety show.”

“No, that’s just what you get when you put a bunch of superior athletes together. Anything is possible.” We both laughed.

“God, the variety show seems like it was just yesterday. That was so much fun,” Amy said.

“I always loved it. Playing in the jazz band, sitting on stage for all the acts. This year doing the kickline was a blast. I guess that meant I arrived.”

“Oh, you probably arrived, for real, last summer. I was so happy I got to be in the women’s kickline. I felt like a Rockette.”

“You know the best part of the two-week run? When you finished the kickline on the last night, and you ran over to me, paused, stripped your garter off, and put it on my arm. I swooned.”

“You make me swoon,” Amy said. We kissed.

“Ames, I know you just said you are ready to finish high school and start your life. But are you really ready?”

“I mean, yes, I think so. It’s kind of scary, though.”

“Um, that would be an understatement,” I said.

"So you're scared, too?"

"I'm terrified, Ames." We approached a bus stop bench. I sat down, and Amy sat beside me.

"What's making you so scared?"

"Failure."

"What kind of failure?" she asked.

"Any kind. What if I fail at life?" I asked.

"Why do you think failure is in your future?"

"Maybe this is just me being melodramatic, but isn't failure of some sort part of everybody's future?"

"Wow, that's a depressing thought," Amy said. "I get your point, but it is still depressing."

"Senior year has been incredible," I said. "I have enjoyed every minute of it. I seemed to have hit my stride. Being with you made it so much better. But what if this is it? As good as it gets? Is this the peak? Did I peak in high school? What if I end up being an absolutely shitty adult? What if I screw things up so bad, I end up alone?"

Those words hung in the air for a pause that seemed like a week. Amy just held my hand. Then she leaned her head on my shoulder. We sat in silence, both thinking about what our lives would become after this imminent rite of passage: graduation.

She reached up and gently touched my cheek.

"I will always be here with you," she whispered in my ear.

—x—x—x—

Amy and I worked in companionable silence as we prepared the Christmas Eve feast for the family. When we were married, Dad and Mom would have joined us. Today, though, Dad felt listless, really missing Mom. He sat in the family room, quietly reading, actually pretending to read, in his chair.

I put the finishing touches on a pan of lasagna that would go in the oven an hour before dinner. The turkey was already in the downstairs oven, cooking away. Mom had installed a second stove years ago to make it easier to cook these big family feasts, where one oven never quite did the job. For Christmas Eve, just like Thanksgiving, we did a mix of traditional American beside something Italian. Lasagna ended up being the something Italian that became a Christmas Eve tradition, just like tree trimming. Truthfully, I could have eaten it for every meal.

Amy was peeling the potatoes. A green bean casserole was cooking in the downstairs oven, too. When the lasagna went in the oven, I would slice the Italian bread, butter it, and shake garlic powder on each slice. We also would have a salad and carrots sweetened with just a bit of brown sugar. For dessert, we had baked pies the day before—two pumpkin, one pecan, and one chocolate mousse. It would be a feast, but it didn't seem like it would be much of a celebration.

Christmas music played in the background, and Amy hummed along.

"This is nice, us making the traditional meal together, cooking the traditional Christmas Eve dinner. It feels like old times. It feels good," I said.

"It does. I'm happy we're doing it despite the generally somber mood weighing down the house," Amy said.

"Everybody misses Mom. I know I sure do."

"I miss Mom, too," she agreed.

We lapsed back into silence for a moment. "Ave Maria" came up on my playlist. I didn't know the words by heart, but the song always gave me a feeling of contentment. "Mom loved this song," I said. "She would always go silent and still whenever this song played or someone sang it. She disappeared into some reverent place deep in her soul as she listened."

"I know. I remember watching her. Everyone else would go silent and still, too, watching her. It was like we couldn't bear to disturb the peace this song brought her," Amy said.

After the song ended, we both pulled out a chair at the kitchen table and sat, letting the mood continue.

"I've never told anyone this," I said quietly, "but before Mom died, we had one of those life-changing talks in her hospital room. Truthfully, I think she had one with all of us."

"She did with me," Amy said.

"I didn't know for sure, but I thought so. Would it be wrong to share with you what she said to me?"

"No," Amy said, barely shaking her head. "I think that's what she wanted. Ultimately, she wanted all of us to share her message. Obviously, I don't know what she said specifically to each of us, but I know in some way what she said to all of us came down to love. That was always her message. That was how she lived her life."

I nodded. I had picked up an orange from the fruit bowl. Even though I knew I likely wouldn't eat it, I started peeling it. The act kept my hands busy instead of just fidgeting. I resumed my revelation to Amy.

"She told me how much she loved me, how much she had always loved me. She said love is the greatest thing a person can have in their life. She said we should cherish that love, nurture and protect it at all costs. And that we should spread that love to as many people as possible."

"See," Amy said. "She talked about love."

"She did. But she told me one other thing, and she made me promise to do this one thing." I paused, maybe for dramatic effect or to stoke my courage.

"She said, 'Make things right with Amy.' So I promised."

I now held a peeled orange. I split it in half. I looked up at Amy, who just stared at me. I handed her half the orange. She cupped it in her hands.

"During 'the troubles,' I screwed things up so bad, and I didn't have any clue how to make things right with you." I paused, still looking at Amy.

"Your mom definitely had an outcome in mind," Amy said. "When we had our heart-to-heart, she talked about you, stressing that you had a good heart. She said to me, 'I know time has passed, and I know you both have suffered. Promise me you won't give up on Robb.'"

Again silence. We both just kept looking at each other.

"I never gave up on you, Robb."

"I know. But I guess I gave up on myself. I was so lost. Not to get sappy or anything, but now I'm found."

"Are you going to start singing 'Amazing Grace' now?" Amy chided gently with a sweet smile.

I smiled back and continued. "Since Mom died, I had been wracking my brain to find a way to make things right with you. I had nothing. Then wham. Thank God, TJ fucked things up."

That last comment just popped into my head.

Amy started chuckling, and then it became a belly laugh and a gut buster. I laughed right along with her. After the laughter simmered away, I continued.

"I know I might have just been a bit irreverent and callous, but we had to come together to save our son. And we did. At first Dad's plan terrified me. But these past few months have been my best in years. I want you to know how much I have loved spending this time with you."

I paused. I could leave it at that—a nice statement of gratitude and appreciation. That didn't go far enough, though.

Weeks, maybe even months ago, shortly after the forced family time started, I began contemplating how to make good on my promise to Mom. It also became a promise I made to myself. That wouldn't just happen, though. I knew I had to take the next step. I had to lay it all out there. I had to tell Amy what I was really thinking and feeling.

It likely would end with a polite but fond rejection. It would be safer not to say anything. Safe is the easy way to go. You know what will happen when you play it safe. Good and bad happen when you don't play it safe.

Our high school graduation speaker delivered a powerful message that still sticks with me. He said people always told him to be careful, avoid risky chances, and avoid challenging people. Don't do this. Don't do that. Just don't. Don't. No, really, don't. But when you don't, nothing ever gets done. When you stop listening to all those don'ts, and you actually do, you can certainly fail. But you might not. What you want to do, you might actually do.

I had to do the next step.

"Okay, so I'm going to just put everything in the open. I want to continue family time. For real. I want family time all the time. The kids. Dad. You. Me. Together. All the time."

I took a deep breath and slowly exhaled. I looked away briefly, and then I looked at Amy. Enough playing it safe or stupid. Time to do.

"I truly never stopped loving you. I want us to be together again as a whole family. But mostly, I want you and me to be together again. Here in this house. Our family house."

Amy kept looking at me. She peeled off a slice of her half of the orange. She held it up and brought it to my mouth.

I opened my mouth and started chewing the orange she fed me. Then I peeled off a slice and put it in her mouth.

She chewed thoughtfully.

"What exactly are you asking me, Robb?"

"Amy, will you marry me? Again?"

She took another slice of orange and fed it to me. I mirrored her movements. She chewed thoughtfully. We fed each other the rest of our orange halves.

Amy gently touched my cheek. Then she took my hand, still sticky from the orange, and smiled.

"I'm going to marry Robb Cesario. Again."

"So, that's a yes?"

—x—x—x—

We sat down to dinner about two hours later. Steam rose from the food just pulled from the oven. It seemed every square inch of the table was covered with tantalizing dishes of food. I had pulled out a nice bottle of wine from the pantry. I knew Dad would have a glass with dinner. I figured Amy and I would, too. But I also placed glasses in front of TJ's and Jessie's plates. Jessie raised her eyebrows. TJ smiled. I poured a glass for Dad first, then Amy's and mine. Into the kid's glasses, I poured about a thimbleful.

"Wow, slow down, Dad. What are ya trying to do? Get me drunk?" TJ said, laughing. Obviously, he knew now what it took to get drunk. Jessie just rolled her eyes at all of this.

I started to speak, working toward a toast. "There are a lot of reasons why this Christmas is a hard one," I said, pausing and looking at where Mom would have been sitting. "But there are a lot of reasons why this Christmas will be special." During this pause, my gaze found Amy. She smiled. Then we both looked at our children. I turned my attention to Dad. He leaned back in his chair, smiling like a wise philosopher who had just seen his best student understand it all.

"The past few months have been difficult and joyful," I said. "The joy has arisen from all of us being under the same roof, from learning how to function as a family again and thriving in that environment. We have had to recalibrate our lives. But we have done that successfully. We have found joy together again. I want to thank Dad for generously welcoming all of us into his home, now our home. I want to thank your mom for bringing us stability. I want to thank you, kids, for always loving us, even when you roll your eyes at us like you're trying not to do now!" Here, everyone laughed.

TJ thought the toast was over and started to bring the wine glass to his lips. "Not yet, son!" *God*, I thought. *I sound just like my dad.* I looked at him. He smiled behind shimmering eyes.

"Amy and I have been talking a lot about things lately. And, well, really talking today. We are so excited and happy to announce that we are getting married. Again. And you're all invited."

Jessie put her hands over her mouth. TJ raised his glass. Dad touched his hand to his heart and smiled. Amy stood, stepped to me, and took my hand. She leaned in and kissed me. It was the best kiss of my life, well, except for the first time she kissed me.

The kids hooted and whistled.

Dad clapped. He stood and walked over to Amy and enveloped her in a long hug. Then he came to me. He took me into his arms. Then he gently touched my face.

"Your mom would be so happy. As happy as I am. Sometimes life gives you a do-over. I'm glad you have made the most of it," Dad said.

With my arm around Amy, I raised my glass. Everyone else did, too.

"To family. Always. And to love. Always." We looked around the table. Everyone made eye contact. Then we sipped the wine.

Jessie set her glass down. "Group hug!" she shouted. We formed our family scrum, holding tight. Smiling.

After some time, Dad slowly broke from our tight family grasp.

"Who's hungry? And will someone please pass me the mashed potatoes?" He said, ushering us back to our seats.

"Yes, my loves. Let's eat," Amy said.

I took her hand and said, "Good, good."

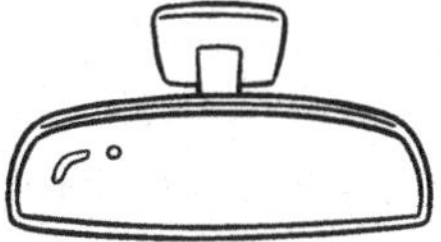

ACKNOWLEDGMENTS

Many people have encouraged and supported me in writing this novel. I am indebted to them

Thanks to Kristin Mitchell of Little Creek Press, who saw the possibilities of this novel and agreed to publish this work, designed, and produced the book, and brought it to the public. Much gratitude to Shannon Booth, whose editing guidance led to a better story and a better piece of writing.

I am grateful for my students through the years, who listened to my stories and encouraged me to tell more. Their motivation centered on a belief that they were distracting me from my pursuit of lesson plans. They didn't realize that I was using stories that would connect to the literature and their lives.

Jim, Chip, and Steve, who are all storytellers, initially encouraged me to start telling stories, so I had to learn how to tell stories to participate in conversations with them.

Many thanks to dear friends Mark Dziedzic and Kelle Adams, the first readers of this manuscript. They offered honest suggestions for improvement and told me I had something readers would enjoy.

I spent many hours at family gatherings sitting in the kitchen listening to my relatives talk, laugh, argue, reflect, and remember. The real action was around the kitchen table, where everyone told stories about their lives. That's where I learned to love stories.

Mom and Dad always encouraged us to work hard and pursue our passions. They supported my career as a newspaper journalist but were most proud when I went into the family business of teaching. They would burst with pride knowing this novel has become a reality.

Special thanks and much love to Trisha, Lynne, Mike, John, and Heidi, who offer love and support in all my endeavors.

ABOUT THE AUTHOR

Mark Nepper is a former award-winning newspaper reporter and state and nationally honored high school English teacher who has spent much of his life helping students find ways to tell their stories. He continues mentoring writing teachers in his role as a co-director of the Greater Madison Writing Project. He also directs "Writing your Life," a series of writing workshops with senior citizens to help them tell their life stories. He now shares his own stories and has written his debut novel, *Glory Days in the Rearview: A Story of Love, Redemption, and Hope*. He is an avid bicyclist and woodcarver and is exploring the frustrations and joys of painting with watercolors. Mark lives in Madison, Wisconsin.

—x—x—x—

Printed in the United States
by Baker & Taylor Publisher Services